WAKE NOT THE HANGMAN

By Woden, God of
    Saxons,
        From whence comes
            Wensday, that is
                Wodensday,
    Truth is a thing that ever I will
        keep
    Unto thylke day in which I creep into
    My sepulchre——

CARTWRIGHT.

WAKE NOT THE HANGMAN

Deborah Leigh

DARROW PUBLISHING | LOS ANGELES

LOS ANGELES, CALIFORNIA

A DARROW PUBLISHING – JURIS BOOK
DESIGNED BY THE AUTHOR.

2015 Darrow Publishing Trade Paperback Edition

Published in the United States by Darrow Publishing.

Sketches and text by Washington Irving originally appeared in *The Sketch Book of Geoffrey Crayon, Gent.*, published in serial fashion in 1819 and 1820.

ISBN 978-0-692-44768-0

1 2 3 4 5 6 7 8 9 10

www.darrowpublishing-losangeles.com

For Jeremy, brave and funny,

and

Steph T., the first Thornton Guthrie I ever knew.

Contents

PART ONE

Fallow Ground

*From childhood's hour I have not been
As others were—*

—Edgar Allan Poe

1

THORNTON GUTHRIE kept one eye on the Hawken rifle his father pointed at him and one eye on the black-capped chickadees that nested in the eaves of the barn. Both scared him. If he let the birds swoop in and fly away with the spring wheat seeds he had just broadcast, his father might suspect a crop-theft conspiracy between Thornton and the birds and shoot Thornton, the bigger, slower, easier target.

Marcus Guthrie had done it before, had shot his son. Thornton was seven and had milked the family cow just a half tick too slow. The animal had been ornery. Thornton had tugged on her teats far too long after sunup, and his back hurt. He sat up for a second, as he figured a fellow had a right to do, and learned he was wrong. His father's Hawken cracked in his direction. Marcus missed the cow but took off a piece of his son's right ear. The half circle at the top had a permanent indentation where flesh and bone had once been.

At fifteen, Thornton was mildly ashamed in front of himself to admit that up until a year before, he had rubbed the little notch every night to help himself drop off to sleep. When he had still been in the practice, he remembered each night as if it were a new thought how there hadn't been much blood, with it being the bony part of his ear and all, but how it hurt like his father had used half his head to touch off a match and let the flame catch his hair. He remembered each night, too, that he had wailed for his mother, who walked and didn't run, to bandage the wound.

"Get them kernels buried good and deep."

"Yessir."

He shifted the dirt back and forth over the seeds with a little extra elbow. He wasn't about to get shot for some gluttonous bird, not with the Hawken or the pepperbox revolver his father kept tied to his belt with a piece of kitchen string. The revolver was mostly for shooting snakes and other varmints, but his father counted him among such creatures, and Thornton never felt as though the gun couldn't be turned on him. It shot three bullets at a stretch. One of them was bound to hit Thornton if his father wanted it that way.

Thing was, his father was a lunatic, not an idiot. The wheels of his foolish mind turned constantly in search of the slight, the infraction against him. Often, he was right, for most folks around and about Columbia, Missouri hated Marcus Guthrie. There were exceptions, Hezzy Jones and the like, fat men with rude lives, but the rest avoided him like horse droppings on the sidewalk. He was shrewd enough to know when a body had it in for him and scheming enough to carry out his crazy notions.

His disposition usually meant calamity for those around him, but it had served him well. For more than ten years, he had built up Guthrie Farms with his guns, ill temper, and overlarge size. He had turned a ramshackle wooden structure that felt like the inside of a pine box coffin during the summer and whose walls leaked when it rained into a seven-room farmhouse with upstairs bedrooms and an indoor privy. To Thornton's great relief, he had done so without slaves. Marcus coveted owning a few, but he was too cheap to buy any.

Marcus's bullish ways were ironic since nothing pleased Thornton more than farming. The guns were too much, *de trop*, as they said all over Missouri, where folks used French more than English half the time. Thornton figured if he didn't do right by the land, she'd scorn him and refuse to grow anything. He courted the land with attention to detail no farmer in Missouri could match, even whispered a little French to wilting crops in need of sweet talking, which was more than any real girl let him do.

And the land, as it turned out, made a fine sweetheart. The eighty acres Thornton tended to requited his love and bore him plenty of fruit. Each night he put the earth to bed, he looked forward to the sun rising up the next morning to beckon him and the soil to make something together. The Hawken rifle was nothing more than a deadly competitor that threatened to come between Thornton and the land. And the use of slave labor would be an affront to the couple.

Thornton recalled a poster he saw once at a mercantile on a rare trip with his parents to St. Louis that advertised a two-hundred-dollar reward for the return of four Negro slaves. A man, his wife, and their two children. The announcement said the man stood erect, dressed well, and went by the name of Winston. His wife had a beautiful name, Mary. Their children were four and six. The family hoped their escape route would get them to Chicago, the poster said. Thornton thought they sounded like a fine family, one that was much nicer than his. He couldn't understand why anybody would hunt them down like criminals. He always liked to think they made it to Chicago.

He glanced up at the sun with open scorn. It was a hundred degrees outside, and the summer of 1834 was still on its way. The sun cooked his dark hair. His neck burned, and his lips fried. A spiky crust of dead, dry skin formed on his mouth. It hurt to run his tongue over his bottom lip, but he did it every few seconds anyway. He was desperate for moisture and hoped the very next lick would give him a different result.

He checked once more on the birds and the Hawken. The rifle lay on the ground next to the block where his father chopped wood. Thornton didn't know which was more unsightly, the Hawken or the cleavage that appeared at the top of his father's pants every time he bent over for the next piece of wood. Marcus Guthrie was well over six feet tall. His ass-crack was long and deep. Hair made the gulley dark, although sweat helped somewhat. It shimmered in the sun on the walls of the crack's valley.

A rogue chickadee flitted in and took two daring pecks for seeds. Thornton jabbed his rake in the air to shoo it off. The bird made one last peck-grab for a seed and flew back to the barn. It waited for Thornton to turn his back long enough to give it another try.

"When you figure on getting around to finishing with them seeds, stack my wood and wash down the outhouse," Marcus said.

The outhouse would give off a special kind of stink on a day that scorched so bad, which his father knew, and Thornton had several more rows of seeds to broadcast and cover, but all he said was, "Yessir."

The bit of interaction required another check of the guns. To Thornton's relief, the Hawken traveled to the farmhouse slung over his father's shoulder. The pepperbox gun headed that way too, on his father's belt. As sometimes happened when the work got tedious and the clouds stayed gone, the job of overseeing bored Marcus and he relied on the mere idea of his guns to make his point. On those days, he nipped on fruit liquor and fell into his bed upstairs in the farmhouse for an afternoon nap.

It always brought to Thornton's mind a story, "Rip Van Winkle", which his mother read to him when he was a small child. Images of the Kaatskill Mountains clothed in blue and purple and the gray vapors around the summits the sun's rays lit up came to him.

He thought about Rip, who ascended a mountain with a stranger and came upon odd-looking personages who played at ninepins, silent, peculiar, melancholy men with exaggerated fashion and strange ways. As a child, he had wondered how loud the peals of thunder were that their ninepins created. Could Rip truly hear them from so far down the mountain?

As he grew older, the story brought more sinister thoughts. He considered Rip's twenty-year nap and the harsh Dame Van Winkle whom Rip, an otherwise lazy gent, worked so hard to avoid with favors doled out to all corners, and imagined falling asleep in his father's fields and waking up twenty years later. With no twinges of guilt, he tended to assume that, like Dame Van Winkle, his father would be dead and his mother would be somewhere far from Guthrie Farms, realizing the dreams her adulthood had robbed of her girlhood.

He began working the land at five and rarely saw his mother. It cost him a little understanding he should have aimed her way. He convicted her of a crime she had no choice but to commit: She put up with Marcus Guthrie. Thornton felt guilty. It was a transgression of circumstance, the result of a life his mother had no means to escape, but she had turned into a shriveled bud he would have snipped if it had tried to grow on something healthy he cultivated. Thornton wished she could find a way off Guthrie Farms, even if she left him behind.

He thought often of what she must have been like as a young girl, but his mind failed to conjure a clear picture of his mother before she became Marcus Guthrie's beleaguered wife. For some reason, he saw her through the eyes of a child. The vision was at once clear for its childlike simplicity and foggy for its unsophisticated view. He wanted to know the girl who had lived on her father's farm, who spoke French to her mules and hid with her dog in her father's tall crops. He wanted that girl to chatter with him as they dropped rows of seeds and to harass the horses with him and conspire to rankle his father. He wondered to distraction whether her impressions of his father were the same as his and whether she found Marcus Guthrie to be as merciless as he did. The bruises that covered her face and arms all the time told him she must have, but he needed to hear it. He hoped the girl might emerge from the adult he knew and be his playmate, his cohort, his accomplice in forbidden thoughts about his father.

Alas, he never made the acquaintance of that girl. He imagined she had existed but had no proof. All he could do was probe her about things he knew were real, knew had happened, like bad weather and clean laundry, the only ground she would give.

He dragged his tongue over his bottom lip and his rake over another patch of seeds and contemplated the three Guthries—his father, his mother, and himself—set apart like points on a triangle, each tending to his or her domain without much interaction with the others for the sheer length of the lines that separated them. He thought again about Farmer Van Winkle, too. The promise of a twenty-year slumber and all one could escape gnawed at Thornton. He hoped that, like Rip, when he came out on the other side of the long, dead sleep that was his childhood, when he woke up to begin his adult years and came down from the mountain, he would be emancipated from Marcus Guthrie's shackles and step out of the shade his father's ill temper cast over him so that he might blossom like the crops he tended to.

And yet, something nagged at Thornton when he thought about a future without his father, and just as he pulled weeds that sprouted between his crops, he labored to remove from himself the ever-present notion that his freedom from his father would come at his own hands.

The chickadee darted in, grabbed several seeds, and flew off, unbothered by Thornton's rake. Thornton didn't notice. He was consumed with thoughts of what would happen to his father when Thornton one day awoke.

The faint sound of feet on the porch steps brought him down from the Kaatskill Mountains. His father and his Hawken headed his way. As it turned out, Marcus hadn't napped. He had probably just used the indoor privy and needed a little extra time to move the stew he'd eaten the night before. Thornton groaned and counted himself lucky that in the process of his father taking care of business Thornton hated to dwell on, the pepperbox revolver had somehow stayed back at the house. He only had to keep his eye on one gun.

2

THE HEADBOARD on Marcus Guthrie's bed slammed against the wall in a steady rhythm. Rose Guthrie clinched her teeth and let out a "Huh" that came from way down in her belly with every thrust. Marcus enjoyed seeing her wince. He had tried, when they were first married, to wait for her to come to him, but some nights, after long days of chores and working the land, he leaned over to touch her and got the low, steady breathing of a person in a deep sleep for an answer. After a while, he no longer waited to find out if she wanted him and just climbed on her every night and took her.

"That's right. That's right. That's right," he said with each forward motion.

He was done. He crawled off her and glanced away. He didn't see the look of relief that washed over her face, but it was there, he was certain. He had seen that look once and made sure he never saw it again. He blew out the lamp light and waited in the dark.

"Night," came the small voice.

For three seconds, Marcus mused to himself about how he could always count on Saturday nights to bring out the dog-tired in him. One more second passed, and he let out the first of what would be an eight-hour procession of loud snores. He marveled at how he always heard the first one.

———◆———

Marcus aimed to stay gone all day. He figured God loaned everybody the excuse of Sunday to fish, hunt, drink, and screw, and he used it every week.

He had a hard time figuring why folks disapproved of whoring on Sundays when the way whores looked and smelled

on Saturday nights, the fishy stench of other men hiding up
their dresses, their faces all dusted with powder to cover up
the streaks the previous man's slobber had left, their bundled
up hair loosened by some sweaty farmer's desperate and clumsy
hands, was too much to ask a man to tolerate. He tended to
end up with bones whose meat had been picked clear off. Just
witness, he would argue if a man let him, his pasty, stringy
wife and his ne'er-do-well son. He didn't need the evidence of
his always coming up short to look and smell like it while he
did a simple thing like whoring.

By the time he got to Columbia that morning, Madeleine
would look as fresh as a churchgoer and betray the lavender
secrets of her bathwater, her bedizened front room tidied
especially for him. She operated out of a fixed up shack on
the edge of town where there was an enclave of similar
shacks. Together, they formed an interesting neighborhood in
which no man lived for more than a few hours and
coincidentally every woman toiled away at the same job.

Madeleine's hut was on the outer edge of the cluster.
Marcus spotted smoke in her chimney and sat up in his saddle.
It meant she had heated water on her stove and taken that
bath he had counted on. If he hurried, he might even be able
to catch her before she got dressed and save her the trouble.
He jabbed at his horse, Blackie's, sides just thinking about it.

Three minutes later, a slender but curvy brunette answered
a door dented in the middle from the hammering of men's
hands. She wore just enough negligee to avoid an indecent
exposure charge.

"Why, hello Marcus." She sounded like she hadn't expected
him, as though she was pleasantly surprised he had called on
her. He stepped over the threshold, tore off her gown, and
piled his own clothes on top of it on the timber floor.

———◦◦◦———

"I said get out!"

It happened more often, Marcus noticed. Just as he settled in for the long summer afternoon, Madeleine asked him to leave, tried to downright kick him out.

"I told you, I ain't leaving until I'm ready." Even he didn't sound convinced. His large, naked body in the middle of her one-room shack made him feel conspicuous, like he was more naked than an average-sized man.

He made it worse. He begged. "Please don't send me home, Madeleine." She stood there in the negligee she had worn earlier, half his size and twice as powerful, and witnessed his portly, grotesque pleading. The garment no longer hung open, like she had meant to be nude and simply forgot about the thin layer of clothing she wore. She overlapped the front pieces of the gown and held them closed with her crossed arms. The gesture made him too afraid to advance. She pushed him, though.

"You're worse than a stray dog. At least a mutt will move on after it eats."

He struck her hard on the side of the head. His naked body moved in strange ways from the force he put behind the blow. His waist was one big collop, and bits of tight-rolled lard jiggled everywhere. His shrunken manhood flapped around his groin. His shame grew. He loathed himself. And he hated her.

"Get out! And don't ever come back!"

He had been about to land a blow to the other side of her head, but those words froze his arm mid-air. He couldn't explain it to himself, but he was terrified that she might stick to what she had just said, might never let him come back.

He slid into his pants as quickly as he could, shoved his feet into his boots, and suffered one more humiliation: His feet gave off a putrid odor. He grabbed his socks and shirt and left the glorified lean-to with his chest bare. He mounted Blackie in the same state. Atop the animal, he dropped his socks in the street. They slid through the planks placed there to cover the dusty road. He put his shirt on and rode off. His unbuttoned chemise flapped in the wind.

He rode that way for several miles, still stung by Madeleine's accurate rebuke. He *was* a stray dog. Sometimes he happened upon the feast of a dead cow he had all to himself. Most times, he wandered for days with not even the feet of a rotted chicken to dine on.

Madeleine didn't know that before he tripped, literally, into owning Guthrie Farms, he had spent seventeen years as a low-wage farmhand, who got fired at fairly regular intervals from one Missouri farm after the next, but it was as if her seeing him naked revealed more than just his hairy skin. He had worked hard to appear the lord of his manor, the farmer who had fatted himself on his own land, but she smelled it on him that he was a mutt, a hard-traveled dog, who had worked for poor white farmers for just a little more than the nothing slaves earned.

He had passed through the Missouri Ozarks, the Great Rivers region, and the northwest tip, and had even dipped down into the Missouri Bootheel with nothing of his own to show for it. He'd planted and grown and harvested other men's sweet corn, soybeans, rice, watermelons, beets, spinach, sweet potatoes, collards, pumpkins, carrots, and cabbage. He'd worked in tyrants' apple orchards and planted their tobacco. He'd picked his fair share of lazy men's cotton too. For years, he got thrown off, fought off—and in two cases, shot off—of property, accused of being ornery, belligerent, and crooked, and Madeleine, who knew none of it, possessed the feminine savvy to be aware of it, to sense it, nevertheless. He had stumbled onto the deserted land that eventually became Guthrie Farms and declared himself king, but Madeleine understood that he was the jester of his fields and that his son, Thornton, was emperor.

She also lorded over him his ugliest secret: He had been unable to complete the deed he had gone to her to complete.

And it wasn't just in Madeleine's bed where he came up empty. Since he had married Rose, he had tried every woman in every shack on that end of Columbia, until they died of some disease or gave up their profession and new females moved in. His manhood had let him down every time. He had convinced each woman that it was a one-time occurrence, that he had been too tired or drunk to be up to the task. So long as he moved on to the next woman, his secret was safe.

Madeleine had been the last and had seen through him. She told him he loved his wife too much to be able to do anything with anyone else, which was likely why he finished the deed with Rose whenever he felt like it. He had slapped Madeleine's face that day too.

He reined Blackie to a stop and fastened his shirt. He relived with each button he closed the humiliation of being kicked out of Madeleine's ramshackle abode, half-dressed. He counted himself fortunate that as he stumbled into the street, the men who ran Columbia and who looked down on him were either in church or in their parlors and unaware that he had been deemed unfit company for a prostitute.

He kicked Blackie into a slow trot and dreaded returning home, especially to Rose. He hated to think she would know he had failed with Madeleine. He never told her outright how he spent his Sundays, never spoke another woman's name to her, but that didn't matter. He had been unable to draw firm conclusions with a woman, an embarrassment that carried over to Rose. He might as well have failed with her. He would have to show her different, would have to prove to her it hadn't happened. There was only one way to do that.

He kicked Blackie into a gallop. It was time for Rose to make what happened with Madeleine go away.

3

ROSE GUTHRIE primed the water pump in the compound. She could have used the indoor pump, but it flowed too slow, and she was in a hurry. She had only one thing on her mind that Sunday afternoon and that was to wash away the filth her husband left in her the night before. It had dripped into her underclothes and turned sticky and rancid.

She yanked on the pump handle and pondered how, in sixteen years of marriage, she had suffered through eight hundred Saturday nights of Marcus's bad breath and heaving body. And that was just the Saturdays. She never got used to the stink the deed left behind. She thanked God every week for Sunday and the image of her husband's back as it rode off to visit a lady friend. It gave her time to move about the farm and fumigate her body.

She had known for years Marcus sought man-pleasures with the women in the shacks on the edge of town. She was grateful to whoever the current female was, the one Rose privately referred to as Lavender, who relieved her of her duties to Marcus, even if just for one day a week.

Rose knew Marcus had whittled down his tastes to Lavender because the previous winter, he smelled like cinnamon one week and lilacs the next and peonies the next. That changed, and for several months, he gave off the same waft of lavender. Rose envied the woman only for her right to smell good. She hoped Marcus and Lavender stayed busy long enough for her to steal a short bath.

In case they didn't, she pumped faster. Marcus didn't like her to be outdoors except to tend to laundry on the line behind the house or to kill a chicken for his supper or to fetch wood and water for cooking. Even the outdoor privy required explanation once he built the indoor privy. She accompanied him on the occasional trip to Columbia, for appearances, or to a neighbor's, for the same reasons, but otherwise, Marcus became irate if he looked for his wife and couldn't find her. Staying in the house seemed like the best way to avoid rankling him.

She had no excuse for needing the water. She didn't need it for cooking. It was three o'clock, too late for dinner and too early or supper. She never did laundry on Sunday. She could abide mild chores to take care of things for Marcus and sidestep trouble, but it was unseemly for clothes to flap on the line on Sunday. She avoided that whenever she could, and Marcus knew it. She had no reason to be outside if he came home.

She hefted the full, heavy pail and mounted the farmhouse steps. Her bucket bumped each one and cost her a bit of its contents, but she hurried on. Her son Thornton appeared on the porch.

"Let me help you, Ma." He reached for the pail, but she freed a hand just long enough to wave him away and walked past him into the house. It aggrieved her to ignore him, but she had to for both of their sakes.

The stove fire still popped and crackled from the noon dinner she had shared in silence with Thornton. She filled two large pots with water and set them on the hot burners.

She glanced out the kitchen window and spotted something she had seen too many times. Thornton kicked a rock around the compound and talked to himself. Farm work was out of the question on Sunday, although sometimes he sneaked to the edge of the rows and tended to a struggling crop, and she pretended not to notice.

His serene exterior caused her to fret over his interior. He wore the same countenance on all occasions so that no one read what lurked inside. She wondered how much loneliness loomed beneath the perennial calm he displayed.

When he was younger and less guarded, he begged for mates, for somebody to play jackstraws or hoops with. She once dared to play a game of huzzlecap with him, using some old coins she found in Marcus's desk, but that had just been once. She hadn't had the courage to risk it twice. For weeks, he had asked every Sunday, "Ma, can we play huzzlecap again?" Her answer was always the same. "No, Thornton. Go on back outside and find something to do." One day, he stopped asking. He had outgrown the question, as he had so many others a young son would ask his mother until age usurped the interest in asking them, and they had never again played huzzlecap. So often, she wished he would ask her just one more time. She would have said yes, even knowing the risk.

The first time Marcus took his rifle and pepperbox revolver to the fields, Rose received his message. Thornton's life became a bargaining tool. Marcus wouldn't hesitate to make her trade it in for bad behavior. She never experienced a relaxed moment on Guthrie Farms once the guns appeared. She watched Thornton as closely as she dared without raising the temperature on Marcus's temper and lived in constant fear of a gunshot cracking through the air and her son dropping in the fields.

When Thornton was seven, Marcus had shot so close to his head, he had taken off a piece of the child's ear. Rose had run to the front door and forced herself into an awkward stroll once she was in view of Marcus, relieved to hear Thornton wail, for it meant he was alive. She had torn her apron into bandage strips for a makeshift remedy for the bleeding and kept her trembling hands out of Thornton's view. Marcus had stood by with his Hawken and watched.

A large pocket of air in the stove popped. Rose jumped, afraid of the sound. She checked the liquid in the pots. It began its slow swirl on the way to a rolling boil. She willed it to hurry.

The steam drew her gaze. She thought about a different Sunday, the day she had met Marcus. He had strolled onto her father's farm in search of work. He had let his reprobate side straggle behind him by just a few weeks. That had been just enough time, and she had married him, for three reasons, all bad. She had reached eighteen with no prospects, Marcus had stumbled into thirty with no wife in sight, and those two things meant when it was time for him to ask somebody to marry him, he asked her and she accepted. It had helped that he was tall. She was five feet, ten inches herself, and most men were shorter than she was. She had counted herself fortunate to marry a man who was taller than she was.

Had her mother, an iron Frenchwoman, still been alive, the marriage never would have taken place. The answer would have been a simple, "*Non*," and Marcus would have ridden off to become the bane of some other women's sorry life.

After a five-minute wedding ceremony, they rebounded to a farm where they lived in a dingy room. Within four days, Rose understood she had made a grave error. Marcus had mauled her on their wedding night. She bit back screams so her landlords wouldn't hear.

By the end of the first week, she doubted his fidelity and cared not at all. He drank and hunted and fished more than he farmed, and Rose had no idea how long he'd keep his job or the stuffy hole they lived in. It turned out to be just an extra week beyond their first week as man and wife, time she learned her landlords gave them because they felt sorry for the young bride.

Although she hadn't loved him when she married him, she had had the romantic notions of a teen girl that the forced togetherness of marriage would bind their hearts. She learned two days after she took her vows his pitiless nature wouldn't allow it. She thought longer than a new bride should about setting out on foot and making her way back to her father until she missed her cycle a mere three weeks into the marriage and realized the child she carried would make her Mrs. Marcus Guthrie for life.

As the years wore on, she came to terms with her bad bargain. She sought refuge in books, in thought, in silence, and avoided mirrors. Her hair hung in strings, and her eyes sank too far into her head for her to bear the mousy image that stared back at her. She felt she looked fifteen years older than thirty-four, her true age. She often thought back to the day before her wedding in 1818 and wished she had not woken up that next morning.

The water was ready. She carted it to the privy and emptied it into the tub and followed up with a pot of cold water from the indoor pump. Her bath wasn't as deep as usual for a Sunday, but it would suffice to wash the stench off her. On her final trip to the kitchen to return the pot that had carried the cold water, she looked out the window and stopped in her tracks.

Marcus rode into the compound, his face flushed and his shirt untucked, and headed for the barn with his horse. She had pushed it, but he was at least two, if not four, hours ahead of his usual return time. She had hoped to have his supper stewing and almost done by the time he got home, to disguise her bath and other misdemeanors she had planned.

Thornton stood at attention near the water pump, caught off guard by his father's sudden presence. Even from the kitchen window, Rose could tell that he watched Marcus's Hawken. He had chosen the water pump as his waiting place in case he needed something to duck behind.

"What are you standing there like an idiot for? Get in there and tend to Blackie," Marcus said to Thornton. He muttered a, "Pfft. Dumb kid," and strolled into the house. "Rose!"

"Here." Her answer came in such a hurry, she almost talked over his calling her name.

"Get upstairs!"

By the time she got to the bottom landing, she was a staircase-length behind him. The scent of lavender trailed in his wake, but something had gone terribly wrong on the shanty side of Columbia.

A moment later, she stepped one foot into their bedroom, and he snatched her the rest of the way. He tossed her and the Hawken onto the bed.

She knew what came next and shrank from it. He yanked off her clothes. The pungent scent he had left behind the night before and that had fermented throughout the day accosted her. Marcus didn't seem to mind. He was on her within seconds. The headboard banged against the wall harder than ever. The Hawken bounced up and down beside her.

She wanted it done, wanted the bath she wouldn't get until Tuesday, or maybe Thursday. The predictable "huh, huh, huh" came from her gut. She commiserated with herself about how, later, she would bail out the unused cold bathwater and ignore the odor that would accumulate over the next several days. Next Sunday, she swore, she would start her bath sooner.

The headboard showed no mercy. It clacked and clacked against the wall.

4

THORNTON EYED the water pump near the front of the house. It was another sizzling day. His thirst demanded he answer it with a ladle-full of water, but his father hovered. The situation required finessing. He could ask, but if Marcus said no, that would be the end of it. It was better to end up at the pump and hope his father was too lazy to react. And if he did react, at least Thornton may have gotten a few sips of water before things went sideways. He sidled up to the pump, unhooked the ladle, and pushed and pulled hard on the handle.

He slurped up the water and spotted something ugly over the brim of the cup. Hezzy Jones's wagon approached on the north edge of the property. Thornton groaned into the ladle.

He hated Hezzy Jones, not because he resembled a toad and smelled of tobacco mixed with cow manure, but because he owned over twenty slaves, an affront to Thornton's existence. His father and Hezzy Jones got on brilliantly, another mark against both of them in Thornton's mind. Other than his distracting Marcus, Hezzy's presence was never good news.

The wagon pulled into the yard, and the men greeted each other with lizard grins. Thornton picked at the bits of verdigris on the water pump base and kept an ear on his father's conversation.

"Hey, now, Hez."

"Marcus." Hezzy reined his horses to a stop. All four of them wore streaks of sweat salt, overworked under the infernal sun by their overstuffed driver.

"Who's watching all your niggras while you're out gallivanting?" Marcus chuckled.

"Heh-heh. I got Jedidiah on 'em."

It sickened Thornton to hear his father and Hezzy talk about Hezzy's slaves like they were animals that might get loose. He pumped himself a second ladle-full of water.

"Which brings me to why I'm here. Got a couple of pickaninnies that won't act right. I'm willing to sell 'em to you for cheap if it'll get 'em off my hands."

Thornton's hand froze halfway to his mouth with the full ladle.

"What's the catch?"

"One of 'ems uppity. Fancies himself the king of the great state of Missouri or something. Caught him reading."

"Pfft. You kiddin'?"

"Nope. Liked to have shot him except I paid good money for him. Couldn't see shooting my investment through the head."

"I guess not."

"Cut his ass wide open with my cat-o'-nine-tails."

"Serves him."

Thornton brought the ladle to his mouth and forgot to drink the water inside.

"Yep. Another's lovesick. I don't mind my niggras breeding me up some free labor, but Jedidiah's taken a liking to the girl 'ninny, you know, for special comfort, if you know what I mean, heh-heh, and I don't need Henry getting it in his chimp head to try to do anything about it."

"Mm-mm, I hear you. One thing's sure. Only a niggra would be dumb enough to try something."

Thornton bit down hard on the tin ladle.

"You can say that twice. Third one got away from me. Tried to take a fourth one with him. Cost me two of my dogs to run them down. With more 'an twenty others to watch, he's getting to be more trouble than a turd stuck halfway in and out. Handles horses real good. Almost hate to give him up. Figure with your bunkhouse ready and just three to watch, with your boy helping you, he oughta stay put. Don't forget. I'm sellin' 'em cheap."

Thornton's teeth dented the ladle.

And it happened. His brain couldn't seem to pull the reins on his mouth, something that had occurred more and more since he turned fifteen. He blurted out, "We're not gonna be wanting any slaves on Guthrie Farms, Mr. Jones."

As soon as the words drifted into the air, his eyes went straight to his father's rifle. He stunned himself with how brainless he had been for talking for his father. If he lived long enough, he'd ask himself why he'd done it.

Too afraid to look away for fear of missing what his father planned to do next, he heard but didn't see his mother step onto the porch. He was at once hopeful and concerned she may intervene on his behalf.

Marcus behaved as though Thornton hadn't spoken. "Sounds like a mighty fine deal, Hez. Do me a favor, will you, and give me a few days to ponder on it? Don't go offering 'em to somebody else."

"You know I wouldn't." Hezzy stood as tall in his wagon as most people sat. He snapped his tired horses into motion. Thornton heard him snicker, no doubt, at his gaffe. He hated the guts of Hezzy Jones.

The Hawken had two triggers, one in back to cock the rifle, and one in front, the hair trigger, to fire it. Marcus pulled the back trigger. A moment later, he stood just thirty-three inches away from Thornton, the exact length of the Hawken. The rifle's barrel came up in one, swift motion. Marcus pressed the cold edge of it hard against Thornton's forehead. The only thing left for him to do was pull the hair trigger.

Thornton steeled his bladder, which was close to emptying of its own accord, and locked his gaze on some infinite point on the horizon just over his father's left shoulder. It was the closest his father had come to putting a round of ammunition through his head. Even his ear had been a farther target than his forehead. He listened for his mother's footsteps, for some sign of her protection. The ensuing silence turned the buzzing of a nearby fly into a cacophony, and he knew her feet hadn't budged.

He was on his own.

Several minutes passed without any Guthrie moving. To Thornton, they looked like statues placed there to greet visitors with an intriguing scene, one that remained static, he hoped, and that didn't play out and result in his head getting blown all over the compound.

He contemplated the fuzzy line where the land met the sky in the distance behind his father's big frame. He felt the barrel of the rifle form an indentation in his forehead. He banished thoughts of the hair trigger and how, over the years, he had seen the rifle go off with the slightest wrong move.

His father dragged the end of the rifle down Thornton's forehead and let it rest above the bridge of his nose. Sometimes, if he touched himself in the spot between his eyes and right above his nose, it tickled. The Hawken didn't tickle. Its weight hurt. Sharp points stuck out of its rough tip. A spiky piece of iron nicked his skin. Tears stung his eyes. He hated for his father to think he cried because he was afraid.

His bladder felt thinner, weaker. He fought against it bursting down his pants with all the resolve he could muster. He did his best to stand up straight and look to the low hills.

Without preamble, his father unstuck the Hawken from Thornton's moist forehead. The place where the sharpest piece of the tip had dug into his skin felt like he had been jabbed with a sewing needle. He stifled the urge to rub the spot.

Marcus slung the Hawken over his shoulder and walked away.

Rose Guthrie crossed the threshold of the main house and closed the door behind her. Thornton didn't know which Guthrie male she had been concerned about, but with both of them still standing, she returned to her chores.

The horizon blurred in the distance. Thornton stared at it for fifteen more minutes. The flies and his mother's indifference buzzed all around him.

His bladder seemed to have emptied from inside. It no longer posed a threat of overflowing, even though he had not actually relieved himself. The sewing needle pain had also become a faint memory. He had recovered from the shock, had been left to return to what he was doing before he stopped for the drink of water. He took small comfort in the fact that his father hadn't actually tried to kill him. He had only threatened to do so, same as he did every day, only from a much closer distance. He rubbed the notch in his ear and shook off the incident.

But something still stunk like urine and stuck like a barb. Thornton realized instantly what it was. His father hadn't declined the offer to buy Hezzy Jones's slaves.

5

"JERE*MI*AAAH!" THE voice called. A sharp-tailed grouse clucked his response. The woman yelled again, like a fast-beaten drum. "Jere-uh-*my*-uh!"

"Yup!"

"It's time! Come on in!"

"Yup!"

For the fifth time in his life, Jeremiah Barker had been called in from the fields because his wife's child labor had reached the tipping point. He and Dorinda lived on a remote patch of land in the Unorganized Territory west of Missouri, a notch too far from the Missouri border, where no doctor had bothered to set up practice.

Flora Perkins and her sister Amy Pierson had arrived three days earlier to play mid-wife and nurse, their sole qualifications being that they had also given birth on desolate farms hundreds of miles from any physician. The notion that childbirth was so easy any woman who had been on the giving end would naturally know how to receive a baby into the world seemed simpleminded to Jeremiah. Flora and Amy were all he had, though.

He headed to the house and looked out over the vastness beyond his farm. He asked himself why he kept his family on such an invisible plot of land. Only God and a few far-flung neighbors saw them. Not even the Kansa peoples who had settled the land centuries before Jeremiah and his kind had invaded bothered with that particular corner of the territory. They were farther north. The Osage were to the south. Jeremiah's small clan and the families of a few others had slotted themselves in in the middle.

Jeremiah had no family to speak of anywhere in the territory. When he was three and his mother died, he went to live with the man his mother said was his father, Tanner Guthrie. Five years later, in 1799, another man, Francis Barker, showed up and announced he had fathered Jeremiah.

The resemblance between the reflection in Jeremiah's mirror and Francis Barker told Jeremiah his mother had lied about Tanner Guthrie. Jeremiah left with Francis Barker, and the two wandered all over the east for twelve years until Francis Barker choked on a piece of jerky and died by the campfire. Jeremiah was twenty. It was 1811 and just in time for the coming war with Britain over Canada. Jeremiah joined the fighting for no reason he could remember and wandered all over the middle territories when it was done. The best thing he got out of the ill-spent time was meeting a young Dorinda in St. Louis on his way west.

At Tanner Guthrie's, Jeremiah had left behind the bad-tempered boy he had called his brother for five years, Marcus, who had three years on Jeremiah. Tanner Guthrie had a strong preference for Jeremiah and spared neither the rod nor the power of his knuckles when it came to rearing Marcus.

Jeremiah still considered Marcus his brother. He had tried to keep in touch with him over the years, but Marcus had drifted all over Missouri. The last he heard, his brother lived with a wife and child on a farmstead near Columbia, Missouri, too far for either man to be any kind of support to the other.

Jeremiah missed having a brother nearby through various calamities, like the tornado that hit in 1831 and destroyed a third of his crops or the winter that didn't see enough snow to keep his meat frozen, which made it hard to keep his family fed. Marcus would have helped him rebuild, would have shared his stores, would have listened to and told big lies that made them both feel masterful. Jeremiah felt things he figured only another man could understand. Who better than a brother, he often lamented.

Near the farmhouse, he heard the familiar noises of merriment and mischief coming from his gaggle of children. "Now, that's enough, y'all! Ethan! Jane! Edward! Julius! Now that's enough!" he said on his way into the house. "I want y'all to stop runnin' around in here while your mother's in there struggling to have this baby. Now, out of the house, now. Do like I tell you."

"What if I don't want to leave?" It was his eldest boy, Ethan. The nastiness that lurked in the distance when Ethan was six and seven and eight had edged its way into his character by his ninth birthday. Jeremiah and Dorinda alternated between kindness and strict punishment and kept it from creeping too close to the family campfire.

Ethan, who had turned eleven, with thirty apparently not far off, had sniffed weakness and exploited it at his leisure. In their private moments, Jeremiah and Dorinda admitted to themselves that raising Ethan felt like they swallowed bitter medicine to cure an ill. Getting him to adulthood required living with the awful taste of the effort, but they were better off with him as their son.

Jeremiah steeled himself and issued a false threat he hoped sounded real. "You don't want my belt to leave you crying louder than that new baby when it comes, do you? Now all of you move."

The three youngest Barker children ran their boots over the hardwood floor and out the door. It sounded to Jeremiah like hail on a rooftop. Ethan chuckled and followed at a slow stroll.

Jeremiah stood at the front door and watched them head for various preferred play spots. They got just out of earshot when their mother screamed.

"Aaaaahhhh*uuugghhh*!" It came long and deep and slow and sounded like the growl of a half-dead bear. Jeremiah took two great strides to the bedroom door and met Amy Pierson coming out of the room. She reminded Jeremiah of someone who had been slapped hard in the face. He made a move for the door.

"Uh-uh, Jeremiah."

He grabbed Amy Pierson by her arms, lifted her off her feet as easily as he hoisted a dead deer, and set her down, away from the door.

"I said no, Jeremiah." She pulled his arm. Dorinda's screams came like shrill pants. "Right now she needs to concentrate on the business of bringing this baby into the world. She can't be tending to your worries. Let Flora help her."

"What's wrong?"

"The feet. They're coming out first."

Dorinda shrieked behind the door. For a moment, the sound nailed Jeremiah's boots to the floor. Dorinda burst into tears. "No, no, no, no, no." Deep sobs followed. "Jeremiah...."

He pushed through the door. "Dorrie?" He wanted to go to her. The image before him froze him dead.

Blood and fluids soaked the entire bottom half of the bed. A large something that Jeremiah didn't know what to call sat in the middle of it all with the cord he always heard talk of connected to it. With his eyes, Jeremiah traced the length of the cord to the other end. It was wrapped like a hanging rope around the baby's neck. The child was blue. And dead. It was a boy.

Dorinda held his son to her breast and rocked side to side.

"Dorrie...." He took a few unsteady steps forward and knelt at the side of the bed. He wrapped his arms around his wife and baby and looked down at the son he lost. "Dammit."

"Watch your language around our boy." Her voice was pinched tight with tears.

"Why'd he have to come in the wrong way?"

"It's not his fault." She wailed right into the baby's lifeless chest.

The muffled sound of tears flowing into flesh grated on Jeremiah. He wanted to run outside and scream, but not even God listened out there. Nobody knew where they were, and it was his fault. If only Dorinda would stop crying into his dead son's belly.

"I'm sorry, Dorrie." He cursed inside his head. It sounded to him as loud as his wife's cries. His son hadn't experienced even five minutes of life, would return to the earth on the day he was born because his father couldn't do better. Jeremiah wept.

"Flora. . . .the children."

"I know, Jeremiah. My sister and I 'll handle it. Just you don't think about it."

Jeremiah was suddenly grateful Flora and Amy lived all over his house that week. He was ill prepared to deal with four children.

Dorinda was still. She held the baby's chest close to her face. Her tears had collected in the concave part of the newborn, bony chest and rolled down the child's bloated belly. Jeremiah cradled her and the baby in his bulky arms, still on his knees.

They remained that way for hours, Jeremiah unable to feel his legs after a time but not willing to disturb Dorinda's razor-thin grasp on her composure. Like those times when he felt food catch in his throat and knew the slightest intake of breath would set off a coughing spell, he feared one false word from him, one wrong sigh would touch off a sorrowful bout of wailing.

Night fell. He hammered together a makeshift casket. He cleaned the baby, swaddled him in bed linens, and buried him, without obsequy, in the yard. He couldn't yet carve a tombstone. He and Dorinda first needed to name their dead son.

6

ETHAN BARKER flew his cloth kite higher than he'd ever seen it go. His father, Jeremiah, ruined the fun and called him back to the farm. He pretended not to hear and ran on with his kite. His father would see the kite travel in the wrong direction, but he didn't care.

Shouts of "Ethan!" followed him down the dirt path and trailed him to Coffee Creek, a rail-thin rivulet so shallow, the water appeared brown from the mud at the bottom. A little mire didn't bother Ethan. The temperature nudged a hundred degrees, and he was thirsty.

He reeled in the kite, on his own terms, and lay face down at the edge of the creek under his favorite shade tree. He stuck his face in the flowing water and slurped at it. Faint calls of "Ethan" sailed over his head. He drank on.

Why did they refuse to leave him alone, he wondered. Since he could remember, Janey, Edward, and Julius nipped at his heels. A year separated one child from the next, but their parents treated them like all four children arrived on the same day. They wore each other's clothes—even Janey, who preferred britches to dresses—and got shoes mixed up. He could never shake himself loose from them. He didn't mind Janey. She lagged behind by just a year and could do all of the things he could do. But at eight, Julius struggled to keep up with the pack, and Ethan got tired of slowing down for his brother and explaining the same thing again and again.

"Are we gonna do chores?"

"Yes, remember that's why we're heading to the barn?" Ethan would answer Julius.

And, "Did it snow yesterday?"

"Yeah, remember?"

"Oh, yeah!"

And, "Did the puppies come yet?"

"No, we'd see them out there in the barn if they were born already."

And, "Is that a flea bug?"

"Well, it's just a flea."

"Oh. . . ."

And so on, all the time.

He sprang to his feet with a bellyful of creek water. He dreaded it, but he trekked back to the farm. On his way, he stopped at the old Dawson place. Ethan had liked the Dawsons. They had staked out the patch of land next to the Barkers' farm five years earlier. They erected a cabin and planted crops, and generally made a big fuss over their first year as Official Farmers. On a random Tuesday, around dinnertime, Mrs. Dawson revealed she hated everything about farming. By Friday, they were on their way back to St. Louis. They hadn't even gathered their first harvest.

Ethan and his younger siblings turned the Dawson cabin into a playhouse. Ethan dropped his kite off in the main living area and headed across the fields to the Barker farmhouse. On the way, he passed his stillborn brother's grave. "JUSTUS BARKER. JULY 22, 1834 — JULY 22, 1834," the tombstone said. It had been a month since Justus had come into the world dead, and all Ethan could think was that he was relieved it hadn't been him. He hated living in the middle of nowhere, but at least he was alive to ponder his options.

He didn't want to be a farmer. He respected his father's work well enough, but whenever he looked down the dirt path, he wanted to walk it all the way to its natural end and not look back. If he could have flown, like his kite, he would have.

"Didn't you hear me calling you? Where you been?"

Ethan stifled a sigh.

"Down by the creek. I guess I was so busy with my kite, I didn't hear."

"Go on and get to your chores now."

"Yessir."

———◆———

Jeremiah knocked on the door of the room Ethan shared with his brother Edward. He planned to go hunting that morning and would take Ethan with him, even if he had lied the day before about not hearing his father call him while he flew his kite.

Edward opened the door rubbing the sleep out of his eyes.

"Where's Ethan?"

"Right there—" Edward stopped short. Ethan was gone.

"Where did he go?"

"I don't know."

"I'm not playing, now. Where is he?"

"I don't know." Edward squirmed like someone who told the truth and worried he'd be taken for a liar and have no way to explain himself. Jeremiah believed him.

He walked outdoors and surveyed as far as his eyes could see.

No Ethan.

He checked the outhouse.

Empty.

Irritated, he went to the Dawson cabin and pushed the door open with more force than needed.

It was also empty.

The sun peeked over the horizon. Jeremiah looked to the sky for some sign of the kite. The wind stood still.

No kite.

He went to the barn and saddled up his horse. A minor panic set in. He would ride to the few places his son might be: the fishing hole, the shade tree at the creek, Jess Tander's place. The Tanders lived a few miles away, near Hec Pierson's farmstead. Ethan may have hoped to get there early, while it was still cool, to see if their boy Curtis could play.

Jeremiah set out on the road. There was no trace of Ethan along the trail.

At the Tanders', he spotted Jess Tander in his fields, working early to beat the sun. He dispensed with the usual greetings. "You seen my boy, Ethan?"

"About a week ago."

Jeremiah rode to the Pierson place next. Hec Pierson had a similar report.

The fishing pond held placid, untouched water, and the shade tree cast its shadow over the creek's edge but not Ethan.

Jeremiah ran out of places to search. Desperate, he rode farther down the length of the creek in a last-ditch effort to see if Ethan had somehow walked along it and lost track of the time and distance. Jeremiah traveled several miles. So early in the morning, Ethan could not have made it any farther. Jeremiah found nothing.

He turned the horse around and set it into a full gallop for the house. He prepared himself to wake Dorinda and tell her something about their oldest boy he thought might kill her.

Ethan Barker had vanished.

7

THORNTON REFUSED to believe his eyes would play tricks on him when he hadn't suffered sunstroke. The summer of 1834 had blazed, but that day the temperature barely broke eighty degrees. The sun felt like a warm cup of coffee.

And yet his eyes plotted something, for right before them, his father drove the family wagon onto Guthrie Farms with three Negro men riding in the back.

Marcus despised Negroes. He would no sooner give them a ride anywhere than he would invite them over for an afternoon of drinking liquor and napping on the porch, like he sometimes did with Hezzy Jones.

It hit Thornton. He swayed in the middle of the field and leaned hard on his hoe to keep from landing face-first in the dirt.

He had done it, Thornton said to himself. Goddammit, he had done it, he said again. *His father had bought Hezzy Jones's slaves.*

Thornton's midday dinner rushed up his throat. He clinched his teeth and choked back the vomit. The gooey mess slid back into his stomach.

Slaves.

Everything slowed. Each second that passed felt like two to Thornton.

The wagon came to a stop in front of the bunkhouse. His father stepped down, not at all in a hurry, strolled to the back, and snatched down the man closest to the open end of the wagon. Thick chains around the man's ankles connected him to the two men in the wagon. The slack was too short, and the man landed in the dirt.

Thornton started forward but his mother's hand appeared like a bear claw around his upper arm.

She caught him by surprise. He hadn't heard her step onto the porch and make her way to him.

Neither spoke a word. Rose held fast onto his arm. They stared at each other for several seconds.

"Ma...." He thought a hundred things and could express none of them. "Ma...."

"I—"

"Ma." He seized on one thought, on a faint memory.

"Thorn—"

"When I was six, back when I still had all of my ear," he said, and wished he hadn't and pressed on, "and Pa and I would ride into town, past those farms with Negroes working on them, at first I didn't think much of it except to appreciate they were farming land same as me. I liked them for it."

He was thankful his mother kept her grip on his arm, for it made her as much his captive as he was hers. She would have to listen. "I didn't have much to say to Pa on those trips, so I looked at the fields, at those men instead."

His mother's grip slackened, but Thornton allowed himself to stay trapped. It felt wonderful to talk to his mother. Years had passed since they had discussed anything less perfunctory than chores, supper, or lessons. It took his father being preoccupied with slaves to give them enough time to talk without Marcus breaking it up with his guns. It was Thornton's lone chance to tell his mother how he felt.

"One day, I stopped looking at the men just so I could avoid Pa. Instead of glancing in no particular direction, or hoping for weird-shaped clouds to roll in, I really looked at them. I noticed on some of the farms, the men were chained to each other."

His mother's face hid her thoughts. He kept talking.

"I wasn't much. Just a farmer, like now. Those men were farmers. I couldn't understand why they weren't free to roam the fields, to walk over and touch any part of the earth that called to them, to do what I had done so many times when Pa was asleep and lay down in the cool dirt in one of the grooves between the planting rows to take an afternoon nap."

His mother let go of his arm. He pretended not to notice.

"Those shackles scared me, made my mouth kind of water up with nervousness. It was the strangest feeling."

"Thornton—"

"I thought about what it was like for two men working chained together. I mean, neither could use the outhouse, rest for dinner in the fields, or even duck out of the way of bird droppings or chase a butterfly without contemplating the other. It was even worse seeing women chained up."

His mother looked at the ground.

"One time I asked Pa why the men were shackled. He said it was the way it was supposed to be. They weren't like white men. God didn't intend for them to walk about like white men and do the same things white men did. He said they couldn't think much better than monkeys. He said God didn't put them on earth to start businesses and build things. He said they weren't capable. They were here to carry out the white man's work, plain and simple."

"Lord. . . ."

"I was only six, but I tried to tell him a man had to be smart to farm right. I told him if those men were farming, they were smart and, either way, God wouldn't create some men just for the purpose of serving others. I tried to tell him I thought lazy men needed a reason to have somebody else do their work and needed to find a way to hide the fact that they were just mean, plain and simple."

His mother looked right at him.

"I was stupid enough to tell him it reminded me of seeing him whip a horse already pulling as hard as it could, like he was doing it just for fun."

His mother gasped. "Thornton, you—"

"I know. He backhanded me so hard, I thought he broke my jaw." He rubbed his cheek. He remembered how his father had punched him with such force, his neck twisted and his chin jerked way past his shoulder. It had been the last time he told his father what he thought about anything.

He was grateful his mother had held him back. He had no real recourse against his father, no means to stop what unfolded in front of him. If his mother hadn't thwarted him, he would have walked into calamity.

She had also given him the first real conversation he had had with any human being since a time he no longer remembered. If the sight of him hugging her wouldn't have gotten them both shot, he would have risked it, even knowing she probably would have rebuffed him.

He looked back at the spectacle his father made across the compound. The other two men stood next to the wagon along with the first man.

"Get goin'," Marcus Guthrie said. The three men moved toward the bunkhouse in a clumsy walk. The jangling sound of the ankle chains made Thornton want to grab them up and strangle his father with them.

Marcus pulled open one of the double doors to the bunkhouse. A moment later, all three heads disappeared through it. One of the men was taller than Marcus, by quite a bit. Until that moment, Marcus Guthrie had been the tallest man Thornton had ever seen.

Marcus followed the men into the bunkhouse and slammed the door behind him. Thornton looked back at his mother. He wanted to finish their conversation, to say a million things while they had time. But she was already headed to the main house. She had given their interaction her customary brand of unnatural conclusion and returned to her chores.

As usual, Thornton was on his own to figure out what to do next. He began a slow walk to the bunkhouse.

8

THORNTON CREPT close to the bunkhouse doors. He stopped about three feet away. He spotted a crack in the middle of the doors where they didn't quite touch. The gap was big enough for him to peer through. The problem was, he had no idea when his father might open the doors. He feared they would swing into his head if he leaned in to peek through the opening in them. He had to know what happened inside, though, so he took the final step and squinted into the crack.

No door opened in his face.

His eye adjusted to the limited line of vision the small space afforded him, and all four figures in the bunkhouse came into view. The three shackled men were lined up and faced his father, whose back was to Thornton. Marcus Guthrie stood to Thornton's right. Thornton could see all three men to what was both his and his father's left. He suddenly felt exposed until he remembered the only thing visible through the hole he peeped through was his eye.

It was the first time Thornton had ever looked real hard at a Negro man. Other than the color of their skin and the texture of their hair they looked like any other men he'd seen. As soon as he finished the thought he felt like an imbecile. Of course they looked like any other men!

"So we're clear, if the sun's up, you're up, and outside working," his father was saying. He swung a heavy set of keys from a ring he must have had the entire time.

"Now, just like you had at Hezzy Jones's place, you get a cot each, and one blanket, winter or summer, which you keep clean, winter and summer."

Hezzy Jones. Thornton still couldn't believe what he saw, couldn't fathom the three men or his father. It wasn't a question of some perceived compassion in his father. Marcus coveted slaves.

But the bunkhouse had stood empty for four years, had double doors so it could pose as a second barn, if necessary. His father had outfitted it with bunks, farm tools, seed bags, a water pump, a stove, and eating implements with a mania his laziness belied and which Thornton never understood since his father was too much of a miser to pay hands to work and live on his farm or to buy slaves. He had even built for it its own, separate outhouse that was distinct from the Guthrie outhouse. Between the two outbuildings and the indoor privy, all three Guthries could go at once, if it came down to an emergency.

Thornton had come to see the bunkhouse and all its appurtenances as nothing other than a symbol of his father's need to display success and prosperity. He never imagined men his father *owned* would sleep in it.

He turned his attention back to the men, using his door-crack advantage to study them in detail. Each man wore a different attitude from the other two. The man to the far left stared over Marcus Guthrie's shoulder at nothing in particular. He looked bored. He was unwilling to give the man who had just bought him any more than he had already taken. It struck Thornton that the man was what people would consider handsome.

"Wood stove is over there," his father kept on. "You get three logs a day, winter and summer. If you wanna stay warm, better think about how you use 'em."

Three logs? There was no way a body could stay warm on three logs through a long, Missouri winter night. The temperature tended to hover around some mark well below zero degrees.

Thornton's next thought was outlandish, but he thought it anyway: He'd see about that. The idea scared him. To see to it the three men got more wood, against his father's will, to do anything contrary to his father, was a grand notion in Thornton's world. It worried him that he considered it.

He had learned never to afford for himself mutinous moments of small victory that might interfere with his way of muddling through his plight, of tiding himself over and getting over until he could disappear for good if the occasion arrived. His father was a thunderstorm. Thornton was adept at jumping between the raindrops. One bit of insurrection and Marcus Guthrie might sweep him up in his tornado, carry him for a few miles, and drop him wherever he saw fit, leaving him there to die.

And yet....the idea of undermining his father exhilarated him. It sparked something in him he couldn't quite place. It reminded him of escape although it wasn't that exactly. It was the closest he had come to feeling like he was out from under Marcus Guthrie in his whole life.

"There's an outhouse back there. You tend to it and see that it doesn't offend. The first one of you monkeys that doesn't look after it will spend the night *in* it to get reminded."

That pronouncement got the attention of the man on the left. The man kept his body still but moved his gaze from the wall to Marcus Guthrie's face. He worked hard to stifle incredulity. The reaction lasted but a few seconds. The man went back to staring at the wall.

All his life, Thornton had watched no one but himself and his mother and the occasional townsfolk interact with Marcus Guthrie in polite and artificial ways. It was an odd relief to see another human being look at Marcus Guthrie with the same disdain Thornton felt. Thornton cracked a smile that was more wonderment than mirth.

He shifted his glance to the man in the middle. The man looked right at him.

Thornton flinched. At first he thought the man's eyes just happened to rest on the crack in the door. His own tiny eye couldn't be visible from across the bunkhouse. But the man leveled his gaze right at Thornton. Thornton's body must have cast a shadow where the thin line of light in the crack in the door should have shone on the bunkhouse floor. He moved a bit, and so had his shadow. It was a dead giveaway, one he was lucky his father couldn't see with his back to the shadow.

There was no way the man could tell, but Thornton turned impish. Still, he looked right at the man. He was taller than the others by a good bit. The others weren't short. It was just that the man in the middle was taller than most men, even taller than Marcus Guthrie. The man held his back as straight as a piece of building timber, and if Thornton hadn't seen the shackles, he would have sworn the man owned Marcus Guthrie, so regal was he in his demeanor.

It was strange, but Thornton envied the man. He saw a confidence he himself was unable to display in front of Marcus Guthrie. Thornton gave the appearance of being self-assured with feigned indifference, but it was an act he developed young to survive life as his father's son.

The man in the middle *was* confident. It was no act. For a brief moment, Thornton forgot about the chains and wondered what it felt like to stand in front Marcus Guthrie, loathing him, which the man must have, and not fear what would happen if his face revealed it.

Deep in thought, Thornton's eye had dipped, but it looked back at the man in the middle one more time and examined him hard. He had to be sure of what he saw. The man held Thornton's gaze. A moment later, as if to revoke permission to stare, he turned to look Marcus Guthrie right in the eye. With that, Thornton was dismissed and forced to turn his attention to the third man. His father continued his tirade.

The third man also looked right into Marcus Guthrie's eyes, but it seemed to Thornton it was for a different reason. Thornton didn't like what he saw. Where the other two men made it clear they tolerated Marcus Guthrie because the shackles dictated it, the third man appeared subservient. He lifted his eyebrows in servile anticipation of Marcus Guthrie's next words, as if to reassure his new owner he planned to follow orders and therefore had better not miss a word.

The man's cheeks bore symmetrical scars. The scars looked as though they had been made at the same time with the same instrument, which seemed odd to Thornton. A moment later, he remembered punishments for slaves who misbehaved included everything from whippings to removal of digits with a sharp blade to mutilation and hanging, even though many of those punishments were supposed to be against the law.

Thornton also recalled Hezzy had said one of the slaves he wanted to sell had tried to run. It must have been the scarred man. It took Thornton a minute, but he realized the third man had suffered a barbaric punishment and preferred to give his new owner the impression he had learned his lesson and would be the exemplary slave. His rapt attention was an act.

Thornton wondered why the three men didn't rally together and strangle Marcus Guthrie. They could overtake him inside of four seconds. He leaned forward a little in anticipation that it might happen.

Marcus wound down his rant. Thornton readied himself to step away from the bunkhouse doors.

His father threw the keys at the bored man on the left. The man unlocked the cuffs around all three men's ankles and gave the keys back to Marcus. The scarred man on the right pulled the entire chain-and-cuff arrangement off the floor and hung it on a peg on the wall near the bunks. Both men had small, ragged sacks tied around their waists.

The tall man moved. Marcus stopped him. "I'm watching you, chimp. Hezzy told me about his most uppity darkie, who thinks he's so eloquent because the good white folks in St. Louis let him read and write. Careful, or I'll cut your backside so wide open, you won't even remember the goddamned alphabet." He had to tip-toe to reach the man's ear. He was close enough to it to spit on it when he talked.

The tall man stared straight ahead until Marcus Guthrie was done. He never blinked. He did wipe his ear once Marcus had turned away. Thornton brushed a hand over his own ear to remove the feeling it contained his father's spit. His stomach churned.

The two shorter men waited for the tall man to move toward a bunk. He chose the one closest to the back wall and farthest from the door—and the wood stove. He placed his sack at the head of it. The others made their way to two of the three remaining bunks. They seemed to make a tacit agreement as to which man would take which bunk. Without hesitation, each one placed his sack at the head of a bunk without any worry from the other. A fourth bunk sat empty.

Thornton pondered what would happen next, wondered how slaves spent their first day on a new owner's farm.

He had no time to contemplate the question. His father moved toward him. Thornton turned away from the door and spotted his mother on the main house porch. Thornton darted fifteen feet away from the bunkhouse doors in four big leaps and turned around and strolled back toward the bunkhouse. He saw his mother retreat into the house. By the time his father came out of the bunkhouse, she would be deep inside the farmhouse, maybe even rolling out some pie dough to make it look good.

Marcus Guthrie walked out of the bunkhouse. Thornton replaced the look of loathing on his face with perfunctory pleasance aimed at the birds above, but he was sure his father caught the contempt.

Marcus strutted through the compound toward the house and took the front porch steps two at a time. For show, he sashayed over the threshold. As though he were a phantom, he disappeared into the darkness of the large wooden abode.

Thornton turned for the bunkhouse. He was done peeping through door cracks.

9

ALL THREE men turned toward Thornton. It startled him. He had thought he would sort of wander into the bunkhouse and strike up a conversation, one at a time. Instead, like soldiers in a battlefield, they lined up as they had earlier with his father and gave him their full—and silent—attention.

Thornton had nothing to say, he realized. He had gone in there on impulse. Since his father might return with his guns, it had been a stupid move.

With the three men staring at him, he couldn't remember why he was there. In the crevices of his mind, he seemed to recall being outraged but couldn't move the feeling far enough to the front of his mind to overtake his shyness in front of the men. Every three or four seconds he expected his father to walk into the bunkhouse. If Marcus Guthrie found him there, it would be bad for him and worse for the three men.

Inertia set in. His mouth refused to form any words.

"Sir?"

For a second, Thornton thought the tall man addressed his father, who must have come back to the bunkhouse. His heart pounded at the base of his neck and all the way up into his ears, which were hot inside. He whipped his head around. No one was behind him. The tall man had addressed Thornton.

Thornton looked back at the man, annoyed that he let his fear of his father show. He had just come far too close to giving away his lifelong plot to appear neutral toward his father. Marcus hadn't been behind him, but if he had been, he would have seen for the first time in years a dread of him his son had worked a lifetime to hide.

There was one upshot to his mistake, however. His irritation with himself had resuscitated his initial indignation.

His apprehension waned and just enough gumption filled in the gap. He turned his full attention to the three men. "I'm Thornton Guthrie. The man who was here earlier is my father."

He sounded strange to himself, like he had been called on in church to recite some biblical passage he didn't understand, with the congregation hanging on his every word for their salvation, but somehow all three men looked at him the same way they had regarded his father. They presumed authority. His thoughts were a patchwork quilt for the moment, but that notion bothered him like a stray thread he couldn't quite find to snip. He told himself he'd figure out later exactly what it was.

The bored, handsome man who had been on the left earlier was on the right. Before the slave owner's son, he looked downright comatose. Thornton pretended to accept the man's posture on its face. He had seen the man's reaction to the prospect of sleeping in the outhouse. Thornton had also seen the way the man had looked past his father instead of right at him and understood it for the survival tactic it was. The man gave more of the same to Thornton, which was fine by him. He had no desire to interfere with a trick, even one used on him, that he had himself utilized with Marcus since he was four.

The man with the scars was on the left and had the same look of subservient anticipation he had shown Marcus, although Thornton gave it no credence. He refused to make eye contact to spare the man the need to try to please him.

The tall man was again in the middle. The three seemed to have an agreement it was his rightful place. To Thornton's mind, it was, although he couldn't say why. It was the tall man he had centered his attention on when he introduced himself.

He looked at him. "Would you please tell me your name?"

"William, Sir." Thornton wished he would drop the "Sir".

"And your family name?"

The man called William looked at Thornton as though he hadn't heard the question right. His half-squinting expression seemed to say, "Huh?" His brow was furrowed just enough to add an air of, "Are you sure you meant to ask that?" He appeared to Thornton like a schoolmaster about to call a pupil to task for dim-wittedness.

Trepidation crept back to Thornton's mind, like a house robber at a window staking out his prey, and started to break into Thornton's head. He remembered he needed to avoid panic and mental paralysis in case his father came back to the bunkhouse and forced himself to return his attention to the men.

"Your first name is William. What is your last name?"

"Guthrie is what they said."

"I'm sorry. Say again." Thornton figured he'd heard wrong.

"Guthrie."

It hit Thornton like a blacksmith's anvil had dropped on his head. His father's ownership of the men meant they carried his name. "Guthrie," he repeated more to himself than to affirm the fact for the man before him. He wanted to spit, unsure what it would accomplish, except that maybe the gathered saliva would cleanse his mouth for speaking the word.

"And your name?" Thornton asked the man with the scars. He sounded listless, like he had needed a nap for several hours and just hadn't been able to find the time to take one.

Thornton figured the man must have picked up on his defeated posture because he dropped the subservient manner and said with no emotion, "Ronan."

"And you, Sir?"

All three men flinched in unison at the "Sir". It took the bored man a moment to recover and answer, "Henry."

"William, Ronan, Henry....Guthrie."

Thornton felt wretched. He wanted more than ever to be done with his father. At lessons, his mother had taught him about exponents in mathematics. He had likened it to taking the profits from one crop and turning it into not just double the crop, but maybe eight times the original crop. In the face of those men, his hatred for his father grew like a large number multiplied by itself a sky-high number of times.

He left the bunkhouse. He wanted to take a twenty-year nap.

10

IT HAD been twenty hours since Thornton's father had brought the three men in the bunkhouse to Guthrie Farms. William. And Ronan. And Henry. *Slaves.*

Thornton wore his work clothes and stared out the window of his room at the back of the second floor of the Guthrie farmhouse. He braced for the bizarre day that lay ahead and wondered what the men thought at that moment. Were they asleep, or had they dreaded, through a restless night, what they would face that morning? He pictured them waking up in a strange place that was no better than the previous place in which they woke and imagined they calculated how they might overtake Marcus Guthrie, kill him and his, and run north or west.

Had they already figured out the Guthries had no dog to give chase? Were they concerned Thornton was tall, like his father, and much younger, making it harder for them to overtake him? Had they seen his mother, and did they wonder whether she was handy with a rifle? Those were the things he would think about if he woke up on Marcus Guthrie's farm a slave. Those were the things Thornton *hoped* the men thought about.

Thornton had beaten Marcus out to the fields every day since he was seven. The sky was no longer black and had shifted to a dark blue. He knew he had better move.

He left his room and stopped cold on the upstairs landing. A thought popped into his mind.

He banished it.

It came back.

He stood still for a long moment. The thought heated up. It terrified him. He tried to forbid it from branding itself into his mind because once it was there, it could not be removed. He would have to live with it, would have to do something about it.

Yet, he just stood there in the dark and aided and abetted the part of himself that wielded the branding iron, which seared the idea into his brain.

It was over. The hot tool lay on the ground somewhere in the back of his mind, cooling off, its job done. The idea rested in his head and lingered like the smell of a snuffed out candle, not to dissipate until he carried it out.

He was going to get them out.

All of them.

William, Ronan, Henry, his mother, and himself.

All he had to do was figure out how, in the face of the law—which said it was okay to kill a runaway slave *and anybody who helped him*—the men's hatred of everybody truly named Guthrie, his mother's reticence, and his father's guns, he was going to do it.

He smelled fresh bread. His mother was up.

———◦◇◦———

Thornton found Rose Guthrie in the kitchen bent over the basin peeling carrots. A stew too hot for summer would simmer in her cast iron crock until dinner at noontime, likely on his father's orders.

"Milk's already in the canister," his mother said, with her back to him. It was her way of saying good morning. It was all she could muster.

"Thank you," he said to her back. She nodded recognition.

The familiar sight of his mother up at dawn preparing the day's meals made him wonder if the day before hadn't been some kind of wicked reverie brought on by the manure fumes he'd breathed all week.

"Those men'll need food. Your father gave me instructions. Take two of those loaves and some jerky and give it to them, will you?"

It hadn't been a dream. The men were on Guthrie Farms and were in the bunkhouse waiting to partake in some kind of meal. It was fantastic to Thornton that within minutes, he would face three men who regarded him as their captor and try to have casual discourse about breakfast.

How one approached his first real conversation with slaves, Thornton had no idea, as he had learned the day before in the bunkhouse. Should he address the fact that he was aware of their predicament, or would that be asinine? They may appreciate his understanding or they may think he was an ignorant worm. And his father might overhear.

Right then, all he knew was that they hadn't eaten since they arrived the day before. They had to be ravenous. He wolfed down his own breakfast and packed two full loaves and the jerky in his seed bag.

All he had to do was work up the courage to get through the open kitchen doorway and out of the house. There was nothing to do but take the first steps. He secured his seed bag and headed out of the kitchen.

"Thornton?" his mother called. Her voice had a tremor so slight he almost missed it.

He turned and she was still at the basin, but she faced him. She appeared more ragged, more washed out and tired than usual. It made him wistful.

"Yes?" He waited like a patient pastor waited to hear confession.

"Those men. Your father."

"Yes?" he said after a long pause.

She waited just as long. "Careful, you hear?" Her eyes looked right into his.

Thornton was fifteen. The last time his mother told him to be careful, he had been three years old and just about to walk under a horse. She had pulled him back and reminded him to be careful.

With her three words of warning—and her willingness to issue them—the gravity of the situation became clear. The men and Marcus's guns made it four against Thornton's one. He thought he must be insane to dare consider what he had talked himself into moments earlier upstairs, let alone take steps to carry it out.

There was no turning back, though.

In a flash, he remembered something his father had said in the bunkhouse the day before and was struck by another inspiration. He hoped he wasn't gathering one dumb idea after the next.

He said, "Yes, Ma'am," and left.

11

WILLIAM ALWAYS knew what time it was without a timepiece. He had an inner clock that kept perfect time. The previous night he hadn't slept at all and knew sunup on his first day on Guthrie Farms was a little over an hour away. An hour and three minutes, to be exact.

He listened to Ronan and Henry breathe in steady, alternating patterns and envied their ability to escape into sleep where they would be free until they woke up to face Marcus and Thornton Guthrie, and maybe more.

He shifted but made no sound. He had shared his living space his whole life. He moved around and left no aural trace with ease.

His stomach growled and threatened to betray his cause of letting his friends sleep. None of the men had eaten since two nights before, on Hezzy Jones's place. Hezzy Jones had refused them breakfast the day before. He said it made no sense to feed slaves that would only be his for a few more hours. Then, Marcus Guthrie had given them nothing. They had all been deprived of food before, and it seemed they would be again.

At least they had had access to the outhouse through the back door of the bunkhouse, with just three men sharing it, although that morning they didn't have much to relieve themselves of. On Hezzy Jones's place, all twenty-seven slaves used the same outhouse. Each of them learned to squat so the only thing they touched in the putrid shack was the floor with their shoes.

He and Ronan and Henry were likely in for it. He had seen the way Marcus Guthrie resented having to look up at him during his tirade the day before. William imagined Marcus

Guthrie had been the tallest man in the room everywhere he went. He probably hadn't bargained on a slave who was bigger than he was and who acted like it.

Through all of his thirty-six years, William had taught himself to keep his back straight and to walk tall, even if it invited peril at the hands of somebody in authority who needed him to be bowed. He promised himself no matter how weary he felt, he would never let himself get worn-out, for he might give in altogether. It proved difficult most days.

Being a slave was so intolerable, he sometimes felt his spirit bend and shift positions in order to be able to better carry the burdens of bondage. Those moments frightened him, for he had seen old men whose spirits were permanently buckled by a lifetime of enslavement.

When he most feared the same fate, he turned to an activity that could get him killed. It never failed to help him stand tall again, though, so he did it every chance he got. He read.

He had learned to read quite by accident. He was twelve when a Tennessee plantation owner bought him at auction in Virginia. Although he was good at farming, he was sold from the Tennessee plantation to a riverboat captain at the age of seventeen.

It was against the law to transport slaves up and down the river, but rogue boat captains risked it anyway. It was a good bargain. The average slave couldn't swim, so overboard escapes were unlikely, although William had seen eleven desperate men drown over the years. Once the boat sailed into shallow waters, there were too many townsfolk in view for slaves to wade in and run for the north. Punishments in towns where slaves tried to disembark and disappear were severe.

When William first stepped onto the river vessel, he was as terrified as he had been when he was sold away from his mother in Virginia. He hadn't known how many days and nights stood between Virginia and Tennessee until he made the journey, and he had no idea how far the boat would travel or what to expect from the owner. He held out hope nothing could be harder than what he suffered in the fields of Tennessee all year.

He was wrong. Stevedores endured rancid living conditions. They traveled up and down the river on boats that made them sick and reeked like vomit and whose heavy cargo they loaded and unloaded with backbreaking relentlessness. Sixteen-hour workdays were common.

There was, however, one advantage to riverboat life. The captain-owner spent much of his time away from his deckhands. He and his men always outnumbered the slaves on board. He cared not what his Negro crewmen got themselves up to so long as when the boat came near the shore, everyone behaved according to what looked right to the local law. The captain was unaware—and didn't care anyway—whether one man taught another to read between ports of call. He just needed his goods delivered on schedule.

William befriended an older Negro stevedore, Archibald Thackeray. Archibald traveled with a library that amazed William for its size, considering Archibald kept it at the bottom of the one cloth bag each man was permitted to have on the boat. The library consisted of tattered books Archibald had collected in towns all over, old newspapers, a worn-out lexicon, and intricate maps Archibald had drawn with the charred ends of sticks of the places he had been on the boat.

William asked Archibald to teach him to read. The old man obliged. By the time William was nineteen, he read fluidly. It was a great gift, for not only could he read signs posted about Negroes in any town where the boat docked, but he was also able to understand the difference between north, south, east, and west. Most slaves who escaped had no idea which way to run. William considered understanding compass directions the most valuable thing he had ever learned.

At twenty, he learned to read clocks and, after a long, long while, to synchronize whatever a timepiece told him with what his body already sensed by nature. He wasn't sure if it was some strange function of his mind or the strain of slavery and his awareness of the slow passage of time. Either way, his internal clock was perfect.

As the years wore on, he scavenged for anything written—newspapers, leaflets, books, posters, playing cards, and theater announcements—and added them to his ever-growing library. He used Archibald's lexicon to look up words he didn't know.

He learned of new slave laws and of the doings of free men, about the lives of Negroes in free states, about what happened in faraway places like Washington, D.C. and Rhode Island and Massachusetts, and about battles in government, shipping tariffs, the Erie Canal, and five-cent elixirs on sale at the mercantile, and ached for a different life. There was a distinct cruelty, he felt, to slaves who worked in cities as janitors, handymen, draymen, and porters, and who often lived side-by-side with freed citizens, exposed daily to how good life could be if they had their freedom.

He was sure rural slaves felt the opposite was true, that they probably envied city slaves their exposure to so many kinds of life and their seeming chances to slip down an alleyway and find freedom. William only knew that wherever he had been, no matter how big the world, he was trapped.

It was especially hard to encounter the occasional free Negro wearing spectacles, for he knew there was a man who didn't have to hide his ability to read, who wore his capability right on his face.

Sixteen years after William left Tennessee and stepped onto the riverboat, the captain retired and sold his slaves. A thirty-three-year-old William had been sold in one direction, Archibald in another. Each took with him a library at the bottom of his bag.

Hezzy Jones had purchased seventeen slaves in one day. He shuffled bodies around between the bunkhouses, and during the confusion, William stashed his library under his living quarters. For three years, he unearthed the treasures at scattered intervals, unnoticed, until one day Jedidiah Jones— Hezzy's older and nastier son—caught him with an old map.

Hezzy took charge. He promptly burned the library. He beat William half to death with a cat-o'-nine-tails dipped in kerosene. He sold William to Marcus Guthrie the minute William's wounds healed and he could fetch a good price.

William hadn't read a word since Hezzy Jones set fire to his library. His wounds had mended, although the kerosene sometimes burned and itched his back skin at night. He had survived the humiliating spectacle his flogging had been. The entire Jones clan and twenty-six slaves had watched Hezzy torture William in the Jones compound.

It was seeing his library destroyed that crushed his soul. Much of his life with Archibald had gone up in a blaze. All recorded proof of their friendship was in ashes. He would never recover what was lost, and he starved for something of substance with which to feed his mind. He needed to feel the rays of knowledge again. His mind grew cold without them. He held out no hope for an opportunity to warm it up on Guthrie Farms. Marcus Guthrie had made it clear William should stay far away from the written word. William could still feel Guthrie's spit on his ear.

With less than an hour to be outside, William went over in his mind the landscape he had spied the day before and wondered whether there was a way off Guthrie's land with a day's head start built in. He had figured out there were no dogs on the property because if there had been, he would have heard one of them bark, the same way Hezzy Jones's hounds barked every morning at the first sound. And he noticed the crops were the finest he'd ever seen, which made him think many hands tended them. The only slaves he saw were Ronan and Henry. He wondered if there were other, white farmhands with whom he'd have to contend. He hadn't seen anybody, but he wouldn't be sure until sunup.

Young Guthrie—Thornton—also occupied his mind. The boy was peculiar. He had looked downright wretched when he left the bunkhouse the day before. William wondered why. Old Guthrie had called the men monkeys, chimps, apes. Young Guthrie had used the word "sir", which stood out, to be sure. He had been deferential, had behaved like he would be in trouble for disrespecting his elders if he slouched when he talked to Ronan and Henry and William. William had never witnessed such an attitude coming from any white man toward him in his entire life, but he wouldn't let it stop him from fleeing.

He hoped to run west, to the Unorganized Territory, his safest bet, he reckoned. There were free Negroes in Missouri, but the government was determined to maintain strict control over the Negro population in the state. Every place, including church, where it was thought Negroes gathered was regularly searched for runaways.

St. Louis had almost three thousand slaves. It would be difficult to masquerade as a free man. Negroes without proper documentation were locked up in jail. The sheriff could advertise the fact that he held a slave for a month and sell the jailed slave to recuperate his expenses.

Heading west would be much harder in the beginning. He would have to avoid detection during his escape through miles and miles of Missouri. Until he reached freedom, he faced the danger of recapture every minute he was on the run.

But he imagined once he made it to the kind of liberty the west offered, with no patrols to evade or papers of freedom or jails or slave auctions or a free market for him to be sold in, he could truly live free.

The obstacles seemed insurmountable, though. Which route would he take? How would he travel? By stolen horse? There were likely enough horses for Marcus and Thornton Guthrie, and maybe others, to give chase. With rifles.

On foot? Improbable at best. Walking and running would be slow-going. It would mean his journey would be long and would take him into the cold, cold Missouri autumn. Spring was no better. The thawing winter snow would turn the roads into a thick mud. The ideal time to run would have been at the beginning of June, but it was almost September.

The other problem could be the two men who slept next to him. Would they join him? Ronan had a family relation at Hezzy Jones's place, and except for an actual ceremony, Henry had left a wife there. Slaves didn't usually get married, but mating was another story. Slave-owners turned a blind eye to relations between slaves, for somewhere down the road, it produced free slaves for the owner.

Colleen was a girl who had been born on a plantation in South Carolina. Henry fell in love with her the day she arrived at Hezzy Jones's. The feeling had been mutual. William didn't think he'd ever forget the look on Colleen's face when Marcus Guthrie's wagon hauled Henry away. Henry had spoken only the most necessary words since he had been separated from Colleen.

Hezzy Jones's farm was east of Guthrie's place. The Unorganized Territory was to the west. Even though they could never be together, it might prove difficult to get Henry to leave if it meant traveling farther from Colleen. He probably considered himself fortunate that he hadn't been sold to some Georgia plantation, an eternity from Colleen.

William hoped his friends slept like dead bricks, their minds thick with nothingness. He wished for Ronan and Henry that no distorted images of their loved ones came to them and disturbed the blessed respite sleep gave every slave, even if they only had a few more minutes to revel in the slumbering reprieve. William's internal clock told him that in thirty minutes, the three men had to be outside to face their first full day as Marcus Guthrie's slaves.

12

THORNTON'S MOTHER had given her son the germ of
an idea. It was a gamble, but instead of heading outside, he
had raced back up to his room and retrieved something he
thought might help him make inroads with the three men. It
would make the perfect weapon against his father and was
small enough for him to tuck inside his seed bag, right in
between the two loaves of bread. With the rifle between them,
Marcus tended to keep away from Thornton and his seed bag.
Thornton should be safe until it came time to take the item
out of the bag.

He stepped onto the porch. His father was nowhere in
sight. Neither were the men. In a few more minutes the sun
would be all the way up.

The bunkhouse doors swung open. Thornton's heart
thumped.

The men emerged.

They walked three astride, with the tall one, William, in
the middle. Thornton was not surprised. It appeared he was
their unofficial leader, which was a good thing. Thornton
figured his plan had no chance at all, except if the other two
men—Ronan and Henry—deferred to William, in which case
he figured he had about the same chances as a chicken did on
a winter day that it wouldn't be the one they came for come
suppertime.

They each had seed bags slung over their shoulders the
way Thornton did, a bit of good luck. It meant his plan
might work. They must have seen the tilled rows and known
what tasks lay ahead.

The spring wheat had been harvested, and they would plant buckwheat. Thornton had spent several days turning over the soil where the spring wheat had grown.

Most farmers planted their buckwheat closer to the beginning of August, but Thornton had insisted on waiting until the end of August so the buckwheat would mature faster and flower in the cooler nights. He'd get more seeds from the flowers and have enough for next year's crop. The other farmers thought he went about it the wrong way, thought he got lucky with a good result, but he never cared. Even his father recognized that Thornton produced the best crops in the state and never questioned his son when it came to the way he went about crop management. He had profited too well to interfere with his son's system.

Thornton heard the distinct sound of horses pulling a wagon near the edge of the property. Who could it be at that hour?

He saw who it was.

His father drove up in the Guthrie wagon. Three bloodhounds and a fourth dog whose breed Thornton couldn't place rode in the back. Thornton gawked in disbelief.

Marcus hadn't been asleep. He had been up for hours and had retrieved from Hezzy Jones's place a pack of guard dogs.

The fourth dog most resembled a wolf, with its pointy face and ears and narrow-set eyes, but its coat was longer and shaggier and bore the marks of battles with other animals. It was missing fur in places shaped like long cuts where scars had formed. Even with its mouth closed, the bottoms of its long fangs were on full display. Thornton had no doubt the other animals the feist had tangled with had met a certain and well-executed demise.

Marcus pulled the wagon all the way into the yard. The wolf-dog barked loud and hard at nothing in particular. The bloodhounds declined to join the chorus. They surveyed their surroundings instead.

"Shut up!" Marcus barked back.

The wolf-dog fell silent. Thornton felt sure the beast would have ignored him if he had given a similar command. He was positive the animal would have torn him to pieces if he looked at him wrong, let alone if he tried to shut him up.

He hated the dogs on sight. He couldn't decide which he despised more, the bloodhounds or the wolf-dog. The sole purpose of the wolf-dog was to terrorize the men into forgetting all thoughts of running and to chase them down and kill them if they tried. The bloodhounds, meanwhile, would use their keen sense of smell to hunt the men for days over land and water and give the wolf-dog his quarry.

Thornton sneaked a look at the men. They looked at the dogs with mild interest and nothing more.

"Get over here and get these dogs." The order was aimed at Thornton. Marcus held up four leashes. "Put these on 'em and hitch 'em to the barn door for now. I'll drive a post in the ground near the bunkhouse for a regular hitching spot."

Thornton had no fear of wild horses, cows, hogs, field snakes, or hungry hawks. Dogs gave him pause. Something in their countenance made him question whether he could trust them. Their eyes betrayed their constant assessment of people as possible prey. He thought people who romped and played with dogs were foolish.

He took tentative steps toward the back of the wagon. The wolf-dog let out a low growl from deep in his throat, not willing to buck Marcus, it seemed, and launch into a full bark.

His father didn't command the dog to stand down in any way. Thornton steadied his hand and took the leashes from his father. He started with the three bloodhounds, all males. He assumed because they were quieter, they might also be friendlier. He was right. One by one, each let him loop a leash around his neck. Thornton felt triumphant, but only for a brief moment. One dog remained.

He aimed the fourth open loop at the wolf-dog. The animal snarled and tried to clamp his mouth around Thornton's forearm. Thornton snatched his hand back just time.

"Heh, heh. Almost got your arm, there."

Thornton felt the eyes of the three men on him. If they were going to see him as any kind of match for his father, he had to prevail over the vile dog.

He was smarter the second time. He stared right into the eyes of the beast and refused to blink. The wolf-dog sized him up, but he seemed more reluctant to howl. Something tentative appeared behind the animal's eyes. Thornton took advantage of that fraction of second's worth of weakness in the dog he was sure he would see never again and reached over and threw the leash around the wolf-dog's neck. The canine had no time to protest.

Thornton pressed his advantage. He lowered the back flap of the wagon.

"Down!" he yelled at all four dogs and tugged on the leashes. They sprang, one by one, off the wagon and onto the dirt. He looked back at no one and strolled to the barn door with the dogs in tow. He hooked their leashes on the door handles.

He turned, and all four people in the compound stared at him. Even his father looked impressed. Their expressions told him he had won the moment. He headed for the three men, careful to avoid the path of the wolf-dog, who eyed Thornton's ankles.

He was relieved his father had not only approved his next move, he had ordered it. It made the transition from the dog moment easier and gave him an excuse to talk to the men.

"My mother baked fresh bread this morning. It's still warm." He handed one loaf each to Henry and Ronan. He was careful not to jostle the item sandwiched in between the loaves in his seed bag.

Ronan inhaled to catch a whiff of the aroma that floated near his loaf. Thornton worked hard not to stare at the man's scars.

"There's jerky to go with it." He handed the meat to William.

The men ate in silent unison. Thornton lost the battle with himself not to gawk at them. He was fascinated by the texture of their hair and thought under different circumstances he may have asked one of them to touch it to see if his hand bounced off of its thickness.

Six holes in the knees of their pants gawped at him, and the shoes of the one called Henry had two open toes. Thornton had no idea how the man had farmed at Hezzy's with no leather on the fronts of his shoes. He would have to do something about Henry's shoes.

None of the men had bathed in a healthy while. Thornton wondered if they were waiting for permission to use the pump in the bunkhouse. He would find a delicate way to clear that up for them when the time was right. He would also ask his mother about patching the knees of their britches, a conversation he expected to be awkward, but that he would have, nevertheless.

"Goddammit!" Marcus yelled from the barn. The dogs took it as a signal to yap. Thornton hated the sound.

The horses fought with Marcus. Thornton thought it was best not to push his luck. He returned to the barn to help his father.

As soon as Thornton appeared, Marcus grabbed his rifle off the wagon seat, ready to take his leave of the barn. "From now on, it's your job to feed all the animals, including them monkeys *and* them dogs." He strutted toward the barn door. "See that they work till sundown." He returned to the farmhouse. He had been up far too early not to need a nap.

Thornton finished with the horses and went back to the men. He felt better-off than he had imagined he would when the morning began. By mistake, his father had handed him his first advantage. He had given Thornton regular access to both the men and the enemy dogs.

All he had to do was find a way to let the men know he was on their side. It was time to turn to what was in his seed bag.

13

WILLIAM SPOKE first. "Mr. Guthrie, Sir."

Thornton recoiled at the "Mr. Guthrie" and at the "Sir". Just ninety seconds into their first day together, Thornton made a decision that would rankle his father but not quite enough to warrant rifle play. A little disrespect thrown his son's way, even from slaves he felt had no business getting out of line, might please Marcus. Thornton would risk it.

"It's Thornton. Call me Thornton."

The men gave him cautious stares. They had no intention of calling him by his given name.

"William, was it?"

"Yessir."

"It's Thornton."

William nodded. Clever way around using his name, Thornton thought.

To the man with the scars he said, "Ronan, correct?"

"Yess—," he said.

"And, Henry?"

"Yes." An improvement. Thornton would take it.

"Generally, my father and I work out here together, but sometimes if I'm planting, he's tending to other jobs. He makes most of the trips into town for supplies, although if there's a lot to heft, I go with him."

The men had finished breakfast and just stared at him, so he kept on. "We grow potatoes, squash, sweet corn, tomatoes, kale, collards, mustards, winter and spring wheat, and as you'll see today, buckwheat. We have lots of hogs and a milk cow. Some chickens. A few horses too." He paused and added, "And now four dogs."

Ronan perked up at the mention of horses. For the second time, Thornton recalled something Hezzy had said about Ronan, the man who had tried to run. He was good with horses.

"Mind if I ask what you men did on Hezzy Jones's place?"

Silence.

Finally, Henry spoke. "Harvesting more than planting."

He had cracked the first layer of dried mud on the conversation, and Thornton was grateful.

Henry kept on. "Chop wood real good. Fix things too."

"Stables," Ronan said. "Work with horses mostly. Don't farm much." His face barely moved. The scars held his cheeks in place.

"The women did most of the planting on the Jones place," Henry said.

"Bit of everything," was all William said about his own skills.

Thornton wished he'd offer more. He moved on, though. "Soil for buckwheat's prepared. We'll plant one inch deep in long rows, about six inches apart." Ronan and Henry frowned in confusion, and Thornton realized they must not have known what one inch and six inches looked like.

William demonstrated with his hands and said directly to Ronan and Henry, "About this deep, and this far apart."

The two men nodded. The exchange made Thornton understand that Ronan and Henry couldn't read.

"If you men want to take a moment in the bunkhouse and wash up at the pump after your meal, please feel free. You can use the pump any time. We'll meet here directly."

They headed back to the bunkhouse single-file, with William at the head of the line. Thornton was becoming used to the pattern of Ronan and Henry deferring to William. It seemed perfectly natural that he should lead the way back to the bunkhouse.

Thornton was proud of himself. He had hid his
nervousness well. He didn't pace up and down in front of the
men, like he itched to, and he had solved the bathing problem.
His idea might work, after all.

——•◇•——

The boy was nervous, William thought. Ronan pumped
cold water over William's hands that he doused on his face.
William had done the same for Henry, who had pumped the
water for Ronan. William was the last to wash up with the
little cake of soap someone had left near the basin.

He rinsed the harsh soap from his face and pondered
Thornton Guthrie's discomfort. He had never seen a white
person—not man, woman, or child—look nervous in front of a
Negro man. William had been ordered around by calm five-
year-olds and carried out those orders as if they had come
from a fifty-five-year-old and as if his life depended on it
because it had.

But Thornton Guthrie was without a doubt uneasy.
William noted keen differences between the countenances of
the older and the younger Guthries. It seemed impossible, but
the young man was polite to him, something William had
never seen a white man be to anybody but other whites.

Nonetheless, he wasn't ready to take any comfort in
Thornton Guthrie's quiet demeanor. William's inclination was to
hate him, as he hated the young man's father.

He dried his face on his dirty shirtsleeve and thought
about how he would scrutinize the younger Guthrie and look
for what he should avoid. A slave got so he recognized who
would give him a backhand to the jaw, who would make him
sweat a day in the fields without water, who might kill him
for looking the wrong way.

The other shoe would drop on his head soon enough, he was sure. He would watch the son closer than he would the father, for it was the baffling white men who required the most caution and who tended to catch a man off guard.

———◦◦———

Thornton and the men had worked for over five hours on the men's first day on Guthrie Farms, but no one spoke. The morning's sparse chatter had been the beginning and the end of all conversation. The men didn't even speak to each other, although Thornton figured they must have talked with one another in the bunkhouse.

It was Thornton who cast the pall over the conversation. He would have to change that.

They planted the seeds in a crisscross pattern. Each took a long row to himself, with two traveling their individual, long row in one direction, and two, the other. Thornton had rigged it so that he and William traveled in the same direction and worked their rows side by side.

Thornton found it hard to fathom there were three other workers at his side after all the years he had worked alone with his father. It would take some getting used to.

He had bigger problems, though, than learning how to share the fields. He needed to get close enough to William to give him what was in his seed bag.

His father had returned to the yard. He pounded a large post into the ground near the bunkhouse and mounted four heavy hooks into it, one for each dog leash. His Hawken rested against the bunkhouse door.

Thornton had wasted five hours. He had lost his nerve and was disgusted with himself. He reached into his bag for another handful of seeds and was immediately reminded of his plan again when his hand bumped into the item he hoped to slip to William.

It was no use. For the first time since he was five, he was distracted from farming by something other than Marcus Guthrie's guns, his bladder, his bowels, or his thirst, even if what was in his bag was just as deadly as the Hawken, depending upon whether his father discovered it before William could get his hands on it.

"About fifteen minutes till noon."

Thornton jumped at the interruption in his thoughts as though they had been overheard. William talked to the dirt more than to anybody in particular, but Thornton still answered him. "Pardon."

"It'll be noontime in about fifteen minutes. Fourteen to be precise." William spoke to the dirt again. It was more of an observation than a statement designed to elicit a response. Still, William carried no timepiece. Thornton wondered how he knew what time it was. He was also grateful for the conversation.

"How can you be sure?"

"I always know what time it is." He pushed another seed into the ground.

Thornton never carried a timepiece either. Timepieces were for rich men in Columbia, not Thornton Guthrie. Besides, it would get in the way of his work. But Thornton had at least seen a clock earlier that day to have some reference. The most recent clock William had seen had been at Hezzy Jones's place.

His mother brought dinner every day at the stroke of noon, or else she'd hear it from his father. He'd know soon enough how well William had guessed the time.

About what felt like fifteen minutes later, the large bell on the front porch rang. Thornton's mother came down the farmhouse steps with a tray full of food. Thornton looked at William and wondered how he had been so accurate about what time it was.

He headed for dinner, but the men kept working. He groaned. He wasn't going to last long if every move the men made had to be sanctioned by him. He thought the best way to settle the matter was to refuse to give the men orders and to refuse to give in on that. He said, "Dinner time," and walked away.

It worked. William said to Ronan and Henry, "Take your sacks." The only true planter among them, he likely knew birds loved unattended seed bags. All three men slung their bags over their shoulders and followed several paces behind Thornton. For the second time that day, someone did him a favor without meaning to. He needed the men to keep their bags with them for what he planned to do next but thought if he suggested they do so, it would sound like an order.

His father and the Hawken ambled to the farmhouse. Marcus had been up early. He had napped after he came home with the dogs, but Thornton expected him to be that special kind of ornery that came from being tired and ravenous. He dreaded him all the more.

He also had a problem. If Marcus sent the men to the bunkhouse, Thornton would have no access to their bags. With that new wrinkle, he estimated he would have no more than two minutes to pull off his plan.

All five of them reached the food at the same time. His mother had brought a second tray, with a heavy crock, three bowls, and bread on it.

William, Ronan, and Henry waited to see how things would go. The wait was over in four seconds.

"I don't eat with niggras," Marcus said. "Take your food to the bunkhouse, and be quick about it. Every one of you better be back out in the field by the time that bell rings again in a half hour. That includes bringing the tray back where you found it. If you can't tell time, you better guess and guess right." He gave the rifle an absent-minded twirl. William, Ronan, and Henry glanced at it.

Marcus's directive gave Thornton just about fifteen seconds to make his move. Thornton was left-handed. His seed bag rested on his left side. William's rested on his right. He had an idea.

William turned for the bunkhouse, and Thornton slid into his pathway, walking with his head down to appear too preoccupied to see William coming. It forced William to bump into him.

Thornton pretended to trip and caused more commotion. He leaned on William for support, and while they were tangled, their bags were nose to nose on their hips. Thornton snatched the item from his bag and slipped it into William's. He was sure not even William saw him do it. William was too busy taking a giant step back. "Pardon me, Sir," he said.

Thornton let the "Sir" pass. That was not the time to expect the men to call him by his first name.

William headed for the bunkhouse. Thornton picked up his bowl of stew. His face went white. His father glared at William. "Hey!" Marcus yelled.

William stopped. He turned to face Marcus.

"Yeah, ape. Hang on just a minute." Marcus stalked over to William, Hawken in hand. Thornton felt his knees about to buckle. Had his father seen him make the drop?

Marcus stood in front of William and looked him up and down for a full minute. It felt like an hour to Thornton. He focused on the seed bag and tried not to faint.

"Watch where you're going. This ain't the jungle," Marcus said. He turned back to his dinner.

Thornton ducked his head into his stew and breathed such a huge sigh of relief the steam floated back up into his face and burned him.

William continued to the bunkhouse. He looked like he had encountered a minor interruption on his Sunday stroll. Henry and Ronan followed him with the tray.

Thornton had recovered. All he could do was hope William discovered what was in his bag and understood what it meant.

He took his food and, as he had done for ten years, sat as far away from his father as possible.

14

WILLIAM'S SEED bag bumped against his right thigh and felt heavier than it should have. A solid object hit him every time he took a step with his left foot and the bag swung down against his right leg.

It was crazy, but he was sure young Guthrie had dropped something into the sack. William had sneaked items in and out of places his whole life. He recognized a "drop" when he saw it.

He also thought old Guthrie knew a drop when *he* saw it and had been about to find out what his son had slipped into his slave's bag in the yard. That hadn't been the case, though, and William bumped his assessment of old Guthrie's intelligence down a few more notches.

Ronan closed the bunkhouse doors behind them, and Henry set down the tray on the stovetop. William was surprised Mrs. Guthrie had prepared their food. He had expected to divvy up cooking with Ronan and Henry. In his entire life, he had never eaten a meal fixed by anybody but a slave or some other servant. William chalked it up to old Guthrie being new at owning slaves. Once he got the hang of it—and his friends found out his wife cooked for three Negro slaves—they'd be cooking their own meals.

Nobody mentioned what had just happened outside. Conversations about incidents with owners and overseers were a waste of any slave's time unless they served to warn a fellow captive. The encounter had already cost them three of the thirty minutes they had for dinner.

William sat on the edge of his bunk with his back facing his two friends. His seed bag sat in front of him on his bunk, hidden from Ronan's and Henry's views. He let them serve themselves dinner and took advantage of their preoccupation with the large crock of hot stew and the second loaf of fresh bread they would eat that day to find out what was in his bag.

He peeked into it, hoping to figure out what was inside without pulling the item out, but it was too dark to see anything, so he reached in and felt around. His hand came upon something floating around in the buckwheat seeds. He recognized it in an instant.

A book.

He thought he must be dreaming.

He made a furtive glance in the direction of Henry and Ronan. They had advanced from the stove and dug into large bowls of stew they balanced on their laps. Big chunks of bread peered over the tops of the bowls. As each man stirred his stew, his bread appeared to glide from one side of his bowl to the other. The two lapsed into an easy conversation, as William had expected they would.

The sight of the food and the smell it sent throughout the bunkhouse should have made William hungry, but he was too stunned by what Thornton Guthrie had dropped into his bag to think about eating.

His heart pounded, both because he was excited to be touching a book and because he wondered why young Guthrie would go to such lengths to give it to him. Did he want old Guthrie to find William with it? William doubted it, although he wondered why he presumed good intentions from Guthrie the Younger when all he had ever seen in white men was their worst. Even abolitionists wanted Negroes nowhere near them once they got their freedom. He had seen abundant evidence of that in St. Louis, where the law enforced segregation with guns.

Still, he found it hard to imagine the boy setting up a slave for a beating or a bullet through the head. He had seen how young Thornton had eyed his father's rifle. He dreaded it as much as Ronan and Henry and he did.

He glanced over his shoulder one more time. Ronan and Henry had gotten all they could from their bowls with their spoons and slopped up stew with their bread. Ronan did most of the talking. Henry missed Colleen and was not up to much chatter.

William turned back to the bag and pulled out the book. His hands formed a kind of hug around it. He rubbed it in disbelief. He held it low to keep the others from seeing it.

The letters stenciled on the cover had faded, but William easily made out the words: "The Sketch Book of Geoffrey Crayon, Gent."

He knew that book! He had read about it in a St. Louis newspaper. The author was a fellow named Washington Irving, and his sketch book and stories were known all over. William never dreamt he would hold a volume in his own hands.

He flipped through the pages and was astounded to see that the book contained at least three dozen stories! He read titles like "The Voyage", "A Royal Poet", "John Bull", "The Boar's Head Tavern, Eastcheap", and "The Legend of Sleepy Hollow". The author had sprinkled throughout the pages sketches that William presumed depicted the stories.

He lost all sense of where he was. He forgot about dinner, Ronan, Henry, and what waited outside and ventured into the book.

He landed on a clump of consecutive pages with their corners bent. The name of the story on the first bent page was "Rip Van Winkle". William had never heard of anything called Rip Van Winkle, but something told him the corners of those pages were bent on purpose and that he was supposed to read that story first.

He read the first line: "*A posthumous writing of Diedrich Knickerbocker.*" He read on through a stanza by Cartwright about Woden, the God of Saxons. Before long, he traveled up the Hudson River to a small town nestled in blue and purple mountains settled by the Dutch. It seemed one of its citizens was a popular figure called Rip Van Winkle, a good neighbor and a henpecked husband, whom women and children fancied.

William's eyes took in the words at a swift pace. He devoured several pages. A few moments later, he fought to come back to himself and remembered Ronan and Henry. They dragged their last chunks of bread across the bottoms of their bowls. The pieces came up almost white. Each bowl had been scraped clean.

William felt sure he could trust them if they saw the book, but they would worry. It was unfair to saddle them with trouble, especially Henry.

Even though time flew, William hadn't lost track of it. With great reluctance, he shut the book. He turned his mind to Thornton Guthrie and wondered why the boy had given him such a gift. He thought back to the way young Guthrie had behaved since he and Henry and Ronan had arrived. He called them "Sir" and avoided his father. He looked downright grim at the prospect of owning slaves. He had given them no orders since they had arrived, not even the slightest command in the fields or timetables for using the outhouse. He had simply shown them how to farm.

When William had bumped into him on the way to the bunkhouse, it was the boy who stepped aside for William, and not William who was required to move for him. William had done so without thought.

William also remembered seeing the boy eavesdrop on his father's diatribe through the crack in the bunkhouse doors. William was certain Thornton Guthrie had heard his father warn William not to read. The boy knew William could read.

The more William thought about it, the more he realized what was going on. Thornton Guthrie was not only against slavery in general, but it seemed he was against his father owning in particular Ronan, Henry, and William. He could try to convey that with spoken words, but the men may not believe him, and his father might overhear him.

Young Guthrie had chosen the most covert way to deliver his message. It was also the most dangerous in the long run. What if his father asked about the book to read it himself or found it in the bunkhouse on a surprise raid? The danger convinced William. By choosing that way to put across his message—a *book* Marcus Guthrie's son had given a slave who was warned not to read—its truth was unmistakable. The three men had an ally in Thornton Guthrie.

The realization stunned William. He had never been on the same side as a white man in his entire life. The younger Guthrie had caught him off guard, indeed.

He was unsure what to do next, how to act. He had no idea how he would proceed in the fields that afternoon, how he would let young Guthrie know he understood his message, how the two of them would behave once he made it clear.

He slipped the book under the mattress of his bunk and went to the stove for his stew. To save time, he scooped it into his mouth with the large piece of bread the men had left him. The three had just seven minutes to be back outside with the tray.

15

THORNTON STARED at the bunkhouse doors. He had no idea what time it was, but he figured the thirty minutes his father had given the men to eat were just about up. He watched for them to emerge from the bunkhouse. He wanted to make eye contact with William and try to read his face for clues as to whether he had gotten Thornton's message.

He was scared either way. If William *had* gotten the message, it forever put at risk Thornton's ability to manage his relationship with his father on his own terms. There would be somebody who could, whenever the urge arose, betray him to his father, albeit at his own risk. Until that morning, he never dreamt he would relinquish that control. It had been too vital to his survival. Even if William never intended to sic Marcus on Thornton, he might do so by accident if he was careless with the book.

On the other hand, if William had gone straight for the stew, without looking inside his bag, the first time he might lay hands on the book could be out in the open field, when he reached into his seed bag, with Marcus in full view. That would be a disaster the perils of which Thornton had no reference to calculate. He had never pushed his father like seeing a book in a slave's hand would push him.

William, Ronan, and Henry emerged from the bunkhouse. Thornton's mother hadn't yet rung the bell, but somehow the men knew it was time to come back outside.

William walked past the spot where Thornton sat. Thornton stared at him. He hoped the man would feel Thornton's eyes on him and look in his direction. He wanted some sort of signal from William that he had found the book, but William faced forward. He didn't acknowledge Thornton.

Thornton's heart sank. It also began to thump. He had no idea whether the book was still in William's seed bag.

Marcus stood up.

Thornton expected his father's next words to be, "Let me see those bags." Instead, he barked orders about everybody getting back to work and returned to the dog-leash post.

Thornton breathed a little easier and executed the other plans he had come up with earlier in the day. He had retrieved from a trunk in his room a pair of boots he had outgrown that he thought might fit Henry. He would hand them to him right in front of his father, in so blatant a fashion, it could only mean he wanted the man to work harder for Marcus. His father would be pleased, and the exchange would distract him from Thornton's maneuvering to get William alone. It would also make Henry's feet feel a lot better. "Henry?"

The man had been headed to the fields and appeared startled to hear his name. "Yessir?"

Thornton let it go. Marcus looked on. "I got you these boots." He hated what he needed to say next. It would give the men the impression it had taken him just half a day to settle into his role as slave-master. He had no choice, though. "They'll help you get more work done." He made sure his father heard him.

He continued, for good measure. "You men take up where you left off with those rows there." He pointed in the general direction where Ronan and Henry had worked earlier. He felt stupid since they were headed that way anyway, but it kept him from giving them the order to their faces. "William and I 'll get these rows." He searched William's face for a sign of recognition that Thornton angled to get him alone so he could probe about the book, but all he got was William's back. The tall man obeyed Thornton's order and returned to his row.

Not far enough away, the dogs barked. Thornton scowled.

———◦◇◦———

An hour later, Thornton agonized. All four bodies worked their rows. William, Ronan, and Henry put much more effort into the job than Thornton, who sweated for a different reason.

He suddenly hated his brilliant book idea. It was about to explode in all of their faces. What had he been thinking?

For the second time, William's voice broke into his thoughts and startled him.

"Rip sure is a funny name to give a man." William again talked more to the soil than to Thornton, but his words stopped Thornton in mid-planting motion. He stared at William, who pushed seeds into the ground and acted like he hadn't just spoken.

Thornton's bafflement disappeared. The message was clear. William had not only seen the book, but he had found the folded pages that flagged "Rip Van Winkle".

It was also clear William understood Thornton had given him the book as a sign he was on the side of the three men. If he had thought it was a trap, he would have burned the book in the bunkhouse stove and would have never referred to it. He would have left it to Thornton to bring it up if Thornton wanted retribution.

Thornton adopted William's nonchalance. He poked seeds into the ground. "His name's the least of his problems," he said to the dirt. "Wait till you meet his wife."

For the first time that day, Thornton and William each had something he was sure he could be happy about. They looked each other square in the eye and grinned.

16

THORNTON CARRIED on a dodgy conversation with
William. He took advantage of an odd situation. He would
have never thought it possible, but two months after William,
Ronan, and Henry had arrived at Guthrie Farms, Marcus
allowed him and the three men to figure out how to divide
the work on the farm, with the overseers being Marcus's
guns, his dogs, and Missouri law.

The first week the men were on the farm, Marcus
engaged in lots of rifle practice. He took shots that hit
targets less than five feet from where Ronan exercised a
horse and clipped Henry's hammer from fifty yards just
seconds after Henry stepped away from it. He shot leaves off
crops, nicked wood in the yard, put a hole through the water
pump ladle, and generally reminded everyone who was in
charge.

As time wore on, however, the ownership of slaves became
a mundane chore. It required more engagement than Marcus
could muster. In typical fashion, Marcus ceded the particulars
to his son. The specifics of who worked which row, who fed
which animals, and who cleaned the outhouse involved much
more consideration than Marcus cared to bother with.

He had spent a lifetime farming with every kind of man.
He'd worked on crowded farms and empty ones and shared
such tight sleeping quarters, men slept in shifts and rotated
in and out of the same bunk over twenty-four hours. He had
never worked with Negroes, but three more men on a farm
was nothing new to Marcus Guthrie. The work would get
divided, somehow, as it always did. He preferred to observe
from afar, show up at odd times, and lord his authority over
all of them at unpredictable intervals.

It had been a boon to Thornton. He used his father's apathy to get closer to the men. Wherever he could find a minute or an hour or a fleeting moment spent on common ground with any of them, he seized it, whether it was about dreading the repair of a fence or having no desire to herd the hogs.

Extreme weather patched together any dry spells in the conversation. A three-day heatwave in September had been a windfall. Nothing could get a man to pile onto a conversation faster than complaining about the weather. Thornton made sure that he and Henry never let the others hear the end of how awful the heat was.

A man needing to relieve himself also helped. It forced *some* discussion as he announced his departure from the general area.

Over time, Thornton found he needed fewer pretexts to gain entry into their world. He genuinely liked all three men, and after years in isolation, he enjoyed their company and cultivated a rapport with a mind as much toward friendship as escape.

He gently inserted himself into their banter and laughed at their subtle humor, which was more hidden, out of necessity, but all the funnier, Thornton found, for its lack of obviousness. He sometimes perpetrated the joke and made sure they felt relaxed enough to laugh with him. It was critical to Thornton that they pay no penalties if they failed to maintain their guard. If something went wrong or was misunderstood, Thornton took the blame.

Little by little, they loosened up. He pressed and enlisted their help to take advantage of Marcus's absences with minor conspiracies around the farm. He made sure he was always the instigator, the first to act up and misbehave.

The "Sir" battle took the longest to win. He triumphed by purposely stepping just far enough away that if they needed to get his attention, they would have to call him *something* and could not just start talking. Over time, after so many

admonitions, "Sir" became conspicuous. "Thornton" slowly
replaced it.

For them to trust he recognized they were equals, he
could not ask them to revert to "Sir" in front of his father.
Still, Marcus Guthrie wouldn't hesitate to punish any one of
the men despite it being Thornton who insisted they not call
him "Sir". He appealed to the self-doubting part of his
father's nature and convinced him the only way they would
know who was really in charge was if they reserved "Sir" for
one man: Marcus Guthrie. He wasn't that obvious, though. His
father would know something was afoot. He took the long
way around. "I don't answer when I hear 'Sir'. I think they're
talking to you. Slows things down," he had argued, albeit to
Blackie's rump, which he was brushing while making his
point. The argument was weak, but its subservience shrouded
that from Marcus for just the few moments Thornton needed
it to. It worked.

"If you wanna let chimps talk familiar to you, what do I
care?" had been all Thornton needed to hear.

He *had* to cross that frontier, had to eliminate any sense
that he had reserved for himself a passageway of authority or
hierarchy, or a separate set of rights, if he ever hoped to be
real friends with the men, which he wanted more and more.

He found he worked easy with Henry and could talk to
Ronan about horses and day-to-day farm life. Ronan exuded
pragmatism. He was the person Thornton most wanted to talk
to for clever solutions to mundane farm problems.

It was with William, though, that he had something extra
in common. They delighted in talking whenever they could
about the stories Thornton had given William on that first
day. Often, their conversations turned from fiction to real life,
and Thornton found himself admitting things out loud to
William that he had never recollected even mentioning to
himself, inside his own head.

That day, though, they discussed something much direr.

The two of them were on their knees harvesting the kale Thornton and his father had planted over the summer. It was the dead of autumn. Thornton's father hated cold-weather harvesting. For years, he had refused to kneel in any temperature below forty-five degrees to harvest, hammer, or heft anything. He had years earlier relegated the autumn harvesting to Thornton. Without help, it had always been slower going—Thornton's normal effort and half again to pick up his father's slack, which was worth only half of the average man's efforts—but it kept his father at a more pleasing distance. Thornton loved cold weather.

It was an ideal time to talk to William about escaping Guthrie Farms. They were alone. Henry chopped firewood, and Ronan tended to the hooves of every horse in the stable.

William snatched too hard on a fistful of kale leaves. The bud at the center of the plant popped out. The plant was as good as dead. William tossed the bunch of leaves to the side.

He was nervous. Thornton thought he should be. The notion of escaping terrified Thornton. Running had to have put ten times the fear into a man who had been flayed for reading. Thornton's own back itched every time he thought about William being torn open with kerosene-dipped rope. He had wanted to sleep for a century the day William had told him what Hezzy had done.

He waited for William to say something. He used a gentle hand to pull up his own kale stalks.

William finally spoke. "Escape? Just *vanish*?" The second question ended on a low tone and dripped with skepticism. Thornton heard no genuine wonderment in William's voice. "It's too chancy."

Thornton suppressed a groan. He wasn't just up against his father, the law, and any weaknesses in whatever plan they might come up with. He also had to fight William's past, and Ronan's and Henry's, and all the retribution they had suffered for either daring to step out of line or accidentally doing so. It wasn't going to be easy to ask them to conspire with him to do anything beyond the small, more manageable risks involved with minor deception around the farm.

For them, he may have been a white man who would turn on them at the first sign of trouble. He couldn't blame them if they felt that way. He may take them just far enough away to be exposed to every law, rifle, and dog in the territory and desert them for safety if his own head was on the block. He tried a straightforward approach. He had nothing to lose.

"If you're worried I'll backstab you, I won't."

William said nothing.

"It should be obvious by now my father is as much a threat to me as he is to you." He let that percolate for a moment. "To him it doesn't matter that he bought you, sired me, or married my mother. We're all just possessions to him. What good would it do me to switch my loyalties to him if we're caught? He's proven he'd kill me if he was bored enough on a Sunday and let his mind ponder the idea for too long." He paused and took a deep breath. "I mean, look at this." He pointed to his dented ear. "My father shot that bit out aiming for my head. I was seven."

He let that sit. William was ever so slightly less blithe. He stared hard at Thornton's ear. Thornton felt he might just have said the right thing. He pushed home. "And, anyway, I don't feel that way toward him." It was the first time he had ever spoken the words out loud. He was surprised by how good it felt to tell someone that he felt no allegiance to his own father.

William said, "Four people—"

"Five. My mother's coming with us."

William raised his eyebrows and gave a slow nod. Thornton felt his first small victory.

"Five people, three of them Negros, can't just promenade through Missouri like they're going to Sunday service. We wouldn't last two hours. They'd find us and hang us."

Thornton tugged on a stubborn bit of kale. William watched his careful technique. "Think about it," Thornton said. "A little over a hundred miles to the west, and you'll answer to no man but yourself for the rest of your life. You can read and, I don't know, maybe get married and become a father. Don't tell me you've never thought about it." He retrieved more kale. "We just have to come up with a way to appear to be traveling with my father's permission."

William continued to nod approval, taken in, it seemed, by the prospect of not having to harvest someone else's kale while that person got drunk and took a nap in a warm farmhouse the law gave him the enviable right to own. "Ronan and Henry and I know how it is with you and your father," he said. "We know what you think of our predicament. That's not the problem."

Thornton was gleeful. His friends trusted him. "That faith takes us a long way, though."

"Yes, but the only way we leave here without your father giving chase is to kill him." He looked Thornton right in the eye. And the ear, his dented one. "Are you prepared for that? I don't even know if I am." He grabbed the next bunch of kale leaves and pulled on them using Thornton's method. They pulled right up. "I got a notion if I killed somebody, even a man as guilty as your father, or Hezzy Jones, something out there would be watching, would note it somewhere, and it would make sure to balance things out. I'd pay for it somewhere in some fair time. Archibald always said if you see a sleeping hangman, don't wake him." He pulled up bunch after bunch of kale with no effort. "And even if that thing watching me let me get away with it, I wouldn't know. I'd spend the rest of my life waiting for it to catch up with me to take it out of my hide. I'd be waiting for the hangman to wake up and put my neck in his noose. I'd never be free."

William's talk of the hangman chilled Thornton. He had pondered a hundred ways to get past Marcus, and every time he came to the conclusion they might have to kill him, he pushed the notion aside and refused to abandon the idea of running. Archibald and William were right, though. Killing Marcus was no guarantee of freedom and could be the promise of much worse.

"We could find a way to keep my father trapped for just enough time to get over the state line. If he caught up with us, he'd have to commit murder to stop us."

"It would be murder in the case of you and your mother, and then only maybe. For certain he'd have the right to kill Ronan and Henry and me."

Those words frightened Thornton. He was just about to drop the entire idea.

"Not a word to Ronan or Henry," William said. "Until we come up with a plan that won't get us all killed, we better keep it to ourselves."

It was too late. Thornton had just taken his first steps off Guthrie Farms. So had William. Thornton couldn't turn back and leave William stranded beyond the property line.

He was scared to death.

17

THE COLD autumn air gave Jeremiah Barker a chill. He preferred not to leave his fields for any reason, not even for a cup of coffee to warm him up. The day promised to be strange, though, so he broke with tradition and went to the house.

In the parlor on the way to the kitchen, he caught sight of his wife Dorinda. She listened to Amy Pierson, Flora Perkins, and Julia Tander drone on about Jess Tander's gout over a quilt they had started at dawn. He had no idea in whose house the quilt would land. He lost track of what order they went in several quilts before that one.

Jeremiah recognized the expression on his wife's face. Dorinda wanted to scream. Jess Tander's gout and all of the details about his hot, red big toe and how large it had gotten, and how the painful heat of it kept him and Julia up at night, were of no interest to Dorinda.

It had been several weeks since their son Ethan had disappeared. There had been no trace of him. Dorinda had begun to lose her mind. Jeremiah feared that if Ethan didn't one day walk back up the path to the Barker farmhouse, Dorinda might lose all reason.

The year of 1834 had been the worst of their lives, and it wasn't over yet. They had lost Baby Justus and Ethan in the span of a few weeks. And Jeremiah hadn't touched Dorinda the way husbands touched their wives since Justus had died. He was terrified he would give her another child who wouldn't survive birth.

Not that there hadn't been close calls, moments between them that they had experienced ten thousand times in so many years of marriage that signaled what should happen next, like the day she had stayed out till sundown pondering near Justus's grave and he had brought her shawl to her and beckoned her to come inside for fear of threats from the night that might hurt her. She had looked at him as a beau who'd come courting, hoping that his small gesture of tenderness might lead to more, but he had turned away and said, "Not too much longer out here," over his shoulder on his way back to the house. She didn't know he had gone straight to the window to keep an eye on her, ready to pounce on any raccoon, wild dog, or man who threatened her. By the time she returned, though, he was hard at work shoveling ashes out of the fireplace, and she went about the business of putting supper on the table. He had wanted her, but he had been too scared to act on it.

The distance had put a strain on them both. Something would soon blow, whether it was their entire marriage or Dorinda's sanity or both. He stared at her over his coffee cup and searched her face for a sign of which it might be.

If Ethan returned, that might stave off the madness. They loved Justus, had grieved all he would never be, but with Ethan it was different. Jeremiah could barely remember a time when he hadn't known Ethan, when his oldest hadn't been there. For a spell, short though it was, Ethan had been his only child, had been the only offspring who had seen him be a father, and they had a special link because of it, even if Ethan had turned irascible. Jeremiah loved his children the same, but he afforded Ethan a different status. Janey had arrived just a year after Ethan, but Jeremiah and Dorinda always thought with fondness of the first child to witness their life together. The others, no matter how much their parents loved them, had missed part of the show. They had each joined something already under way. The later they were born, the more they had missed. They would never know as much as Ethan had known.

That awful summer morning Ethan disappeared, Dorinda had refused to hear her husband. He told her he had hunted

for Ethan everywhere it was logical to look in his first
search, but Dorinda had threatened to mount up and ride the
entire territory to look for her son herself. Jeremiah told her
that would be unnecessary. He said he and Hec Pierson and
Jess Tander and some of the other men would ride out and
track Ethan all year, if they had to. And they did look, for
two weeks, riding out in one direction, and doubling back
after several days and heading out in the other.

It had been no use. Ethan hadn't turned up, and the men
needed to get back to their own farms and children. Jeremiah
set out in a third direction and stayed gone for another two
weeks but came home alone. No one risked heading in the
fourth direction since it was unexplored territory and the men
couldn't be sure whether they would end up stranded without
water.

Jeremiah hoped wherever Ethan was, he wasn't there. He
prayed Ethan had marched along the creek and ended up
somewhere harmless and that it was just too cold to return.
That was magical thinking, though. Ethan had likely died at
the hands of a violent man or in the mouth of a four-legged
beast.

Jeremiah finished his coffee and strode through the
parlor and out the front door without speaking a word to the
women. He dreaded what he had to do next.

———◆◇◆———

Jeremiah entered the abandoned cabin next door and
stepped into what had been the Dawsons' parlor. He surveyed
the room. Janey's slingshot lay on the ground in the corner.
An ongoing game of jackstraws sat in the middle of the floor.

Jeremiah looked for one item. At first glance he didn't
see it. He knew it was there, though. He walked through the
rest of the small house in search of it.

In the back room, he spotted it against the wall. The
sight of Ethan's kite leaning there as if his son planned to

come back at any moment and fly it down to the creek crushed Jeremiah.

He carried the kite to the parlor. He had brought with him to the Dawsons' a hammer and two wooden pegs the size of nails that he had whittled. He set the kite down near the jackstraws and hammered the pegs into the wall above the fireplace, slightly out of line. He lifted the kite and rested it on the pegs.

He stepped back and stared up at the only tombstone, the only resting place he could offer his son until he knew for sure what had been his fate. The kite hung sideways, just a little, on the out-of-line pegs. It mimicked how it looked in real flight. A rock formed in Jeremiah's throat.

"Good-bye, son," he said. He left the Dawson place for good. He had paid what he feared were his final respects to his oldest boy.

18

THORNTON AND Ronan herded hogs. It was afternoon on an autumn Wednesday. Marcus was just inside the barn tending to the horses. Ronan normally groomed the horses, but since it was a cold day, he was sent to work outside, while Marcus enjoyed the relative warmth of the barn.

Thornton wanted to find out more about Henry. Both men were his friends, but neither of them spoke much about themselves. Ronan was simply a quiet man not given to go on about any subject. Some questioned and pondered all the time. Ronan spoke in answers, in solutions. Henry, however, could go days without speaking a question or an answer. He seemed to Thornton to be permanently distracted by some additional horror on top of being trapped on Guthrie Farms.

"How long have you known Henry?" It was a sensitive question. It required Ronan to reflect on being a slave.

"Handsome Henry. Heh-heh. Long time. Mr. Jones bought us at auction on the same day."

At that, Thornton shut up.

Ronan stepped to his right to round up three stray hogs. He veered back to his left and fell into step with Thornton. "He left his woman behind at the Jones place. Colleen. As soon as Mr. Jones brought her to the farm, Henry made sure every fellow kept away from her. He didn't have anything to worry about anyway. His looks had us all beat." Ronan sounded matter-of-fact and not at all bothered by the notion that he hadn't stood a chance with Colleen.

Despite the scars, Ronan was not an ugly fellow. The scars were evil because they had been done to him, but as far as his appearance was concerned, the scars added to his resolute nature more than they detracted from his looks. He and Henry were both younger than William. Thornton guessed they were just past twenty-five. Unlike William, who knew he was thirty-six, Ronan and Henry were unsure how old they were, but it was clear they were of an age to find a mate. Ronan had likely had his chances. It was just that Henry was striking in how handsome he was.

Thornton took the opening. "So, he's pining for her. I understand." He didn't understand as much as he claimed, for he had only ever been in love with his fields. He was unfamiliar with how a man felt when he longed for a woman. He guessed it was akin to how he figured he would feel if his crops refused to grow.

"You know how menfolk are."

Thornton didn't, not the way Ronan meant. All he had ever witnessed was the way his father had treated his mother.

"He's worried she's moved on to some other fellow with him gone."

That Thornton could relate to. He had always felt his mother would replace his father if she could. Thornton figured Ronan meant it another way, for Colleen probably missed Henry and would move on by virtue of the circumstances, whereas his father deserved to have his mother desert him if the chance ever arose. He and William were in the process of arranging for that very thing to happen.

"A man stays up nights imagining the worst, knowing a rifle and dogs and all the miles he'd have to run stand between him and his woman. It's a lot for a man to bear."

Thornton picked up a rock and tossed it hard. He tried to skim it across the fields, but it stopped dead in the dirt. "Seems to me slavery wrecks every life it touches."

Ronan stared long at him. "I'm willing to swear you never told a bigger truth."

"How about you? Are you missing someone back at the Jones place? A woman?"

"No, I thought too much about runnin' to take up with any lady folk. Tried to run. Didn't make it though."

"Did Hezzy....?" Thornton dropped the question.

"Yeah. Dragged me to the middle of the compound and cut me, real quick like. Made his point. Didn't need to do to me what he did to Will. Branded a runaway wherever I go."

Thornton rubbed his ear. "Ronan, I'm shameful for never telling you this, but...."

Ronan's scars stared harder at Thornton than the man who wore them.

"I'm sorry."

The two walked on behind the hogs in silence.

"I'm going to Hezzy Jones's place to see about Colleen for Henry."

They prepared the final corner of a patch of land for planting the winter wheat.

Both shovels stopped. Each man stood his upright in the earth.

"What?" William leaned on his shovel, his face blanketed in disbelief.

Thornton leaned on his shovel too. His father had gone into Columbia for supplies, and they were free to speak. It was the day after Thornton had talked to Ronan about Henry, and overnight, he had made up his mind to find out what he could about Colleen. It sounded strange, but he hoped to bring back news that she was just as miserable as Henry was, that she missed him the way he missed her. He also planned to use the outing to assess how hard it would be to bring Colleen with them when they escaped. He kept that from William, though, and only relayed the part about Colleen's misery. William seemed doubtful about the venture.

"Hezzy Jones isn't going to let you just ride up on his property and start asking about his slaves. Even if you pretended you were interested in buying more, as soon as you start fishing around about Colleen, he'll know what you're up to and tell your father the minute he gets the chance. Or he may just decide to ask your father about the extra slaves he's supposed to be interested in, and you'll be found out *that* way."

William was right. Thornton had to get to Colleen without Hezzy Jones knowing it.

"I'll sneak into her quarters."

William threw up his hands. His shovel fell. "And just how do you plan to do that?"

Thornton leaned harder on his shovel, for moral support. He was losing the argument. "I'll wait until my father is asleep on fruit liquor and ride over there in the middle of the night."

"Not if I have anything to say about it. There's only so heavy your father sleeps. Must have been six or seven times he's come into the bunkhouse in the middle of the night, checking to make sure we're still there. I lost two brand new newspapers in the wood stove because of it."

Just about every week, Thornton had sneaked William a copy of the *Missouri Intelligencer and Boon's Lick Advertiser,* a newspaper his father picked up in Columbia. William used the papers not only for his own pleasure but also to teach Ronan and Henry to read. William burned each copy within days of getting it. With what William said, Thornton understood he had been forced to set fire to two papers he hadn't even gotten to read.

His father's midnight raids appalled Thornton. He couldn't even forewarn his friends. His father gave him no hint when he planned to carry out a search. His father didn't suspect him. He presumed his guns kept Thornton heeled. It simply was not his way to include Thornton in his actions.

"And besides. How will you get past Hezzy Jones's dogs? His hounds sleep in front of the bunkhouses there just like your father's do here. Where do you think your father got the idea?"

Thornton knew. His father had forced Henry to build a large doghouse like Hezzy's, warm enough for winter. It sat right in front of the bunkhouse.

"You'll never get through." William's tone was more matter-of-fact than pleading. He picked up his shovel and went back to work.

Thornton hated to hear any opposition, but he appreciated William's protective inclinations. "Look, I know it's crazy," he said, "but it's the only way I know to help Henry not worry about Colleen as much, if that's even possible."

"It's not." William dug hard with his shovel. "Besides...."

"What?"

"Never mind." He kept digging.

Thornton thought he was sure what was on William's mind. "I know."

"You know what?"

"That I'm the only thing standing between my father and you and Ronan and Henry. Believe me, I've thought about what might happen to you three if something happened to me." Thornton didn't tell William he had spent hours and hours pondering just that question. "But it doesn't mean I shouldn't try to bring Henry some good news if it's in my power to do so."

"You think that's it? I'm thirty-six years old. I've seen everything. There's nothing your father can do to me short of killing me that I haven't had done to me already. Publicly. Hiding behind a fifteen-year-old wouldn't be how I'd work my way out of trouble. Ronan or Henry either."

Thornton was thoroughly chagrined for what he had said, especially in light of the flogging and maiming William and Ronan had suffered, but he was also exhilarated. He had never met a man like William.

"It's that...." William shifted some more dirt with no purpose.

"It's what?"

"It's been a long time since I had a friend like Archie, someone to talk to about....things, about books, about life."

It was the first time in his whole life Thornton had heard anybody use the word "friend" to describe him. Despite a life in bondage, William had had Archie. Thornton had never had one friend.

William had finished every story in *The Sketch Book of Geoffrey Crayon, Gent.*, and Thornton had slipped him *Ivanhoe*, by a fellow known as "The Author of *Waverley*". Invariably, whether they talked about reports on Congress in the newspaper or pondered Rip's slumber or wondered about twelfth-century England, their banter always lapsed into deeper musings on life. William's declaration about what it meant to him overwhelmed Thornton and made him feel responsible and joyful at the same time.

"Which is why I have every intention of coming back," he said. "With information for my other friend Henry about....his wife, when you think about it." He dug his shovel into the dirt in front of him, hoping he had settled the issue.

William continued to dig too. "Not a word to Henry. Better not to get his hopes up."

Thornton nodded and kept digging.

"She's in the bunkhouse closest to the edge of the field. If you tie your horse to a tree a ways away and walk up slow on foot, you may not wake up the dogs. They're used to some moving around by the folks in the bunkhouses."

Thornton nodded again.

"Go to the window at the back. Tell the first woman you see you have a message from Henry for Colleen, or she's going to think you're a friend of the Jones family there for another reason, and I can't have that. You have a message from Henry for Colleen. Those have to be the first words out of your mouth."

Thornton nodded slower that time, horrified by the implications of what William had just said.

"Let me know what night you plan to go. I'll distract your father if it comes down to it. You are not to leave without me knowing."

Thornton contemplated the gravity of William's offer and dug harder. He was as scared as he had been when they first talked of escape and the sleeping hangman, but he had no intention of suggesting they call it off. He hoped he could make it and that William wouldn't have to intercept his father. He nodded one final time.

The shovels scraped in rhythmic fashion. The two friends had survived their first disagreement not about books. Thornton wondered whether they would survive his reconnaissance mission to the Jones farmstead.

PART TWO

Crop Rotation

My overcoat is worn out; my shirts also are worn out.
And I ask to be allowed to have a lamp in the evening;
it is indeed wearisome sitting alone in the dark.

—*William Tyndale*

19

THORNTON WALKED his horse, Ashes, out of the barn
at the pace of a snail's crawl. It was one o'clock in the
morning. The ride to Hezzy Jones's place would take forty-five
minutes by lamplight. The lamp was absurd since horses saw
better at night, but Thornton had to see which way to guide
Ashes.

He would snuff out the light about a hundred yards out
from Hezzy's farmstead, hitch Ashes to a tree, and sneak onto
the property on foot. He hoped to spend no more than five
minutes there. He factored in problems like a reluctant horse
or a recalcitrant bunkmate of Colleen's and planned to be back

in bed by three o'clock. He tried not to factor in being caught and shot by Hezzy Jones.

William had attempted to talk him out of going right up until sundown on what was technically the previous day, when William, Ronan, and Henry were forced to retreat to the bunkhouse. Thornton imagined William tossed in his bunk and kept perfect time in his head, with Thornton's exact location at every minute fixed in his mind.

Thornton had learned his friend's claim to always know what time it was had been true. With a regularity that sometimes unnerved Thornton, William predicted events down to the second. It was he who had figured out the travel times for the night ride to the Jones place. He remembered the distance between the two farmsteads from the day Marcus had brought him to Guthrie Farms in the back of his wagon. If Thornton were late by even a minute, William would know something had gone amiss.

He closed the barn door and mounted Ashes. He walked the horse until he was out of earshot of the property to keep the dogs' mouths shut. Far out, he set Ashes into the fastest gallop he could achieve with the awkward lamp situation. He had been to Hezzy Jones's place enough to know the way. He had also been fortunate his father had dragged him along his whole life on his horseback errands. Marcus forced Thornton to tote dead animals intended for supper and chase down stray hogs. It made him almost as skilled a rider as he was a farmer. He gave Ashes another kick to speed up the ride.

About forty minutes later, he thought his right arm might fall off. It was numb from carrying the lamp. He was sick of holding it aloft, but he was close to the Jones place. He rejoiced at almost being done with the journey.

A light shone in the distance. It came from the Jones place.

They were awake. At that hour?

Thornton pulled Ashes to a stop and hopped off. If he could see their light, they could see his. He snuffed out the lamp and assessed the situation. The light was all the way to the right of the string of buildings he was just able to make out in the dark. According to William, from the direction he approached, the main house was to the right and Colleen's bunkhouse was all the way to the left. It meant the light he saw was in the main house. If he was lucky, whoever was awake was far enough from Colleen's bunkhouse not to hear what was about to happen.

He tugged on the horse's rein and walked until he reached a good hitching tree. He looped the rein around a low branch, hooked the dark lamp over another one, and girded himself for the precarious trek to Colleen's bunkhouse. He walked in crouched fashion.

A few moments later, he reached the edge of the property. He glanced at the light in the main house and wondered how he had gotten himself into such a situation. He crept closer to the bunkhouse. He looked at it and at the light in the main house. He looked again at the bunkhouse and again at the main house.

Bunkhouse.

Main house.

He must have looked back and forth over a hundred times. He skulked on.

He looked at the main house one more time. He never got another proper look at the bunkhouse.

Ashes let out a long neigh under his tree in the distance. The dogs went wild.

Thornton had just enough time to duck behind the far side of Colleen's bunkhouse. He dove to the ground and lay flat against the bunkhouse wall. He hoped he blended into the wood in the pitch dark. Unless somebody from the main house came out with lamps and searched not just in the bunkhouses but also around them, for slaves who may have run, he might go undiscovered. It was fortunate he worked in dirt all day and paid no mind to how filthy the ground was as a hiding place. He ignored some cow manure he sniffed not more than a foot away.

The dogs howled on. Voices approached from the direction of the main house.

Somebody fired a rifle.

The dogs became strident. Ashes neighed at a higher pitch and presented an additional problem. If whoever fired the rifle discovered his horse, he was doomed. He sweated and hugged the wall of the bunkhouse with his back.

He heard several voices. They belonged to people who ran. The sound of them moved along too fast to belong to people who walked.

"I thought I heard a horse!"

"One of ours?"

"I don't know!"

"Obadiah, I'll get the men's bunkhouse! You get the barn!" Thornton recognized Hezzy Jones's voice commanding his younger son to check the barn. "Jedidiah, check the women's bunkhouse!"

"Yep!"

Jedidiah Jones. Hezzy Jones's older son, the one who had taken a liking to Colleen, Thornton suddenly remembered Hezzy telling his father the day he had offered to sell Marcus his slaves. Thornton knew Jedidiah well. He was just about five years older than Thornton and handy with a rifle. Both of Hezzy Jones's sons were. The bunkhouse he was assigned to check was the one Thornton hid behind.

Another rifle cracked.

Ashes neighed louder, but in the confusion, it was difficult to tell where the sound came from.

Thornton's face was drenched in sweat. The dogs continued their cacophony.

The door of Thornton's bunkhouse banged opened. From where he lay on the ground, he saw a light come through the window above him. The inhabitants had been braced for the intrusion, Thornton assumed, because they made very little sound when Jedidiah rushed in and demanded, "Which one of you tried to run?"

Thornton heard a hard slap to a face. A woman shrieked. Thornton was sure she fell to the ground. He clinched his fists and prayed it wasn't Colleen. He felt awful for putting her ahead of the others, but he cared most about Colleen.

Thornton heard a woman say, "None of us, Sir. We're all here, Sir." He wondered if it was Colleen. The voice was young.

The head count must have satisfied Jedidiah because the next thing Thornton heard was him yelling, "All the women are here! It must be one of the men!"

"Nope! All the men are here too!" Hezzy said.

"Barn's clear!" Obadiah said.

It was the moment that would decide Thornton's fate. If they believed no one had tried to escape, they would return to the main house and figure the dogs and maybe one of their horses had gotten spooked over nothing. If they thought a runaway from another farm had tried to take refuge during the night on their farm, they might search the entire surroundings of the property, in which case they would discover either him, his horse, or both of them.

He held his breath.

Sweat dripped sideways down the bridge of his nose, but he was too afraid to reach up and wipe it off for fear his arm might cause a rustling sound that would get Jedidiah's attention. It was an irrational fear since the dogs still barked and made too much noise for Jedidiah to hear Thornton's sleeve shift in the dark, but he held still anyway.

He rolled his eyes up and saw the lamplight leave the bunkhouse. He braced for it to make its way around the side of the building where it would discover he lay there in a pool of muddy sweat.

The light never came.

The voices retreated to the main house. They traveled at the pace of a walk. One of them ordered the dogs to shush.

With the exception of an occasional yap, the dogs quieted down.

Thornton stayed where he was for at least another half hour. He couldn't risk moving around until the dogs had fallen asleep.

Thornton despised dogs.

He wanted to make a slow crawl back to his horse and leave without talking to Colleen.

It took him half a second to dismiss the thought. He had come too far to leave without getting a message to Colleen. And he could never gather how difficult it would be to help her escape until he talked to her and got a gander at her living quarters. He and a band that included three slaves and his mother would probably set off a maelstrom of dog and rifle madness if they approached the Jones property. He had to know how hard it would be to get Colleen off Hezzy's farmstead to join them.

Still, if the dogs howled a second time, the lamplight would come for him. He dreaded his next move.

He rolled over and up onto all fours, careful not to land his hand in the pile of manure, and waited a moment. He posed like a four-legged animal and felt just as dumb. *Why had he gone there?*

The dogs stayed quiet. Ashes was quiet too. Thornton stood up in a long, slow motion. He looked like he had a backache and practically did have one.

He stood flat against the bunkhouse wall for five more minutes, he reckoned, until he accepted he had to summon the courage to tap on the window. He noticed for the first time how high up the window was cut into the wall. It was not as high as the window in the men's bunkhouse on Guthrie Farms, but it was just as impractical. Most windows were cut low, so folks could easily lean out of them. Thornton thought it was absurd that it was different for slaves. He was just tall enough to reach his chin to the bottom of Colleen's window.

He hoped the women inside were still awake after Jedidiah's raid. It would mean he wouldn't have to knock on the window too hard, and the dogs may remain asleep.

He gave the window a soft tap. Unless the women were tall like he was, they would have to stand on something to reach the window. Thornton figured they had a stool they used regularly to open and close the window. He hoped it was stationed somewhere near the window. If it was so heavy they had to drag it, it might wake the dogs or even alert Ashes and cause him to nicker.

To his great relief, a face appeared in the window just a few seconds after he tapped it. It belonged to a young woman who jumped at the sight of his face.

He mouthed, "Open the window."

Without hesitation, the woman opened the window. Thornton remembered William's stern warning. He whispered, "I have a message from Henry for Colleen."

Two more faces appeared. They stood on a long bench that accommodated all three of them.

"I'm Colleen," whispered one of the new faces.

She was stunning.

Thornton understood why Henry worried nights about Colleen. He directed his words toward her and tried not to let her loveliness distract him.

"My name is Thornton Guthrie." He hadn't known he could whisper so softly. "Henry lives on my father's farm." He felt guilty for referring to Henry's slavery as "living" on Guthrie Farms, but he pushed through and said, "He's my friend. He wanted me to tell you he is doing fine." In reality, Henry had no message for Colleen because he had no idea Thornton was fool enough to tap on her window in the middle of the night. He also wasn't "fine." He was a slave. But Thornton figured if Henry could give Colleen a message, he would want her to be reassured he was well. "He eats well every day, has a clean bunkhouse to sleep in, and has suffered no illnesses since he arrived at our farm."

Colleen scrunched her pretty face into a cry and somehow managed to remain beautiful. Her sobs were soft. She sounded at once relieved and sad. Thornton hated his father at that moment more than he ever had.

He had to press on, though. He took advantage of the quiet dogs to deliver more news. "Please let everyone know William and Ronan are fine too." More lies, since they were also slaves. "They also have a clean place to sleep, eat well every day, and have not been sick since they came to my father's farm." He left out that they all worked at gunpoint.

The second new face said in a whisper lower than Thornton's, "Ronan is my boy. How is he? Is he taking care?"

Thornton was flabbergasted. *Ronan's mother was there?* He knew Ronan and Henry came to Hezzy Jones's place on the same day. He had no idea Ronan's mother must have been with them. He realized that the day he asked Ronan whether he left a woman like Colleen at the Jones place, he hadn't asked about other relations. Since Thornton wasn't one to talk about his own mother, the subject between him and Ronan never came up.

His heart became heavier than it had been even just moments earlier with Colleen's tears staring at him. One thing was sure. There was no way he would help Colleen escape and leave Ronan's mother behind. The band of runaways had just gotten larger.

Or smaller. Ronan may be unwilling to run if he thought his mother had to stay behind with Hezzy Jones. She must have been with him when he ran the first time, the "fourth slave" Hezzy had told Marcus the third had tried to take with him but who was not, in the end, for sale. Hezzy's solution was to maim Ronan and separate mother from son.

Thornton said, "Yes, he's taking care, Ma'am."

He was afraid William had a woman who might be concerned about him, but none stepped to the window. He was relieved. He asked Colleen, "Do you have a message for Henry?"

Colleen opened her mouth but said nothing. Thornton waited. Sweat cascaded down his forehead. His wet face looked at hers and pleaded for her to hurry.

After a long moment, she said, "Please tell him I am going to have a baby, and it will arrive I reckon around Christmas."

Thornton's jaw dropped. He was stunned. He did some swift math. The day his father had carted Henry away, Colleen had been carrying Henry's baby for over four months, and Henry had never had the chance to know. Colleen must have covered it well. A couple of more weeks, and Henry would have known for sure.

Thornton recovered and said, "I will tell him."

He turned to leave but realized he had forgotten something crucial. He risked one more whispered message. He hated to scare the women, but what he had to say was vital. "Sometimes I travel to this farm with my father. You can't ever let on I was here tonight. He might kill me or Henry or Ronan or William. And I mean it." All three faces mimed a silent gasp. "You have to pretend you never saw me. No greetings of, 'Hello, Mr. Guthrie, Sir,' or anything like that, all right?" All three ladies nodded. "I must leave now. Close the window as quietly as you can."

He ducked and walked low in the dark back to Ashes. He was a farmer. He stooped for hours at a time. Hunch-walking to evade Hezzy and Jedidiah Jones was another thing altogether. His back and neck ached by the time he reached Ashes, whose light coat he spotted easily since his vision had thoroughly adjusted to the dark.

He patted the horse's nose to keep him from snorting in recognition of Thornton and gave him a little frown of disappointment in his unwitting betrayal. He untied the horse from the tree, walked him slowly in a half circle to turn him around, grabbed the lamp, and headed toward home. He wished he had William's internal clock. He had no idea what time it was. He was way behind William's schedule.

As he trod through the dark, he pondered what folly it was to expect seven people—five from Guthrie Farms, Ronan's mother, and a pregnant Colleen—to tread over the same terrain in the same blackness without Hezzy Jones, his dogs, and his sons hunting them into oblivion. Feelings of despondency crept into his mind like ivy climbing a wall. He snipped at the thickest vines of negative thoughts, but there was nothing he could do about the thin shoots of worry that worked their way up his mind.

He was far enough out. He mounted Ashes, lit the lamp, and set the horse into a gallop. Near Guthrie Farms, he snuffed out the light in case his father was awake. He refused to make it so far and get caught in his own barn.

He went to the back doors and avoided waking the dogs. William startled him in the dark barn.

"Where have you been?" The question came as an urgent whisper.

"I'll tell you all about it in the morning. I'm lucky I wasn't shot. Wait. What are you doing out here?"

"You're fifty-five minutes late!" William whispered louder.

Naturally, William would know with precision just how late he was. He was probably fifty-two minutes late or fifty-seven minutes late, and William rounded to fifty-five to not pick nits at four in the morning, or whatever time it really was, which he was sure William knew. "I was held up by rifles, dogs, a clan of toadish men, and a disloyal horse. How did you get past the dogs to come to the barn?" Thornton was nervous again.

"Jerky. I'll sleep in the barn and head over to the bunkhouse at sunup. The barking won't matter by then."

"Okay." Thornton let out a big sigh.

"Did you talk to Colleen?"

Thornton hesitated.

"Well?"

He had to tell William what he found out. "Colleen is going to have a baby at Christmas, a tad later at the most, as far as I can calculate how much she showed it when Henry left."

William was silent for a long while. Finally, he said, "You can't tell Henry."

"What? I have to tell him. He has a right to know. Besides, I have a message from Ronan's mother too. You failed to mention her, by the way. Now, how can I have a message for Ronan from his mother but have no news at all about Colleen? Once I tell Ronan about his mother, Henry will ask about Colleen."

William had no good answer and struggled to come up with one. Finally, he said, "Don't tell either of them. For now, we'll have to keep it a secret you saw anybody at the Jones place."

Thornton couldn't believe it. He had just risked the lives and limbs of several people, and he was not about to let the circumstances thwart him. He avoided William's suggestion and unsaddled Ashes.

"You know I'm right."

Thornton did, but he couldn't fathom how they would keep from Henry that he was going to be a father. And what about Ronan? He had a right to know his mother fared satisfactory under the awful circumstances and had sent greetings his way. He must have missed her terribly.

Still, if Henry learned about Colleen, he may do something desperate. Thornton hated to admit it, but William was right. They had to keep his night ride and all it revealed a secret. He felt bad for Ronan and worse for Henry.

"I risked my hide, your hide, everyone in Colleen's bunkhouse, Ronan, Henry, and Ashes just to come home and get two hours of sleep and tell nobody I made the trip."

"An hour and forty minutes."

"What?"

"It's an hour and forty minutes to sunup."

"Thanks."

Thornton left William in the barn. He crossed the compound to the farmhouse. The dogs in front of the bunkhouse were sound asleep. He tiptoed into the main house and shut the door behind him. He didn't make a sound. He climbed the stairs.

At the top of the staircase, he heard his father snoring through the bedroom door on the left. He went to his room on the right. The door was shut. He ducked behind it, closed it, and fell onto the bed wearing the clothes he had rolled around in in Hezzy Jones's dirt. Suddenly, he had all the luck in the world.

He was asleep in one minute.

20

"WHERE'RE YOU going with that wood, anvil-brain?"

Thornton stopped dead. He had thought his father was sound asleep in his room upstairs in the farmhouse. Marcus Guthrie's breath on the back of his neck sent a heat all over his body. He felt his cheeks, neck, and arms shift from pale to crimson. He turned to face his father.

"Sir?" He stalled and racked his brain for an answer, angry with the dirt for the first time in his life. It had masked his father's footsteps and set a trap for Thornton. He felt he deserved more loyalty than that.

"How dumb are you? That's wood you're carrying. Up to your stupid neck. I asked you where you're going with it. Wood bin's that way." Marcus pointed toward the main farmhouse. Thornton was headed toward the barn.

Winter was about to show up, and Thornton and Ronan had devised a plan. Thornton would slip firewood behind the stall where Ashes was kept. The stable would act as a kind of wood shed for the bunkhouse. All Ronan had to do was wait until Marcus slept off his noontime liquor or rode for supplies in Columbia, and he could move a few pieces as needed into the stove in the bunkhouse. Once the wood burned, Marcus would have no idea how many logs were in the stove, even on a raid. It was safer, they had figured, than if they stored the wood right in the bunkhouse stove. That day was their first crack at executing their plan, and it was about to be an unmitigated failure. Thornton opened his mouth to form the beginnings of a mumble.

Over his father's shoulder he saw his mother stumble onto the porch of the farmhouse. She clutched at her chest and took three or four stilted steps forward. Her boots clacked hard on the porch wood. Her face was screwed up in what looked like a terrible pain. Thornton's mouth froze mid-mumble. He stared across the yard at his mother and tried to figure out what was happening.

His father turned just in time to see Thornton's mother attempt to take the first step down the porch and miss it altogether. She tumbled down the remaining steps and landed square on her face in the wet dirt. Thornton heard the thud of her forehead all the way from the barn.

For three or four seconds, no one moved, not even William, Ronan, or Henry, who should have at least made a pretense of working at something. Thornton shook off the stun, dropped the wood where he stood, barely missing his father's feet, and ran to his mother. He knelt next to her and gave her a gentle shake. "Ma?"

She remained still.

Was she dead? His mind flashed forward to a funeral and a life with Marcus Guthrie and without his mother, and a panic set in. It was not the ending "Rip Van Winkle" had promised him his whole life.

He shook his mother harder and yelled, "Ma!"

She remained in a silent, still heap. Thornton's father had walked the length of the yard and towered over both him and his mother. He said nothing. He watched Thornton attempt to revive his wife.

Marcus appalled Thornton and nudged his wife's shoulder with the tip of his boot. Thornton almost snatched his father's boot heel and tripped him backwards onto his ass. He shook his mother again.

She stirred and let out a low moan. Thornton followed with a low sigh of his own. He kept his immense sense of relief to himself. He composed his face and gave his mother another gentle shake.

"Hmmm."

"Ma?" He helped her into a sitting-up position. Mud covered her forehead and nose.

"Hmmm, yeah?"

"What happened? Did you have an attack?"

"I don't....know. Felt like an elephant walked into the kitchen and stepped on my chest."

"Let me get the wagon and take you into town to see the doctor," Thornton said. He brushed a little of the dirt from her face.

"No, no, I'm fine." She waved his hand away.

"Well, get up." Marcus rocked forward on his feet and leaned into his directive. The day was cold but bright. His figure cast a shadow over the lower half of his wife's face. She looked up at her husband and squinted into the sun.

She gathered herself to get up. It annoyed Thornton that she hurried. He reached out to help her up, but she rejected his hand and rolled over onto her hands and knees and pushed herself up. Thornton saw her legs wobble underneath her and reached around her waist to steady her. She had no choice but to accept his help up the porch steps.

"You need to lie down."

"No, I'll be fine."

"Do like the boy says," Marcus said.

Thornton was surprised to hear those words. He looked back to see if it was his father who really spoke them. Marcus stood on the same spot where he had towered over his wife moments before. He exuded indifference.

"I got crops to worry about. I can't be taking time to haul you out to the doctor. Lie down a spell so I don't have to bother with problems later."

That sounded more like his father. He continued into the house and let his mother use him for support. They walked in a crooked line up the stairs and stumbled into his parents' room, a place Thornton felt was strange and therefore rarely entered. He steered his mother to what he assumed was her side of the bed, but she suddenly let go of Thornton and said, "I'm fine." She shook him off and stood straight. She no longer wobbled. Her cheeks were full of healthy color. Come to think of it, he realized, they had been all along.

"What do you mean?" Thornton was confused.

"I mean I am absolutely fine."

Thornton sensed more coming. He waited.

"The next time you want to defy your father with the men, make sure he's nowhere on this farmstead. Do you hear?" There was no irritation in her voice. She sounded matter-of-fact.

Thornton's mouth fell open and his jaw hung in the air.

"You took a terrible risk with that firewood. Good thing I had the kitchen window open. If I hadn't shown up, there's no telling what your father would have done. You're lucky he'll be too drunk tonight to remember you were headed to the barn with that wood. While you were fussing over me, I caught a glimpse of Ronan gathering it up. If your father doesn't see it, he won't remember it."

She knew. She knew what he had been up to with Ronan and had faked her attack to keep his father from finding out, had taken a willing tumble down the steps to help them all avoid disaster.

"You should get back to work. I don't want your father trailing after us. I guess I'll lie down for a stretch and get that rest we told your father I needed."

"Ye-, yes, Ma'am." He left his parents' room and bounded down the stairs, two at a time.

His mother was on their side. And she proved she'd be wily enough to be more asset than hindrance when it came time to run.

He couldn't wait to tell William.

21

A WEEK had passed since Thornton's mother had faked her attack. Thornton had told William how his mother had helped them, and they had begun to work out the details of their escape. They had agreed Ronan's mother and Colleen would join them.

It would come down to Thornton, they had figured. He was the only one who was both strong enough to execute whatever plan they came up with to restrain his father and able to gain the access needed to do so. William, Ronan, and even Henry could probably kill Marcus with their bare hands, but the Hawken wouldn't let them get close enough to do it.

Thornton wanted to head toward his Uncle Jeremiah Barker in the west, but it would make for an awkward hideout if his mother came with him. Jeremiah was his father's brother. Thornton could always explain why he had come alone. It would be harder to explain Rose being there without Marcus.

Still, his father and his uncle were not what anyone would call close. Neither family had visited the other in Thornton's lifetime. All Thornton knew was that if he traveled west on the main path, not far beyond the Missouri line he would come upon his aunt and uncle's farmstead along something called Coffee Creek.

At least that was how his mother said his Aunt Dorinda had described it in a letter years before. There was no telling how accurate Aunt Dorinda's description was or how much the area where she and Uncle Jeremiah lived may have changed since his aunt wrote that letter. He wasn't even sure they still lived there or anywhere. They could all be dead. His idea was to head up the road and see what happened.

The north was safest for William and the others, but how they would get there Thornton wondered all day long. Maps of the area to the north were crude or nonexistent, and Thornton took only small comfort in William's—and, to an extent, Ronan's and Henry's—ability to read sign posts they encountered along the way.

Getting their hands on enough horses for everybody to ride so they could flee at high speed was improbable. Staying ahead of the pack that chased them on foot would be impossible. They had to worry about their conspicuousness in the face of strangers they encountered and the weather they would have to fight along the way.

Thornton wielded his hoe at the rain-hardened turf. He turned over in his mind a couple of different ideas, not happy with any of them. He needed to get William alone to discuss it.

"Boy!" his father yelled across the yard.

A groan audible only to the few mice that scampered around the field in search of a meal the rain may have unearthed escaped his chest. He donned a veil of indifference and answered, "Yessir?" His voice dripped with reluctance to engage with Marcus.

"Put that hoe down and ride over to Hiram Elliot's and ask him if he's got wolves."

Thornton went to the barn, his way of letting his father know he would obey. He refused to say the words out loud.

His head hung low. He needed to meet with William, and his father's idiotic request got in his way. Marcus could go to Hiram Elliot's himself but wouldn't because he loathed the man.

Hiram Elliot refused to own slaves. Marcus hated to be in the company of men who disagreed with him or the things he did. He wasn't about to stand in Hiram Elliot's parlor and chat about wolves while Hiram thought, "Why can't you do your own work or pay the men who do it for you?"

Ashes perked up at the sight of Thornton. The two were always glad to see each other. At least Thornton would have good company for the trip to Hiram Elliot's.

———◆◇◆———

Ashes had languished too many days without exercise, the result of Marcus taking horse duties from Ronan, who would have been embarrassed by the way Ashes ran that afternoon if the horse had been in his charge. After a balky couple of miles, Ashes found his stride and cooperated with his impatient rider. Thornton sent the horse sailing over a large boulder he had no time to sidestep. He rode into the gray clouds on the horizon at an uneasy gallop, anxious about what his father might do to William, Ronan, and Henry while he was away at Hiram Elliot's place.

Since the men had arrived at Guthrie Farms, they had never been left alone with his father, which allowed Thornton to run a steady interference between his father and the men. His mother may have helped them with their wood scheme, but her presence mattered little when it came to protecting the men. She had no control over Marcus, and there were only so many heart attacks she could fake.

Thornton had no control over Marcus either, but he distracted his father from the men by virtue of his annoying existence. Without him there, too much of his father's attention would turn to the men, with the usual reserved for his mother. He didn't like any of it.

He pressed Ashes hard, running him at a full gallop. He tucked in his tall body to maximize the horse's speed. Ashes wheezed with the effort.

Thornton refused to relent. Horse and rider moved at top speed. The rider employed a lifelong deftness at steering horses to get the animal to sidestep thick-rooted plants, jump logs, and miss boulders. They raced through the fields dotted between the Guthrie and Elliot farms. The breath of man and horse floated behind them.

After two lifetimes, Hiram Elliot's enormous farmstead had the decency to appear in the distance. Thornton tried not to let being impressed with the large main house distract him. Three other buildings, each the size of the Guthrie farmhouse, were strewn about the property in random fashion, as if Hiram Elliot could take or leave them and used them only when he got around to it. Thornton had always heard that a mile away, elsewhere on Hiram Elliot's property, he had a large bunkhouse for his men, none of them slaves. They walked in every day to work his farm but had their privacy at night. Thornton realized there was another reason his father hated Hiram Elliot.

Envy.

He had no time to ponder the issue, though. He had to get back to his own farm.

He headed for what looked like the barn, distinct from the other outbuildings with its flat front and large double doors. Its fine-sanded hulking wood shell gave it the air of a farmhouse.

He had only been there once, when he was six years old. He remembered three older sons and a much younger daughter, who was also six at the time. He knew none of their names because they attended a different church than the Guthries, although it might not have mattered since the Guthries rarely attended church anyway. Mrs. Elliot had died several years earlier.

He had guessed right. Thornton brought a hard-breathing Ashes to a halt near the front of the barn. The doors stood open. He spotted a girl who was almost a woman mucking out the stalls.

It was the loveliest sight he had ever seen.

His gut felt like somebody had rammed a fist through it, he was so taken by the image in front of him. Long dark hair swung in all directions. The body wearing it moved like a swan. Thornton forgot about his father, William, Ronan, Henry, and his mother. The wolves and Hiram Elliot were a distant memory too.

He hopped off Ashes, walked him into the barn, and tied his rein to a hook where some tools hung. He said nothing and grabbed a rake and got to work.

He wasn't sure if she didn't know what to say or if she just didn't care. From side view, he saw her look at him for a moment. Uninterested in what she saw, she mucked some more manure. Several men roamed the farm. Maybe she thought he worked for her father.

He was too afraid to look at her. He raked and appeared more interested in the dung he moved than the girl whose animals had dropped it.

He screwed up his courage and asked, "'s your name?"

She jumped at the sound. "Fidelia." After a moment, she added, "Elliot."

The six-year-old, who, to Thornton's delight, was fifteen like he was. He made no reference to their first meeting nine years earlier. He said, "Thornton Guthrie."

"Hello."

"Hello."

They raked on in easy silence.

Twenty minutes later, Thornton remembered why he was there.

"Is your father home? My father sent me to ask him about wolves." To his own ears, he sounded like an idiot. He must have looked like one too. He had raked out her stalls with a purpose when he obviously had a different reason for being there.

"Go on up to the house. You can talk to him there. I'll look out for your horse."

"Thanks. His name's Ashes."

"Ashes," she affirmed.

He replaced the rake and headed out the barn doors taking care not to walk stupid in case she watched. He was sure she did. Her rake didn't make a sound. For the first time in his life, he hoped the seat of his pants was clean. He racked his brain trying to remember if he had sat on anything dirty earlier that day. He probably had.

——◆——

Hiram Elliot gave Thornton a bit of information he cared nothing about. The Elliots had lost some livestock to wolves. Mr. Elliot was a keen shot and had removed the threat in quick fashion. It was beside a much larger point: Thornton had met in Hiram Elliot's enormous byre the woman who would one day be his wife.

She wasn't in the barn when he came back for Ashes. He mourned her absence and wondered where she had gone.

He mounted Ashes and raced home. He suddenly remembered William, Ronan, Henry, and his mother. He had no idea how he would break it to William that they had just added an eighth person to their band. There was no way he'd leave Missouri without Fidelia Elliot.

22

"DID YOU look it up?"

"Yeah. Found it on the same page as 'vermin'. It means 'to have the appearance of the truth, to depict what's real, to be probable'. Seems like that's what they should say." Thornton swung his ax down hard on a large log and sliced it in two.

"Verisimilitude is shorter." William swung his ax and gave the same treatment to his log.

"Verisimilitude is *shorter?*"

"Heh-heh."

"Change of subject, and promise not to laugh?"

"Why would I laugh?"

"I met a girl."

Both axes stopped.

"Say, now."

"Fidelia."

"Fidelia. Fidelia what?"

"Elliot."

"Hiram Elliot's girl?"

"You know her?"

"Know of her daddy. Used to see him from time to time on the Jones place. No slaves, as far as I know."

"No. Has hired hands. Looks as though he gives Fidelia her fair share of chores too. Her mother's gone. Her brothers live in other territories. It's just Fidelia and her father. Good sized farmstead."

William gave Thornton a sly grin. "I don't want the history of the Elliot farm, son. Tell me how Thornton Guthrie met Fidelia Elliot."

It was fifteen degrees outside. Thornton's father kept warm in front of a fire deep inside the house. Ronan and

Henry were on the roof of the barn. They checked for any holes that needed repairing so winter would be a bit easier on the animals.

Thornton leaned down to pick up the next block of wood. A shot rang out in the cold winter air and blew his hat off.

The sound was unmistakable to Thornton. He had heard it far too often. It was his father's Hawken.

He snapped his head in the direction of the farmhouse, where the shot came from. His father leaned out of his bedroom window, Hawken in hand. Heavy puffs of breath came from his gaping mouth and evaporated into the freezing air.

"Now, that's enough chit-chattin' with niggras." He seemed larger than usual looking down on Thornton from the upstairs window.

Thornton stood frozen in place. He stared up at his father, afraid to move in any direction. The spot where he chopped wood was not close to the house, and yet his father had put a bullet through something attached to his moving body on the first try.

The Hawken was accurate up to two hundred yards. All the animals his father had put on the supper table with one distant shot and the piece missing from Thornton's ear reminded him his father was a keen enough shot to take him out on the second try, with him pinned down and standing still.

His mother appeared on the porch, just as she had the day Marcus had held the rifle to his forehead. Also, just as she had on that summer day, she remained where she stood. There would be no fake attack to come to his aid.

William whispered in a way that sounded as though his lips didn't move. "Just stand there. Let it pass. It'll pass. Don't make any sudden moves. Wait him out."

It was hard to have faith he could just wait it out, especially with his father drunk, which Thornton could tell he was from the slur in his speech. He took William's advice, though, and stared in the general direction of the house.

His father reloaded the rifle. From as far away as the chopping block, Thornton heard his father cock the back trigger. All he needed to do was pull the hair trigger. A light tug would do the trick. Sweat dripped down Thornton's face. The wind blew against it. The cold bit his face.

Thornton also found that on top of the fear, he was deeply embarrassed in front of William, Ronan, and Henry to have them see his father treat him that way. All the years he had been alone with his father, the terror had been bad enough, but at least his mother had been the only witness. That day, he was a spectacle.

Another shot rang out. The bullet just missed Thornton's right foot. Snow kicked up next to his boot.

"Don't move," William said.

He and William became garden statues, pinned down by Marcus. He could only imagine Ronan and Henry were similarly fixed to one spot on top of the barn behind him.

After a long moment, Marcus retreated from the window. For another long moment, nobody moved. They all wanted to be sure Marcus wouldn't emerge from the window again.

It became clear he had made his point and didn't plan to fire a third shot. Thornton exhaled a long breath and steadied himself.

Rose strolled back into the house.

William bent down and picked up Thornton's hat. It had a hole the size of a half dollar in it. He handed it to Thornton, who refused to put it back on his head. He muttered, "Thanks," and stalked to the barn, hat in hand.

Five minutes later, he came out with a saddled Ashes in tow, and without the hat. His ears were already bright red from exposure to the cold.

He mounted his sleepy, grumpy horse and lit out for Fidelia's to tell her his father had tried to kill him. He had no idea whether she would care, but he had to tell her. For some reason, he needed her to know.

23

FIDELIA OPENED her front door and found Thornton there. Her face looked as strange as he felt. They had only met once since that first time when they were six, yet he stood before her with bright red ears, one of them severely dented.

Hiram Elliot had a fireplace tall and wide enough for an average sized person to stroll around in. Six-foot-long logs blazed in the cavern, and the open door brought in wind from the outside that made the fire roar. The heat reached Thornton's face all the way at the threshold of the house.

Thornton froze, and with nowhere near enough shame, he left Fidelia at her own front door and walked straight to the fire. A second later, he turned to her and blurted out, "My father just tried to kill me with his rifle." He could see Fidelia believed him. For one, she closed the door and staggered into the parlor. For another, she held her hands in front of her, in search of something to hang onto while the shock set in.

He should have been mortified, as he had been in front of the men. He wasn't. He wondered why, especially since he cared very much what she thought about....everything.

As if she had known him forever, she offered a plausible reason for the incident without any of the preamble a stranger would feel obligated to include. "He must have been drunk. Or aiming at something else?" It was part question, part suggestion.

She was half right. He had been drunk. "No, he was aiming at me." Fidelia plopped down on the chair behind her. She didn't seem to care how she landed.

"How....why....did he shoot at you?"

"He didn't like me talking to one of the....slaves on our place." Belated embarrassment kicked in. He hated to admit the Guthries owned slaves. He was thankful Mr. Elliot was not in the room, although that didn't change the atrocious facts.

"Fidelia...." There was so much he wanted to say to her. In his mind, she was going to run away from Missouri with him, and they were hardly acquainted. He wondered how he could advance her thinking to match his and not sound like a lunatic.

She got up from the chair and joined him in front of the fireplace. "Thornton...."

He stepped closer to her and took hold of her hands. It heartened him that she let him. Her regal countenance belied her approachable nature.

He stalled in telling her how he felt about her and kept the subject on his father. "On the way over here, I got to thinking he had missed on purpose, like he just wanted to rankle me and put fear in me." He didn't tell her he had a dreadful feeling his father would one day hit his mark. It may take another week or another year, but the day was coming when his father would summon up the spite, drop the rifle three inches, and put the bullet through his head instead of his hat.

He was just about to speak up on the subject of the escape. With the help of the fire, the warmth of her eyes, and the feelings that traveled between their hands, he would make her understand, even if it took all day. He hoped it would take all day, for he didn't want to be anywhere else but in front of the Elliot fireplace with her.

As it turned out, he wouldn't get all day or even three minutes. Hiram Elliot interrupted.

"What's going on here?" At five feet, six inches, Hiram Elliot was more than half a foot shorter than Thornton, but he had the mien of a giant. He ruled his roost, his land, and his children with quiet authority. Thornton sensed that he never bellowed his point. Thornton's respect for Hiram Elliot skirted the edges of a healthy fear. He dropped Fidelia's hands and stood at attention.

"Nothing, Sir."

"Nothing, Pa." They answered in unison.

Thornton was irritated. The mood was just right for him to make his case for why Fidelia should abandon everything and follow a fugitive farmer to the west. The incident with his father almost helped his cause. It proved he needed to get away and might garner her sympathy. But he couldn't talk in front of her father. Not only was Thornton too shy to express his romantic feelings in front of a stranger, but if Hiram Elliot had any inkling Thornton's life was in danger and that he planned to break the law, he would want to keep Fidelia as far away from Thornton as possible.

"I'm not sure why you came by, Mr. Guthrie, but Fidelia isn't receiving visitors this afternoon." He stared at Thornton, who understood the hint. Thornton should have left but made no move toward the door. He was desperate to finish his conversation with Fidelia. "Good day, Mr. Guthrie."

"Sir, if I might—"

"Good day, Mr. Guthrie." His tone was quieter. The implications were ominous. Thornton wouldn't oblige him to make his point a fourth time. Three times had been too many. He had no choice but to leave. He suddenly wished he had his hat, hole and all. The ride home would be cold.

———◦⋄◦———

"I'm telling you, you need to burn them books right now." Ronan was adamant.

So was William. He responded with an unequivocal, "Over my dead body."

"Well, that's what it'll be if you ain't careful, except it'll be three dead bodies. Didn't you see him try to kill his own son? He'll have killed us all if he finds them books in here."

Ronan rolled into his second hour of trying to convince William to throw *The Last of the Mohicans* and *The Sketch Book of Geoffrey Crayon, Gent.* into the stove with the wood William and Thornton had chopped just a few hours earlier, in the line of gunfire. Ronan's diatribe tired William.

Henry had stayed quiet through most of the argument, but he sided with Ronan. He had offered the occasional, "That's right," when Ronan hammered home some point.

It was dark outside. Thornton was back from the Elliot place and in the main house. The temperature had dropped below zero, and all three of the men made their contributions to the debate from under the covers of their bunks. A fire blazed in the nearby stove. William thought the scene would have been cozy if they hadn't been slaves talking about how best to avoid being shot.

He was unfair to both friends, but he just couldn't part with his books. It was bad enough the situation forced him to burn every edition of *The Intelligencer* Thornton had slipped him. His old friend Archibald would cry if he knew that.

"I'm telling you, he'll never think to look under the floorboard under the bed."

Henry finally had a point to make. "You don't think old Hezzy Jones told him where he found your books at *his* place? Pfft. C'mon, now."

William didn't consider himself the smartest of the three, but he was the most reasonable and measured among them. Ronan had the scars to prove he had had at least one serious lapse in judgment, and Henry was likely to light out for Colleen, with no plan, if he discovered he had a child on the way. It was William who avoided histrionics. The scars on his own back were there because he had been found out and not because he had behaved in a rash manner.

Yet, on that evening, he was the most unrealistic of the bunch. Except for *The Sketch Book of Geoffrey Crayon, Gent.*, which Thornton had gifted William, Thornton was careful to give William only one other book at a time, to give him less to hide. William was diligent about moving the two books around to different places in the bunkhouse and the barn, but Ronan and Henry were right. Marcus Guthrie already made night inspections. Earlier that day, he had shot at his own son. William held to himself, lest Ronan continue for a third hour, that Marcus Guthrie's Hawken had chipped Thornton's ear. Anyone could be next.

"I'll find a way," was all he could promise. Ronan and Henry would give him a little more time to come up with a solution. Not much more time, though. If he waited too long, Ronan, in particular, would lift the floorboard, retrieve both books, and throw them in the burning woodstove.

24

ROSE GUTHRIE placed a spoonful of the white clover leaves Thornton had grown, picked, and dried for her into a small bit of cheesecloth. A cup of long-steeped tea would go perfect with her favorite activity of the day: She gazed out the window at William and watched him work.

She had sneaked a look at the bill of sale between Marcus and Hezzy Jones. She learned William was thirty-six. He was two years older than she was, but years of marriage to Marcus made her feel ten years older than William.

She didn't know to what aim, but she brushed her hair with more care and matched shawls with dresses. For years, she had taken refuge in her washed out plainness. She held out hope it might work to keep Marcus away from her.

She was no longer as willing to accept her diminished looks. She felt self-conscious any time William came within close proximity of her, to pick up a meal tray, bring firewood to the bin on the side of the house, or draw water from the pump just as she filled a tub for the wash.

When he was near, she felt things in the most private parts of herself. She had no idea her body had the capacity to respond to a man the way hers did to William.

The only awareness Marcus gave her of her body was pain, the time it took for bruises to heal, and the amount of pressure her bones could withstand without breaking.

It was more than an attraction to William's countenance. She observed the affection he seemed to have for her son, the gentle way he tended to the crops and the animals alike, and the quiet manner he adopted when he listened to anyone who talked to him. It all made her feel for him the way she had hoped all those years earlier she would feel for Marcus.

She was in love with William.

Her newfound feelings made her at once ecstatic and miserable. She had access to the man she loved any time the sun shone, but she would never be with him in the one way she wanted to, would never be close to him when it was dark. The two would never share an afternoon in the woods or touch each other's skin. They wouldn't lend each other courage to get through life's travails or give and accept tenderness. She had to love William from afar.

She knew some of the secrets he shared with Thornton. The books terrified her the most, although they had no idea she knew. They had conducted several careless conversations when Marcus was in Columbia, unaware she paid attention through an open window.

As scared as she was, she was also proud her son defied his father in any way he could when it came to the men. She had even helped protect their secrets. Sometimes she distracted Marcus for one or two minutes on the porch, just after he stepped outside, to give the cohorts a chance to cover up anything they should not have been doing.

There wasn't much anybody could teach her son about farming, but there were times when Thornton and William gathered around the same patch of land and knelt down to examine some detail. She had no idea who taught whom, but the sight was a blessing. Thornton no longer talked to himself in the compound.

"What are you lookin' at?"

Rose spun around.

Marcus had watched her watch William.

The teapot she had been about to fill slipped out of her hands and crashed to the ground. The blood drained from her face down to her toes. Her feet were weighted to the kitchen floor. They felt like they were under flour sacks.

She said nothing. Marcus took one big stride toward her and yanked her hair loose from its bun. He wound a chunk of it around his hand two or three times and tugged hard on it.

He dragged her to the kitchen table and forced her down into a chair.

He kept hold of her hair. He pulled her head far back, using her mane for leverage. His fist had just enough room to fit in the space at the base of her neck. She felt the calluses on the side of his hand rub its nape.

Her eyes rolled up to the ceiling. She tried to beg. The position of her throat made it impossible for her to get out any sound.

"Let....go," she managed to gurgle.

"Shut up!" He hunched over and punched her hard in the ribs.

She moved to double over from the pain but couldn't. He still jerked her head back with her hair. All she could do was bring her hand up to her ribcage and rub it. It was small comfort. And it didn't matter. Three more blows followed in rapid succession, all to the ribs.

"Admire that tall nigger?" He delivered two more blows to the space between her breasts.

She gurgled her cries. Tears streamed down the side of her face to her temples and into her hair, which Marcus still had wound around his hand.

"Where do you think you are? Your daddy's farm? Just a whore looking at the next farmhand coming through? Looking at some nigger I own? I *own* him."

He was homicidal. He wrapped his free hand around her jaw and squeezed it as tight as he could. Years of farming had made his huge hands as strong as a vice. She thought her jaw would break.

She murmured, "Thor....un." In the past, he had tried to keep what he did to her from Thornton. There was evidence he brutalized her, bruises and hunched-over walking, but Marcus had been careful to keep his actions behind closed doors. She thought if she reminded him the boy was right outside and could come in at any time, he'd let her go.

He leaned over her face and said, "I don't care if that boy comes in here. I don't care what he sees. You didn't seem to mind him catching you gazing at a nigger." Spit drops landed on her forehead.

She looked into his eyes. Through his dreadful breath and clinched yellow teeth, she saw what was coming next. She recognized the look. She was horrified. She couldn't believe he was about to do what he was about to do right in the kitchen.

She braced herself. He snatched her up by the hair, turned her around, and slammed her face onto the table. He broke her nose, she was sure.

He hoisted up her skirt.

He fought with her undergarments.

He forced himself on her from behind. He jerked forward so hard again and again, the table slid four or five feet. Its legs scraped across the floor, and her legs followed in an awkward walk. She was penned in by Marcus. She let out a low grunt with each drive forward and spit-breathed through clinched teeth so she wouldn't scream.

She caught sight of what was outside the kitchen window. Or, who.

William.

He stood paralyzed, transfixed by the shocking scene that unfolded in the kitchen. Rose never shut the window during the daytime, summer or winter. It was wide open. William not only saw everything. He heard it too. He must have heard the teapot crash and come to investigate. She hoped Marcus's words were grunted too low for William to make them out.

He wore a look of sheer horror. There was nothing he could do to stop the attack, short of getting himself killed, but the look in his eye said he so pitied her, was so outraged by what he saw, he just might take the risk and confront Marcus.

Her humiliation was enormous. She wished Marcus would kill her right there.

William turned away. She didn't know why, didn't know what would happen next, but she was grateful he no longer watched what Marcus did to her.

As the violence wore on, she shrieked with every movement Marcus made and stared into the nothingness beyond where William stood, with his back to the window. Tears and blood puddled on the table next to her cheek. Her ribs felt broken. She didn't think she could take anymore.

William leaned down and reappeared in the window a few seconds later. He faced her, and to Rose's horror, he had a large piece of wood in his hand. He planned to come into the house and bash in Marcus's head.

Things got worse.

Thornton approached in the distance.

William started to move away from the window and toward the house.

He suddenly turned in Thornton's direction. Her son had called William's name. He was farther away than William, and it was faint, but Rose heard him. In a flash, William dropped the wood, took several big strides toward Thornton, and distracted him. The two walked out of earshot of the window.

And just that quickly, Marcus stopped. He climbed off her, fastened his pants, and left the kitchen. She heard his boots make their way up the stairs.

It was over. She had survived the most violent assault he had ever visited upon her. She had looked at a Negro the way she never looked at him, and he had punished her.

She lay bent over the table for a long while.

She caught her breath and labored to stand up straight. It was unbearable, but she couldn't sit down either.

She compromised with herself and hobbled around the kitchen, trying to get back her ability to move. Her feet crunched on the teapot shards.

She rubbed her ribcage and cried silent tears. Slobber and mucus and blood covered her face. Hot liquid dripped down her legs. Her blood and Marcus's seed. She limped a few more circles around the kitchen.

She was afraid to go to the window, not only for fear of what Marcus would do, but because she was unsure whether William was still outside. She was ashamed to look him in the eye after what he had witnessed. She had to know, though, whether Thornton had seen or heard anything. She took the risk and stumbled to the basin in front of the window.

To her great relief, she saw William with Thornton by the east fence. The two were repairing a post. William had no doubt made the awful choice to walk away from the attack to protect Thornton. She felt an odd conspiratorial parental bond with him.

She had no idea what would have happened if William had entered the house with his wooden weapon, but as mortified as she was, it meant more than she could measure that he had wanted to protect her, even at the risk of his own life. It was a lot more than the law would do for her.

A wife was expected to give her husband what he wanted no matter how he took it or the level of humiliation it caused to give it. There was no crime to report if he beat out of her intimacy between them. Rose's sole protection from Marcus was whatever restraint he decided to show.

With a fierce bitterness that sent new tears down her face, she thought for the millionth time how unfair and unsafe the laws were for women. Every woman in the land was at the mercy of her husband. Where was her protection? Short of murder, a husband could do almost anything to his wife right in front of the eyes of the law. Even some killing was deemed justified, if a husband's self-respect was bruised by the presence of another man. It was no matter if that same husband took a different woman every morning, noon, and night of the week.

Rose would never forget William had been willing to make Marcus answer for something he would otherwise always get away with. She was relieved, for William's sake, it hadn't come to that.

More blood and mucus oozed from her nose. She tried to wipe it with her hand, but even the softest touch stung. She would need to tie a binding around her entire face to keep her nose in place so it could heal.

She would also have to stay in her room for a week until the worst of her wounds healed. Marcus would allow it, despite his earlier bravado. He had had his way. That was good enough. He would not want Thornton to see the extent of the damage he had done.

She had fashioned her hobbling into an awkward walk. Blood drops were mixed in with teapot shards all over the kitchen floor.

She tilted her head back, shuffled to the indoor privy, closed the door behind her, and tended to her wounds. She would worry about the kitchen floor later.

25

WILLIAM WAS in a quandary. After what he had witnessed in the Guthrie kitchen earlier that day, he and Thornton needed to finalize their escape plans and get everybody off Guthrie Farms straightaway. He'd leave that night if he could.

He alternated all afternoon between conjuring every few minutes the dreadfulness he had caught sight of and straining to forget it. He had never expected when he went to investigate the sound of glass breaking to see Rose Guthrie in the midst of being tortured. The horror had paralyzed him, had frozen him in the dirt. By the time he gathered himself, Thornton had been on the horizon. He had been forced to strand Rose Guthrie with a maniac in her kitchen. It was an awful choice he had had to make, but Thornton was only fifteen. William couldn't let him see what his father had been doing to his mother. He knew what it was like to have the degradations he imagined his mother suffered haunt him every, single day. He couldn't saddle Thornton with those same torments.

He had no idea how things would have ended if he had been allowed to use his wooden bludgeon on Marcus Guthrie. He had only known how he felt when others watched Hezzy Jones cut him open with rope and kerosene. He understood that they could do nothing on his behalf, but he felt abandoned. Rose Guthrie had looked abandoned, and William had reacted.

On her own, she had survived, but William held out no hope that she wouldn't face more terror eventually, or that Marcus Guthrie wouldn't shoot Thornton or Ronan or Henry. Or William. They had to leave.

The problem was that winter was upon them, and the only way William would be able to convince Thornton to risk the escape in the dead of winter, with a band of eight people, nine if Colleen had her baby somewhere along the way, was to tell him what he had seen. If Thornton knew what Marcus Guthrie had done to his mother, he'd not only leave that night, he might stop to kill his father along the way and put himself in trouble with the law.

William usually had no sympathy or consideration for how white folks managed their affairs. He had seen them steal from each other, cheat on their wives with women in taverns, and run their own sons off their property. If they wanted to stab each other in the back, he was happy to let them. There had to be kind white folks all over the earth, but the faces of the men who bought and sold him and his mother interfered with his ability to see them.

Thornton was another matter. So was Rose Guthrie. William saw her as a prisoner of Marcus Guthrie, different from himself because the law recognized her as a free citizen, but identical to him since the law gave her husband the right to beat her, rape her, and end her life under certain circumstances with impunity.

He appreciated that, within the limits of what she could get away with, Rose Guthrie had come as close to treating him and Ronan and Henry with kindness as was possible. Kindness was not a word he usually used to describe how anybody white had ever treated him.

Thornton, meanwhile, was his best friend, his brother, his son even. From the first day, Thornton had recognized the dignity that he and Ronan and Henry carried within them, and he had made a point to tell them all when he gave William "Rip Van Winkle" and the other stories. Thornton was one of only three or four human beings William had ever encountered who treated him like a man and not like a child. Or an animal.

When he arrived there, he had been prepared to endure until he figured a way out, no matter how long it took. But the fever had risen on Guthrie Farms. He and Thornton talked every day of escape, and it enticed him. After what he saw in the Guthrie kitchen, and knowing Henry was about to become a father and the annihilation of the next generation would soon get under way, he wanted them all freed. He didn't think he could wait another day.

They couldn't flee until the first thaw. Thornton ran reconnaissance and interference, spied and schemed, diverted Marcus Guthrie, and sought to free his father's captives. William would keep his own eyes on Ronan, Henry, Thornton, and Rose Guthrie.

It was going to be a long winter.

———◆◇◆———

Henry stopped what he was doing. Ronan followed suit. A moment later, all four of them—Thornton and William and Ronan and Henry—no longer worked. They stared at the bedraggled figure that had just entered the gate of Guthrie Farms.

Thornton gauged it—the figure—to be a child of no more than eleven or twelve. Boy or girl, it was hard to tell. Its hair was too long and its feet wore nondescript, raggedy boots. Its clothes were tattered. It looked like it was unable to talk, as if it was something mechanical that had broken, so dirty and disheveled was it. It was more blob than person, with two eyes poking out of the donut-shaped dirt smudged all around them.

It trudged along, the figure, making a straight line for the water pump, not to drink, but to sit down on its large base.

The child ignored Marcus, who sauntered over with his rifle. Thornton decided the child was a boy. It was the indelicate way he slouched that tipped the scales.

Marcus aimed the Hawken right in his face. The boy just sat there. All five men stared at him.

He appeared to have mustered some energy and spoke. "I'm looking for Marcus Guthrie." He pointed right past the rifle and said to Marcus, "Are you him?"

Thornton glanced at William. The two had a whole conversation with their eyes that said, "We'd better watch out for what this is."

"Don't point at me, boy." Marcus concurred the child was a boy.

"My name's not Boy."

"Oh, it's not, is it?" Thornton was surprised Marcus seemed more bemused than bothered.

"No."

Marcus let his rifle relax.

Thornton and William gave each other a longer glance.

"Do you mind telling me what your name is, if it isn't Boy? I think I have a right to know who's on my property." Marcus set the rifle down and leaned it against the pump.

"Ethan Barker."

Thornton and Marcus both gasped, though Thornton understood not in a unified way. It was just coincidental shock. Thornton thought it couldn't be possible his cousin Ethan was on Guthrie Farms, when he had planned to escape to Ethan's place.

What did it mean? Where were his Uncle Jeremiah and Aunt Dorinda? The child looked like he had walked to Columbia, Missouri all the way from the Unorganized Territory by himself. Were Thornton's aunt and uncle dead?

William had seen Thornton's shock and his own face asked Thornton a thousand questions. Thornton gave him a look that said, "I'm not sure either. Give me a second." First he needed to find out himself what was going on. His father helped.

"Ethan Barker? Jeremiah's boy?" Marcus asked.

"Yessir."

"That's not possible. I mean, look at you. And where's your mama and daddy?"

Thornton dreaded the boy's answer.

"I ran away. Got up in the middle of the night and took the road along the creek east. By the time it was light out, I was farther away than my pa likely rode looking for me. I'm sure he figured I hadn't gone far and just looked around my usual hiding places. I reckon by the time he gathered up enough men to really come searching, I was too far gone." No one said anything. He kept talking. "I took a guess they'd go west first. The Tanders and the Piersons live that way. I'm friends with their boys. Heh, heh. Pa's predictable, you know? Whole farm is, really. Whole territory, when you think about it. Anyway, by the time, I figure, they searched east, I was deep into Missouri. Too late to find me."

Thornton looked at William again. His face said, "Yes, this *is* going to be a problem for us."

Ethan kept on. "I been in the backs of wagons and on the backs of horses. Walked, camped out, slept with strange families. One fellow tried to load me off on a family heading west, but I warned him I'd just run east again as soon as they weren't looking, so he let me ride as far as he was going. Finally met up with a couple of drifters who took me all the way into Columbia. Big town. Slopes downward if you approach it right. Anyway, I asked around without telling anyone who I was. Didn't want some concerned idiot to send word to Ma and Pa where I was. Folks there told me how to get to the Guthrie place. No one's told me yet. Is this it?"

"Yeah, this is it. I'm Marcus Guthrie. Your uncle, and your pa's older brother."

"I figured. Since you aren't real brothers, you don't look like him. Gave me my first inkling I might be in the right place."

Thornton braced for Marcus to blow.

Nothing happened. A smile tugged on the corner of his father's mouth.

"Tell you what. Go on inside and see your Aunt Rose. Tell her I said to fix you something to eat and to give you some clothes and to do something about that hair."

Most people who dealt with Marcus knew on instinct not to trust what he said. There always came that moment, after he let a person pass, when he'd stick his foot out and trip them. Ethan had no idea what his Uncle Marcus might pull. The boy walked past Marcus toward the house. Thornton expected his cousin to feel a slap across the back of his head for telling Marcus to his face Jeremiah was not his blood brother, but again, nothing happened. Ethan bounded up the porch steps without a care, clearly replenished by having reached his destination, and disappeared through the front door.

Thornton and the others went back to work. Thornton managed to give William one final conspiratorial look that said, "Don't worry. I'll figure out what this is gonna do to our plans."

William must have thought all the things he did. How would they machinate an elaborate escape plan with a savvy youngster under foot, one who maybe eavesdropped and who would tell his father what he overheard? Would his own parents send his cousin home, or, worse, would his aunt and uncle come to Guthrie Farms and even out Marcus's odds?

If not, if Ethan stayed, when the time came to run, how would they get a child so bent on staying in Missouri to travel west with them, right back to the place *he* had, in his mind, escaped, and would he play along if they encountered the law on the road?

Would he defend Marcus and get in the way when the hour came to make their move? Had he come to Missouri because he treasured slavery and wanted to be Hezzy Jones when he grew up? Would they be able to continue their schemes around the farm, like pilfering wood and padding rations with Ethan around?

And on the other hand, did he know the best route west? He had just traveled on foot, by horse, and by wagon the roads they would use to escape. He had to know which method of travel had been best, but could they approach him and ask him for his opinion on the subject? Would he go so far as to be their guide and map?

Those were the things Thornton and William needed to know. Thornton would start that night at supper.

26

AUNT ROSE was going to work out just fine, thought Ethan. He helped himself to a third portion of her beef stew. It was loaded with carrots, potatoes, and onions, and slopped up great with her biscuits. He smelled apple pie he was eager to sample after supper. Earlier, after his hot bath in the indoor privy, while he had been sitting in a chair his aunt dragged into the kitchen and getting his hair cut, he spotted various kinds of homemade jellies, jams, and relishes he would help the family eat.

Uncle Marcus was fine too. He was a burly man who didn't talk too much. Ethan loved his father, but nobody would say Jeremiah Barker was good at keeping his opinions to himself. Ethan appreciated that Uncle Marcus seemed to reserve opening his mouth for those moments when it was absolutely necessary to speak, like when he gave directions or talked about how good the fishing was or something like that.

Ethan was the oldest at home, so the idea of Thornton was strange to him. He figured, though, he was going to like having someone older bear the brunt of the responsibility when things went wrong for the adults and they needed a child to blame.

His road to Missouri had been a rough one. At times he would admit to no one, he had cried for both his mother and his father, especially the day he had turned twelve with nothing but the dirt path to tell about it. He had even almost stayed with one couple who picked him up, whose daughter added a "bratty younger sister" element to the situation, who had no intention of going all the way to Columbia desperate was he to be part of a family, but he forced himself to push on for Guthrie Farms.

He was glad he had. Aunt Rose had cleared out a spare room for him downstairs. It would be all his own. He had never had his own room. And the privy was inside, for Ransom's sake. A fellow wouldn't need to feel like he was going to freeze certain crucial parts right off his body when he relieved himself in the middle of a winter night. Already, he had pissed once, saved some up, and pissed again, just to see how doing it indoors worked.

He'd have to do some farming, but what did it matter with a booming town like Columbia so close by? And Uncle Marcus had slaves. He wondered if he would be allowed to boss them around. He would find out the next day after a breakfast of Aunt Rose's fresh bread dripped with honey.

———◦◇◦———

Marcus liked Ethan from the start. The boy reminded him of himself. He was restless and wasn't about to let anybody force him to plant roots where he didn't take a liking to the land they had staked out for him.

He thought about Jeremiah, somebody who hadn't crossed his mind in years. Ethan was his image. It was as if he saw Jeremiah again. Marcus didn't hate the man who had been his brother in childhood, but he still resented that when Francis Barker showed up to claim Jeremiah, it left Marcus alone with *his* father, Tanner Guthrie, the nastiest man Marcus had ever known.

If Marcus was honest, he also had to admit he appreciated that Ethan seemed to like him too, unlike Thornton, who turned on Marcus when he was still a baby. Thornton lived in a fortress. He would never lower the drawbridge for his father.

Ethan had appeared to give Marcus a chance at being liked. He made eye contact when Marcus talked, engaged in easy conversation, seemed excited when Marcus told him he'd ke him fishing and show him Columbia, and offered without being asked to take over whatever chores Marcus assigned to him, so long as Marcus would let him stay. He got the impression the boy wouldn't question the occasional bruise on his Aunt Rose's face or interfere with the way his uncle handled his slaves.

Marcus scooped more stew into Ethan's bowl. The boy could stay as long as he wanted, and nobody, not Rose, his son, or even Jeremiah or Dorinda would have anything to say about it.

———◆———

Jeremiah and Dorinda must have been worried to death about their boy, Rose thought. Ethan had told her his story of running away while she cut his hair in the kitchen earlier that day. She thought the entire situation was frightful.

She said, "Your ma and pa must be real worried about you. How about we write them a letter tomorrow and let them know you made it to Missouri safely?"

Ethan stopped chewing. "Ma'am?" he said, with a mouthful of stew. A biscuit he had poised for a bite remained in mid-air in his right hand.

"Don't you think we ought to let them know you're here?"

"Um. . . .no, Ma'am. If you do that, they might want me to come home, and you wouldn't want to be bothered with all of that."

"It's no trouble one way or the other. You're welcome to stay, but it doesn't seem right letting them think you're dead in a ditch somewhere when you're eating stew and headed for a warm bed tonight."

"I guess you're right. It's just that. . . ."

"It's that," Marcus said, "you don't need anybody, especially not some woman, telling you what's best." Marcus turned to Rose. "If the boy wants to drift, let him drift." He looked at Ethan for good measure and said to nobody in particular, "The boy stays here. Jeremiah's my brother, and I'll decide who sends him any letters. Since the boy is, in fact, safe, that's all that matters. I'll have no more talk of letters complicating things, you hear?" He looked right at Rose. Ethan was too young to understand the look in Marcus's eye and what it meant when he gave an order. Rose nodded and ate a bite of stew.

———●◇●———

Thornton was afraid of what he heard at supper. The minute he saw his father grin at Ethan where he would have coldcocked him had he been anybody else who told him to his face who his rightful kin were, and watched him scoop more stew for the boy, Thornton understood Ethan was there to stay.

Thornton had no desire for Marcus to mete out to Ethan the brand of treatment he reserved for him and his mother. But with the escape becoming more complicated, Thornton wished his cousin had not decided to "drift" to Guthrie Farms.

The situation was dire. Just a few weeks earlier, Thornton's father had turned his mother's entire face a strange shade of blue-black. He had beaten her so bad, he had almost turned her nose inside-out.

Thornton had no idea what had set off his father, hadn't even seen how it happened. His mother simply "took sick" one afternoon and stayed in her room for a week. She didn't even come out to use the privy. In uncharacteristic fashion, his father tended to her. He brought her the meals Thornton prepared and emptied her chamber pot.

Thornton had thought she really had been sick with some kind of flu. When she emerged after the long week, Thornton was horrorstruck. She was stooped over and looked like a horse had trampled her face. His mother hadn't been sick with a cold gone awry. His father had thrashed her and tried to cover the worst of his crimes, even as he felt no need to hide that he had perpetrated them.

If his mother looked that bad after a week, how bad had it been when she first retreated to her room? She had only returned to her normal self a few days earlier. Thornton was convinced if she did just the wrong thing, she wouldn't survive the next beating.

It killed him that he had no way to protect her. His father had all the might in the form of his guns. The only time Thornton fired any gun was when he hunted with his father, who stood, sat, or crouched right beside him with his own gun. Otherwise, he was perpetually unarmed. The only way to defend his mother was to help her run.

Meanwhile, Colleen was about to deliver her and Henry's child into bondage and put it at the mercy of Hezzy Jones and his swine sons. Boy or girl, the child's life would be treacherous. And Thornton looked his friend in the eye every day and didn't tell him. He was disgusted with himself that he kept the awful secret, but if Henry knew about the child, he might put himself, Colleen, and the baby at risk with rash heroics.

Still, Thornton knew he was guilty of one of slavery's worst sins. He treated Henry like he was a child. If Henry wanted to risk his life to save his wife and child, he should be the one to make that choice. But Thornton and William had discussed it and figured they did their friend a favor when they didn't torment him about a child he might not get to raise, a family he may never again see. They told themselves it would be a wonderful surprise for Henry if they pulled off the escape and presented him with his child.

Thornton questioned their wisdom, though. The birth of the baby loomed. Thornton wasn't sure how much longer he could keep the secret from Henry. If the plan went south, Henry might never lay eyes on his child. If he controlled own fate, he may one day find a way to see his child, ev just once. How long could Thornton and William continue to make that choice for their friend?

And there was Ronan's mother. Her life was in every bit of danger—and from more sources—as his mother's was. If they needed to get Thornton's mother out, they needed to get Ronan's mother out too. Thornton's initial desire to run away from his father had become almost insignificant compared to so many other priorities.

Ethan threw a large hoe into the spokes of his wagon wheel just as he and William had worked out some of the details.

They would run at the first sign of the winter thaw. The days would be shorter, and they would have more darkness to hide in than if they waited until the long days of summer.

They figured individual horseback was the best way to travel since it meant they could scatter and force those who gave chase to spread their resources.

Less clear were details like how they would subdue his father, get past Hezzy Jones's dogs and sons to free two women and a crying baby, and find enough horses for all of them to ride.

With Ethan there, they would have to conspire around a twelve-year-old who already owed Marcus his loyalty and who was wily enough to walk from the Unorganized Territory to Missouri and live to tell about it.

Thornton had to admit that what also bothered him about Ethan was good, old-fashioned envy. He had been just a year younger than Ethan was when he had tried to walk the same route Ethan had taken, in the opposite direction, to his aunt and uncle's farm, only to be apprehended by his father and marched home at gunpoint. It had been humiliating. His father had taunted him about it for two years afterwards.

He admired Ethan for being craftier than he was. He had figured out how to stay several steps ahead of Uncle Jeremiah's posse.

He wished Ethan was on their side. They could use him.

27

IT WAS William's twenty-fourth Christmas without his mother. He hadn't seen her since the worst day of his life, when he was twelve years old and they sold him away from Virginia, away from her, to a slave-master in Tennessee.

He wondered where she was. He felt guilty. He sat with Ronan and Henry in the bunkhouse and dined in the warmth of the stove on a Christmas goose Thornton had procured for them, how, William still didn't know, and that Henry had roasted for them. He hoped his mother, wherever she was, ate well in a warm place.

He wondered often what she looked like. She had been bookish when he knew her, with a tall, lean frame. He wondered if she had the same grace all those years later or if decades of servitude had buckled her. He worried about the humiliations she had been forced to endure that made him want to kill the men who violated her and hoped she was still alive. His father had been sold shortly after William was born, so William had been all the family his mother had had when they sold him away from her.

He pondered every day whether she would know him if she saw him. He missed her terribly. He ached to have a conversation with her, to bathe in the warmth of the smile he remembered, to take refuge in the fact that no matter how miserable he was, no matter how much his life remained at stake, there was a person on earth who loved him, and for whom he had value. He hoped she fared well.

He hoped Rose Guthrie fared well too. It had been weeks since the incident in the kitchen, and as far as tell, Rose hadn't endured any more beatings, although h no idea what she had to put up with in her bedroom.

He contemplated more and more what went on in her bedroom. It was a fool's game and a dangerous one, but whenever he could find reasons to be near her, he risked it. He lingered in front of the kitchen window longer than necessary and hoped for a glimpse of her. Since that horrible day, he had only seen her twice in the window. Both times, she turned away and walked to another part of the house.

He hadn't even tried to figure out what had provoked Marcus Guthrie to be so violent. There had been no immediate warning. If William hadn't gone to the window, he wouldn't have known it had happened.

But he did know. He had seen it all, seen too much.

He thought often about the way she looked at him through the window while her face was pressed against the table. He wanted to rescue that woman, to treat her with kindness, to take care of her.

All his life he had been either sold away from a place and therefore unable to form a bond with a woman, thrown in with nothing but men, which had happened when he was a stevedore, or faced stiff competition in other men. He had never learned how to talk to females. If he encountered a woman he might dare to talk to, as soon as another fellow showed up, William retreated. It had been impossible to mate under conditions of confinement and bondage.

Many slaves went their entire lives without love, mating, or romantic human touch. William had assumed he would be one of those slaves. He had never had relations with a woman and expected to die never knowing how it felt to get lost in a woman and maybe have a child with her. His sudden desire to bond with Rose came out of nowhere and astonished him.

He figured like Thornton, who had been happy with his land until Fidelia had come along, William's first love, books, no longer fulfilled all his needs. He wanted more.

He kept his feelings from Thornton. His friend had enough concerns. He had to get nine people out of Missouri. It would horrify him if his mother moved on from his father to his best friend.

When it came time to run, Rose would travel with Thornton. Both of them would want it that way. But lately William wished there was a way for Rose to travel with him. He was foolish, but he had heard during his time on the boat that there were places far to the north where no one had a care about what people who lived together looked like. There were small villages, smaller than the one Rip Van Winkle lived in, where outcasts as unwanted as the scapegoat sent to pasture in Leviticus could make a life. He thought every day about how he and Rose might share an existence in a faraway place like that.

Many obstacles lay ahead of him. Rose had no idea how he felt and sure enough had no plans to take up with a runaway slave in some cabin in the woods. He had no means to approach her, no safe way to hint about what could be.

Ethan was also a problem. Everywhere William looked, there was Ethan. The boy watched him and Ronan and Henry without any shame about it. Slavery and the men trapped in it fascinated him. His curiosity about slavery like it was a choice the men had made incensed William. And he didn't need the boy to report back to Marcus Guthrie that his Aunt Rose talked to the slave Marcus hated most for his friendship with Thornton.

He was grateful Thornton had laid down strict rules for the boy. He was not permitted to give one order to the three men or tell Thornton's father Thornton had issued that order lest he find his older cousin would feel the need to write to the boy's parents and tell them where Ethan was.

They had to be careful with that threat, though. If Ethan caught on that he was supposed to stay away from the men because he might otherwise accidentally witness something between them and Thornton, he may turn their blackmail around on them and threaten to tell Marcus what they were up to if they didn't give him what he wanted.

Thornton and William were smarter than the twelve-year-old, though, and he had followed the order not to boss around the three men.

William checked his internal clock. It was seven-forty-five in the evening. He wondered how the Christmas celebration in the main house went. He ate a little more Christmas goose.

Later, he would risk reading aloud to Ronan and Henry a story from *The Sketch Book of Geoffrey Crayon, Gent.* called "Christmas Dinner", and the three would play a few rounds of Gleek with the deck of cards Thornton had slipped them. Ever since Ronan and Henry learned to read numbers, the three of them engaged in the distraction the three-man card game offered as often as it was safe to chance it. Christmas in a snowstorm seemed like a safe bet. Marcus Guthrie was getting drunk and fat in the main house, William was sure. What was Rose doing, he wondered.

———◆———

Christmas was different, Thornton reflected, although not for him or his mother. They exchanged no gifts. She had knitted him a sweater, which she did every year. She gave him nothing that had no practical value whatsoever but that would be a delight to receive, like a jackstraws set. Likewise, he gave her no shawl or fancy hat. He had no money, and she wouldn't have accepted such tokens anyway.

The difference was with his father, who finally had a drinking buddy of sorts in Ethan. Thornton's cousin listened with rapt attention to his drunk Uncle Marcus's stories of farms he'd caroused his way through in 1815.

Ethan sat in the big chair next to Marcus's in front of the fireplace and refilled his uncle's glass from time to time. He made sure it never had less than two or three swigs worth of liquor in it. He wore the sweater his Aunt Rose had knitted for him for Christmas. It looked absurd under the idiotic expression on his face that revealed he couldn't wait to grow up and steal, cheat his bosses, and violate farmers' daughters, so that he could get run off of farms like Thornton's father.

Uncle and nephew made a happy pair. Thornton still couldn't believe Ethan knew his parents thought he might be dead and didn't care to clear that up for them. Thornton thought their Christmas must be dreadful.

He listened to his father guffaw at one of his own bad jokes and thought if he could just silence the gurgling in his bowels for two more months and go through with his escape plan, he would never again have to hear that cackle.

* * *

"Merry Christmas. Well, day after Christmas." Thornton always felt as though he sounded stupid around Fidelia. He couldn't even wish her a happy Christmas without stumbling.

Hiram Elliot was off visiting far-flung neighbors, spreading post-Christmas tidings. His own father was in Columbia, probably drinking his way through town. Thornton had taken advantage of their gadding to bring Fidelia a small gift, one that suddenly struck him as. . . .stupid. It was a sack of clover tea that he had grown especially for her and placed in a bag he made out of some fancy material he found in his mother's sewing things. He tied the brocade sack with a piece of ribbon he found in the same box. It had seemed like a grand idea until he stood on her porch toting the sack. He figured she probably had her own clover tea or hated tea altogether.

"Merry Christmas, Thornton. Come in!"

Many Sundays, when his father was away, he sneaked over to the Elliots and met Fidelia on some far corner of the property outside the view of her father. Fidelia hadn't banished him. It was by his own choice that they met outdoors. He found it much easier to talk to Fidelia in the open air. He had to admit, though, that it was a nice change to be walking into her front room. And warmer too, although no fresh fire blazed in the vast fireplace. The embers from what was probably the fire from the night before still glowed. They were hot enough to keep the entire downstairs warm.

"Here. I mean, I brought you this, for Christmas." He handed her the tiny bag. "It's tea. Clover tea." He sounded dumber by the minute.

"What a treat! I haven't had clover tea since before my ma died. She used to grow enough to keep the whole farmstead steeped in tea. Ha! Get it?"

He did. It was funny. He relaxed and felt less dumb.

"I'll make some for us this afternoon. I have something for you too. I hope you like it." She flashed him a bashful smile and he loved the present before he saw it. "It's a riding scarf. For when you ride Ashes. To come see me. On cold days. I knitted it myself."

"It's perfect." Lately, they had experimented with kissing, had tried it out here and there to see how it felt between them. Thornton had thought it felt wonderful. He thought they should try it some more. He leaned across the settee and kissed her. It never failed to surprise him when she kissed him back, as she did then.

"How was your Christmas?" she asked.

"Well, it's different at our place."

"Because of the men, and your father?"

"You could say that. And, well...."

"Well, what? No use in hiding it. If I have to tickle you in all the wrong places to get it out of you, I will, you know." She laughed good-naturedly.

She beguiled him. He wanted so much to hold back and have it tickled out of him by her, but he couldn't contain himself. "I'm keeping a dreadful secret from Henry."

"A secret? What kind of secret?"

"Well, Henry, he left a wife on Hezzy Jones's place, and if everything went according to nature, she may have had a baby yesterday that Henry had no idea was on the way."

"A baby!"

"Thing is, if we tell him, William and me, that is, he may go rushing over there and get himself killed."

"William knows too?"

"Uh, yeah." He felt exposed. He talked past the awkwardness of his and William's sharing such a strange secret. "We have an idea about when to tell him, but it's not time yet." And it's not just Henry's baby that I'm scared to talk about, he wanted to say.

He should have told her that in eight, or, at the most, ten weeks, he and William planned to run for it. They had worked out more details. They would borrow an idea from Ethan and leave in the middle of the night to put distance between the hunters and the hunted while it was dark. The initial band of five fleeing Guthrie Farms would use all four Guthrie horses for their getaway.

The most brazen part of their breakout would be the Hezzy Jones stretch of the trip. Thornton and William had kicked it around for weeks, and there was no way around it. They would have to march right into Hezzy's house and announce they were there to take Ronan's mother, Colleen, and the baby. If they helped the three flee undetected, those who remained behind might be punished as conspirators. It was safer for the women in Colleen's bunkhouse if the escape took on the form of a raid.

It meant they would have to hold down Hezzy and his sons the same way they did Marcus and try to walk out right under their noses and not get shot. They'd have to show up with saddled horses to get away fast.

Hiram Elliot's horses. William got it into his head that they could pick up from the Elliot farm a few saddled horses so that they could get in and out of Hezzy's place with greater speed. It was the thing Thornton was most scared to tell Fidelia, for it included a marriage proposal. His to her. It terrified him. Not marriage. He couldn't wait to be married to Fidelia. It was the proposal part that petrified him. Involving Hiram Elliot would be an enormous risk. He lived by the book. He hated slavery, but he dealt honestly. He would be reluctant to help the group flee, let alone to allow Fidelia to join a bunch of scalawags who were as likely to find themselves at the end of a rope as they were to end up in free territory. If he balked, he might take it a step further and turn them in. It meant Thornton would have to include in his proposal asking Fidelia not to tell her father until the night they fled and to first break several laws with him and flee the state before the ceremony.

Thornton and William would surprise Hiram Elliot on the night of the escape, just as they would Marcus Guthrie and Hezzy Jones, only they wouldn't subdue him with violence. They would show up and plead their case, and hopefully leave with a few of his horses. And his daughter.

The problem was, Thornton hadn't screwed up the nerve to ask Fidelia yet, and time was running out.

"I think you should tell Henry," Fidelia said. "Seems to me he ought to decide for himself whether he wants to get killed. How do you keep it from a man that he's a father? I mean, what are you waiting for? And, anyway, how did you find out?"

Thornton dreaded that question because he couldn't tell her about his midnight ride to Colleen's bunkhouse without spilling the entire plan and making his outlandish marriage proposal, and yet he refused to lie to her. It made the answer harder. "I can't say."

She looked hurt. It hurt him right back.

"I'm sorry, Fidelia." There was so much he should confess. He lacked the courage. "I'm asking you to trust me. I have a good reason for not being able to tell you right now, but I promise I will tell you one day. Not just that, but everything surrounding the reason we can't tell Henry yet."

"One day? Hm. Seems to me you're keeping lots of secrets, from Henry, from me. I see."

"Please don't say that. I wish you wouldn't say that." He was scared. He felt her retreating.

"Well, what should I say?"

"You have every right to feel how you do. I don't mean to be a heel, but I am one. All I can say is I have a good reason. It seems when a fella....loves a girl, there ought to be some understanding when he's honest and asks for it up front. You know, like trust."

"Say that again."

He knew which part she meant. "I love you." He had never said it outright before.

"Oh, Thornton, you're not a heel. I guess I just feel left out, is all. When you're ready to tell me, I'll listen. I just don't want it to always be this way between us, you deciding when you'll tell me things. When a girl loves a fellow, it seems he shouldn't have secrets from her."

"I promise this is the one and only time, the first and the very last time. Wait. Say that again."

"I love you."

"Will you say one more thing again?"

"Always, between us? Always. Between us. Always."

"I love you, Fidelia."

"I love you, Thornton."

He should have proposed right then, should have told her about the escape, but he didn't. Instead, he kissed her. She made tea, and they drank and talked and kissed all afternoon.

28

IT LOOKED to Rose like 1835 would be as tedious as 1834 had been, as dreary as every year with Marcus had been. It was the middle of January, and there was no letup on the snow.

Winter was always hard. There was not much to do on the farm, and she was trapped inside the house most days with Marcus, with no Thornton to run interference since what work there was to be done by a Guthrie, and not the three men, was done by her son. Marcus hated to work outside in the cold. He relegated most winter chores to Thornton.

Rose pined for William. She no longer watched him through the window and instead relied on the glimpses of him she caught on the few occasions they were in the yard at the same time. Once or twice she could have sworn he stared at her a little longer than necessary, likely because what happened in the kitchen made her a strange sight to him.

There was one thing she tried to see as an improvement in her life. Ever since Ethan had arrived, Marcus hadn't hit her too often. There was the occasional slap to the face in their bedroom, or the twist of her arm in the kitchen, or a single sock to the jaw when nobody looked. And he still forced himself on her just about every night.

But Ethan had distracted Marcus, for the time being, from having nothing to do but torture his wife. She hadn't been subjected to any out-and-out beatings. Once Marcus got used to Ethan being around, he would again look to her, and she would be in for it. She dreaded it and soaked up the respite, even if she realized how absurd it was to be grateful for slaps to the face and socks to the jaw.

She laced up her boots and bundled up to go outside. She needed to wring the necks of a couple of chickens and pluck them for a soup.

Marcus had taken Ethan to Hezzy Jones's place so the boy could see what a farmstead with two dozen slaves working it looked like. Marcus would expect a warm meal waiting when they returned, especially after riding in the snow, which he usually shunned but agreed to do for Ethan.

Rose was surprised Thornton had joined them. She knew how he felt about his father and Hezzy Jones, but he had gone along on the ride.

She stepped onto the porch and took deep breaths of icy air. It felt like seventeen or eighteen degrees. She headed to the coops that kept the chickens high and dry during the winter.

She learned as a girl on her father's farm not to form any attachments to chickens or pigs. It made it much harder to set a table with them when the time came. Without hesitation, she chose the first chicken and walked toward the barn. She would wring its neck and pluck it there and eviscerate it in the kitchen.

The chicken squirmed under her arm, but she pinned him tight. He was headed for Marcus's stomach, whether he liked it or not.

She pulled hard on the barn door with her free hand and encountered William. He sat on an anvil and read *The Last of the Mohicans*.

He sprang to his feet. He made a weak attempt to tuck the book into his coat, but it was too late. She had seen the book, and he had seen her see the book. He stood there guilty and caught, but his back was straight, and he looked her right in the eye from his much taller vantage point. He was the handsomest man she'd ever seen.

His mouth moved. It tried to provide some answer, she figured, some excuse for why he sat in her barn and read her son's book, but no words came out. He stared at her.

"Don't worry. I know," she said. She went to the far side of the barn, where her tools were. She was too mortified by what he had seen through the kitchen window to engage him in conversation. She busied herself with the chicken.

"Ma'am?"

"It's okay....William, right?" It was the first time she had ever addressed him directly. She had said his name a thousand times in her head. She imagined conversations with him several times a day. In real life, she had only watched him talk to Thornton. She envied her son his right to banter with William any time he chose.

She knelt down over the wooden bin she would use for the chicken. "I know my son gives you his books. I'm guessing you figured the sound of the horses driving up would give you some warning."

"Uh, yes, Ma'am."

She wished he would call her Rose. "I guess you hadn't figured on my coming out here in this cold. I probably should have coughed or something, you know, to warn you. If I had known you were out here, I would have." He didn't answer. She glanced up and risked him looking into her plain face. His height didn't scare her like Marcus's did. It was a thing to behold. She noticed for the first time how thin and worn his coat was. She looked down again and went to work on the chicken. "Why not read in the bunkhouse? Has to be a good deal warmer, with the stove and the extra wood." She wanted him to know she was aware of the extra wood and was glad about it.

"My reading makes the other men nervous. I try not to do it in front of them."

The chicken's neck had been through the worst. Rose had been quick about it, another thing she had learned from her father. She started the tedious task of plucking its thousands of feathers.

"I see." Heat rose up her cheeks. She was sure they were as red as coals in a fire. "Where are you from, William, originally I mean."

He waited a long moment to answer. "Virginia, where my mother is, or at least where she was when I last saw her. I was twelve when they sold me to a man in Tennessee and seventeen when I came to Missouri."

She looked up for a brief moment when he mentioned his mother. It saddened her he should have been separated from her so young. Her own mother had died when she was thirteen, and she still missed her. She couldn't imagine if she had been sold away from her and had been left to wonder every day whether she was alive or dead and what she endured.

Rose was curious about what William had done all those years in Missouri, after he left Tennessee—and with whom. She probed, and the story of the boat and his friend Archibald tumbled out. At first he had hesitated, but after a while, he became comfortable and talked real easy with her. She was pleased he made no mention of a wife, or even a casual woman, in his story.

She was done with the first chicken and ready for the next, but he kept her with a question of his own. "How about you, Ma'am? Have you always lived in Missouri?"

"My whole life." She made quick work of cleaning up the chicken mess. She surprised herself with how she managed to forge through a conversation with him after what he'd seen. She told him about life on her father's farm, her parents, and the day Marcus had shown up. They talked and talked.

———◦◦◦———

"We've been talking eighty-seven minutes, Ma'am," he said. They had been the best minutes of William's life. He was having his first real conversation with a woman who wasn't his mother.

"Eighty-seven minutes?"

"Yes. Shouldn't we, I mean, what if your, your husband comes home?" They sat on anvils right in the middle of the barn.

"We'll both listen for the horses. If they come home, I'll leave out of one door, and you got out the other. Please finish telling me about St. Louis. You know, my mother lived there."

"Hardest part about St. Louis, besides the back-breaking work and the bad smell all over the boat, was seeing free Negroes everywhere. Must have thought more than a hundred times about mugging free men for their papers. But I couldn't take another man's freedom."

"I know what you mean. Those aren't just words. I truly know what you mean. The few times I have traveled off this farm, I have envied just about every woman I've seen. Wondered how the man she was with treated her."

William gathered the courage to ask the question that had been on his mind for weeks. "Ma'am?"

"William, will you do me a favor? Will you call me Rose?"

His heart thumped. "Rose." He tried it out, on its own. He dared a bit more. "I have to know, Rose. What happened that day?"

She held her head up but lowered her eyes. "He caught me staring at you. Through the window." She raised her eyes and looked right into his. He stared back. For the first time in his life, he didn't care how much time went by. His mind kept track anyway.

Their anvils rested so near to one another that his knees touched hers. He had never been so close to a woman in his entire life. He was terrified, but he refused to let it show. He reached out and grabbed her hands. "It was because of me?" He sounded guilty.

"No, it was because of him, and his need to....treat me like he does. Any excuse'll do, most times. The first time he hit me, I don't know. I—. Well, I don't know." He squeezed her hands. They leaned closer to each other. "William." It sounded to him more like a sigh than a statement.

"Rose. You'd better go inside and start your soup, and I'd better get back to the bunkhouse. As it is, I'd guess you're down one chicken." She didn't let go of his hands.

They stared at each other for two more minutes, his clock told him. He moved his hands to pull away. She gripped his harder and leaned in and kissed him.

It was an awkward kiss, William's first.

He was unsure what to do. He kept his mouth close to hers. Their lips remained together for several seconds. She adjusted her mouth, and he realized it was part of the kiss. He moved his mouth in similar fashion. They kept at it for several more moments.

He tore himself away. "Rose."

"You're right. I'd better get back to the house."

He wanted to kiss her again, but he didn't want to be forward. He stood up. He still held her hands. He helped her up and gave her hands one more squeeze. He let go and walked past her and out the back door of the barn.

He wanted to murder Marcus Guthrie for more reasons than he could count. If he had encountered him on his way to the bunkhouse, he would have killed him on the spot with no thought of the disastrous consequences.

He walked between the buildings through the snow. He brooded over how he would tell Thornton he was in love with his mother and that she would be going with him, north, when it came time to escape.

29

"A BOY?"

"A boy," Thornton repeated. "As handsome as Henry. And so small."

Thornton knew, even if William didn't, that they were about to have out the Henry situation. It was sure to be a nasty difference of opinion.

They hid in plain sight and shod horses right under Marcus's nose in the barn. They left the barn doors open to give the impression there was nothing to hide.

Ronan and Henry fed the livestock and cleaned out the men's outhouse. Thornton hated to leave them with the outdoor chores while he and William worked in the barn, but for that day it had to be that way.

It was the morning after Thornton had suffered through spending the day with his father and Ethan at Hezzy Jones's place, and he had grave concerns about his and William's approach to Henry's affairs. It was bad enough that the entire way to and from Hezzy's, his father and Ethan bantered like two eighty-year-old men who swapped stories of fighting in the War of Independence. They exaggerated and blustered up and down the road. To hear Ethan tell it, he flew his kite so high, people in the Qing Dynasty could see it. It had grated on Thornton. But what he had seen at Hezzy's as it pertained to Henry had so disturbed him, he hadn't slept at all the night before.

It was true that the trip had been an unexpected godsend. Without the need for midnight rides, Thornton would find out how Colleen and her baby fared and get a look at how Hezzy Jones ran his farmstead in the winter, information Thornton and William would need to raid the place.

With his father as his usher, Thornton carried the presumption of good intentions. Hezzy granted him a tour, led by Jedidiah, of the bunkhouses and barn, eager to help Marcus Guthrie's son learn how to manage his own three slaves and "grow his crop," as Hezzy had put it. True to what Thornton realized was his nature, Ethan had tagged along.

It felt strange. On instinct Thornton wanted to dart behind buildings whenever he encountered a Jones. With an eye focused on reconnaissance, he counted horses—Hezzy had seven, unless more were off with bodies they carried hunting—and noted where they were kept, found out how big the dogs were that had shouted the night he visited Colleen, and learned where in the house Hezzy's sons slept.

He hid how eager he was to see the female quarters. He pretended to be thoroughly bored by the tour by the time they arrived in front of Colleen's bunkhouse. Jedidiah Jones led him through the shack and talked about the women like they were livestock. Thornton almost punched him.

He worried the women might accidentally give him up, which would have been all the more disastrous with Ethan under foot, but they had remembered his admonishment from his night visit and pretended not to know him while he and Jedidiah surveyed the bunkhouse. Jedidiah blurted out that "one of his females" had given birth to a boy on Christmas day.

At that pronouncement, Colleen emerged from the back of the gathering of ladies with her son in her arms.

He was so tiny. Thornton was taken aback. The baby lay in his mother's arms, a slave, and slept sounder than Rip Van Winkle. His awakening would be much ruder, Thornton feared, and it wouldn't happen twenty years from then. The child had probably already faced undue separation from Colleen in his short lifetime.

A weird sense of dread had begun to overtake Thornton. He felt guilty standing two feet away from Henry's son, especially since Colleen didn't know that Thornton had never told Henry about their child. She sent him a message with her eyes that said, "Please tell Henry how beautiful our son is." Thornton was unable to muster a return message with his own eyes. He half-grinned at the baby and asked Jedidiah a question whose answer didn't matter to him.

Jedidiah was aware that Henry was the father but didn't mention him. Henry was nothing to Jedidiah Jones but a bull who provided the seed for his newest slave. A desire for Thornton to deliver congratulations to the father never entered Jedidiah's mind.

Standing there in Colleen's bunkhouse with Jedidiah, Thornton had remembered something. He had no idea why he kept forgetting it. *Jedidiah had taken a liking to Colleen.* Thornton had felt queasy. He had not only kept Henry from being able to do anything about being an expectant father, but he had done so knowing that Henry's inability to get to Colleen subjected her to Jedidiah Jones. He and William had usurped Henry's entire right to manage his own life and problems his way, and Thornton had spent a restless night mulling over how to tell William he could no longer do it.

He relayed to William the easiest part of the information that he had gathered the day before. William seemed distracted and appeared to not be listening to Thornton, as if something bothered him besides all of the obvious.

"Thornton?" It was Henry. Ronan was with him. They appeared in the barn from nowhere.

"Hi, fellas." He acted natural.

"You were at the Jones place yesterday?" Henry asked.

A sense of doom lurked. "Uh, yeah." Thornton maintained an upbeat tone.

"Did you by chance encounter any of the women-folk? You can't miss Colleen. She has a way of drawing a fellow's eyes." Henry sounded resolute, sad.

Ronan didn't ask about his mother outright. In typical fashion, he simply waited for Thornton's answer about whether they had seen any of the women, and he would ruminate on that information and proceed from there. If Thornton admitted seeing the women, Ronan may have waited two more days to ask about his mother. Either way, Thornton was relieved that for the moment, Ronan let Henry seek answers.

Thornton felt William's eyes boring into the side of his head. It was a point—a day—of reckoning for Thornton. He could confess to Henry all that he knew and had seen, which would put him right with Henry, Colleen, their son, and himself. He'd be able to tell Ronan about his mother and unleash to Fidelia much of what he had been keeping from her.

Alas, his confession would take down William, and he couldn't do that without first telling his fellow perpetrator. William deserved fair warning. "Uh, we saw their bunkhouse, but I didn't actually speak to any of the ladies," which was the truth. "Sounds like I would have known if I had seen, Colleen, was it? She sounds lovely, Henry. The ladyfolk I saw all seemed fine, though."

"All right." Ronan and Henry went back to work, with their heads hung low. They each looked three inches shorter.

Thornton waited until they were out of earshot. "I'm telling Henry today. That man has a son."

"I know that. We're not telling him."

"He's somebody's father! Hezzy Jones's most fragile slave is Colleen and Henry's little son!"

"I know."

"And Jedidiah Jones is hunting Colleen! Henry deserves to know what's happening, to take matters into his own hands, to decide for himself what to do."

"He'll get killed. It won't do him or his boy any good."

"But, Jed—"

"You think I don't know?! You think Henry doesn't know about Jedidiah Jones?! Why do you think Henry neve~ ˙ ˉ Thornton? You don't want to know what we know, seen women taken right on the ground behind dogh҄ of dog manure and in broom closets that had mice r around in them by men who snatched what they thought they had a right to."

Thornton dropped onto an anvil with his head in his hands. He couldn't stand what William had just said. And yet, it never failed. Every time William called him "son", it calmed him. William never condescended. It was always with spontaneous affection that it slipped out, and it repurposed Thornton enough for him to see logic. William was right. *Of course Henry knew about Jedidiah Jones.* His countenance revealed that fact all the time. If Henry knew he had a son who was subjected to Jedidiah Jones, on top of Colleen already being at the pig's mercy, it would give him a thousand more reasons to rush headlong into disaster. As sickening as it was, it remained better for Henry not to know about his child. "Dammit," Thornton conceded.

William heaved a sigh. "I know."

With great reluctance Thornton returned to practical matters. "I didn't get the boy's name, but he looked healthy."

"How about the dogs?"

"Down to five, like you guessed."

"That means even if we go four separate ways, they can put a hound on each of us."

"It just means the horses will be all the more crucial."

"How many did you count? I mean, in case we can't get what we need from Hiram Elliot." William worked on a hoof of the horse Thornton thought of as his mother's favorite.

Thornton caught the forlorn sound in William's voice. "Seven, I think."

"No, it was eight."

Thornton and William swung around hard, in unison, at the sound of Ethan's voice behind them. They looked caught in the act of something they should not have been doing. Those damned open barn doors, Thornton thought. Ethan had walked right through them. How much had he heard?

Thornton fished. "Eight what?"

"Eight horses at Hezzy Jones's place. In case you can't get what you need from Hiram Elliot."

He had heard that much, maybe more, including what they had said about the different routes and the dogs, and worse, Henry's son.

Thornton had to be careful how he handled the next two minutes. He used the hard-ass approach. "Excuse me, but what the hell are you doing listening to adults carrying on conversation?" He waved his farrier's nippers in the air for good measure. They were much longer than a wrench, with large clawed tips, and perfect for hitting someone over the head, which Thornton wouldn't do, but Ethan would have to wonder whether he might. He hated people who threatened children, but he had come to believe Ethan was a man in disguise. It was hard to remember he wasn't.

He leaned forward as though he might have to walk over to where Ethan was and get better answers to his questions. The routine worked. Ethan recoiled.

"I—, I wasn't listening on purpose, I swear. I just happened to hear."

"Well, if you *happen* to repeat what you *happened* to hear, I will *happen* to tell your parents where you *happen* to be. Now get on back to the house, and next time announce yourself if you come into any room I'm in. Clear?"

"Yessir." The word flew out of the boy's mouth.

"Sir is right. Now go."

Thornton waited for Ethan to reach the farmhouse. "What do you think?" he said.

"I think he heard everything and knows more."

What a ridiculous predicament, Thornton thought. For months they had gone undetected, and some pipsqueak who had walked out of the Unorganized Territory on a whim had planted himself in Thornton's business, and, like stinkweed, his noxious scent was everywhere.

———◆———

They planned to escape. Ethan was sure of it. He sat in his favorite chair next to where his Uncle Marcus sat evenings and thought about how much he hated people who treated him like he was stupid just because he was a child. He was almost twelve-and-a-half.

It was obvious they planned to run. Why else talk about dogs following them if they went "separate ways"?

And it wasn't just Thornton and William who planned to run. He had heard them talk about as many as four different routes. Ethan guessed that meant Ronan and Henry intended to join them.

But if that was the case, why involve Hezzy Jones's horses at all? He remembered they only planned to use Hezzy Jones's horses if they couldn't get what they needed from Hiram Elliot. It sounded to Ethan like they intended to swing through Hezzy Jones's place to pick up other people who would run with them on horses they got from Hiram Elliot. It made sense. His uncle had bought his slaves from Hezzy Jones, and his besotted cousin moaned and groaned about Fidelia Elliot all the time. William, Ronan, and Henry most likely had family on the Jones place they didn't intend to leave behind, and they would use Thornton's connection to the Elliot farm to help their escape.

It hit Ethan. He had heard his cousin and William talking about a healthy boy whose name Thornton didn't get. He had almost heard more, but Ronan and Henry had gone into the barn, and Ethan had waited several minutes until after they left to be sure they wouldn't come back. In that time, he had heard raised voices and was annoyed that he couldn't approach to hear what Thornton and William argued about.

The first thing he heard was the tidbit about the boy. One of the three slaves on Guthrie Farms must have been connected to the slave woman who had had her baby on Christmas. But Jedidiah Jones hadn't mentioned who the father was. How had Thornton known who he was unless he had been to the Jones place on his own and figured it out? Ethan bet himself his uncle had no idea his son had been to the Jones place gathering information about the women and children of his three slaves.

Ethan could tell by the talk in the barn that the baby wasn't William's, but Ethan had never overheard even one syllable from Ronan or Henry about a baby left behind at the Jones place. Whichever one it was didn't know he was a father.

Ethan felt sure he had figured it all out. He had to decide what to do with the information. He was tired of Thornton bossing him around. He had expected his older cousin to be a barrier between him and the adults, the way he had been for Janey, Edward, and Julius. It hadn't turned out that way. Instead, Thornton gave him orders and set boundaries for him. It was like his father was there. Ethan would love to tell his uncle what he had overheard in the barn.

He believed Thornton's threats, though, to send his parents a letter that told them where he was. Even if it took the letter a year to get to his parents, it would still mean his time on Guthrie Farms would end. He didn't want that to happen. Already he had been to Columbia with his Uncle Marcus three times. There was no way he would give that up to return to flying his kite through the wilderness where his mother and father lived.

He was in Missouri to stay. And, anyway, if Thornton did run, it would leave more room for him. He wanted his cousin gone. The escape was a happy turn of events.

He would keep his mouth shut, both for his own sake and to help make sure Thornton left. But he liked having something to hold over his cousin's head. If he was backed into a corner, he wouldn't hesitate to use it.

30

"THE BOOKS were bad enough, but this is too much. The answer is no."

"Absolutely not. Have you lost your mind?"

William figured Ronan and Henry would react that way. He *was* crazy to try to plan a clandestine meeting with Rose in the bunkhouse while the two of them slept in the barn. He had thought about nothing but her kiss since it happened. He was desperate to be with her and knew of no other way.

The middle of the night offered his best chance to meet her. On any given night, Marcus Guthrie would be dead drunk by the stroke of twelve and wouldn't come to until after three in the morning. Days when Marcus was gone wouldn't work because there was no way of knowing whether Thornton would visit Fidelia Elliot or whether Fidelia's father would send Thornton home with no further notice, causing Thornton to appear unexpectedly.

Thornton had sneaked him pencil lead and paper. He used it to teach Ronan and Henry how to write. William thought he could use the writing materials to slip Rose a note. He would invite her to meet him in the bunkhouse. He planned to end the note by asking her to burn it.

He had it worked out down to the smallest detail and had even come up with a way to handle the dogs. He and Thornton had discovered the hard way that bribing the dogs with jerky was a risky proposition for the hands. Ivan the Terrible—as they called the wolf-dog—had tried to eat the Thornton's fingers and had angled for his thumb one when Thornton had made a mistake and fed Bluebeard, .erre, and Caligula—the bloodhounds—first.

Ivan the Terrible was too moody to be trusted with a jerky bribe. Instead, William and Thornton had given the dogs fruit liquor. They figured if it put an oaf like Marcus Guthrie in a deep slumber, it could disarm the dogs on the night of the escape.

They had tried various amounts. A jigger had been too much. Robespierre stumbled around suspiciously the next day, while Bluebeard and Caligula crawled around on their bellies looking sick, and Ivan the Terrible needed till noon to sleep off the drunk. A quarter-jigger made them too happy. They yapped all day. A half-jigger was the perfect sedative for all four animals. Once they dozed off, a man could walk by their tiny doghouse barn a million times without notice, but they woke up spry as ever—and on schedule—the next day. William would use fruit liquor on the dogs the night he met Rose.

Ronan and Henry were unconvinced. They were also right. If Marcus had tried to kill Rose for staring at William, what would he do if he found William's note in her pocket, or, worse, her in William's bunk?

He convinced himself they could get away with it one time. He feared once they all ran, she would insist on going with Thornton. If he could spend one night with her, he would embrace that for the rest of his life and never give himself to another woman. It would be enough to comfort him through what was sure to be an eternity without her.

He made his bunkmates an offer. "What if I told you I could guarantee you will see Colleen," he said to Henry, "and you will see your mother?" he said to Ronan.

They remained immovable, which they communicated with dead stares and silence.

Henry was also furious. He began a steady march around the bunkhouse floor and let William have it. "Have you lost *all* your good sense talking to me about Colleen?" William started to speak, but in a rare reversal of roles, Henry held up his hand and silenced him. "I spend every hour of every day thinking about that cuss Jedidiah Jones sniffing around

Colleen like the mangy dog he is. Thought about riding over there and shoving a hoe up his ass. Don't you talk to me about seeing Colleen when you know that's not possible."

He stood right over William, who sat still at the edge of his bunk. William had no intention of engaging Henry in a physical debate on the issue. Not only would it be an unfair contest in which he would prevail within seconds, but he sympathized with his friend and understood his rage. He had just explained it to Thornton not long before in the barn, when they had argued about not telling Henry about his son. William dropped the subject.

Ronan picked it up again. "How serious are you? Are you telling me I could really see my mother? Thornton was just over there, and he didn't see her."

William felt too guilty to look Ronan in the eye about Thornton's recent trip to the Jones place. Where he had been eager earlier, he turned subdued. Henry was on tenterhooks, and he refused to push it. All he said was, "I promise you I can arrange it. Give me about four weeks, and you'll see her." He turned to Henry. "And you'll see Colleen."

He pushed away a feeling he couldn't shake that their escape plans were going to collapse around them and end in catastrophe for them all. He needed them to work, both to keep his end of the bargain he made with his friends and because he could not spend a lifetime as Marcus Guthrie's slave and watch Rose spend her nights with Marcus while she suffered beatings during her days.

He looked them straight in the eye. "I promise."

Nobody spoke for sixty-two minutes. Each man lay on his bunk with no acknowledgment of the others. William resolved not to say anything more on the subject. He had tested them beyond reason.

Under different circumstances, *The Last of the Mohicans* would have tempted him from the deep place inside his pillow where he had stuffed it, but he was just about to attend the literary funerals of Uncas and Cora, two possible but improbable lovers who were slain, and he didn't need the fictional reminder of his real predicament with Rose.

He stared at the knots in the wood slats of the ceiling above him, unblinking, until the dark images faded into the timber around them and his mind went into a kind of dreary blankness. On the outer fringes of his thoughts he had a vague awareness of Ronan and Henry. He expected if one of them spoke, it would be Ronan, but Henry broke his silence first.

"If I don't see Colleen by the end of the winter thaw, you don't want to know me." He rolled over and faced the wall.

"Write your note," Ronan said.

William came out of his trance and cracked a small smile of appreciation. He had asked for four weeks. His friends had given him three months. He wouldn't need it, but he was pleased they had been willing to let him have so much time to make good on his promise. They would let him see Rose.

He reached into his seed bag—still a perfect hiding place and second only to his pillow—and pulled out his lead and paper. He thought for a long time about what he should say. The invitation had to be perfect.

31

ROSE STOOD over the woodstove in the kitchen. A fire blazed in the oven's bowels. Rose held William's letter. Every time her hand moved to within a couple of inches of the flame, she couldn't bring herself to toss the message into the fire. She read it again.

My Dear Rose,

I have lived my whole life in confinement. As though I were a chicken in a pen, I have poked my head through any holes I could find in my cages in Virginia and Tennessee and Missouri, thinking if I could just stick my head out far enough, I'd be free. It took me a long time—but less than my lifetime—to realize that no matter my ability to get my head through the various openings I discovered over the years, my being was still trapped, and I'd live inside a cage for the rest of my life. Many people passed by without freeing me, and the dreadful truth sank in.

I realized it was hopeless. 315,000 hours in captivity on a clock that never winds down on slavery is unbearable. And I have only lived 36 years. I have known slaves who have traveled 80 years on this earth. They've spent more than 700,000 hours in bondage. What does it feel like, I wonder, to be free for 700,000 hours? For one hour?

I have been passed around for less money than it costs to buy a milk cow. I have never had a friend I didn't have to fear being sold away or killed. Control over my own body is a freedom I have not enjoyed. I have never been acquainted with the love of a woman or

*known what it feels like to enjoy her good counsel and
her warm embrace. I have kissed a woman but once in
my life, and in her husband's—my owner's!—barn.*

*Before I came to Guthrie Farms, Rose, a day I swore
to fend off with all that was within me arrived. I
turned my back to the cage door and resigned myself
to eating right off the bottom of the muck-filled pen.
I no longer stuck my head out for fresh water, good
seed, and the hope of human touch that didn't poke at
me through the crevices. I've always been weary, but all
those hours had made me too worn-out to fight.*

*A glimmer of something I feared to call hope
appeared on the horizon, headed my way. It was a
person who was sympathetic to my troubles. He
wandered by my pen and took a long look at the life
trapped inside.*

*He was not standing. He crouched to hide himself
from view. His name was Thornton, and he was himself
a prisoner. He had had the fortitude to sneak out of
the cell his father built around him to get to mine—
and Ronan's and Henry's—so he could ease our door
open a crack.*

*We owe him a great debt, Rose, for in giving me
just enough room to slip out of my coop, using books
and conversation and dignity when keys were not
available to him, he allowed me to peek into the doors
that kept you trapped. For one afternoon, we roamed
free together, shared an embrace.*

*Roam with me again, Rose, for one night. Let us give
each other something we can take back to our jails and
hold close to us as we endure the confinement
architected by men like Marcus Guthrie. I can speak
only for myself when I say that while captivity will*

never do—it is only a life if you are free to live it—I could survive eternity never free to feel your touch again if you give me one night to know every bit of you in the one way that sets love matches apart from all other connections. I am not boastful enough to presume the same will suffice for you, but I am bold enough to try to make it so because I love you, Rose.

I know from all the yarns I have read that I should have waited to tell you that until I was sure you felt the same way, but my kind of life risks being too short to remain silent and dare you never knowing that I love you.

If you will grant me an audience, the men I am cooped up with have agreed to leave us be. I will ensure the dogs are quiet when you arrive.

I apologize, Sweet Rosaline—I pried your true name out of Thornton—that I cannot sail with you to an island or carry you up the mountain, to Rip Van Winkle's purple world—Heaven, really—and give you all the things a free man longs to give the woman he loves. I do hope to change that, although I cannot say more on the subject at this time.

If you are inclined to do me the honor of meeting me, wear the blue scarf I have seen you don but twice, the one I envy for the privilege it has to be so close to you and that makes your face all the more beautiful. A mere glimpse by me of the scarf in the morning will ensure I am alone in the bunkhouse and waiting in the evening.

Observation tells me we should meet no earlier than midnight if we are to escape Marcus Guthrie's detection. My hope is he will be in one of his liquor-induced stupors and that oblivion will set in long enough for us to be together for more than just a few moments stolen in a barn.

If you agree midnight offers us our best chance to turn moments into hours, I promise I will know when the clock has struck twelve. You need have no fear I will not be aware of the time. (Remember those eighty-seven minutes I kept track of!) I promise, too, I will know when the clock has struck three more times, and when the hour has arrived when we must part, so you may make a safe return to the farmhouse. I have chosen those hours when I feel your jailer will not stir while you are outside of the house.

I am unable to take my leave. I am giddy with the anticipation of tomorrow or the next day or the day after that.

The world will have no color, and my eye will not see the difference between the white clouds in the sky and the red coals of the fire until I spy the azure garment adorning your shoulders. If I should never again set eyes on it, I will take the hint and say no more. I will not burden you with my grief.

Burn this note. Take no risks, my love.

Your William, now and <u>always</u>.

Rose folded the note into its worn creases and tucked it into the pocket of her dress. She would never burn it.

32

THE LAST thing Thornton needed was to catch the cold he felt coming on. He had bedded down a few hours earlier, but his stuffy nose had woken him up. He figured it was just about midnight. If he could get back to sleep, he'd be in fine shape for his usual early rise.

At supper, he had thought the one good thing about feeling poorly was that it gave him an excuse to skip mealtime with his father and Ethan. He hated to leave his mother with the pair, but he had been glad for the reprieve, even at the cost of a cold.

Hours later, unable to achieve that perfect breathing rhythm that would lull him into a hard-working farmer's sleep, he would happily exchange his cold for an hour of his father's and Ethan's hog slop.

He swallowed a couple of times to test his throat to see if it was sore. He felt a twinge of something. He groaned. It made him wish Fidelia was there. Everything made him want to be near Fidelia. He missed her all the time. Feeling sick made it worse, made her seem farther away.

He wondered if the stove in the kitchen had enough embers left for him to toss on more logs and get a real fire started. He wanted to bundle up next to it and set a pot of water for clover tea. He'd have a bit of trouble straining it. His mother had dropped the teapot and broken it a while back, in a turn of uncharacteristic clumsiness, but he could make do with hot water, cheesecloth, and a cup. With a little honey, it would be perfect.

Alas, that sounded like a lot of work for a fellow with a cold. He was too tired. He tried to go back to sleep.

Several swallows later, all he could think about was his throat and the clover tea. He would have to get up. He moaned.

He dragged his trousers back on. He didn't bother with his shoes or a lamp. He could find his way in the dark.

He pulled the blanket off his bed. It would make a warm wrap while he drank his tea at the kitchen table. He felt better just thinking about the sweet, hot water gliding down his throat.

He opened his door and saw a light in the hallway. It trailed down the stairs. The stairway had walls and obscured whatever the source of the light was.

He ducked back into his room and tossed his blanket onto his bed. Much slower, he opened his bedroom door again. The light was still there, although it had traveled farther down the stairs. All he saw was a glow that grew fainter.

That was strange. It wasn't his father. Thornton had seen how drunk he was after dinner.

Could Ethan be prowling around the house? Thornton doubted it. His cousin had full access during the day to everywhere but his parents' bedroom and Thornton's. Creeping around in front of their rooms at night, with the occupants inside them, would get him nothing. He'd have a better chance if he snooped at noon, when the rest of the folks in the house tended to other matters. Thornton had already figured his cousin had done just that.

It had to be his mother, but he couldn't figure why she was up at that hour or why she needed a lamp. She knew her way in the dark as well as he did.

He took advantage of his quiet bare feet and made big strides through the hallway to get to the top of the staircase as fast as he could. He set his foot on the top step. The sight in front of him froze him in his tracks.

From his vantage point at the top of the stairs, with the ceiling overhang in his way, Thornton could just see the skirt of his mother's best Sunday dress swing and swivel once in the entryway to the house. She appeared to check behind her to be sure no one saw her leave. The dress disappeared through the doorway, squeezed out by a creaky, slow-moving wooden door his mother inched shut. It was obvious she wanted to be sure there was no sound from the latch. He heard it click though.

Where was she going? The outhouse was out of the question. There was no way she would walk right past the indoor privy in January to sit in the dark on a cold, wooden, unclean bench. She would defeat the whole point of the indoor setup. And she would be wearing a nightgown, not her best dress, if she had just gotten out of bed.

And, what was that smell? The strong scents of bergamot, lemon, and sandalwood floated around the staircase. She wore her perfumed water. He could remember just one other occasion when she had worn it: her father's funeral. Was somebody dead?

He waited a moment, glanced at the bedroom door his father slept behind, and prayed his father was the drunkest he'd ever been in his life.

He went down the stairs. He had to know where his mother was going. He grabbed the rail and took the steps two at a time.

He paused at the bottom landing. Maybe his mother had gone out for a moment of fresh air. She might open the door and find him standing there. He didn't want her to know he had seen her. If he went to the kitchen, she'd have to pass by the door on her way up the stairs, and she would know he had known she had been outside in her best dress.

He realized he should go back to his room and wait there. It was out of the question, though. He took a chance and eased open the front door of the farmhouse. What he saw next staggered him. His jaw dropped and hung there.

In the pitch Missouri darkness, he watched the shadow of his mother in the light of the lamp she carried make a steady course for the bunkhouse doors. She slowed her walk near the doghouse. Thornton waited for Ivan the Terrible to growl and snap at her feet, which would set off a chorus by Bluebeard, Robespierre, and Caligula and wake his father and his Hawken.

He braced for disaster, but no noise came from the little wooden structure. She strolled right past it. The dogs were sound asleep.

There was only one way those dogs could have slept while his mother's Sunday dress rustled by.

An odd feeling came over Thornton. It was part dread, part impending doom, part grief. A deep sense of loss set in, but he couldn't trace its roots.

His mother arrived at the bunkhouse doors. She took a moment to straighten her dress and adjust the blue scarf he just noticed. She never wore it, but he remembered she had donned it earlier that day. He had been so focused on the cold he was trying not to catch, he had not paid full attention to the mundane specifics of his mother's wardrobe. He understood, though, what it meant. It hit him like a bundle of hay falling on his head.

His mother opened the bunkhouse doors and slipped inside. The windows his father had set high up in the building glowed from the lamplight that shone far beneath them in his mother's hand. Not more than five seconds later, Thornton saw the light go out. The windows darkened. The faintest glow from the fire in the stove far below the windows seeped out of the cracks in the doors and up to the bottom edges of the windows.

Thornton stared at the bunkhouse for a long time. After several minutes, he forced his jaw to close and made a heavy realization: His mother wasn't coming out anytime soon. In a daze, he shut the farmhouse door and stood in the entryway, unsure what to do next.

After a long moment, he ambled to the staircase and took the steps one at a time. He contemplated his mother in the bunkhouse with each footfall. The stairs creaked under his heavy feet, but his father was too sound asleep to hear them.

His mother never would have dared such a brazen act if he weren't.

On the top landing, he glanced at his father's bedroom door once more. He had no sympathy for the drunken boar who slept behind it. Seventeen years with his father had aged his mother a lifetime and made her turn to what—or who— was in the bunkhouse.

William, he presumed. Ronan wouldn't take the risk, and Henry would never betray Colleen. William was the only one who knew to use fruit liquor on the dogs.

Henry and Ronan must have known about his mother and William, however, and cleared the way for the clandestine meeting. He was sure they were in the barn.

Thornton turned right and went to his room, the tea and the warm fire a distant memory. His throat no longer hurt. His nose cleared. The shock had knocked the cold right out of him. He closed the door and went to bed in his trousers. He stared at the pitch-black ceiling.

His mother and William took an unfathomable risk for everyone. If his father carried out a night raid and caught the lovers, he would work lethal mayhem up and down Guthrie Farms.

Thornton understood something much more than convenience was going on between William and his mother in the bunkhouse. He realized they felt about each other the way Henry and Colleen felt for one another and the way he and Fidelia felt about each other too. If it were nothing more than a hankering, neither would take the risk they took.

They were in love. They had to be. Somehow, through proximity and the occasional interaction Thornton must have missed, his best friend and his mother had fallen in love.

It made sense. William had never been allowed to form a bond with any woman, not even his own mother, much less a woman with whom he could dare a romantic pairing, so his heart was free to fall for a woman with whom he had a lot in common. They had the same quiet manner, albeit for different reasons, enjoyed the same books, and were gentle, even as they kept their distance from others. Both had been brutalized by authority figures and had no seeming way out of their predicaments.

Thornton had mixed feelings. Aside from his anger with William for putting them in peril when he knew they planned to escape in a matter of weeks, he couldn't help thinking his mother had stolen his best friend.

He realized the odd sense of grief he experienced earlier was jealousy. *He* had discovered William, had finally found a confidant, a brother, *a father*—a much better one than his mother had provided—and she had swooped down like a hawk on field prey and stolen William, who, it appeared, had been happily taken. Despite all the surreptitious looks that plotted entire schemes, the whispered half-conversations dropped at a comma and picked up three days later as if there had been no pause, and the subterfuge that advanced their plot, his friend liked his mother better.

He wondered if they talked about him behind his back the way parents who got along well sometimes discussed their children when they were behind closed doors. They were, after all, the same age while he hadn't yet turned sixteen. Were they laughing at him for his childish notions about Rip Van Winkle and the way he felt about farming and the sweet smell of the soil?

He tossed onto his left side and realized he was foolish. He thought back on all of the hazards he and William had risked to organize the escape, how worried William had been the night Thornton rode to Hezzy's, how desperate William had sounded when he ordered Thornton through clinched teeth to wait out his father when Marcus shot off Thornton's hat. William was his friend, who would no more mock him than he would mock Ronan or Henry.

William was in a quandary. Thornton remembered how distracted he had been lately. What was really going on

William loved both him and his mother, and with the escape imminent, he faced separation from them.

Thornton brought his blanket closer to his chin. He was happy for his mother. Her joining with William revealed that the girl he had always suspected lived deep inside of his mother really was there. The happy-go-lucky youngster who ran away when his mother met his father had returned home to his mother's being. He was grateful to William, who cajoled her to return, even if, like a young person, she felt an invincibility that caused her to take foolish risks.

The specifics of their liaison were more than Thornton could cope with, so he mulled over what it would mean for the escape. He tossed onto his right side, unable to sleep while his mother was still outside. He contemplated the best way to tell William he knew what was going on between him and his mother and listened for his mother's return.

* * *

Marcus Guthrie sat in the dark in a chair he had moved to his bedroom window. He had seen the lamplight in the bunkhouse go out and waited for Rose to return.

He held his rifle in one hand and a worn piece of paper in the other. He needed no light to go over the words he had read on it after he found it tucked in Rose's bible. They would forever be etched into his mind and were as permanent as the scars on a whipped slave's back.

He had come in from hunting with Ethan and saw Rose slam the good book shut. He made a note to himself to find out why his wife was suddenly afraid to be caught reading the bible.

She had cleaned up the kitchen after supper, and he had snooped between the book's black covers, not knowing what he would find. He expected to come across a dog-eared page with some passage about forbidden biblical mating. It had excited him.

The folded up piece of paper that slid out of the book and landed near his feet took him aback. The words the nigger slave had written to his wife enraged him.

He stared at the bunkhouse and thought about talk of cages and two people roaming in the night and blue scarves. He remembered she had worn the scarf all day and realized she had been signaling to that black ape that she would let him touch her in the same way he himself had touched her. Madeleine had been right. Rose was the only woman he could be with all the way, yet she preferred a mangy vermin's fondling to her husband. If he didn't have his gun, he felt sure he would choke her to death with that scarf the minute she skulked in from lying down with that monkey.

He fingered the note and felt how soft the paper had become. She must have read it a thousand times, must have thought for days and weeks about the words in it even as she had been private with her husband.

He suspected the chimp wrote the note with lead and paper his traitor son had provided, since Rose had to ask Marcus for any such things to keep her from writing letters to stray relatives without his knowledge. Thornton had always been permitted to keep a small supply for his schoolwork. The way his son had his nose up the nigger's ass all the time, he was probably the culprit.

He gripped the Hawken hard and thought about how he had feigned being drunker than he was, how he had pretended to be asleep, how he had let her leave the house, wondering whether she would really betray him. Not only had she done so, but she had made a cuckold of him in front of his son. Not long after she left the farmhouse, he heard the stairs creak and the front door open and close a second time. Thornton had been awake and had likely also seen her go into the bunkhouse. The mortification was more than he coul tolerate. He would not allow the embarrassment to stand

The clock struck one. She had been gone an hour, been doing Lord knew what in the bunkhouse for an h had allowed that nigger to put his mouth all over her and touch her private places for an hour, had intended to give that piece of manure as much as he wanted, as much as he could take in the time they stole, more than she ever gave her husband. She had never given him anything. He had always had to take it.

He refused to confront them in the bunkhouse, the barn for his slaves. He wouldn't suffer the humiliation of having to hunt down his wife on his own property, couldn't face finding their naked bodies entangled in a grotesque heap of wickedness, even if he shot them dead seconds later.

The farmhouse was his castle. The bedroom he shared with his wife was his throne room, the bed the throne itself. It was there where he had reigned best over Rose Guthrie. It was there where his death warrant issued against her would be carried out.

He had teetered on the precipice of murder during the episode in the kitchen, and she dared tempt fate anyway. She slithered over mud and evaded hounds to lay down with a black dog.

Had she loved the nigger? He was afraid to answer his own question, the dark room too small and lonely a place for him to face the truth. He thought she had simply been curious about what an African looked like up close. He hadn't appreciated, though, the impression it gave, her gaping through the window, and he had had to beat out of her any further inclinations to stare. He had made a mistake in not ending her life that day. He would have had some explaining to do, but he could have concocted an excuse that would have satisfied the law, and it would have saved him the disgrace of that night.

He would wait as long as necessary for her to return. He would line up the perpetrators and witnesses and kill them all. That time, he would get it right.

33

ROSE TRIED not to compare, but she couldn't help it. Lying with Marcus felt like being attacked by a rabid dog. Loving William had been as easy as having wind blow across her skin in the compound on a mild summer day. Even if two people with nothing but a carnal desire came together, it need not be as brutal as Marcus made it.

Where Marcus had kneaded and handled and squeezed and pinched her body, William had caressed her skin and stroked her hair. He had also been shy and tentative, not always sure what to do, not able to get guidance from Rose, who had never come together in love with a man, and who had only been used by Marcus for his own pleasure. They found their way.

She was thankful Marcus had been too drunk to take her at bedtime. If he had, she would have refused to meet William and left him wondering why she had worn the blue scarf and not shown up.

She was relieved to be able to sneak into the privy for a short, warm bath. That had been around eleven. She had slipped into her best dress but had been too afraid to leave without checking one more time to see that Marcus was indeed asleep. She had tiptoed up the stairs and ducked her head in the door. Marcus had snored. She had lit her lamp and ventured down the stairs. It had taken all of her courage.

She was overjoyed she had risked it. She and William lay face to face. The fire from the stove gave them light and warmth. They talked and kissed and braved the subject of his back scars and her ribcage bruises.

"Do you remember in my letter I said I had bigger plans for us?"

His mention of his love note aroused her guilt about not burning it. All she said was, "Yes," and rested her hand on his face. He took hold of it and let both their hands lie on his cheek.

"I know I sound foolish, but if I told you it might be possible for us to make that life together, without thinking about all of the problems, would you do it?"

"But since it won't ever be possible—"

"Would you do it?" His voice was soft. He smiled and moved his hand to her face. His callouses didn't bother her. They only reminded her of how hard he worked and how unfair it was. She hugged him closer. They weren't kissing, but her mouth was right on his.

"Why talk of what can't be? Why make me wish—"

"Wish what?"

His mouth moving on hers felt divine. "That we could. . . ."

"Get married?"

"Yes," she said after a long while. "You talk as if you're proposing."

"I am," he said.

She looked him right in the eye and said, "William, don't tease me."

"I'm not. I want to marry you. I have plans to do just that, if you'll have me."

He was serious. He was huge and beautiful and warm and kind and gentle and serious.

"Tell me, Rose, please, if I could arrange a miracle, would you leave Guthrie Farms and go someplace with me where you could end your marriage to Marcus and marry me?" He pressed his forehead to hers and waited for an answer. He was nervous. Her own heart thumped hard in her chest.

"Yes," she said.

He closed his eyes and exhaled.

Their mouths still touched. He kissed her, and they were intimate again. She wished he would give her a baby. She wanted his child.

After another long while, he spoke the words she dreaded to hear. "It's almost three in the morning. Two-forty-five, to be exact."

"How are you so sure?"

"I just know. And it means we have to end this. I want you to be able to get back inside the house. . . ." He frowned. He appeared to forget she was there for a moment. He rolled onto his back and said to the ceiling, "I hate to think about you going back into that house. Just a few more weeks. . . ."

She had the feeling he really contemplated running away. She thought it best to distract him from such notions. Such thinking would only frustrate them both. She leaned over and kissed him and said, "Don't worry about what goes on in. . . .the house."

"I can't help it. I love you. I can't abide you spending one more minute in that house."

"It's different now, though. I love you, too, and have loved you for a long time. I'll find a way to make it different." She heard her own words and wondered how she would change anything between her and Marcus. It was folly to think he wouldn't have his way with her by sunup. She dreaded Marcus.

She forced herself up. William reached for his trousers, but she said, "Don't. Just let me go."

Moments later, she lit her lamp and walked out of the bunkhouse. Outside and away from the security of William's presence, she stared at the large farmhouse in front of her.

It was formidable.

She had feared it so much of her life. She had put on a brave face for William, but if she could have run that night, she would have. She had never shrunk from crossing the threshold to the farmhouse as much as she did in that moment.

She steeled herself, tip-toed past the sleeping dogs, and ventured across the yard, grateful William had kept such good track of the time. Marcus was still asleep, she was sure.

34

THORNTON HEARD a noise. He closed his eyes and listened hard. He couldn't tell if the sound came from across the hall or down the stairs. Then he heard the distinct sound of the wooden legs of a chair. They slid across the floor of his parents' bedroom.

His eyes opened. His father was awake, and his mother was still in the bunkhouse.

His heart banged.

He got out of bed, threw on a shirt, and paced his room. He had to warn his mother. He had no idea, though, how he could get to her before his father did. If he met her on the downstairs landing, it would likely be too late. His father would know she was in the house and there would be no time to talk and come up with a plausible reason she had been *out* of the house. His father would pounce. If Thornton sneaked to the bunkhouse, there was no telling what he might interrupt.

He was suddenly furious with his mother and William, who took a ridiculous risk and left it to him to keep guard and figure a way out of their mess. He hammered his right palm with his left hand several times in rapid succession to get the anger out of his system. It didn't work.

He had no time to find something that *would* work. He had to get to his mother.

He put on his boots. He had a feeling he'd need them, even though it would be much harder to get around the house undetected.

He crept to his door and put his ear to it. No sound came from anywhere. He had no choice but to open the door and peak his head out.

He suddenly couldn't remember whether his door creaked. He'd opened and closed it for ten years and never paid attention. "Dammit," he whisper-cursed. It looked like he and his father were both about to find out how dry his door hinges were.

He turned the knob and opened the door no more than an inch. It slid open without a sound.

From what he could see, there was no one on the upstairs landing. It looked like his father was still in his room.

Thornton opened the door another foot, yanking it hard to force it past any possible squeaking sounds it wanted to make. His luck held out. The door hadn't betrayed him.

He worked up the nerve to venture into the hallway, taking exaggerated steps to control how his booted feet landed. At the top of the staircase, he debated what to do. He had no time to come up with an answer. Both of his parents appeared.

His father stepped onto the upstairs landing with his Hawken in his hands and his pepperbox revolver tucked in the front of his pants, which Thornton could see because his mother came through the front door of the farmhouse with her lamp still lit. It cast enough light for Marcus's guns to be on full display.

It all happened at once.

Thornton saw what his father was about to do and lunged for him.

"Nigger whore!" Marcus fired his Hawken down the stairs at his wife.

Rose fell back against the front door.

———◦◇◦———

In his room on the first floor, Ethan heard the gun blast and ran out to the main room.

———◦◇◦———

In the bunkhouse, William was still wide awake and sat straight up at the familiar sound of the bang of Marcus's rifle. He hurried out of bed and got dressed even faster. He snatched his boots on and ran out of the bunkhouse. He paid the dogs no heed. He would kick Ivan the Terrible's face in if he so much as showed his teeth.

He ran as fast as his feet would take him toward the main house. Behind him Ronan stepped out of the barn and called in a low, hard whisper, "Will!" but William ignored him and kept running.

———◆◆———

"Ma!" Thornton saw his mother stumble backwards against the door and figured she had been hit. Ethan arrived in the main room with a look of panic on his face. Thornton wanted to run down the stairs and check on his mother, but his father had been fast with the rifle. He cocked it in preparation for a second shot.

Marcus had had more years of farming than Thornton had, but Thornton had farmed hard for over a decade and was much younger than Marcus. It was difficult to say who was taller or stronger. One thing was sure. Thornton was as furious as his father.

Marcus's hand slid over the hair trigger. Thornton surprised him with a hard backhand to the jaw.

Rose's lamp remained lit but hung way down by her calves and shone far below the upstairs portion of the house. In the weak light, Marcus's big body cast an eerie shadow all over the walls around him. He stumbled on his heels but stayed on his feet and held onto the rifle. He steadied himself and aimed the gun right at Thornton on the half-lit landing. He pulled the hair trigger. Thornton ducked. The shot flew over his head and into his bedroom door.

Marcus cast aside the empty rifle. Thornton could just make out his father reaching for the revolver in his pants.

He hesitated a half-second too long making the switch in guns. Thornton charged him.

Thornton's hands landed on the pepperbox revolver at the same time his father's did. Father and son drew the weapon from Marcus's pants and stood nose-to-nose. They struggled over the gun, which Thornton knew had three shots in it, enough for Marcus to kill him, his mother, and William in the bunkhouse without reloading.

He glowered at his father. Something washed over him. He looked directly into his father's foul face for the first time in his life and refused to look away, refused to retreat.

Neither released his grip on the gun. Time seemed to stop until all four of their hands shifted onto the trigger and the clock ticked again.

Thornton made a snap decision. He sacrificed a hand and punched his father in the gut. Marcus doubled over. Thornton snatched the revolver out of his father's hands.

In one swift motion, he took a step back, cocked the gun, and aimed it right at his father's head. Marcus froze in the shadows.

"You all right, Ma?" Thornton held the gun steady on Marcus's face. He stood close enough to see him in the weak light and take perfect aim at the spot between his eyebrows.

"I'm fine. I stumbled, but I'm all right."

"Thornton!" It was William. He was on the bottom landing with Thornton's mother. "Careful now, son. Think about what you're doing."

"I am. It's either him or us. If I give him back this gun, he'll kill us all, if not now, tomorrow or the next day or the next day. We'll never be free. We'll never be safe." Tears streaked down his face. He kept the gun trained on Marcus's head. "We were fools to think we could get away."

"Killing's not the answer, son. You'll never be free that way either."

"Look at the monkey calling you 'son'." Marcus laughed. "You better shoot me now, or else I'm gonna kill that niggra, your whore mother, and you, first chance I get."

Thornton heard William climb the stairs what had to be three at a time. Of the three of them on the upstairs landing, William was by far the strongest. He took one giant step forward and punched Marcus so hard, he knocked him out. The big farmer and his shadow fell backwards. Marcus landed flat on his back. The bottom of the wall supported his head at a slight angle. He looked like a man sleeping on a hard pillow.

Thornton lowered his arm by a foot and kept the gun aimed at his father on the floor. He was ready to pull the trigger.

"Hand me the gun." William spoke with authority.

"No." Thornton took two steps toward his father. He was close enough to Marcus to guarantee if he pulled the trigger, the bullet would go right through his father's head. "Since I was five, I was less afraid of snakes, wild dogs, and getting trapped under horse hooves than I was of him. Goblins could have walked through the fields at night and chased me to bed, and I would have felt safer with them than with him." He wagged the gun in Marcus's direction. "When I was seven, he fired his rifle so close to my head, he took my ear off. All my mother could do was bandage me and wash my soiled pants. He's terrorized us our whole lives, and I can put a stop to it right now. He *owns* three human beings. Five, really. He doesn't deserve to live."

Thornton was tired in his dark end of the hall. His mother's funeral perfume hovered and reminded him of death. He thought about Rip Van Winkle and how nice it would be to go back to his room and sleep while somebody, anybody dealt with his father.

But he held the gun. And he was in the best position to claim he shot his father in self-defense. The law wouldn't listen to a woman or a slave, but it might believe the situation had come down to him or his father, especially since it was true. The bullet in his door proved it.

If his father regained the upper hand, he would kill them all. Who would care, Thornton thought, if he got the events a little out of order and shot his father first to preempt catastrophe?

Thornton had never been able to protect his mother, but he could give her the gift of killing Marcus and take the consequences with the law. He saw no other way.

His ears rang. Tears drenched his face. He gripped the gun tighter and thought about all the hours he had shared the fields with his father without getting so much as a three-minute respite from the terror. His mother's bruises and silence and abandonment came to him, and the dread in the men's faces the first day they arrived. He could put an end to all of the misery if he summoned the guts to end the man who lay there.

His father's eyes opened. He looked right at Thornton and the gun. He would see it coming. There was enough light for him to know what—and who—had hit him.

An object revealed itself in the half-dark just as Marcus pulled it from his pants pocket. He brandished it with a relaxed hand that rested on his belly.

A third gun.

Thornton recognized it the minute it came into view. His father had retired the small gun years earlier, had nicknamed it The Hammer because, he said, it pounded nails better than it shot. It was a fine gun, but his father always spoke ill of it. Thornton had thought he had melted it down and used the liquid to build tools. He realized that Marcus had stored it in his room all those years.

Thornton was aghast to realize his father's condemnation of The Hammer was a ruse. He wanted a small and convenient gun handy in case he wanted to use it against Thornton's mother. The Hawken and the pepperbox revolver lived under his father's side of the bed at night, but Thornton figured by the time he moved his burly, drunk body to reach for them, his mother could get out of the room. The Hammer had obviously been hidden in the drawer of the nightstand next to Marcus's side of the bed, where he could easily reach it. The implications horrified Thornton.

A standoff ensued.

Thornton trained the revolver on his father. Marcus aimed The Hammer right at William. Thornton kept his eye on Marcus's gun hand.

No one had the upper hand. Either could pull the trigger and kill his target.

It happened. A finger moved. And another.

Two gun blasts reverberated throughout the house.

In unison Ethan gave a startled shout and Rose screamed. No one upstairs uttered a sound. One of them couldn't. He was dead.

To Thornton's great shock, he still had a father.

PART THREE

Harvest

There is a certain relief in change, even though it be from bad to worse; as I have found in travelling in a stage-coach, that it is often a comfort to shift one's position and be bruised in a new place.

—Washington Irving

35

ETHAN STOOD downstairs in the Guthrie farmhouse and called upstairs to Thornton with information Thornton already knew. "He's dead."

"I know." It had not surprised Thornton. He was an excellent shot. The bullet he fired had gone straight through Marcus Guthrie's head. He knew it would when he fired it.

What stunned him was that Marcus had missed his mark. William stood on the upstairs landing, right where he had been when Marcus fired the shot that forced Thornton to pull the trigger on his own weapon.

Thornton had seen Marcus's finger move. His own finger moved an eighth of a second later. He had been terrified he was too late.

He looked at William with great relief that he had been on time. The noise from his gun must have startled his father enough to alter his hold on The Hammer. It had ruined his aim. And the man Thornton had come to regard as his father was still standing.

The next several hours felt to Thornton like molasses but passed like water that flowed downhill with heavy ice floes pushing it for emphasis.

Within moments after the upstairs gunfight, he and William had snapped into action. They left Marcus upstairs for the time being, and in half-unison, explained to Rose they were all leaving Guthrie Farms. In three minutes, the entire plan—Colleen, a baby Henry still didn't know about, Ronan's mother, and Fidelia—spilled out of their mouths.

Rose appeared stunned at first. They provided more details, and she regarded William with a kind of recognition. Thornton understood William must have told his mother he planned to run.

They all avoided what had transpired between Rose and William. They knew Thornton knew. More needed not be said.

It was about zero degrees outside and colder than it might have been had they waited a few more weeks to leave. It meant everything would be worse. The ground snowier and unkinder. The freezing temperatures harder for the horses to push through. Tracks much trickier to cover unless fresh snow fell, in which case travel would be all the more punishing.

'hey had no choice. People expected to see Marcus
ie places. Rose could explain his absence for only so
he couldn't claim he had abandoned the family or had
l dead of a heart attack because Ethan had witnessed

the shooting and would never cover for the group. From Ethan's childish perspective, Thornton had killed once and he might kill again. It would be better for Ethan, from his standpoint, to go to the law.

And even without Ethan, if they stayed on Guthrie Farms, it would mean Henry and Ronan would never reunite with their loved ones, and his friends would never make it to a slave-free territory.

His own freedom no longer mattered. His emancipation from his father did everything *but* set him free. In the eyes of the law, he had committed murder. Killing a white man to defend a slave would be impossible to plead as some kind of justifiable defense of another. All they could do was leave and not give a crafty Ethan the chance to sic the law on them.

They would make preparations throughout the day and depart near sundown. The first stop would be Hiram Elliot's. From there, they would time their arrival at Hezzy Jones's for after bedtime to catch him and his by surprise.

Thornton had thoroughly blown it with Fidelia. He had thought he'd have a few more weeks to propose and ask her to run with him. He had squandered the chance to quietly make his case while things were calm. The last time he saw her, there had been benign chatter about nothing remarkable and an embarrassing instance of jealousy. "On cold days like this, I sure do miss Calvin," Fidelia had said in Hiram Elliot's apple orchard.

"Well, maybe you'd be better off with him," Thornton had said. He had mounted Ashes and ridden out. Fidelia let him get far enough to feel extra dumb.

"He's my oldest brother," she called after him.

He had set Ashes into a droopy half-trot that took on the right measure of slinking and headed back to the orchard. As it turned out, Fidelia and Calvin had played hide-and-seek on cold days because the running around kept them warm. Cold days reminded Fidelia of how much fun it had been and made her miss her brother.

In the end, Thornton had been a fool on that day on two accounts: his jealousy of Calvin and fairly guaranteeing Fidelia wouldn't go with him because he hadn't asked her. His appearance at her house later that night would come as a complete surprise.

Until it came time to leave, each person on Guthrie Farms would carry out an assignment. His mother, who no longer wore her best dress, would pack food and clothing and keep an eye on Ethan. Thornton remembered how she faked her attack. Ethan would not have an easy go of it if he rebelled in any way.

William would go through the farmhouse and round up as much ammunition for the three guns as he could find. He would also gather from every corner of the property the most helpful supplies for the road.

Thornton would dig his father's grave after sunup with the help of Ronan and Henry. He had handed William his gun and gone to find the two men, who, he thought, must have heard the gunfire and wondered who had been hit.

They had a long day ahead of them.

———◆◇◆———

Thornton had shot Marcus at three-twelve a.m. The clock on the wall had told him so. William appeared and told him and Ronan and Henry it was just about thirty minutes past twelve noon and time was running out.

Thornton was unprepared for what happened as he dug his father's grave. He felt something akin to grief. He didn't mourn his father. But he had been steeped in one way of life, and the sudden and violent way things had changed meant he would leave all of it behind, both the good and the bad. Tending to his crops. Enjoying a bowl of his mother's stew on a Sunday when his father cavorted somewhere not on Guthrie Farms. Discussing books with William. Riding Ashes.

He thought about how he had wanted to sleep twenty years and wake up with the problem of his father solved. All his life he had looked to the horizon for answers and escape. He had expected if he liberated himself from Marcus, he would not just look to the horizon, but he would travel to it and explore all he imagined it offered, just as Rip Van Winkle had traveled to the mountaintop.

But there had been no odd personages, like the ones Farmer Van Winkle knew, to lead him away to the crest of some mystical mountain while others solved his problems. He had pulled the trigger. He had ended his father's life. And none of it had been a dream.

He had always assumed the moment he was free of his father, he would feel nothing but jubilation. But trepidation about what would come next cast a pall over his mood.

If he had just been able to plan for it, to leave on his own terms, to walk out on Marcus and make him watch his son leave, he may have felt less of a sense of loss, less fear about his future, less contemplation about the import of his own actions and what they might portend.

And there it was, the belief he was unable to escape. Killing his father would be a presage of something, but what? If whatever kept track of a body's deeds had noted THE SHOOTING OF MARCUS GUTHRIE BY THORNTON GUTHRIE on the Grand Ledger, it may record it as a credit that balanced against all of Marcus Guthrie's wickedness.

Or, it may record it as a debit against Thornton.

If God created men like Marcus and men like Thornton, each as different from the other as a rat was different from a foal, each bearing His imprimatur by virtue of his existence, whose side would He take? Thornton would never regret that he shot his father and saved William, but he remembered Archibald's warning to William about letting the hangman sleep. He couldn't help but wonder if he hadn't disturbed the hangman's slumber with his actions in the shadows of the upstairs landing of the farmhouse.

He reflected on the expression on his mother's face when he and William had carried his father down the stairs and out the door to the front porch. His mother had looked at Marcus as though she watched a dead dog that rested on the shoulder of a farmer who carried it somewhere he was about to bury it. There were no tears, there was no remorse, not even elation that an animal that kept them cornered for a lifetime had been put down. Marcus was just a dead dog and nothing more.

Thornton and Ronan and Henry shoveled out, in turns, small mounds of frozen dirt from the hole that would become Marcus's final resting place. White-capped sparrows caroled from atop the barn and offered the only funeral song any being would sing for Marcus Guthrie, whose body lay in the snow nearby.

Thornton didn't look at his father's corpse but not because he wanted to avoid his father or the reality of how he died. The odd grief for parts of his old life he experienced also had nothing to do with it. The fact was, he had mourned his father ten years earlier, the moment the man aimed the first gun at him. His death was a technicality, the burial a necessary chore. The only emotion about his father Thornton had was deriving satisfaction from how much it would gall Marcus Guthrie that he had to wait in the cold while his son and two slaves dug his grave.

Henry and Ronan had joined in not because they thought Marcus deserved a respectable burial, but because, as slaves, they didn't need to be accused of perpetrating Marcus's death. They wanted to hide all evidence of Marcus's demise as much as Thornton and William did. They were angry, though, for being forced into such a mess. They dug hard and silent.

William had brought a shovel to help them finish faster. He groped for idle chatter to cut the tense air. "Horses are about ready."

"So is this hole," Thornton said.

"And *now* what?" Ronan said. He planted his shovel hard in the mud-caked snow.

William glanced at Thornton. He said to Ronan, "We head to Hiram Elliot's for more horses." He offered nothing more.

"And then what? Did you think to ask me or Henry about this? I have a mother not far from here. Do you expect me to just hop on one of Hiram Elliot's horses and ride off without her?" He glared at William. He glowered at Thornton. He scowled at William again.

"And we know you're getting more than just horses at Hiram Elliot's," Henry said. "Seems you've got it all worked out for yourselves."

Thornton realized what Henry meant. Thornton would have Fidelia and William would have Rose while they would be forced to leave everyone behind. He decided to spill the whole plan. He braced himself.

"It's not like that."

"It ain't?"

"No. After we leave the Elliot place, we head over to the Jones place to get your mother," he said to Ronan. He turned to Henry and sucked in a deep breath. "And your wife....and son," he said.

Through the thick winter air, he watched Henry's face transition from surprise, to shock, to wrath. "My....*son?*"

Thornton recounted for Henry and Ronan the details of his night ride the previous autumn and his visit to Hezzy's when he had seen Henry's son. He was nervous and rushed through the story, but the import was not lost on either man. Ronan seemed somewhat appeased to hear someone had gotten a message to his mother and that they had planned all along to get her out. Henry was not as easily mollified. Colleen had had a baby, he was a father, and nobody had bothered to tell him.

"We'll *never* get them out of there! I might not ever see my son! I could have tried if you had told me!"

"How? How would you have possibly made it back to Hezzy Jones's without getting yourself hanged? This is why we didn't tell you. We knew you would try something foolish," William said.

Henry picked up his shovel and swung it hard at everyone and no one in particular. The others stepped back just in time to not get hit. "Goddammit!"

"We don't have time for this. It's twelve-thirty-seven. We'll all be hanged if we don't leave tonight. We still have a lot to do."

"Why should I go to Hiram Elliot's? I'll just take a horse from here and go straight to the Jones place and get Colleen and my son."

"Because you'll be dead before you get to her bunkhouse." It was Ronan who tried to talk sense to Henry. "Thornton can go all the way into the main house and distract folks while we get to my mother and Colleen and the boy."

"And if Hiram Elliot will give us even just one or two more horses, we have a better chance of scattering and confusing Hezzy's dogs if they get loose and give chase," William said.

They waited.

Henry drew a ragged breath. "What's his name? My son, I mean. Did you find out his name?" He was as broken as anyone Thornton had ever seen.

"No, Henry, I didn't. I'm sorry. I'm so very sorry."

Henry ground his teeth. His jaw bulged every few seconds.

They waited again.

Several moments passed.

They still waited.

"Let's get Guthrie in this hole, and let's go. My son is waiting."

The four resumed digging.

36

THEY CONVERGED on the main house. Rose had forced Ethan to keep the fire stoked. It roared when they opened the front door. After the cold, hard work of burying Marcus, the warmth of the house felt good to Thornton.

Ronan and Henry appeared uneasy in the main house. Even though they had just buried Marcus Guthrie, Thornton figured the shift in attitude about the freedom to move around the farm would take a while. By that time, they would be gone.

"I made dumplings."

Thornton had smelled them from the front porch. It made him ravenous. It had been good thinking on the part of his mother. They needed one more good meal, something heavy and hearty. His mother had set a place for everyone.

"You men have a seat. Please eat up."

They all sauntered to the table with a hesitant gait. It mimicked a stroll only in its pace and not its level of easiness.

Thornton noticed his father's seat at the head of the table had no place setting. He felt a pang similar to what he felt while he dug his father's grave and thought about how a lifetime of dreading supper with a belligerent, inebriated father, who dished out socks in the arm and spit food when he talked, had ended suddenly on the upstairs landing, where the man's blood stained the wooden floor. The empty seat provided one more reminder to Thornton that he could no longer hide in the predictability of life with his father, no matter how grim it had been. He would ride into the unknown and face obstacles only a few of which he could anticipate.

Too, whatever budded between William and his mother could only be ignored for a few more hours. He assumed they loved each other based on their behavior in the bunkhouse, the specifics of which he refused to ponder, but that made it no easier for him to decipher where he fit in. That strange sense of grief he had felt when he first saw his mother sneak into the bunkhouse returned. He pushed it aside. He concerned himself with the setting sun and concentrated on getting through the next thirty minutes. Food would help.

With a lot of slow, reluctant, chair-dragging noise, everyone took a seat.

Except Ethan.

He never opened his mouth to protest. He avoided disaster. Instead, he sat in his favorite chair next to Marcus's.

Thornton's mother intervened. "Come on over here and get something to eat. I won't abide anybody leaving here hungry."

With obvious foot-dragging, Ethan moved from the chair to the table and accepted a plate of food from his aunt.

Other than resolving the Ethan protest, the six of them ate in silence.

———◦◊◦———

Ethan wanted to make a run for it, to head to the barn and hop on a horse while they stuffed their faces. It was no use. One of the five adults would snatch him back to the table by the collar if he tried.

Besides, he *was* hungry. And he loved Aunt Rose's dumplings. A better time to try to get away, he decided, would be when they brought the horses into the yard for the trip to what he had learned for sure would be Hiram Elliot's place, as he had suspected the day he overheard Thornton and William plotting their escape.

He would take Thornton's horse, Ashes, and bolt. He would give them no time to gather their wits, and Thornton would have to give chase on a strange horse. He could find his way to Columbia after all the trips with Uncle Marcus and would ride straight for the law.

After the dumplings was when he would make his move.

————◇————

"Henry, Sir?" Rose said. Thornton stood closest to her and barely heard her. He was surprised Henry looked up. The group had finished eating. They gathered items they would take with them in the middle of the parlor. Anything not in the pile would stay behind. They all watched Henry and Rose. Even Ethan was curious.

"Ma'am?"

"Rose. My son tells me you have a baby boy."

Thornton groaned inside at the mention of such a sore subject. He almost left the room until he saw what his mother held out in her hands. It punched his gut and touched him beyond belief at the same time.

His mother handed Henry five tiny sweaters small enough to fit a baby. "These belonged to my son. I've kept them all this time. Silly, I know." She hugged the sweaters. Thornton's throat clogged with a lump the size of a rock from the yard outside. She had cared enough to keep something as insignificant as his first winter clothes.

He stared at them. He would never remember wearing them, but he tried to imagine what life had been like when he had been small enough to fit them. Had she hugged him as close as she hugged the sweaters? He had never seen them. With a chill, he realized he only saw them that afternoon because his father lay dead under the soil outside.

"With it being so cold out, your son will need warm clothing. I thought we could take these along with some of Thornton's wool baby britches and a few extra blankets, if it's all right with you."

Henry looked exhausted, worn down by it all. Thornton figured the sight of the small, small sweaters reminded Henry of how vulnerable his son was, of how much was at stake. He accepted the articles of clothing in silence and placed them in the middle of the pile at the center of the parlor. They would make the trip, for sure.

Thornton glanced at William to trade a look that said, "Whew. We dodged Henry's ire there," but he couldn't get his attention. William gazed in the direction of his mother.

Reality dawned on Thornton.

37

THORNTON LED the way to Hiram Elliot's on Ashes in a repeat of his night ride to the Jones place the previous autumn with one serious difference. The temperature hovered around zero. The mud and snow formed a cold, thick slush. It was hard to get his horse's hooves through it.

Just as he did earlier, he manipulated the reins with one hand and held a lamp high in the other. He could just make out the sludgy terrain. They traveled slower. Thornton's arm throbbed. Tiredness permeated his bones. He went over it to himself how he had woken up in the morning on the day before, worked all day, gotten no sleep the night before while he waited for his mother to return from the bunkhouse, and worked through the night and all day after he shot Marcus. He had experienced sound sleep thirty-six hours earlier. He felt no sleepiness on the insane night ride. He had advanced to mind-numbing exhaustion.

It caused him great confusion. William followed in the wagon, but Thornton was sure the hoof noise of the two horses that pulled the cart came from a horse his father rode. Like Ichabod Crane, who raced through Sleepy Hollow in Washington Irving's sketch book with a headless horseman bearing down on him, Thornton felt Marcus Guthrie just a horse length behind him the entire ride, no matter how hard he pushed Ashes.

He would have thought, as Ichabod did about himself and the horseman, that his father could toss his own dead, smashed head at Thornton. He kept telling himself that in the sketch book it had been a romantic rival with a pumpkin, masked by the dark and Ichabod's imagination, who had chased the skinny schoolteacher through the Connecticut hollow, and not a headless horseman. William, he told himself again and again, was behind him, steering a wagon that carried Henry, Rose, and Ethan. Ronan, not Marcus, was in the rear on Marcus's horse, Blackie.

They had tied the milk cow to the back of the wagon and forced her to trot along to keep up. She could go about three days without being milked. By the fourth day, her udder would swell and become sore. It would be better for the cow if Hiram Elliot could take her and keep her milked than if she stayed behind and suffered. If she slowed them down too much, they would cut her loose. She would be in pain while she waited for her milk to dry, but it was a smaller price to pay than the cost of them getting caught.

The other animals would do fine in the wild or on the eighty acres of Guthrie Farms. Thornton had let them all loose. It had been a good riddance of the dogs. Thornton was especially glad to see Ivan the Terrible head south for parts unknown.

Ethan was going to be a problem. Ronan carried his own lamp and made sure Ethan didn't try to hop off the back of the wagon and escape the escapers. Ethan had tried to take Ashes into Columbia to report The Murder of Uncle Marcus and The Escape of the Slaves and My Murdering Cousin. It was Ronan who settled the matter. He wasted no time. He simply told Ethan to get in the wagon and be quiet. It worked, but Thornton prepared himself for another go-around with his cousin. It didn't matter. There was no way Thornton wasn't going to return to his aunt and uncle the son they thought was dead. Ethan was stuck with the pack.

They neared the Elliot place. Thornton's nerves wavered. Fidelia would already be baffled by his arrival and his request that she go with him. The additional twist that they needed help aiding several slaves in their escape, would take some of Hiram Elliot's horses, and had a criminal explanation for the absence of Marcus Guthrie sent the final meal Thornton had eaten on Guthrie Farms a few hours earlier upwards to the

back of his throat. He ducked his head and let it fly past
Ashes into the earth. He didn't feel any better afterwards.

The shadows of Hiram Elliot's large farmstead formed in
the distance. Thornton spotted the main house. He didn't
delight in seeing it that night. Everything they all had at
stake could fall apart there.

Just a few hundred yards more. The whole party slowed
to a walk. They hoped to arrive noiselessly and catch Hiram
Elliot unawares.

They were twenty feet from the house. Thornton reined in
Ashes and hopped off him. Ronan pulled up beside him and
dismounted Blackie. William pulled in his horses and inched
the wagon as close to the house as possible. Thornton and
Ronan snuffed out their lamps. Darkness shrouded the Elliot
farmstead.

The door of the main house opened. Hiram Elliot stood at
the threshold with a gun. Five fugitives—and their hostage,
Ethan—turned in his direction. Light emanated from the vast
fireplace in the front room. It lit Hiram Elliot from behind
and belied his short stature. His rifle-toting silhouette
appeared giant-like in the doorframe. "Who's there? What is
this?"

Nobody moved in the dark. Ashes leaned in and rubbed
Thornton's head without a snort.

"Speak up or get shot."

"Mr. Elliot? It's Thornton Guthrie."

"I hear a lot more than just you. Who's with you? And
what the hell are you doing here?"

A second silhouette appeared in the doorway.

Thornton stood surrounded by runaways and fugitives and
tired animals, but he thought only of how striking Fidelia
looked in the firelight. Her hair swung to and fro, as if
moved about by a breeze. But the frigid night was still for
the moment. Her hair simply behaved that way.

"Thornton?" She repeated her father's question, without the
profanity. "What are you *doing* here?"

The sound of her voice slayed him. He didn't even attempt to open his mouth to answer. A kind of paralysis set in. Somewhere in the back of his mind, their plan slipped away.

"Answer now, young man. What in God's name are you doing on my farm in the middle of the night?"

Hiram Elliot's voice broke the spell Fidelia had cast over Thornton. "Mr. Elliot, uh, Sir. Uhhh, there's no other way to say this. My father's dead, and we're running. I'm with my mother and the men who live on our farm. And my cousin." His eyes darted to Fidelia and back to Hiram Elliot. They couldn't see him, but he still felt conspicuous. He rubbed Ashes for encouragement, and pressed on. "Sir, we need your help. I know I got no right—"

"What happened to Marcus?"

Hiram Elliot would not accept a bunch of sniveling equivocating, so Thornton said, "I shot him. He tried to kill a man, and I shot him."

Every man, woman, cow, and horse stood silent in the dark. Even Ethan seemed to recognize the moment had arrived when the group's fate would be decided and said nothing. All eyes rested on the two shadows in the doorway.

"Was it a man who worked on your farm he tried to kill?"

"Yessir."

Another long silence.

"Go on."

"As I say, I know I got no right—"

"Get to the point." He waved the rifle for emphasis.

Hiram Elliot had not asked why his father had tried to shoot one of the men on the farm. He seemed not to care. Thornton wondered if he assumed whatever the reason, Marcus had been wrong. Thornton saw it as a small opening, as a hole in the fence Hiram Elliot formed in the doorway that he and the others could crawl through. Thornton did as he was told and got to the point. "We need horses. As many as you can give us. Two of these men have families on Hezzy Jones's place. We aim to ride there next and. . . ." Thornton hesitated but gathered himself and said, "We aim to take them with us."

Hiram Elliot didn't hesitate. "Have you lost your mind? Between Hezzy and his sons, you'll never get out of there without everybody getting killed. Hezzy'll hang half of you for the fun of it and shoot the rest."

Again, Hiram Elliot didn't seem to object to the idea of escaping and concentrated more on the chances of success. "That's why we have to surprise him in the night," Thornton called out. "And have enough horses to get away, so we can scatter in different directions." Fidelia took a half step forward. Thornton hoped it was because she dreaded him scattering in some direction without her.

"I'm kind of used to my horses. And it seems to me the law'll scatter in every direction too. When they come here and find my animals missing, it won't take long to figure I had a hand in everybody running."

Thornton moved toward the porch and became visible in the outer limits of the firelight. Hiram allowed him to approach. "But they won't be able to prove it. You could leave a barn door open. Your horses could get out in the night. You could cry horse theft. The law won't know for sure you gave us the horses outright."

Thornton climbed the porch steps and walked all the way to Hiram Elliot's threshold. He towered over the man, but it mattered not. He was too worried about what the man's daughter thought. Standing so close to her, he caught the scent of sweet peaches coming from her.

"Hi, Fidelia."

"Hi, Thornton."

He wanted nothing more than to reach out and embrace her. He was desperate to know what she thought of what he had just said. He worried what Hiram Elliot would say when he heard the rest, when he discovered Thornton wanted Fidelia to run away with him. He stuck to the subject of the horses.

"One of the men has a wife, Mr. Elliot. Back on Christmas day she had a baby boy." He glanced at Fidelia. "Sir, we gotta get Henry's wife and boy out of there. And Ronan's mother."

"Ronan's mother?" Fidelia asked. Her face was steely.

"Yes," Thornton said. He sounded guilty even though he wasn't. He had told her the day after Christmas there was more to the one secret he had kept about Henry, but until he could talk to her and explain, she clearly thought he had kept a host of secrets from her.

Hiram Elliot's shoulders dropped. He relaxed his hold on his rifle and let out a loud sigh.

"Come on in." He sounded tired. He called into the dark, "All of you come in."

38

THE MOTLEY collection of escapees looked even stranger
to Thornton in Hiram Elliot's front room than it had in the
main house at Guthrie Farms. The group fanned out across the
cavernous fireplace. The six of them stretched end-to-end still
left room on either side for Hiram and Fidelia. Hiram's
daughter chose, however, to sit in a chair in the far corner of
the room.

Thornton had wanted to follow her. He worried she
thought he held her in low regard and had planned to drop
what formed between them and leave the territory with no
consideration of whom he left behind. He needed to explain
that, no matter how things looked, he had never planned to
leave without her, that he had lacked the courage to ask her,
and that he had hoped all along she'd be with him when he
headed west, but the others and Hiram and his horses came
first.

In what was becoming standard practice for the fugitives,
nobody spoke. Thornton felt time running out. "What time is
it?" He had aimed the question at William, but Hiram Elliot
said, "I don't carry a watch in my night clothes." He looked
at Thornton like he was an imbecile.

"No, I meant—"

"Nine-thirty-eight."

Hiram Elliot flashed William an odd look. The others,
even Ethan, who had spent the day watching the group use
William as their clock, took William's answer at face value.

Henry said, "They've long bedded down at the Jones
place." He pounded his fist in the palm of his hand. "We're
wasting time, and we've made it easier for the law to find us
by coming here." He turned to leave, but Ronan stopped him.

Henry worried Thornton only slightly less than Ethan did. He had a small child at stake. He might run out the door and light out for the Jones place at any moment.

"Mr. Elliot, what's it going to be? Henry's right. I know this has been a shock, but we have to get moving. I need to know how many horses you'll give us."

"Hiram," Rose said. "I realize we're relative strangers. Shameful given how close our farms are. And I know how all of this looks. But I promise you if you help us tonight, you'll be doing a good thing."

Hiram shook his head at the ground. Thornton saw him glance up to find Ronan looking right at him. Ronan's scars stared hard at Hiram Elliot.

"I never could abide slavery. Your father knew it," he said to Thornton. "It's why we don't know each other better, Rose. Marcus Guthrie and I would never see eye to eye on the matter."

"Help set these men free," Thornton said, "and Henry's wife and son, and Ronan's mother. I wish I could say I'd pay you back for the loss of the horses, but I can't make that promise. Truth is, no one here can. It'll be a straight loss to you, not to mention any trouble you might have with the law."

———◦◇◦———

Rose had had enough of being at the mercy of men who would decide her fate as they saw fit and at their will. She would lay out the truth for Hiram Elliot. He would either see it their way, or refuse to help. But she wouldn't beg, even if her life depended on it. She wouldn't get in Thornton's way or do anything to endanger the lives of the others. She had no delusions she had secured her own freedom.

But it made no sense to her to get out from under the muddy boot Marcus had stomped on her half her life just to subjugate herself to another man, who exercised power over her simply because he could. Hiram Elliot had every right to keep his horses, but she wouldn't scrape her knees waiting to hear his answer. Regardless of her love for Thornton and William and her empathy for the others, *her* fate would lie in her own hands.

"Hiram, Marcus died tonight trying to kill Thornton, trying to kill William," she said, nodding at her lover, "and trying to kill me. Pulled the triggers of two guns on three of us. Would have used a third gun if Thornton hadn't angled for it and nicked it from him."

"Thornton, are you all right?" Fidelia asked.

"I'm fine. I ducked at the last second."

Rose saw how the youngsters lingered on each other's faces when they addressed one another. She let it hang in the air for a moment before she went on. "And he just barely got out of the way. I nigh fainted," Rose said. She took in a deep breath and felt bigger than she was. "Marcus always thought backwards. He thought the people closest to him deserved the worst treatment while he saved the glad-handing, the favors, and the genuine concern for relative strangers. The bad crop of some farmer he didn't even like worried him more than whether his own wife or child lived to see sundown.

"Since the first night we were married, he's been plucking my feathers. Seeing they were almost gone, after years of beatings and attacks at night, he had moved on to trying to wring my neck. See what I mean? Backwards. If he had wrung my neck first, I would have been spared the pain of watching him pluck everything from me over the years. My son, my dignity, my strength."

The fire cracked loud in the silence her words brought down on the room. William moved and stood right behind her. "When he felt particularly powerless, he fired his rifle at his own son—my son—blithe as you please. I learned to hate the kitchen window. I feared every moment I would hear the gun pop, hear my son cry out, hear him drop in the fields. And yet I had to keep the window open, I had to know. I had to know. How I hated that window, though."

She touched William's arm. "Tonight, Marcus found out I love this man." She didn't explain or justify her bond with William. It was none of Hiram's business. "As I said, he shot at me. Thornton leapt to my defense, and he shot at him. It came down to a standoff. I believe Thornton would have let him win it, would have taken his chances for survival, if my life and William's life weren't at stake.

"I heard a lot through that window, Hiram." She nodded toward Ronan and Henry. "William and these men are the best friends my son has ever had. When Marcus pulled the trigger on the gun he had aimed at William, Thornton had no choice but to fire the gun he had pointed at Marcus." She squeezed William's arm for one final bit of courage. "Hiram, you and I both know the law'll never take the side of a slave, a woman, or my son over a man like Marcus. We need your help to free these men's families and get us all beyond the law. One way or the other, make your decision."

———◦◇◦———

Ethan wanted to shout, "Don't do it! They murdered my uncle!" but he was far outnumbered.

The chimney corner looked like sleeping quarters someone had converted into a fireplace. They might throw him in the fire if he spoke up.

He feared Ronan the most. Of the entire bunch, Ronan was the only one who showed no emotion. Fret and worry did not preoccupy him in the least. He had quietly kept watch over everyone and held those in line whose feelings threatened to get out of control and scuttle the group's mission. Ethan didn't stand a chance with him on guard.

His best opportunity to find allies would come at Hezzy Jones's place. Their plan had a fatal flaw as Ethan saw it.

They had too many differing interests. They wanted families and freedom and horses and women and babies.

They would have to trap Hezzy and his sons in one building and spread out to find and load up the women and child in another building. When it was done, they would run in different directions, some west, some north.

They had to get past Hezzy, Jedidiah, and Obadiah Jones, dogs, falling snow, slush, mud, freezing temperatures, hunger, a crying baby who might give away their location, and the interference of body functions that demanded their attention.

Whether Hiram Elliot provided horses mattered not. They were going to the Jones place next. If Ethan could get to any man on the Jones place in all of the chaos, he was sure he could find safe cover on the Jones side of the battle.

For the second time that night, he would postpone action and hope when he made his move at the Jones place, he would have better success than he'd had on his uncle's farm when he had tried to steal Ashes and Ronan had soundly thwarted him.

———•◦•———

Everything loomed large on Hiram Elliot's farmstead. His barn doors were enormous. He needed two hands to swing the left one open against the front of the barn and had to lean hard into the final few inches to make sure the wind didn't blow the door against his head.

The chilly air gusted through the building and irritated the horses. Several of them shuffled and stomped their feet. Hiram walked toward the horse stalls with Thornton, William, Ronan, and Henry right behind him. Thornton's mother and Ethan had stayed in the house with Fidelia.

Thornton's nerves nagged at him. Hiram had held court in the main house, had speechified, had put the defendants through the ridiculous wait for him to change into day clothes. Thornton didn't think he could take another minute of waiting for the verdict. He hoped Hiram Elliot had brought them to the barn because he agreed to give them even just one horse.

They stopped in front of the closest stall. The horse they convened in front of bellowed at having his slumber disturbed. Ronan couldn't help himself. He reached out and made contact with the horse.

Even as he waited to hear what Hiram Elliot had to say, Thornton marveled at Ronan's gift with horses. Most mounts disliked contact that came too soon from an unfamiliar hand. A state of anger made it all the more true, but when Ronan stroked the animal's cheek, he nickered at Ronan as if he greeted an old friend.

In the house, Hiram Elliot had debated and paced and bellowed himself in the warmth of the fire. In the frosty barn, he got right to the point sans pacing. "I'll let you have eleven of the twelve, on one condition."

The ears of all the men perked up. Ronan disengaged from his equine friend. William and Henry stared hard at Hiram Elliot, scrutinizing his face in search of the possible liar who lurked behind his eyes. Thornton's mouth sagged open in surprise.

He remembered nothing came for free. Hiram Elliot had just offered to give up eleven of his animals, which left just one for himself and his entire farm. Thornton suddenly dreaded the condition Hiram Elliot would place on all of them in exchange for eleven horses. They could get away with five. If the condition proved too harsh, he would bargain for middle ground and decline six horses.

"Get everybody out."

"How's that?"

Hiram Elliot repeated the words. "Get everybody out." The four bodies and the horse set ten eyes on him. No one spoke. "It's not enough for you to go riding over there to get your loved ones out. Hezzy Jones has nigh onto thirty beings enslaved."

"Twenty-four after he sold us."

"Twenty-five with my son."

Thornton and William looked at each other at the mention of Henry's son.

"It's an affront," Hiram Elliot continued. "It's why the people in town, who built up Columbia with theaters and a hospital and an academy where women can study, so dislike men like your father and Hezzy Jones.

"I side with you in considering your families first—it's what I would do—but with no family at stake, I'm bound by larger concerns. I can't in good conscience assist you in making twenty-two people watch three of their own escape while the twenty-two stay behind and stomach the predation, the wretchedness, the crassitude of Hezekiah, Jedidiah, and Obadiah Jones.

"With your horses and wagon, my wagon, and my saddled animals, you can probably get the other twenty-two people out, if some ride double, and you load up the wagons." After a moment, he added, "And you take my rifles. It'll be tight, but I think you can do it. And what a sight it will be."

"If we scatter, we can create enough chaos to guarantee at least half getting to freedom," William said. He went straight to the planning stage. Once he liked an idea, he moved right to the execution of it.

"Of course we want to get everybody out," Henry said. "I detest Hezzy Jones. You think we'd *want* to leave anyone behind? We didn't figure on getting eleven horses. Some of us didn't even know we were *leaving* tonight. For *us*, there was no time to plan." There was a hint of lecture in Henry's tone that Thornton appreciated, even the part aimed at himself. Mr. Elliot had come too close to presuming he understood the depravity of slavery more than men born into it, who stood before him with their lives and the lives of so many of their own at stake. *Henry's newborn offspring was a slave.* Nobody fathomed the depredation of a life spent in servitude better than Henry.

Thornton piled on with a slight lecture of his own. "Yes, if we had known we could have asked for your entire herd, we would have planned for all twenty-five from the beginning." His aim wasn't to justify himself to Henry. He didn't think he could do that. But they had never dreamt of getting eleven horses and had planned accordingly. Thornton was glad Henry had pointed that out to Hiram Elliot.

"Certainly, certainly," Hiram said.

"Still, half of them can't ride," Ronan said. "It will take time to figure out who they are and pair 'em up with someone who can. I don't need to be William to know we're late as it is."

Nobody bothered to explain to Hiram Elliot what Ronan meant about William and the time. "How do we keep that dirty cuss Jones out of the way and get everybody off his farm?" Ronan continued. "And I won't lie. I don't want my mother ending up lost in the muddle. I'm getting her out."

"I hear you, Ronan. No doubt, trapping smoke in a jar would be easier, but I know we can do it," Thornton said. "We have to move much quicker for the rest of the night. Every escaped man and woman driving a horse will have to pound hard to make use of the dark. When day dawns, we can't have people caught right in the middle of some farm where they can be recaptured." And I still don't know how Fidelia will fit into all of this, Thornton thought, but he kept that to himself.

"And with all of these animals, we'll never be able to sneak up quietly," William said. "We'll have to drive in fast and move on the main house quickly. We'll roust everyone in the bunkhouses and give them no more than five minutes to gather their things and come along. And with sunlight chasing us, we can't find ourselves there more than ten minutes."

"Horses alone'll be faster than wagons," Ronan said. "I'll put the best riders bareback on Hezzy's horses, including my mother, who can outride us all. I'll get as many traveling double as I can on these saddled horses," he said, pointing around Hiram Elliot's barn at his animals. "None of them are weanlings, a blessing."

"Yes, they're all adults and well-trained. Good horses," Hiram said, with a hint of bragging in his tone.

"Hmm, yes," Ronan agreed. He walked the stalls and assessed each animal in them. Satisfied, he came back to the group. "The wagons will be for the oldest, anyone who's sick, and Henry's boy." He looked Henry right in the eye and added, "Even Colleen may have to ride a mount and let one of the older women take care of your son. We have to keep the load light."

"Only if *I* drive the wagon my son is in."

"Of course," William said. "Since Thornton will drive the wagon heading west, you'll be in charge of the one going north."

Thornton avoided William's eyes. He dreaded the moment when he and his friend would have to say good-bye. It reminded him to ask William the question he hated most on that long night. "What time is it?"

"Ten twenty-two. We have to *move*."

Hiram Elliot pulled his watch out of his pocket. He squinted at its face in the half-lit structure. "Remarkable," he said. He tucked the timepiece into his pocket and added a simple, "Yes, we have a lot of work to do."

39

HIRAM ELLIOT had one saddle for each of his horses in case he and all of his men, and a few friends, wanted to ride at the same time, he had explained. He and Ronan had placed nine of the saddles on the horses Ronan judged to be the best runners. Hiram Elliot kept the tenth horse. The final two horses were the ones trained as a wagon team. William hitched them to Hiram Elliot's wagon. Thornton strung the nine horses together on one line he tied to the Guthrie wagon.

Thornton would again lead the way on Ashes, and Ronan would again ride in the rear on Blackie. Henry would drive the Guthrie wagon, and William would handle the wagon Hiram Elliot had given them.

The milk cow was sound asleep on the far end of the barn, probably grateful that her cold night odyssey had come to an end. It was a minor point among so many large ones that night, but Thornton was relieved she had found safe quarry.

The folks who had been in the house were in the barn and were aware of the plan. Rose and Fidelia added blankets and other supplies and a dozen rifles and ammunition to the Elliot wagon. Fidelia had donned a practical pair of britches, a woolen jacket, and a pair of boots. Thornton thought she looked wonderful, even if she also seemed cross.

Ethan sat on an anvil and refused to lift a finger.

William announced the time. Five after eleven. The group would leave within the next ten minutes. Thornton had just five to make his case. He found Fidelia rearranging food in a basket so she could fit another jar of preserves in it. It seemed to Thornton that she slammed the jars together more than necessary.

It was late. The direct approach made the most sense. He leaned close to her and whispered, "Come with us. Come with me." His eyes pleaded in a sort of desperate way, but he didn't care. He *was* desperate. Time was running out.

"Go with you?" Her voice carried just a little too far.

"What was that?" Hiram asked from the other side of the barn. All hasty movement by the others stopped. They watched Hiram Elliot traverse his long barn. "What's going on over here?" He stood in front of Thornton and Fidelia. "I asked you a question, Guthrie. What is afoot? Did I hear right?"

"Yessir, you did. I asked Fidelia to come with us." He paused, but not long enough for Hiram Elliot to comment. "I was going to ask her something else, too. I hoped to ask her to be my wife. I want to marry her, to be her husband."

He turned to Fidelia and ignored the observers. "Fidelia, I never planned on it being like this, on asking you to marry me while running from the law for killing my father. William and I had planned it much different all along. It was why I knew about Colleen. I sneaked over to the Jones place to see about her coming with us and found out about her baby and Ronan's mother. We figured on leaving at the first thaw. I thought I'd have time to propose proper and ask you to come with me ahead of the day we'd show up here asking for horses. What happened tonight wrecked those plans." He took her hands in his. They each wore gloves, but he squeezed her hands to let her know he had never intended to leave without her. "You know I love you. I would be honored if you would come with me. When we get to the Unorganized Territory where my Uncle Jeremiah lives, we—"

"She's not going anywhere with you."

"Pa, please. Thornton's talking to *me*."

"And I'm answering. You're not leaving here with Guthrie."

"Mr. Elliot—"

"Look, Guthrie....Thornton. Lord knows my view of you has changed drastically in the last two hours. But if you

expect me to send my daughter into the chaos about to happen
on the Jones place, you've grossly misunderstood my generosity
tonight. I will not now, or ever, purposely place Fidelia in
harm's way. Letting her go with you would do just that."

"With all due respect, Pa, I'm almost sixteen. It's not up
to you to 'let' me do anything anymore."

"And with all great deference to your fifteen years of
gathered wisdom, young lady, Hezekiah Jones and his reprobate
sons have guns. And they won't hesitate to use them when
Thornton invades his farm tonight. Hezzy will see shooting
Thornton and the rest as protecting his property, as revolting
as that is. And the law will see it that way too."

Fidelia looked at her father and sighed. Thornton couldn't
tell if she was frustrated with her father or about to
capitulate to his insistence that she send Thornton on his way.

Hiram addressed Thornton. "I understand what you did on
your father's farm earlier tonight, and I respect what you're
about to do at Hezzy's. I'm more than a little envious I can't
join you. If I had fewer years on me and didn't need to
provide you cover when the law comes around, I'd join you on
my last horse." He cleared his throat with more gusto than
necessary. It gave Thornton the impression he felt guilty for
his position and needed to cover that fact with bluster.

"But make no mistake. For the rest of your life, you will
be a wanted man. By sunup tomorrow you will have willfully
and purposefully broken dozens of laws, one for every slave
you free, for starters. There'll be horse theft once you ride
off on Hezzy's mounts, property theft for his wagon and any
other goods you abscond with, and murder. That's what they'll
call what happened to Marcus. And the hardest decision they'll
have to make is which thing to hang you for."

Hiram Elliot had been the first one to call what
Thornton did to his father murder. Not even Ethan had said it
out loud, although Thornton could guess it was what he
thought.

Thornton had thought it but hadn't been sure. He still wasn't, but to hear the word come from someone who had understood his actions dealt him a blow. It threw his mind off-balance for a moment.

It didn't help that Fidelia didn't say anything in his defense. She stood her ground with her father on her own account, but she had no words of outrage about accusations aimed at Thornton. Did she see him as a murderer?

He felt feeble. "Sir—"

Hiram Elliot held up a hand and silenced Thornton. He turned to Fidelia. "Your mother is gone and your brothers long ago abandoned me. I've always known some beau would show up and leave with you on his arm. I'm as prepared for that as a father can be. But if you expect me to climb the stairs to retire for sleep while you ride up the road to be killed, you need fifteen more years of life to gain some sense."

"Pa—"

"He's right." Thornton had held Fidelia's hands through Hiram Elliot's entire speech. He ended up feeling foolish. He said, "He's right. I don't know what I was thinking. In my mind, if you're with me, nothing can happen to you. But what happened with my father should remind me danger can come out of nowhere.

"I can't ask you to walk through the fire with me. And I can't ask you to join me somewhere up or down the road since I don't know for sure which road I'll travel or whether I'll be alive to meet you at the designated place on a schedule we can't even determine. For the second time tonight, I realize I was a fool to think things would go as I planned them in my head."

"Thornton—"

"Good-bye, Fidelia. Just please know that I have wanted to marry you since the day I mucked out your stalls uninvited. I didn't propose tonight because it was convenient. If I hadn't wasted time being jealous of Calvin, I would have asked you the last time I saw you. That will be a mistake I will live with for the rest of my life." He let go of her hands and turned to William. "Ready? It must be eleven-fifteen by now."

"Thereabouts."

With that, Thornton's shame was complete. The time was never "thereabouts" for William or "almost" or "half past", for that matter. The most he'd let himself round time was "fifteen" or "forty-five", and that visibly bothered him. For him to agree the time was "thereabouts" some random guess meant he so pitied Thornton, he'd do anything to get onto the next thing, even let eight different people have eight different notions about what time it was. It had to be killing him, but he put up with it for Thornton.

"I think with time, you'll see—" Hiram Elliot offered, but Thornton talked right over him.

"The horses are tied to the wagon, Henry. We'll run 'em slow at first and pick up the pace once they're warm. Stay on me." He sniffed a couple of times and promised himself he'd dive under a running horse if he started to cry.

Mostly, he hated that William had witnessed that scene. Thornton had talked about Fidelia for days' worth of hours in the fields, and William had indulged him every time. Hiram Elliot made sure William knew Thornton would never be good enough for Fidelia, that the life Thornton had bragged he would give Fidelia sometime after he awoke from some childish slumber with all of his problems gone would never be.

Thornton wanted to die of shame and embarrassment. He wanted to kill his father all over again, for he kept Thornton stuck and caused him problems even after he was dead.

William shot him a look of deep sympathy. He headed toward Thornton, who couldn't take being anymore of a spectacle than he already was. Out of deference, he would hear whatever William had to say, though, so he hoped he planned to change the subject.

He braced for more embarrassment, but it never came. Once William moved, the others went back to work. Thornton

watched Fidelia take her packed basket across the barn with
her father right behind her and accepted he would never be
with her.

"I know," was all William said. He stared at Thornton for
another long moment and said, "It seems bad now, but you're
just weary, son. You can't let what happened make you worn-
out."

"I won't. I promise."

William rested a hand on his shoulder. He gave it a
gentle shake and a soft pat. "All right, son. All right." Much
louder, he said to the group, "Let's move out. Thornton, good
man, light your lamp and lead the way. It's eleven-eighteen.
Get us there by midnight."

40

THE THRUM, thrum, thrum of fifteen heavy horses announced the runaways half a mile out from Hezzy Jones's place. The snow served as no buffer between hooves and earth. The sound reverberated to the Jones buildings and all around the low hills and back again.

Thornton maintained his position at the front of the pack. Bits of hail fell through the snow and pinched his face. He had no wagon driver to hide behind the way his mother and Ethan did, and he couldn't work with one hand and protect his face with the other, as William and Henry could. They drove wagons and could operate the reins with a single hand at different times. Thornton steered Ashes with his left hand and held the lamp in his right. He had no guard against the weather. He thought Ronan, who was in the same predicament, must be soaked in mud in the rear with the horses in front of him kicking up so much wet earth.

He felt as though he led an army through enemy terrain and into battle, and in a way, he did.

Thornton never thought he'd say it, but he would be relieved to arrive at Hezzy's. Not only did he want to come in from the snow, even if just for the few minutes it would take to raid the place, but his nerves had worked up into a frenzy.

Despite William's warning, he was wearing out. He was sick of dreading what would come next and was ready for it to happen, whatever it looked like.

The events at the Elliot place tormented him. It wasn't just that he felt deep humiliation and sadness about how it ended with Fidelia. His mother had besieged him with her words.

Riding in the half-dark by himself at the front of the band, he brooded over how, for a lifetime, she had listened for him to die in the fields when all the while, he had wondered whether she cared. If he had known about the kitchen window, he would have used it to form a conspiracy with his mother against his father. They could have talked through it. She could have passed him treats, smiled, and whispered, "Don't worry," or simply stood watch, and he could have thrown her looks behind his father's back that said, "He's crazy, not us." He had proven himself to be quite capable of subterfuge. They could have pulled it off. Instead, she had chosen estrangement as her co-conspirator. It had aligned her with Marcus, even if it had not allied her with him. If only she had told Thornton.

The cold, biting ice reminded him of how forlorn and frigid his life had been. Rage took over. He pushed on for the Jones place. He no longer cared whether any of the mob were behind him. If he had to, he would take Hezzy's clan by himself.

Although the plot had changed wildly, the strategy remained the same. Thornton and William would take the main house, Ronan would start in the men's bunkhouse and recruit a few friends to handle the horse assignments, and Henry and Rose would rescue Colleen, the baby, and the other women.

As always, Ethan posed a problem. The group decided he could be best controlled if he went with Ronan, who would have plenty of men to help him watch the wily man-child.

In the near distance, several dogs barked. Thornton figured his posse had a hundred yards to go. The previous autumn, he had left Ashes a distance away and walked the final steps. That night, they would thunder right into the Jones compound as if they owned it. They would come in near Colleen's bunkhouse and drive right past the window he had tapped on months earlier.

Fifty more yards.

Ashes sensed the battle had started. He sped up with no nudging from his rider. The thunder of their fifteen horses rolled in ahead of the band. The Jones animals—dogs, horses, and hogs—went wild.

Ashes galloped over the invisible property line.

They had arrived.

Thornton careened in a hard right turn around the women's bunkhouse and charged up the middle of the compound toward the main house.

The last thing he spotted through the snow was William, who drove his horses extra hard on Thornton's right flank. Thornton figured they would arrive at the bottom steps of the porch within seconds of each other.

—◇—

William refused to fall too far behind Thornton. His friend rode as much away from what had happened at the Elliot place as he drove his horse *to* Hezzy Jones's. William had only loved one woman in his life, but he knew how the prospect of separation from her as early as sunup pained him. He imagined Thornton felt the same way about Fidelia.

If the young man lost his head over Fidelia, though, it could cause a catastrophe for him and the group. For Thornton's sake, and Rose's, William would not let that happen. So, he drove his horses harder than prudence advised. The back wheels on the wagon slid left and right like the tail of a fish. William needed both hands on the reins to control the contraption. He came to a dead stop in front of Hezzy Jones's main house three seconds after Thornton.

—◇—

Henry rounded the same corner Thornton and William had, but stopped several yards sooner, in front of the women's bunkhouse. Rose sat frozen in place on the long, cold ride, but the ice hadn't kept her from plotting her own battle the whole way to Hezzy Jones's.

No matter how foolish it seemed or how much the others would advise against it, she had to carry it out. She couldn't get out of her mind something William had said, and she had to right a wrong. It may result in the law giving chase sooner than if she didn't go through with it, but principle dictated she do it anyway.

She grinned as much as her numb face would allow just thinking about it. She couldn't wait.

———◆◇◆———

Through the white wall of snow the skies erected, Ethan recognized the women's bunkhouse he had toured with Jedidiah Jones and Thornton on the visit with his Uncle Marcus. The main house—where his allies slept—lay dozens of yards ahead at the end of the compound.

The snow was so thick, Ethan couldn't see Thornton's horse or the Elliot wagon William drove stationed there, but he figured his cousin and William had made it all the way to the house. Things always seemed to work out for them.

He scrambled for a way to break loose from Henry and Aunt Rose and run for it. On a cold night like this, he had no idea if Hezzy and his sons would ignore the yowling dogs or at least step onto the porch to investigate the noise. He couldn't wait for them. He had to get to the house on his own.

He heard a baby cry. Henry froze and not because of the icy air. The others had talked enough for Ethan to know he had heard Henry's baby cry. Ethan viewed Henry's besotted distraction with his son as his own chance to dash for the main house. He could find a hiding place near the house and wait for Thornton and William to go in. He could slip in behind them unseen and beg Hezzy Jones for refuge once the confrontation began. He might even alert Hezzy Jones and wreck his cousin's chances to gain an edge.

Ethan, his Aunt Rose, and Henry sat and listened to the
baby cry. Henry was stuck at the reins of the wagon while
Ronan untied the line that held the nine horses to it. Henry
hurried Ronan with a terse, "Let's get on with these horses!"
Ethan's Aunt Rose turned her back on him and looked toward
the women's bunkhouse.

Ethan took his chances.

He hopped off the back of the wagon and ducked down
beneath its ledge. He crawled underneath it and stayed on all
fours in the snow. He looked around and took stock of where
he was. Past the left wheel and across the compound stood the
barn and the men's bunkhouse.

If he darted out to the left of the wheel, he could run
in a direct line to the barn, which was safer than the men's
bunkhouse. It was farther from the main house, though.

He had just two or three more seconds to make his move.
In four seconds, they would realize he was not in the back of
the wagon.

The baby cried louder and the horses reacted. The wagon
wheel rolled back three feet and blocked Ethan's exit from
under the wagon. He shifted to his right and ducked out
through the space between the wheel and the front of the
wagon.

He bumped right into the leg of Blackie. He looked up.
In the snow and mist loomed Ronan high up on his horse.
Ronan had seen every move he had made after the baby cried
and had simply waited for Ethan to crawl into his trap.

Ethan wasted no energy running. He stood up.

"We're going this way." Ronan tucked a gentle but firm
hand into Ethan's collar from atop his horse. "Henry. I got
him and the horses. Please get to my mother and get her to
the barn. And see if you can find out who knows how to
ride."

Ronan hoisted Ethan onto his horse and trotted away.
Ethan bobbed up and down seated in front of a muddy Ronan
on the large horse. They stopped at the barn on the way to

the men's bunkhouse and hopped off Blackie. To save time, Ronan opened one of the doors and slapped the rumps of the nine horses and Blackie to get them to file into the barn. He didn't follow them inside. He'd see to them later. He shut the barn door and closed the horses into the warmth.

Ethan felt his options slipping away.

———◦◇◦———

Rose had packed Thornton's baby clothes where she could easily reach them. She took them and followed Henry toward the women's quarters. The baby cried again. She couldn't believe a newborn had to live in such vile conditions.

They heard several voices beyond the door. The women were awake but in possible various stages of undress. Henry tapped the sanded wood several times with an impatient hand. A woman who looked not much older than Rose opened it. She gasped. "Henry! Wha. . . .?"

Henry fast-walked through the door with Rose right behind him and shut the door. Every face in the bunkhouse stared at them. One stood out to Rose, and not because she held a baby. Her immense beauty overpowered everything else that happened in the room—Henry showing up in the middle of the night, the strange white woman who stood next to him, the baby fussing. The loveliness of the woman Rose guessed was Colleen eclipsed all else.

"Hen— Henry?" At the sound of Colleen's voice, the baby cooed.

Half a second later, Henry had his arms around Colleen and his son.

"What? How?" Colleen asked. The family laughed and hugged and kissed. Colleen's face was shrouded in doubt and disbelief. "How. . . .?" she said again.

"My son." It was the first time since Rose had known Henry that she had seen him smile. And cry. "My son, my son." He alternated between kissing the baby and Colleen.

Rose's heart swelled. It was the only happy moment she had witnessed since she left William in the bunkhouse what felt like a century earlier but what had only been three o'clock on what was by just a few minutes the early morning of the day before. She had seen nothing but death and disappointment and cold ever since. "Tell me his name."

"They named him Josiah. But it was August when I knew for sure he was on his way, so I call him August."

"August." The family hugged and kissed some more, but the rest of the ladies stood motionless and silent. They were torn. They watched the family reunite, and they stared at Rose. Their eyes darted back and forth between the two spectacles. One by one, they centered their attention on Rose. After several moments, Colleen looked at Rose too and froze.

"Henry? Is there trouble?"

"No," Rose answered and took a few steps forward, eager to join the celebration and share the good news of the escape. She also hoped to hold the baby. Thornton had been the last baby she had held.

Except for Henry, they all stepped back.

Rose stopped in her tracks, horrified.

She tried to put them at ease. "Do you remember last autumn a boy came to that window?" Some of the women nodded. "He's my son, and we've brought horses and supplies." She held out Thornton's baby sweaters. The women stared with leery looks on their faces. Rose's mouth dried up. Her voice shook. She remembered Colleen had asked *Henry* whether there was trouble and wondered why she had pushed her way in and answered. Stuck, she prattled on. "My son and William are at the main house and Ronan is with the men."

"Ronan?" A robust but small woman who wore the same face that hid underneath Ronan's scars took a step toward Rose. "Are we being sold? In the middle of the night?"

Rose was horrorstruck.

She said to the woman she recognized as Ronan's mother, "No! Ma'am, your son lived on my farm, but my husband is dead, and Ronan and my son and William are here now." She rambled.

"I don't understand," Colleen said. She hugged August tight.

Rose suddenly realized how to make sense. "Every last one of us is escaping tonight."

The collective gasp made August cry.

———◦◦———

The prospect of the men's bunkhouse and who inhabited it terrified Ethan. He remembered from his tour that twelve men bunked there. At the time, he had looked at them with open disdain. His Uncle Marcus had told him he possessed the social station of a white man, said the men's lives amounted to nothing more than river sludge. On a hot day, he had said, you could soak your feet in it to cool them off, but when it came time to collect good drinking water, you would take special care to leave the sludge behind.

His own father would disagree, and his uncle's words had made him uneasy, but he liked his Uncle Marcus and went along with him. He would face those men and hope they hadn't noticed his pompous attitude the previous time he was there.

"Pick it up." Ronan urged Ethan to walk faster from the barn to the men's bunkhouse.

Ethan stifled a groan and stepped up his pace. He wiped mud from Ronan's coat off his own sleeves. There was nothing else for him to do.

———◦◦———

Thornton and William hitched their horses to the post in front of the Jones house. Thornton had snuffed out his lamp, and they worked in the dark. William felt his way to the back of the wagon in search of two of the rifles Fidelia

Elliot had put there. They were Hawkens, like Marcus Guthrie's.

They agreed to go in with the back triggers cocked. If threatened, they would only need to pull the hair triggers to fire the weapons.

"Here." William tossed one to Thornton, whose arms ached. He bungled the two-handed catch. The gun fell in the snow. Thornton cursed and scrambled for it. It came up covered in ice. He hoped it would fire when he needed it.

He shook off thoughts of Fidelia and his mother and Marcus and said, "Okay, like we planned, we start with Jedidiah and Obadiah. By the time we get to Hezzy's room, he'll have no one to call for help. We'd better hurry. They're not going to ignore the dogs forever." He cocked the back trigger on his rifle. William did the same.

Thornton started up the porch steps. He didn't think to ask himself why the Jones men weren't already outside, with so much dog noise.

William grabbed his arm. "We march them straight to the barn where Ronan and the others can help us pin them down. If it gets out of hand, Hezzy's mine. Are we clear?"

Thornton nodded assent.

They headed for Hezzy Jones's front door. They expected to meet Ronan in the barn with four prisoners no more than five minutes later. William would keep time.

"It's two idiots, their toad father, and their silly mother. We have the guns and horses and men. They have two imbeciles and a man half the size of my father. It's going to be fine," Thornton said. He turned the knob on the front door and strolled into the Jones's parlor.

—◦◦—

Ronan tip-toed into the men's bunkhouse. Ethan had no choice but to follow him. He wondered why they approached in silence. Ronan's enemies slept in the main house. The men in the bunkhouse all felt friendly toward Ronan. Not that Ethan cared, but they would be glad to see him. He stayed by the door while Ronan found the lamp that was probably in the same place it had been when he lived there and lit it. An odor of unwashed bodies hovered over the room.

Ethan realized Ronan had waited until he could assess his surroundings and reserved noisemaking for after the lamp was lit. Once it was, and he knew none of the Jones clan lurked, Ronan walked straight to a bunk against the far wall.

"James. James! Wake up! It's Ronan!" He didn't bother to whisper. They needed everybody awake. James was just the start.

The man called James popped right up. "I'm up. We all are. Dogs saw to that. We heard you come in, didn't know who it was. Are you trying to get us all killed in here? What are you doing here?" Every man in the room was agitated.

Ethan became nervous. He backed farther against the door. He knew better than to try to run. He had learned Ronan always had one eye on him. As if to prove Ethan's point, Ronan glanced at him to let him know he wasn't distracted by James.

Ethan surveyed the bunkhouse. Men with matted hair and dirty feet sticking out from tattered patchwork blankets were scattered in bunks throughout the room. Judging by the dense stink, none of the men had bathed in weeks.

Ethan's insides turned in a strange way for the first time since the entire crusade began. He was uneasy in his mind more than he was in his belly.

For some bizarre reason, he thought about his Uncle Marcus shooting off a piece of Thornton's ear, something he hadn't learned until that night. He had wondered what had deformed his cousin's ear but had been too afraid to ask.

He had to admit he had been aghast to learn his Uncle Marcus had shot Thornton. His own father had never raised a hand against him or Janey or Edward or Julius. When he threatened to, it had always been hard not to laugh. Ethan thought it frightful that Thornton's father had shot his own son. He didn't know why seeing those men should make him think of that.

"What are you doing here? Have you lost your mind?" James ran to the window in his filthy bare feet and peered out of the lower corner. "What's going on out there? *What are you doing here?*"

At once, all twelve men talked over one another. Ethan picked up lots of "Ronan" and "doing here?" and "crazy?" and "Jones." He also caught the occasional "Colleen" and "baby".

They sounded to him like chickens that cackled out of rhythm with each other. Some of them stood up. Ethan was poised to run if he had to.

"Quiet," Ronan said. "Everyone up. Old Man Guthrie is dead. His son and William and Henry and me took his horses and another man's. We're running. We came to get my mother, and Henry's woman and child, and everyone else."

The clucking resumed.

Ethan caught the gist. The men were doubtful, incredulous Ronan would put them at risk, nervous, and even irritated. They questioned Ronan's wisdom and sanity. They cursed him.

Some grinned, however. They understood they were getting out. One by one, the enlightened convinced the doubtful.

Three minutes after he entered the bunkhouse, Ronan had converted every man.

"Let's move, now. Each man pack a sack, nothing heavier than what you can run with tied around your waist. Relieve yourselves anywhere you can in the snow, and go to the barn."

They ran all over the room. "When you get there, the ones who feel okay setting a horse meet at the stalls. The rest of you go to the other side of the barn. Once the women get there, we'll figure out who will ride which horse. Move." He glanced at Ethan and said, "James. Don't let that boy out of your sight."

James, whose sack was packed the quickest, walked to where Ethan waited. He barely looked at him other than to make his presence known, but Ethan's back was pressed against the bunkhouse doors.

He was cornered. Not even the barking dogs gave him comfort.

———◦◇◦———

Thornton was cocky. The mood began on the ride from Hiram Elliot's. He couldn't tell if he wanted to prove Fidelia's father right or wrong in his assessment of Thornton as not good enough for his daughter. Maybe anger fueled him. Or disappointment or the bitter cold weather he expected to be in for the rest of his life since that night was never going to end. A feeling of having nothing to lose swept over him. His attitude was reckless, but he had no control over it.

He and William had strolled into Hezzy Jones's house without so much as a field mouse giving them grief. Thornton thought they could be bolder. He felt around on the table near the entry to the parlor and found a lamp. He reached into his pocket and retrieved the tiny metal box that contained his phosphorous matches. He struck one against the piece of sandpaper glued to the box and lit the lamp. The blown out match would leave a stench, but he couldn't care less. It wouldn't take long. Why work in the dark?

The light came on.

Ten men with ten rifles aimed them at Thornton and William.

In the smelly light, Thornton recognized the imbeciles and their father. It was the other seven faces he had trouble placing.

41

AUGUST APPEARED to Rose to snuggle into his newfound warmth. He wore Thornton's winter clothing, and Henry cuddled him against his breast in the corner of the women's bunkhouse. The baby was sound asleep.

Henry paced a small pattern of three feet up and three feet back. He had waited in the barn while the women dressed but had returned once eleven had trickled into the barn. Rose and Henry's family were the only people left in the women's quarters.

"We have to go," Henry said. "We've been here too long."

Rose had stayed in the bunkhouse with Colleen to dress August in Thornton's clothes, and the two women had lagged and talked. Rose had seen bruises all over Colleen when she changed clothes. They looked identical to the bruises Marcus gave Rose her whole life. Without thinking, Rose asked Colleen about the welts and discolorations.

"Jedidiah," she said. She cried.

"Jedidiah Jones?"

"He took me into the wood shed. In my condition. With Henry's baby. He still does."

Rose grabbed Colleen's hand. "You don't need to explain."

"His manhood doesn't react. He can't...." She sobbed. "He gets very angry and beats me. Henry doesn't know."

Rose despised Jedidiah Jones and every pig like him. She hated to think what Colleen had endured in that wood shed, and yet she had all too vivid a picture. Rose had suffered similar degradations for seventeen years with Marcus.

It was worse for Colleen. She faced being taken by a stranger whenever he got the notion to sniff around. Rose was relieved Jedidiah couldn't complete the deed. It provided no solace, but it meant Colleen wasn't carrying the vermin's child.

Rose had always counted herself lucky Marcus's seed was infertile except the one time, although when Thornton was eight, she missed her cycle. A month later, she suffered profuse bleeding after Marcus had gut-punched her. She had always wondered if she had miscarried his second child. She didn't see it as a blessing. She simply couldn't imagine having more than one of his children. It was William's child she desired to carry. She hoped they had already accomplished that.

She had gone outside and dipped a cloth in the snow. She gave it to Colleen to soothe her eyes before Henry returned. She prayed her son and William made Jedidiah pay when they raided the main house and that Henry would not feel any different about Colleen if he knew about Jedidiah's night visits. She remembered her own plan and couldn't wait to go through with it.

"All right, I'm ready," Colleen said. She had fashioned her small satchel into a kind of hip sack tied around her waist. The crying—and the slight redness it left in her eyes despite the cold cloth—had not interfered one iota with her prettiness.

"Don't forget. I've got plenty more clothes for August in the wagon," Rose said. The two women smiled at each other. Rose hoped Colleen couldn't mount a horse and that she, herself, could barter for a spot in Henry's wagon, despite being a good rider. She wanted to travel with Colleen. She had taken an immense liking to the young girl. "Shall we?"

Henry handed August to Colleen. "Hold onto him tight. I'll walk out first."

"Be careful."

Henry smiled at his wife and touched her cheek. "I'm here now. It's going to be fine. It's never going to be wrong again. I won't let it."

His words and tone were so soothing, even Rose felt calmer and almost optimistic. She figured Thornton and

William should have taken care of Hezzy and his ill-bred sons by then. She hadn't heard one gun fired.

Once she knew William and Thornton had made it to the barn, she would get to her own work. She had wanted Hezzy to see it happen. She needed Jedidiah there too. And Colleen. She would make sure they all saw.

———◦◦◦———

Ronan, James, and Ethan were the final three to leave the men's bunkhouse. Ethan tugged on his scarf but had little success fending off the freezing wind that whistled over the snow in the compound. His teeth chattered, but his lips were too frozen to quiver.

The two men nudged the boy toward the barn. Ethan caught a glimpse of light at the main house and figured the Jones family would be marched into the barn right behind him. Baby cries told him the women and child had already gathered inside the large building.

They had spent fifteen minutes on the Jones property, and the war was almost over. Ethan's shoulders drooped as much from disappointment as from an effort to hunker down to get through the frosty compound.

The three of them went through the doors of the enormous barn, and Ethan remembered it functioned like a large stable. Hezzy had said he liked having enough room for his guests to store their wagons on long visits and during wintertime. Six wagons formed a neat line against the far wall.

A thought struck Ethan. At most, two of those wagons belonged to Hezzy Jones. Where had the other four or five come from?

His eyes darted to his chief captor. The color of Ronan's skin hid the activities of his blood, but Ethan felt pretty sure it drained from the man's face. The look of shock betrayed what his facade hid. Ronan had deduced the meaning of the wagons.

The turn of events brought to Ethan's mind something his father used to say when he got the upper hand on an uncooperative crop: The snow blew in another direction. It made him think of something else. He had options again.

Something was wrong, though. He should have felt elated, should have been glad his face hadn't yet thawed because it kept him from having to stifle a smile, and yet he had no urge to grin.

He hunkered under his scarf and scanned the barn. More than twenty slaves were gathered. They displayed various states of dishevelment, fear, excitement, and gratitude. The room smelled like hay, manure, and sweat. The stink of so much unwashed humanity jammed into one space overwhelmed Ethan. He watched tattered clothes and messy hair and worn-out boots move around the barn and wondered how twenty-five people could find themselves in such a circumstance.

The magnitude of the answer hit him, and he hunched further into his own garments. They hadn't woken up one day and found they had fallen into slavery. Someone, many people, a country had put them there. His thoughts shifted from the captives to the captors, and he didn't like who roamed around his mind. Hezzy Jones, Jedidiah Jones, his Uncle Marcus. Himself?

A baby cried on the other side of the barn. Ethan's eyes sought the source of the sound, and he spotted Henry, who caressed his small son's back as the baby lay across his mother's shoulder. Ethan couldn't believe that if that tiny baby weren't escaping that night, he would work for the Jones clan for the rest of his life as soon as he was old enough to walk and take simple orders. Every slave in the room had once been that small, that innocent.

Aunt Rose stood with Henry's family and grinned at the sight of the three of them. The family was picture perfect. Ethan had always thought Henry a handsome fellow, but he hadn't noticed on the day he toured the Jones place with Thornton and Jedidiah how comely Colleen was. He saw it that night.

Ethan realized, though, that it wasn't their looks that made them a nice family. It was the way they looked at each other that struck Ethan. The scene brought thoughts to his mind of Baby Justus and his own parents and their terrible loss. The realization of the god-awful cruelty he had delivered letting them think he was dead made his head heavy on his shoulders. The weight crushed him.

He suddenly saw his mother roaming the farm with no purpose in the days after Justus died and wondered how he could allow her to think lightning had struck twice, that God was so angry with his parents, He had taken two of their children in the span of a few weeks.

And if his parents suffered their losses, how must it have been for the millions of slaves who daily could be and were moved across whole territories, never to see their families again, and always left to wonder what they endured and whether they were still alive to withstand it or wished they were dead so they wouldn't have to?

Ethan averted his eyes from Henry's family. They landed on the wagons against the wall, the ones that represented an unknown number of enemies who waited for Thornton and William in the main house. Ethan's final hope of achieving a smile vanished. He was stunned.

———◦◦◦———

The longer Thornton stared at the other seven guns—the ones not pointed at him by Hezzy, Jedidiah, and Obadiah—the more he recognized Hezzy Jones's ugly face on each one of the men who held them, some young, some not as young but not old either. Hezzy's brothers and nephews, Thornton figured. It appeared Thornton and the others had interrupted a reunion of the Jones bunch.

A surreptitious glance around the room told him no women had joined them. The telltale signs—quilting patches, needlepoint racks, stray pieces of yarn, hat boxes, shawls, and forgotten spectacles—were missing.

The Guthries led the lives of recluses, but only on the subject of hosting visitors. Thornton had visited a number of parlors over the years, mostly when his father wanted to keep up a false image of the pleasant farmer and family man who called on neighbors just for the sake of the sweet lemonade and good chatter. Thornton's experience had been that the more women in the house, the more likely one would encounter needlepoint and other sewing in progress. A tea set might stand at the ready on the table in front of the settee. Some lady's hat was sure to be lying around.

In the Jones parlor, except for some half-darned socks, the room exuded a stark maleness: snuffed out cigars, six cowhide hats on a side table, three thick riding scarves, like the ones Thornton and William and the other men wore that night, draped over the arm of a large chair. Other than Hezzy's wife, Thornton felt sure there were no women in the house.

The band had interrupted their sleep, but none of the men wore pajamas. They all wore pants with their big shirts untucked, as if they hadn't brought changes of clothes and had been forced to sleep in what they wore on their day trip. The men had likely visited and let the blizzard sneak up on them. Only a band of killers and fugitives would try to make their way through the storm that blew outside. The rest would ride it out in the warmth of their fat uncle's—or brother's—house. They must have lived a bit farther east. Thornton had never heard of them.

William also stared longer than necessary at the hats on the table. His gaze said, "Look at all those hats. There's nothing but men here."

Thornton indicated understanding with a half-blink of his eyes. William answered the half-blink with a slight lift of the chin. It was the same silent communication the two had employed hundreds of times to get around Marcus Guthrie's guns. Not more than fifteen seconds had passed since Thornton had lit the lamp, and already they were in perfect agreement about the situation.

It was two men against ten. And Hezzy's wife. They couldn't discount her. Thornton's own mother lay in wait in the barn with twelve other women.

"You just gonna stand here in my parlor with this nigger, Guthrie, and not say anything, or are you gonna explain yourself? I can shoot you both now or later. It's up to you."

Thornton and William said nothing.

"Guess he thought we would ignore the dogs howling and all that horse noise," a plump brother said.

"Saw you from the window when your wagon came to a stop," Obadiah said.

"Didn't think you'd be stupid enough to come right in. Thought you'd start in the bunkhouses and collect some men first," Hezzy said.

"Leave it to Marcus's idiot son and a nigger to get it backwards, heh, heh." Thornton almost lunged for Jedidiah Jones but restrained himself.

"Speaking of Marcus, where is he? Does your daddy know you're out gallivanting with one of his barn animals? I warned Marcus this one was trouble."

An image of Marcus Guthrie lying face down at the bottom of a sloppy, icy grave came to Thornton's mind. He brushed it aside and glanced at William. He gave his friend a slight lift of his eyebrows. William replied with a nod of the head discernible only to Thornton, he was sure.

They had come to a tacit agreement about what they had just heard. Snow, fog, and ice had protected Ronan and Henry and the others from view. The Jones clan believed Thornton and William were alone.

"Drop those guns. Pick up that lamp, Guthrie."

They did as they were told.

"Both of you turn around and head back out that door. I don't aim to let the blood of a nigger shed all over my abode."

Thornton and William walked toward the front door. Ten pairs of boots clacked across the hardwood floor behind them.

Thornton had no doubt when they got outside, Hezzy would shoot them both. That he was Marcus Guthrie's son mattered not one bit. Hezzy was a sonofabitch. Thornton had brought a Negro into his house to do Lord knew what. And his family watched. If for no other reason than to save face, he would have to kill them both. Ashes too, out of spite.

The three had one final hope. All those men had to have gotten there somehow. Thornton prayed Ronan, Hezzy's old stable hand, would find all the extra horses and wagons in the barn and gather a strange feeling about it.

Twelve bodies reached the porch. Thornton's lamp illuminated a small space. Only Thornton, William, and the tips of the guns of the two or three men who stood closest to Thornton were visible.

Hezzy opened his mouth to say something. A gun fired in the compound shut it. The bullet missed Hezzy and crashed into the front window of the house.

Ronan!

Thornton wasted no time. He slammed the lamp into the ground. The compound went pitch dark.

Shots fired in all directions. Some of the women screamed. Others yelled orders. A baby cried.

Thornton ran down the porch steps, guessing his way in the dark. He assumed the feet he heard next to him were William's. They reached the bottom of the steps and crouched below the line of fire. They held their positions, each with one knee down and one knee up, ready to bolt like horses if necessary.

Thornton's eyes hadn't adjusted to the sudden dark, and with Ashes and his rein being the color of the elements, he could hear his horse, but he couldn't see his way to untether him and set him loose. He hoped none of the flying ammunition struck the animal.

Shots came from everywhere and ricocheted against wood and unintended targets around the compound.

Windows broke. Horses bellowed. Dogs threw tantrums. A rooster crowed. One disembodied voice wailed in pain. The sound came from so deep in the soul's throat, Thornton didn't know if it belonged to a man or a woman. The voice lay stranded somewhere in the snowy compound.

One of his folks, he feared. His mother?

As quickly as the gunfire had started, it stopped. An eerie silence fell about the farmstead. The snow had ceased its fire, as well.

Only the screams of the genderless person, the cries of the baby, and the occasional animal noise penetrated the atmosphere.

Thornton performed some quick math. Forty-one people—Hezzy's twenty-four adult captives, the five conspirators from Guthrie Farms, eleven in the Jones clan, and Ethan—scurried around in an eerie dark the luminescent snow all over the ground fought to light up. Most had guns they just needed to reload. As far as Thornton knew, only one had been incapacitated. Another, Colleen, watched over a baby. The rest were free to fight to the death over horses, guns, supplies, and wagons.

As if they had eavesdropped on his mind and taken his thoughts as instruction to behave accordingly, as if they had been in a racing contest in a church social and the minister had yelled, "Go!" forty people scattered.

Bedlam ensued.

42

"WE CAN'T just sit here!" William called over the din of gunfire, screams, and wind.

William was right, but Thornton had no idea where they could go if they got up from where they hunkered in front of Hezzy's porch.

He took the brazen approach.

He crawled in the general direction of where he thought Ashes was and felt around for the horse's hoof. He had to be careful not to find it just as it shifted and stepped on him. He wasn't even sure Ashes was there since William's wagon full of rifles was clearly long gone and its contents were being put to great use by Ronan. He didn't think Ronan would abandon Ashes, but in the commotion, Ronan may have been unable to see him, let alone chase him out of the way of so much gunfire.

Within a few seconds, Thornton's hand landed on a hoof. He quickly stood up, felt along the length of the rein, unwound it from the post, and shouted, "Ronan!"

"Over here!" The voice came from the direction of the barn.

If we can get to him, Thornton thought, we can find out where we stand.

"Don't move, Guthrie," Hezzy Jones said.

Hezzy's rifle was pointed right at Thornton's back.

Thornton dropped to the ground, rolled under Ashes, and came up on the other side. He yanked on the rein and ran for the barn. Hezzy shot at him and Ashes. He missed.

Thornton looked to his left. William had taken advantage of the diversion Thornton had created with Ashes and had run too. Thornton turned around just in time to see a shadowy figure approach Hezzy from the side and hit him hard across the side of the head with a scantling. Hezzy's squat frame tumbled head first into the snow. He wouldn't be firing his rifle anytime soon. Not only was he out cold, but the elusive figure had run off with the gun. Hezzy remained behind in a heap.

Thornton's night vision had kicked in. He saw things in greater detail.

"This way!" Ronan called out. Thornton and William ran eight or ten yards more and stopped right in front of Ronan. He toted one of Hiram Elliot's rifles. It comforted Thornton to see him, not just because he had the rifle, but because he was okay.

Ashes agreed. Through his own excellent equine night vision, he recognized his old acquaintance and nodded a happy greeting.

In the distance, the unidentified injured member of their clan howled. Thornton still couldn't tell who it was. For the first time, though, he noted a hint of female in the voice. He tamped down his thoughts that the person could be his mother and turned to the men.

All three of them spoke at once.

"How many are there?" Ronan wanted to know. He absentmindedly patted Ashes on the neck.

"Was anybody able to ride away?" William wanted to know.

"Who got hit?" Thornton wanted to know.

The answers to the first two questions also came in unison.

"Seven, besides Hezzy and his sons."

"We were in the barn. I saw all those wagons. We took up rifles and watched the house. No one had time to get away. I got a couple of men holding down the barn though. Hezzy's men'll get shot if they try anything."

Ronan was unable to tell them who had been hit. Thornton's neck got prickly with fear. The sound of rifle shots sailed overhead. The bullets were farther away than the sound they made, but the entire scene still unnerved Thornton. He wanted to know where his mother was. Presumption and panic wouldn't help. He reverted his attention to the problems he knew for sure he had.

"Hezzy's gonna regroup. Let's split up and get every man and woman who can ride on a horse. Tell them each to put anyone they happen to see on the back of the saddle and *ride*. No looking back." Thornton saw his breath float through the night. His night vision improved by the minute.

A tall Negro man ran past the three of them.

"Thomas!" Ronan said to the man. "Come here! Get on a horse and take John with you. You know how the sun comes up every day over yonder?" He pointed east. "Well, take the horse *that* way," he pointed north, "and keep going. No matter where you are or how you have to hide, the sun should be on this side of you," he tapped Thomas's right shoulder, "as you ride straight out every morning. You'll be heading north. You can also head *away* from the sun a ways. That's west. Then turn thisa way," he said, as he mimicked a right turn with his hand, "and that's north again. Just don't ever ride *into* the sun in the morning. That's east. You'll get caught." Thomas nodded.

Ronan gave Ashes one more soft rub on his long neck. "One last thing. Bring this horse to the barn. Cover him with a blanket and put him in the farthest stall in the corner next to the big black horse. Let him sleep. Make sure everybody knows not to take this one or the black one, you hear?" Thomas nodded again and ran off with Ashes in tow.

For the first time since they encountered all of those Jones guns, Thornton felt a sense of order and control return.

He, William, and Ronan split up and searched for the rest of the men. Wherever they found one, they sent him to find a horse and another rider and repeated Ronan's exact instructions about riding north and west.

They helped tenderfoot riders mount up behind the more
skilled riders, and Thornton overheard Ronan give one poor
pair, neither of whom knew how to ride but who insisted on
going together because they were as married as Henry and
Colleen, quick lessons on how to steer and guide a horse. He
wished them luck, bade them farewell, and sent them on their
way, with a rifle and their sacks.

Thornton also witnessed the reunion between Ronan and
his mother, who hadn't been able to greet each other in the
barn. Ronan had had to act too fast. With a forlorn sense of
guilt for intruding, Thornton had watched Ronan hug her hard
and lift her off the ground for what had to be a full minute.
They smiled at each other and stroked each other's faces. He
had never seen such affection between a mother and son.

"Miss Ella, Miss Ella, Miss Ella. Mm, mm, mm, Mama."
In the presence of a loved one, Ronan looked to Thornton like
a happy-go-lucky free man. His big hands rested gently on her
shoulders, and the two were at complete ease with each other.

"I don't like all this, Ronan," his mother had said.

"I know. Don't you worry. We'll handle this and be on
our way. You'll ride with me. It's safer. There's too much
going on in all this cold. Wait in the barn till I come for
you."

"All right, son." She squeezed his shoulder and ran to the
barn in ducked-down fashion.

"Careful, now!"

"I'll be careful!" it sounded like she said. The wind blew
away some of her words, but Ronan's face was calmer than
even the scars usually made it. Still, he waited until she
darted into the barn before he got back to work.

Little by little, the gun fire died down as more and more
pairs rode off. There were teams of men, of women, and of
one of each. With Hezzy's horses, some were able to ride solo.

Through it all, Thornton searched for the injured body.
The more healthy people he saw ride off, the more the process

of elimination meant there was a good chance his mother had been hit.

Where was she? He had cocked his ear and listened for the moaning. Folks hollered and barked good-natured orders, women reminded friends to be careful, dogs yapped. The injured body made no sound.

He would search the barn. Halfway there, he ran into William. "Was my mother in the barn?"

"No." William sounded matter-of-fact, almost dismissive. Thornton took it to mean he was also worried and preferred not to dwell on his mother's disappearance. He carried a long, thick rope and two rifles. He tossed one to Thornton and said, "The only way I see the last of us getting out of here without being shot or followed is to ambush Hezzy's men one by one and tie them up in the middle of the compound."

William was right. The dark, the snow, and the numbers in the enemy camp had caught the Jones clan off guard. They likely gave up chasing Thornton and the rest around the farmstead and regrouped inside the warmth of the house, where they could reload their rifles and come up with a plan.

Thornton figured none of the Jones men had made it far enough outside to realize how many saddled horses the marauders had brought with them. Even if Hezzy hadn't been knocked out in the snow, he would have no idea most or all of his slaves had escaped. When he awoke, he would probably swear retribution only to find he would have no one to exact it on. Still, it would take just a few clean shots to take down someone in their group.

Thornton and William had to press their advantage over Hezzy's stupidity and finish off the Jones bunch. Thornton's search for his mother would have to wait. He took comfort in the fact that he also hadn't seen Henry since they arrived. He hadn't heard a baby cry for several minutes. Wherever his mother was, he hoped Henry was with her and kept her safe.

Despite the chaos and the dark, it had all happened fairly fast, William realized. The arrival, the failed ambush of the house, the shootout, and the rounding up of the men and women and sending them on their way had only taken twenty-six minutes.

Henry, Colleen, Rose, and the baby had disappeared like snow flurries on a fire. That was too much of a coincidence. William hoped Henry had taken them somewhere safe until the gunfire had died down. For his own sake and Thornton's he clung to that notion.

"There's a side door, and a back one. I remember that. They'll be expecting us to use one of them. I have another idea. Follow me."

———◆◇◆———

Ethan had taken the dare, and he thought he might freeze to death for it. Ronan and the other Negroes sprang into action once Ronan figured out that Thornton and William were trapped. Some had protested, had wanted to run while they had the chance, but Ronan reminded the insolent few that they would never make it on foot, that their number gave them the power needed to help Thornton and William and still get everybody out on horseback, and that if it weren't for the two men trapped inside the house, none of them would have the luxury of debating when and how to flee. The straggler bits of grumbling stopped, and the men got in line. Some had even itched at the chance to shoot Hezzy and his brood.

One of them darted across the compound and retrieved Hiram Elliot's wagon. No doubt panicked, he left Ashes behind. Ethan had realized Ronan was unaware of the horse's predicament. He felt sure Ronan would have made a run for it and rescued Ashes if he knew the animal was stranded.

They all stationed themselves in front of Hezzy Jones's house with loaded rifles. Ronan ordered Ethan to stay behind in the barn. Ethan saw his chance to get away.

Ronan had read Ethan's mind. He said, "Go ahead. I dare you. You can't go into the house, and you won't get one mile up the road in any direction. The cold'll get you. You'll wish you stayed with us and the wagon full of blankets."

He hadn't been mean about it. Ethan got the distinct impression Ronan tried to convince him to stay for his own good. He had almost said as much. "You've seen a lot," Ronan had said. "You saw a man get shot, saw him die. You should talk to your father about it. Talk to your mother about it. We're not dragging you just to say we hog-tied you. You need to go home," he had said.

Ethan had left anyway. He walked in a direction he hoped would get him back to Hiram Elliot's place. He would throw himself on the man's mercy and pray for shelter in front of his huge fireplace. He had lived through a lifetime of winters on his parents' farmstead in the west. *He had walked a hundred miles to get to this spot.* He felt sure he could make it.

He was wrong. He had traveled just a quarter of a mile and could go no farther. The wind bit his face, and he struggled to locate the path. He swung his legs at the knee out to the side to achieve a high step over the snow for the first several yards, but he couldn't keep it up.

In the end, he trudged straight through the snow. He walked ten more steps and came to a stop. He would have to turn back, would have to make the journey west with Thornton and the others, would have to go home to his parents. Ronan had won again.

Ethan began to wonder why he and his uncle and Hezzy Jones and men like them thought Negroes were dumb. All Ethan knew were Negroes who got the best of all of them. William was a walking timepiece and used words so big, Ethan struggled to keep up with the conversations between William and Thornton on which he had eavesdropped. Ronan mesmerized horses with his eyes. The magic in his touch was merely a luxury. Henry could build anything right the first time without proper measuring instruments. He never needed to go back and sand some crooked corner or take apart two poorly joined pieces of wood and hammer them back together. How were any of them considered dumb?

Ethan stood stranded in the snow and remembered the pungent men's bunkhouse and the scene in the barn. He thought about Aunt Rose's bruises and how his father had never laid a hand on his mother. He wondered if he'd be freezing in the middle of a snowstorm if his Uncle Marcus had treated his aunt the way his own father treated his mother.

He had to admit that more than once, he had heard Ronan and Henry talking about how much they hated herding hogs or wanted to get out of the cold, often with wry humor, and wanted to join in the laughter. He hated herding hogs and working in the cold too.

And why couldn't a Negro read if he wanted to? Thornton gave newspapers and books to William, but Ethan never told his uncle, and not because his cousin threatened to tell his parents where he was. If he was honest, he couldn't see the harm. It had reminded him of how he dreamt about flying as high as his kite and how his father always made him pull in the toy and get back to sensible farming.

Maybe books made William feel the way Ethan's kite made him feel. Maybe Henry missed his child as much as he guessed his father missed him and Justus. Not for the first time since the nightmare began, he thought about his family, about how his mother thought he was dead. And about something else Ronan had said. "You are very lucky, young man, to have a home." They had been surrounded by the pungent scent of so many men and women who had never had a home. Ethan would bet that each and every one of them had something they were good at, the way William, Ronan, and Henry did, but that they had never been allowed to show it except to put it to use for their owner.

Maybe things like Ethan pondered that night were why Thornton and Aunt Rose and Hiram Elliot treated everybody as though they were the same, as though what a person looked like, Negro or white, had nothing to do with whether he was good or bad or worthy, and as though the good in Negroes existed not in spite of their being Negroes but because of who any one of them was. Ethan realized that how Negroes looked was as much a blessing to them as how Ethan looked was to him because it was who they were.

From the vantage point of his anvil, Ethan had sat in wonder and watched Hiram Elliot and Ronan assess horses in Hiram Elliot's barn like two men in business together, who were about to make an important purchase and who therefore wanted each other's opinion. His cousin and aunt and Hiram Elliot had not wasted time making false separations. They respected Negroes as much as they respected themselves. Could it be that they had accomplished more good because of it?

He stood in the middle of a blizzard where nobody could see him, where he was likely to die since he couldn't find his way back to where the others were, and answered his own question. And what he answered surprised him.

He turned in the direction he hoped would take him back to the Jones place. He took just four slow steps. A horse pulled up next to him. It carried two riders Ethan thought he'd never see on that night. Somebody's luck was about to change.

43

THORNTON AND William shinnied up Hezzy Jones's tree using a hand-off system for the rifles. One of them climbed a few feet without the guns, and the other handed up the guns and inched up the tree himself, and so on.

Just one more round and they would be at Hezzy Jones's upstairs window. They hoped the men were all downstairs and that they could sneak up on them from upstairs and get them to drop their guns at one time. The idea was to march them outside, tie them up with the rope they left near the front porch post, find Thornton's mother and the others, and ride off.

Thornton stood in the crook made up by two tree branches that met at the trunk right in front of the window and peered into Hezzy Jones's house. Blackness stared back. Reconnaissance was impossible. He would have to take his chances and open the window without knowing what—or who—was behind it.

He reached for the bottom ledge and lost his footing. His slow fall from the tree began. In the final second, he held fast to a bunch of leaves and recovered his balance. He grabbed the window a little slower the second time, and it popped right open.

A strong scent of perfume attacked his senses. A woman slept in that room. Would he run into Hezzy's wife, Tildy? He hesitated.

"What are you waiting for? Go on. We've been on this godforsaken farm thirty-four minutes." William said.

Thornton climbed into the window and expected Tildy Jones to stick her rifle in his face, but nothing happened. The room was empty. Thornton waved his hand toward himself to signal to William he could come in.

William handed Thornton the rifles and came through the window. Thornton immediately gave him back one of the guns. They didn't bother to look for a lamp. They preferred the dark.

They walked to the door of the room. Thornton cracked it open, and in a repeat of what he did at his own house on the night of the shooting, made sure no one was on the upstairs landing and tip-toed onto it. William followed and pulled even with him. The two stood and listened for sounds in the house. They heard the voices of six or seven men and one woman downstairs in the same room where they first ran into all of the Jones guns.

Thornton and William moved in tandem and crept down the stairs. Their boots threatened to give them away. The front room was to the right of the staircase. Weak light drifted out of it and made it as far as the bottom landing.

One of the men said, "I'm telling you, they're hiding all over this farm. I say we take 'em."

"Are you willing to get shot? It's dark. They're dark. They'll see us before we see them, and one or more of us could get picked off."

"How in the hell did this happen? Where did all those guns come from? And where's Pa?" Obadiah Jones said.

Your pa, Thornton thought, is outside with his face in the snow.

"Your Pa's probably outside gettin' the lay of the land. I'm telling you, if we wait long enough, the sunlight'll tell us where they are. It'll be a lot harder for them monkeys to hide in broad daylight."

It didn't make any sense to Thornton to let them prattle on. He glanced at William. They gave each other one big nod that said, "Now," and marched into Hezzy's main room. They aimed their rifles high.

"Hands up, every one of you!" William said.

"Drop your rifles or we'll shoot," Thornton said.

The order was unnecessary. None of them carried their guns. Each man's rifle lay next to its owner's feet, where it had been lazily set aside, while the men lounged on a combination of the settee and Tildy Jones's overstuffed chairs.

Except for Hezzy, they were all there. Thornton guessed in their typical arrogance, they figured there was no way any of the men outside would dare cross the Jones threshold. They were mistaken.

That time, it actually *was* going to be easy, or Thornton would be damned.

———◦◇◦———

Thornton and William marched the men to the middle of the compound. Obadiah carried a lamp Thornton had made him light. No one could run without Thornton or William seeing him.

They would tie up the men in such a way that they would eventually get loose. With no horses and nothing but snow to slog through, by the time the men walked into Columbia to report what happened, the escapees would be long gone.

Thornton's friends felt a deadly rage toward Hezzy and his. But they had all agreed at Hiram Elliot's they would shed no more blood than necessary to escape. Ronan, in particular, had said once he and his mother fled, he wanted to be done with Hezzy for the rest of his days. If they escaped into free territory, that would be it. If he murdered Hezzy or had a hand in his death, he would be a wanted fugitive forever. He didn't want that for his mother or himself. Henry agreed that that was no life for Colleen or him either.

Thornton put Tildy Jones in the barn. The only two members of their group still in the barn were Ronan and Ronan's mother, Ella.

Ronan tended to the remaining horses. Ella took an ax to the wheels of the wagons the runaways wouldn't need. Neither of them had seen Thornton's mother. They had been with him helping others ride off when she disappeared.

"Sit down over there," Thornton said to Tildy Jones. "Can you folks keep an eye on her?"

"I'm watching," Ella said.

Thornton rejoined William in the compound. He expected to drag Hezzy Jones out of his heap and throw him in with his clan, but Hezzy no longer lay face down in the snow.

He was gone.

"Goddamn nigga!" It was one of Hezzy's brothers. "You ain't gonna get away with this. I will personally take all the skin off that ugly monkey hide of yours and drag you by the neck for a mile on my horse."

"What horse?" Thornton said. "Except for ours, they're all gone. Every last man and woman on this farm took them. And your food....and blankets and any supplies they could carry. They'll keep what they need and scatter the rest all over the countryside."

"Niggas!" was all Obadiah Jones could contribute.

"They won't get far. Them niggras'll get caught and hanged by sunup," one of Hezzy's brothers offered.

"Shut up!" Thornton placed the end of the rifle right at his temple. "Another word out of your fat ass, and I'll pull the trigger." He tried not to let on he was more than a bit concerned Hezzy was nowhere in sight. "Do you want the honor of tying up these pigs, or shall I do it?" he said to William.

"I think I'll do it."

Thornton held his rifle on the men and watched William the stevedore twist and turn the rope in intricate fashion in and around the men's bellies, wrists, and ankles. It was a complex web only a sailor could untangle. William tied the final knot and stood back and admired his handiwork.

"Way over yonder," William pointed past the farthest outbuilding on the property, "we'll leave you a knife. If you can manage to walk through the snow in the dark and find where it's buried in the slush, you can cut yourselves out."

One of the men hawked a big glob of spit at William. It landed square on his cheek. Thornton moved forward with his rifle, but he had no time to make a threat. With the spittle still stuck to his face, William punched the fool so hard, the entire group went down with him from the force of the blow. They struggled to regain their footing with their ankles bound together. It reminded Thornton of the first day William, Ronan, and Henry had arrived at Guthrie Farms and walked to the bunkhouse with their feet chained together. Thornton appreciated the irony.

William grabbed a ball of snow and washed his face with it. It took every, single thing that had ever lived inside of Thornton to keep him from pulling the trigger on the degenerate soul who spit on William. To be sure he wouldn't do it, he lowered the gun. His hand shook. He willed it to steady.

Relaxing the rifle had been a mistake. The next sound he heard was Hezzy Jones's voice. It said, "Drop it, Guthrie."

44

HEZZY JONES had recovered from the earlier knock in the head and was in a position to reverse the hostage situation Thornton and William had orchestrated. He carried an old musket rifle he must have retrieved from some spot on his farm no one in Thornton's gang had encountered.

The reversal of fortune was obvious to Thornton, but he refused to cooperate. He had no doubt Hezzy could shoot him or William or Henry or his mother—that was, if they weren't already dead—but that was just it. Hezzy could only shoot one of them. Thornton preferred it be him. After Hezzy shot Thornton, his rifle would be empty, and William could take him down. Thornton considered how little he had left to lose, and slid in between William and Hezzy. Hezzy's only shot would have to go through Thornton.

William immediately stepped to the side and pulled up next to Thornton. "You can't shoot us both, Jones. You know you want to shoot me, so do it."

"Oh, I'll deal with you, nigga. Guthrie first, though, for turning on his own."

"You sure about that, Hezekiah?"

Hezzy Jones turned at the sound of his name and looked right into the barrel of Hiram Elliot's Hawken.

Thornton was flabbergasted. Standing there in the snow and the fog and the mist, silhouetted by the lamplight that made him seem more ominous than the light from his fireplace had, was Hiram Elliot. Next to him, riding double on what Thornton recognized as Hiram Elliot's last, lone horse, were Ethan and Fidelia.

With everything that had occurred that night, the strangest thing Thornton had seen by far was Fidelia riding a horse with Ethan on the back of it. The three had emerged from the dark, unseen by anyone in the compound. They had all been watching Thornton and William vie to be the first one shot.

"Drop the gun, Hezekiah. I'll shoot you if I have to," Hiram Elliot said. As he had once done with Thornton, he lowered his voice and spoke slower. "Drop the gun, Hezekiah."

Hezzy withered. Within two seconds, he lowered his gun. Hiram Elliot stepped forward and snatched it from him.

Hezzy couldn't help himself and ran his mouth. "The law'll get you, Hi, for being a part of this."

"Pshaw. I'll deny it, even with these bumpkin witnesses. It'll simply be one farmer's word over the other's. I'm more respectable than you. They'll believe me, not you." Hiram Elliot didn't bother to wait for Hezzy's response. He turned to Thornton and William. "You gentleman have enough rope to add one more to your bunch?"

———◆◇◆———

Rose had bled a slow but nonstop trickle in the Jones storm cellar for thirty minutes. Henry had been shrewd in remembering the cavern. He rushed her into it once he realized she had been shot and had fallen in the middle of the compound. She had moaned, and no one had heard her in all of the gunfire and animal noise.

Without thought, Colleen had rushed into the barrage with August tucked close to her and followed them down there. Even though she and August were safe, Henry had words for Colleen. "I told you to stay put!"

"In that barn? Wondering if you got shot or eaten by a dog?"

"So you bring yourself and August into it?!"

"Yes! To stay together, yes! Don't you tell me, Henry!"

He sighed. "All right, all right." He hugged her. August was tucked between them. "I'm sorry. I'm sorry."

Rose heard the set-to, but she was secretly relieved Henry had braved a solution for her. Henry was the only reason Rose wasn't lying cold and dead in the snow. She was also glad Colleen and August were in the relative safety of the cellar.

They all agreed they'd remain below until they were sure it was safe to go outside.

"Good, Lord, there's nothing in here but fruit liquor and preserves," Colleen said.

"Dim-witted Joneses," Henry said. "Why have a place to come in a storm but nothing to help you if you get sick down here?"

"Give me your scarf." Colleen fashioned a makeshift dressing from Rose's scarf, which was soaked clean through. The blood continued to drain from Rose's left shoulder.

Semi-consciousness set in. It bordered on euphoria. In the distance she thought she heard Thornton call her name, but she imagined it. The pain had tricked her mind, and it heard what it wanted.

"Ma!"

Rose opened her eyes. That time she had heard it for real.

"In here! In the cellar!" Henry shouted.

Rose fell unconscious.

———◆———

Rose had awakened on Tildy Jones's settee. She had bled all over it.

William was by her side. They quarreled.

"I'm fine. With enough blankets and padding, this wound'll heal in no time. We have to go."

The bullet had grazed her deep and sliced a gash in the round peak of her shoulder, but it hadn't gone through her body. Like Thornton's ear, her shoulder would probably have a permanent dent.

Tildy Jones had performed crude surgery with a sewing needle and her thickest black thread and closed the gap in Rose's skin. She hoped to earn goodwill with the group so they'd consider freeing the men.

Colleen had dabbed a medicinal salve she found in the kitchen cupboard along the stitches.

"We can hole up here for a day, eat, sleep, and leave when the sun goes down again."

"That's a bad idea, Will," Ronan said. "There's no telling who got caught and how much the law knows by now. It's better if we ride out while we can."

"I'm not letting Colleen or August spend one more night or day on this property. The three of us leave tonight, even if Colleen and I have to walk," Henry said.

"That won't be necessary," Rose said. "I'm fine, and Henry's right. I don't want to stay here one second longer than I have to either, and I don't want anyone staying on my account."

Thornton was a little less settled on the matter. He worried about his mother. The rest might do her good. He wouldn't mind a catnap himself.

In the end, he felt they should risk the ride. "Henry, you and Colleen are not going to have to walk out of here. My mother is strong. If she says she can make the trip, she can make it. And no matter, anyway, because the wagon is for you and your family. You're not joining us. We'd be following you. I thought that was decided."

"That's right," Rose said. "And I can make it."

"I say we go now," Ronan said.

"All right. We'll go now," William said.

Thornton was glad that was settled, but his mother wasn't his only concern.

Something else bewildered and infuriated him. He wondered what Fidelia was doing there. In all the confusion, he hadn't spoken to her. He wasn't sure he wanted to.

The Elliots—father and daughter—had rejected Thornton, had made it clear he wasn't good enough for Fidelia, and they had done so in front of an audience. If Fidelia thought she could just show up and have Thornton fall at her feet, she could forget it.

Still, he stole surreptitious glances at her when he was sure she wasn't looking. He couldn't help himself. He loved her.

"Will. It's time," Ronan said.

"They're right." Rose stood up. She leaned hard on William. "We've come too far to lose everything now."

"Henry? You ready to push that wagon one last time?" Thornton said.

"You know I am." He gazed at Colleen. August was in a deep sleep on his mother's shoulder.

"Ma, you can lay down in the back. It'll be bumpy, but we'll get you through." He turned to Hiram Elliot. "Mr. Elliot, it seems between your horses and Hezzy's extra mounts, everybody found a way off this dreadful farmstead. They had supplies, blankets, and directions west and north. We kept our end of the deal. It looks like you'll be able to take your wagon home. It's a good thing you showed up." He said to William, "I'll just saddle Ashes and meet you in the compound." He walked toward the door.

"Thornton—" Fidelia stopped herself. Everyone in the room looked at her.

Thornton turned on his heel and looked right at her without saying anything. He waited. And softened.

"Thornton. . . ."

Looking right at her undermined his resolve.

"Thornton, I love you. I don't want you to leave without me."

He was afraid to relax. He had been hurt too badly already.

"Will you take me with you? As your. . . ."

"My what?"

"Your wife."

Thornton shot a look at Hiram Elliot. He expected more humiliation.

"Don't look at him. I'm the one asking, even though I shouldn't really have to."

"Fidelia—"

"If you think back, you never gave me a chance to answer you in my barn. You turned down your own proposal. I said, 'Thornton,' and you cut me off and rejected yourself. If you had let me finish, you would have heard me say, 'Yes. I love you, and I'd be happy to marry you, and no matter how scary or dangerous, I would go anywhere with you.' I told you the day after Christmas, always, between us. Always."

Thornton searched her eyes for the mockery and the lie. Exhaustion and embarrassment told him to go get Ashes and ride west.

But he didn't retreat. He crossed the room to stand closer to her. His mind told his feet, "Stop walking over there," but his feet ignored him. He would kick himself all the way to the Unorganized Territory if he knew there had been a chance to be with her and he hadn't taken it.

He had to know for sure. He would risk it one more time. "Are you really accepting? It won't be easy. We still haven't made it to safety, and we don't know what the snow or law has in store for us or whether the horses won't flat out give up. Are you sure?" He braced for her answer. He had put himself on the line for a second time in front of the same onlookers, something he swore he wouldn't do.

"I love you. I'm sure."

He let out a gentle laugh. "I love you, too. I'd be honored to marry you."

"I know nobody's asking," Hiram Elliot said, "but you have my blessing, young man. Why do you think I rode my only horse over here and gave him to Fidelia? I was prepared to walk home if I had to, so long as Fidelia could join you."

Thornton couldn't believe his ears. "You took a big risk, Mr. Elliot. If Hezzy had prevailed, you would have been caught with the rest of us."

"I'm aware of that, Guthrie. Somehow, I didn't see that happening. Or maybe I felt it was worth the risk. As I said, I envied you your mission. And....I realized Fidelia's mind was set either way. I fear she would have chased you on horseback all the way west. Besides, ahem, you're a....fine young man, Guthrie. Just promise me you'll find the first preacher when it's safe."

At those words, Thornton finally believed Hiram Elliot. For the first time in two days, Thornton smiled a real smile. And he kissed his future bride. In front of everybody.

45

ROSE'S LEFT shoulder felt like a cow had stood on it and refused to move, but the bleeding had stopped. As painful as it was, Marcus had put her through worse.

According to William, it was just past two in the morning. Six minutes after. The group was about ready to leave, but Rose felt there was time to do one more thing. It was the perfect moment. They were all outside, including Hiram Elliot, who wouldn't leave until he saw that Fidelia got off safely. The Jones men were still bound together in the middle of the compound. Rose wondered how far away they were from the spot where Hezzy had cut kerosene into William's back with a rope.

Tildy Jones begged Hiram Elliot for their release, but he ignored her. He preferred to wait until his gang had left. After they were a safe distance away, he would give her the knife William had threatened to plant in the snow, and let her work to cut them out. He would be home. He dared them to cross his property line for retribution.

The wagon was packed. The men had rounded up every gun still on the property. They had set the dogs loose in the wild to live side by side with the wolves. The chickens and pigs roamed the cropland where there was plenty for them to eat. Somewhere in the distance, the milk cow mooed. She would probably return to the compound when her udder was full and she needed a Jones to empty it. Rose was the only one on the farmstead who knew the Jones bunch would soon need that cow more than they ever had in their lives or the cow's.

They had figured out the traveling arrangements save one detail the subject of which Rose didn't yet know how to broach with Thornton. Until she did, she, Colleen, August, and

Ethan would ride in the wagon. Henry and William would take
turns driving it. Thornton, Fidelia, Ronan, and Ella all had
their own horses. The plan was for Rose to ride double with
Fidelia and for Ethan to ride with Thornton when the men
and their families headed north with the wagon and Thornton's
clan headed west to Ethan's place.

Something had happened to Ethan. He no longer tried to
run away or cause problems. When they figured out who
would ride where, Ethan had said, "I'll head west in the
wagon."

No one had said a word except Ronan. "The boy'll be
fine," he said.

Rose found Thornton with Ashes in the compound. She
walked slow, but she was steady on her feet. "Son, hand me
your matchbox."

"What for?"

She held out her hand. That was her answer. He handed
her the matches. "I promise I'll be no more than one minute,"
she said to the group at large. Ronan, in particular, was
anxious, but she hoped he would appreciate the purpose for
the delay.

She retrieved a piece of wood from the shed.

"Ma. We—"

"Just a minute." She had stashed one of the strips of
cloth she used for bandages in the pocket of her dress. She
took it out and wrapped it around the wood and tied it tight.
She snatched the lamp from Obadiah and snuffed it. They had
all been outside for a while and could see in the dark. She
felt sure every eye in the compound watched her.

She opened the top of the lamp and dipped the cloth end
of the piece of wood in the oil for several seconds. She
walked around the bundle of men to the place where Hezzy
Jones was bound to his ugly brother, held up the makeshift
tool, and said, "I hear you like to burn things." At five feet,
ten inches, she towered over Hezzy.

"I hear you burned William's library, that you beat him with a rope and kerosene." She struck a match and set the torch on fire. It formed a small ball of flames. Rose waved it past Hezzy's face, but all the men in the rope recoiled. "Well, you ought to get a kick out of watching the fire I'm about to set."

"Rose Guthrie! Filthy bitch!"

She had to act fast or Thornton and William would have interceded on her behalf. She leaned into Hezzy's face. The Jones bunch tried to step back, but all it resulted in was awkward bumping and shoving. They didn't shift an inch. "You enslave people and treat them like cattle, you separate families, you degrade women. You're a pig, Hezekiah. Your sons are your droppings. This farm is a rotten sty. It has to burn. That farmhouse, these bunkhouses, the barn, it all has to go. It has sheltered too much wretchedness to be allowed to exist." She marched to the barn with the torch.

"Noooooo!"

Rose held the torch with her bad arm, flung the barn door open with her good arm, and touched off the hay with the oily flame. Within forty-five seconds, the barn caught fire. She moved on to the men's bunkhouse and set a straw bed on fire. She crossed over to the women's bunkhouse and repeated the process.

Within minutes, all three wooden buildings were ablaze. Rose thought the soft orange glow was actually beautiful against the snow. In the distance, the cow serenaded the flames and dogs bayed, as if the inferno they saw on the horizon were the moon.

She went to the main house and touched off the settee, the drapes, and all the men's scarves. She ventured upstairs and set all of the beds on fire and rushed downstairs and out of the house. Tildy Jones wept in the compound. Rose delighted in her misery. The woman had helped her husband destroy dozens of lives that spanned three generations. She hadn't been a captive, as Rose had been with Marcus. She had been Hezzy's co-warden, had delighted in the enslavement of twenty-eight people, including an infant. The entire farmstead, and all the misery it abetted, had to go.

She was almost done. One more place had to burn.

She strode across the compound to Colleen, careful to keep a safe distance from August. "The wood shed is all that's left." She proffered the torch.

Ella handed her horse's reins to Ronan and dismounted her animal. She walked to where Colleen stood, took August, and said, "Go on."

Colleen almost snatched the torch from Rose. She sashayed to the tied up Jones clan. She stood in front of Jedidiah and waved the flames up and down the front of his body. The torch hovered at the opening to his pants.

He didn't move.

The torch lingered for another long moment.

Colleen spit on him. It landed all over his face. He tried to blink strings of her saliva out of his eyes.

She set his pant cuffs on fire and moved on to the wood shed. Jedidiah yelped and danced and kicked up snow to put out the flames that threatened to crawl up his thighs. Spit still hung from his face.

A ruckus broke out in the wagon. William had Henry pinned down. Henry had understood the connection between Colleen, Jedidiah, and the wood shed. He wanted to kill Jedidiah.

He and William stood up on the driver's platform of the wagon, and William appeared to use all of his strength to keep Henry from jumping out of the wagon and butchering Jedidiah Jones. Henry broke loose and punched William. William grabbed Henry and regained control.

William said, "It's not worth it. Do you want to slaughter a man in front of your son? In his short life, he's already seen enough ugly. They forced him to be born into it. Don't let them cause you to continue it for them. Besides,

Rose and Colleen are ending it for him right now. Look around you." Henry fought a little less.

Flames roared all over the farmstead. Their faces glowed in the light. "Every Jones is as good as destroyed already. No horses. No slaves to work their crops. No place to live." Henry was still. "We're going that way," William said. He nodded west, away from where they stood. "Don't worry about what's behind you. Look ahead." Henry relaxed his stiff body. William loosened his hold just a bit.

Henry dropped down onto the driver's seat. "If we don't leave in the next minute, I'm gonna murder him. And nobody's gonna stop me." After a moment, he yelled, "Colleen!" His voice cracked. In the firelight Rose saw tears in his eyes. She looked away from Henry and toward Colleen.

The young mother had reached the wood shed. She threw the torch inside and stood there for a moment. She watched it burn like it was her own private fire. After several minutes, she rejoined the enclave of escapees. Henry was silent.

The band faced the inferno and took in the majestic light it painted into the dark night. Only Henry's head hung low.

Every building was on fire. Only the outhouse shared by Hezzy's twenty-seven hostages remained. The entire farmstead would be obliterated.

And Hezzy watched.

46

THE WEARY group had traveled for several hours. For the first hour, any time they turned around, they saw Hezzy Jones's farmstead blaze against the backdrop of the hills on the distant horizon. Hour by hour, enormous flames that sent up smoke that choked the light out of the occasional snowfall became smaller yellow waves that looked like blankets billowing in the wind. Finally, orange embers, probably as bright as stars up close, appeared to Thornton to twinkle no brighter than the tip on the wick of a snuffed out candle. Not long after, the light went out.

For the first time in two days, winter had been a friend. Daylight had broken, but much later than if it were summer. The horses had held out well because it no longer snowed, and Thornton could tell that western Missouri hadn't seen as much snow the night before as Columbia had.

The band had pushed the horses hard, but they had managed to cover almost ninety miles, much more territory in such a short time than Ethan had covered on foot and with campers and drifters when he had traveled in the opposite direction.

It had been easier than they had imagined. They had run afoul of no major obstacles, and their bitterest enemies were the cold and the distance to be covered. Hezzy had not been able to alert the law. No one gave chase.

Thornton worried about how all the others, like Thomas and John, had fared. He tried not to think about how he would never know if any of them made it or what retribution they would face if they hadn't.

The group was quiet. William and Henry gave each other advice about how to negotiate an obstacle in the road but engaged in no conversation. Colleen shushed August if he stirred but talked little. Rose slept on and off, and Ethan uttered not one sound on the whole ride. Ronan and his mother shared inaudible words at the back of the train the group formed. Thornton could only imagine how much catching up they had to do, how many plans they would finally get to make. They had waited a lifetime to be able to do so.

And Fidelia, who had kept him from rejecting his own marriage proposal. He fretted about the kind of life he could give her, but he couldn't wait to try to do right by her, couldn't believe they would be together as husband and wife, with all of the rights to privacy and intimacy and planning it implied. It was a far cry from her father's apple orchard.

Another fifteen miles, or so, and they would be across the border and in free territory. William, Ronan, Henry, Colleen, Baby August, and Ella would break off and travel north to Canada. Everyone agreed it was safest for them to leave United States territory altogether. The rest would head to the Barkers. Thornton dreaded the moment of parting.

—◆◇◆—

William had worried all night about Rose's wound. She hadn't said much in the back of the wagon. She was in tremendous pain and probably kept it to herself for the sake of the group.

He had a fierce admiration of what she had done to Hezzy's farm. He would never forget her face in the firelight.

He didn't see how he was going to turn north without her when the time came. She and her son had just been freed to be a family. She would want to go with Thornton in the wake of what he was forced to do to his father.

William carried a tremendous amount of guilt that it had been on his account. Rose may have understood it when it happened and even as late as the night before at Hezzy's felt her son had done the right thing. William figured all those cold hours later, she had come to resent him and maybe even blamed what Thornton had had to do on herself and her behavior with William. He couldn't ask her to part from her son under those circumstances.

In a little over an hour, they would split forever. He held onto what he had told her in his letter. He had said he would make it through the end of his days never touching her again so long as they could have one night. They had had their one night, and William would never forget it. He had been clumsy, but she hadn't seemed to mind. He hoped his awkwardness wasn't the impression that stayed with her once they parted. He hoped she still loved him. He thought she did. They hadn't spoken about such things since she had left him in the bunkhouse. It appeared they never would.

———◆◇◆———

Rose hadn't yet figured out how to tell Thornton she would head north with William. His entire life, she had betrayed her son, had abandoned him right across the kitchen table. Marcus was dead, and nothing stood between them. She was free to talk to her son, to hug him, to tend to his wounds, to tell him she loved him.

In wicked irony, the opportunity had come too late. It wasn't just that Thornton had Fidelia and was too old, anyway, for his mother to kiss his sore, skinned knees. It was that the previous forty-eight hours had aged her son a lifetime. He was a man, capable, she was sure, of being anyone's father.

He had needed her to be his mother when he was too young to defend himself against Marcus and all the ills of the world. He didn't need her to play mother in the thirteenth hour. In the end, he had had to protect himself, and she had squandered her chance to be a real mother to him. It devastated her, but she could not impose on him to mak feel better and finagle her way into his life with Fidel

She thought about those infamous cages William talked of in his letter to her, the letter she found in the moments after Marcus's death and tucked into her pocket, where it still was. Thornton had been penned in the back of his cage for his entire life. From his own prison cell, he had fashioned an escape, had unlocked the heavy gates on the fortresses that had jailed them all, and set them free.

She could not ask him to walk back into his coop and let her shut the door behind him so she could make up for time she had lost as an inattentive mother. All she could do was rejoice in his freedom and reassure him that if he ever needed her, she would travel any distance to get to him.

She would miss him, would pine for him from one corner of her heart for the rest of her life, but no amount of proximity would close the gap maturity and experience and the wisdom that came with them had rightfully put between him and her. It was a wedge that eventually came between all mothers and their children. A good mother would see the space the wedge created as an opening for her child to walk through, as a passageway to adulthood. At least she would try to see it that way.

Rose was confident Thornton had traversed the full length of the pathway and was in open space on land where he could plant any kind of life. He had shown it in his willingness to leave Missouri without Fidelia. He didn't force her hand the way Marcus would have. Only a man could have accepted the kind of truth Fidelia and Hiram Elliot had given Thornton in the Elliot barn.

She had wanted to tell her son she was proud of him for the way he handled Fidelia's seeming inability to requite his love, but there had been no time. Happily, it had become a moot point. She would tell him nevertheless. He needed to know. It might even help, she liked to think, that he would hear it from her.

———◦◦◦———

In no time at all, Ethan would be home. The first five minutes would be a dream. He would get to see his mother again, would smell all the familiar scents of home, and would share with his sister Janey his adventures on the road. Some of them, anyway.

The first five minutes he was home wouldn't be the problem. It was the rest of his life that followed that would make him miserable.

They inched closer to his farm. He found he envied those going north. Their journey might be treacherous, but the destination appealed to Ethan much more than the Barker farmstead did.

For the thousandth time, he pulled the collar of his coat up around his ears. Dawn had long broken, and he could see his breath coming from his nose. He couldn't remember when he had slept. He should have felt starved, but he had no appetite. The others had eaten the occasional jerky. He had abstained. He felt colder for the earlier lack of nourishment.

The train of travelers came to a stop. He looked up and saw the crude sign. Someone had scrawled "END OF MISSOURI" on a wooden plank. It wasn't an official sign. It had been hammered onto a wooden post likely by a vagabond who wanted to help out fellow wanderers. Ethan had seen it on his way to Columbia months earlier. He wasn't sure the sign was accurate, but he did recall he had encountered it about a day after he left his farm on foot. They were on horseback. Ethan would be home very soon.

He buried himself in his coat and took comfort in one fact: The others had made it out. They were free.

47

THORNTON DISMOUNTED Ashes. The others on horses
climbed down too. William and Henry hobbled down from the
wagon and stalked up and down the front of it, stretching
their legs. Rose, with William's help, and Ethan climbed out
of the back of the wagon and traced their own circles in the
earth.

Thornton couldn't believe his eyes. Colleen scooted to the
edge of the wagon with August, and Ethan beat Henry to the
chivalry and reached out to help her down.

Along the way, the group had risked three stops on the
road. At each one, Henry sought out Colleen and August and
stayed close. Thornton had spied one or two kisses between the
new parents. He pondered his own guilt in Henry's fate, in
his separation from Colleen, in what Jedidiah had done, and
was grateful the two appeared to have found a way to look
forward.

Like nine condemned prisoners, the adults and Ethan
paced the area in silence. They had expected the moment, but a
strangeness hovered. Thornton's group was almost home, but
William and the others still had to head north, through Iowa
Territory, in uncharted land. The trepidation was palpable, even
among those who would go on to his Uncle Jeremiah's farm.

The ground was muddy where they stopped, but no snow
had fallen in the past several hours, if not days. Thornton
wondered what the roads were like farther north.

In an eerie coincidence, all nine bodies stopped at the
same time. Like snowmen erected to face each other, for just
a twinkling of time, they stared into the nothingness between
the people who stood farthest away.

Ethan was the first to move. He surprised Thornton again and trudged to where Ronan stood. The two stared at each other for a long moment. Ethan finally offered his hand and said, "Godspeed."

Ronan accepted Ethan's hand. "If you're ever up north, I expect you to come by for a hot meal and stay put long enough to tell me about your father, about home." The shake part of the gesture had ceased, but they maintained their grasp on each other's hands and looked one another in the eye.

Ethan let loose a sly grin and cleared his throat. "Yessir." He held Ronan's hand for a second longer. "Do you. . . .?"

"It's okay. Go ahead."

"Do you think James made it out?"

Ronan hung onto Ethan's hand. It took him a long time to answer. "I hope so. I think so. I think so." He added a few light shakes of Ethan's hand and nodded to convince himself, it seemed to Thornton.

Ronan finally let go. Ethan walked far away from the group to wait for those who headed in his direction.

Thornton followed his cousin's example. He approached Henry and said, "I'm sorry I never told you about August. He's with you now, but that's no excuse for keeping him from you."

"Thornton, there was no way one man could have stopped any of the Joneses. You kept me from maybe getting us all killed. You did right." His solemn expression transformed his face into an even better version of handsome. "When—not if, but when—we set up home up north, and when August grows up, we'll make sure he knows about you, about the brave thing you did for us."

"Nonsense. Nobody on earth is braver than you and Colleen and William and Ronan and his mother and all the good people I met last night. I just hope there will come a day when that kind of courage is no longer necessary." He leaned in and gave his friend a sturdy hug and patted him hard on the back. "As soon as you can, let me know where you are. I can't wait to get my first letter from you."

"Will do, Thornton."

Thornton turned to Colleen and was, again, struck by her beauty. "It's been a long time since I tapped on your window. I look forward to knocking on the front door of the home you share with Henry the next time we meet." They exchanged a smile, and he walked away to find Ronan.

His mother stepped into his path. "Son, I'm going north with William." She explained to him that he didn't need her, that he would be fine without her, but he barely heard her. She made no sense. It didn't seem real. Just two days before, he woke up and expected to see her at breakfast that day and many more days. He would be outside working the land, and she would be somewhere in the house being his mother.

So much had changed since the previous week—and the previous summer, when he had fought off chickadees who went after his seeds. Dame Van Winkle—his father—had died and it was finally time to enjoy life down the mountain. He realized he thought of fairy tales, but it seemed appropriate. The dragon had been slain, and his mother wanted to separate all the villagers who had been singed by his wrathful fire-breath just when it was time to rejoice in the town square.

Slowly, though, she made sense to him. One at a time, her reasons began to penetrate. At Uncle Jeremiah's, he would have Fidelia, and his mother would have a married son. In the north, she would have an equal, a partner, a friend, and a mate. She could tag along on Thornton's life and be happy in some ways but unfulfilled in others, or she could experience how it felt to love and be loved. She would finally get to live what he always assumed were some of her girlhood dreams.

Since the shooting, he had tamped down in his mind the reality of what bloomed between his mother and William, had thought the horrific event had cast shade over it, but he remembered on the side of that road that, as he had waited in his room for his mother to return from the bunkhouse, he had found he had been happy for her and William. Subsequent events had kept him from realizing the only proper place for his mother was with William. And it meant William would become his father, and he would never have to really say good-bye. He was overjoyed.

"I know you don't need my blessing, but you have it," he said.

"I love you, son," she said.

He had never heard her say those words. "I love you, Ma." He had never said those words to her.

"I'm so very proud of the man you've become." She ignored her sore arm and embraced him with all her strength. Thornton held on for as long as she would let him. In the end, he had been the first one to let go.

He turned to William. With no preamble, he said, "I have secretly wished you were my father almost since the day I met you. Your courage. Your dignity. Your kindness. And now it's to be!" He let out a small, happy laugh. "I've never been privileged to know three finer men than you and Ronan and Henry. You three are my true family, my brothers, my father, and just like a good family, you taught me how to be a man. I promise to make good on it, to be a good husband and, one day, a good father."

William went to the wagon and fished around for something in his bag. He came back with a volume in his hand. Thornton recognized the dog-eared book immediately. It was the sketch book that held "Rip Van Winkle" and so many other stories. He handed the book to Thornton.

"I want you to always have that," Thornton said.

"I know, but I added an epilogue. I want you to keep it. These stories should stay with you. I won't hear argument."

Thornton flipped to the back of the book. William filled the few blank pages that straggled at the end an inside back cover with tiny print. A skim of the words Thornton it was the tale of their friendship. "When yo daughter or son is old enough, read them these stories, make sure to tell them you never went to sleep while somebody else took care of your problems. The story of their father's bravery in the most adverse of times will be all they'll need to know about what it means to have character."

Thornton's eyes filled with tears. His throat was thick.

"Something else, son. I——. I never told Archibald, but I wished I had, and I'm going to tell you now. I love you, son."

Thornton hugged his friend, his father. "I love you, too. I don't know what I would have done, where I would be if I didn't have you to show me the way, even if I hate how it came about." The embrace lasted longer than the one Thornton shared with his mother. Thornton had grown in the previous half-year, but William was still taller. He bowed his head slightly and said in Thornton's dented ear, "You are the finest man I have ever known." Thornton hugged him a little harder.

They finally let go of each other. William leaned back in and whispered in Thornton's ear, "Be gentle with your bride. Never spurn the gift she gave you last night."

"I'll do right by her. I promise."

Thornton turned to Ronan. "I know you'll all make it through with you leading the way. You have a wondrous gift with horses. It was something to watch." They took a few steps toward one another and shook hands heartily. Each patted the other's arm with his free hand, Ronan's way of hugging Thornton. Thornton heard Ethan clearing his throat. "Good-bye, Ma'am," Thornton said to Ella. "Now I know where Ronan gets his gumption."

Her face melted into a warm smile that looked just like Ronan's. "Good-bye, young man." She took his hand in both of hers and held it close to her chest. "I been trapped a long time. Long time." She kneaded his hand. The warmth of her hands felt wonderful to Thornton. "It's been a hard life, hard for me, for my boy." Her gaze and grasp captivated him. "I'm grateful to you."

Thornton sensed the words "thank you" coming. He ˙aded them, for it felt like further degradation. No being

who should have been free all along should have to treat
freedom like it was a favor and not a birthright. He had
helped to right a wrong. He could understand her gratitude,
but he would not ask for her thanks. He deflected her with a
truth. "I'm grateful to Ronan, Ma'am, for being my brother
and for being so courageous. We wouldn't have made it
without him."

She sighed and smiled. A moment later, she headed for
her horse.

Ashes seemed to sense Ronan was taking his leave. He
bellowed for attention, and Ronan strolled his way to calm his
friend and say good-bye.

The sun shone bright on the horizon in the direction
whence they had just traveled. It reminded Thornton of the
directions Ronan had given the others. *Head away from the
sun and turn right. That's north.* "Looks like it's going to be
a nice day. We'll wait here while you push off."

Thornton, Fidelia, and Ethan gathered by the side of the
makeshift road. The others took their places for what would
be another long leg in their journey. Near the wagon, his
mother turned and said, "I'll find a way to write."

Thornton nodded.

William helped Rose into the wagon, where Colleen and
August were already tucked in, and joined Henry on the
driver's bench. Ronan and Ella trotted to the front of the
train on their mounts. They had already turned right. Henry
turned the wagon and followed them.

Rose called again to her son. "Thornton?"

It felt nice to hear his mother call his name one more
time, he hoped not the final time.

"Happy birthday. Many happy returns of the day."

Thornton had never seen her smile as tenderly as she did
at that moment. He nodded again and smiled too. If his
mother hadn't reminded him, he would have forgotten
altogether that it was the twenty-fourth of January and his
sixteenth birthday.

EPILOGUE

Unorganized Territory, west of

Missouri — 1840

It is not in the still calm of life,
or the repose of a pacific station,
that great characters are formed.

—Abigail Adams

JEREMIAH BARKER was terrified. His wife, Dorinda, was having a baby. Six years earlier, on a hot summer day, with no doctor in sight, she had given birth to a baby that came out feet first and died. Baby Justus was buried on their farm.

It was a cold February day, still with no doctor in sight, and Dorinda was deep in labor. Jeremiah prayed the baby would make it out alive and that his wife would be fine. He was sure his malaise matched his wife's, labor pains and all. Dorinda was just thirty-seven, but Jeremiah was forty-nine and far too old for the strain.

They were surrounded by loved ones. The whole family had gathered for the birth of the baby, including three of Dorinda and Jeremiah's older children—Janey, Edward, and Julius—their nephew Thornton, and Thornton's wife, Fidelia. Thornton and Fidelia lived on the farm adjacent to the Barkers' farm, and Fidelia expected her first baby in the spring. Jeremiah had always thought it was a silly form of logic, but he hoped it meant she would have the instincts necessary to help bring his baby into the world. She played midwife.

The only person not in the Barker farmhouse waiting for Dorinda's baby was Jeremiah and Dorinda's oldest son, Ethan. He was seventeen—and almost a half—and lived in Canada with a friend he met in Missouri named Ronan. The man rounded up horses for a living and traveled all the time. Ethan had joined him as soon as he was old enough to make the trip on his own.

Even though Jeremiah missed Ethan, he could recall a time when he thought Ethan was dead. His son was alive, and that was all that mattered.

He still remembered the day his son returned. Jeremiah was in his fields. He spotted three people on horseback near the empty Dawson farm where Thornton and Fidelia had eventually lived. A tall young man had a shorter one on the back of his saddle, the way Jeremiah used to ride with Ethan, only the youngster was a bit taller than Ethan had been. The other rider was a female. Jeremiah would have thought they were a young family, except even from a fair distance, he saw that the man and woman were too young to have a son so old.

They aimed right for his property and right for him. The horse with the two passengers was the color of fireplace dust. Jeremiah hadn't recognized it as belonging to anyone he knew. He remembered thinking he wished he had brought his rifle to the fields.

The strangers were still fifty feet away, but something about the youngster had struck Jeremiah as familiar.

He didn't think it could be, but it was. "Ethan?" he had said.

"Hi, Pa," Ethan had answered.

The reunion between father and son had been stilted at first, full of anger and questions, but Jeremiah couldn't hold onto the resentment. Ethan's return was glorious. The light reappeared in Dorinda's eyes. And Jeremiah and Dorinda began to touch each other again.

They learned that Ethan had been in Missouri with Jeremiah's brother, and that the people he brought home with him were Jeremiah's nephew Thornton and Thornton's bride-to-be Fidelia.

Over time, as Ethan and Thornton and Fidelia saw fit, Jeremiah and Dorinda learned about Marcus's fate. Ethan's parents agreed they had heard a story that was more about courage than crime. Jeremiah was chagrined on the inside to find out the brother he had missed all those years had perpetrated so much treachery. It had been a strange kind of mourning, pondering what he had believed Marcus was, what Marcus had turned out to be, and what Marcus's father Tanner Guthrie's hand in all of it had been. Jeremiah felt twinges of guilt that Francis Barker had turned out to be his father, but he had never abided slavery and figured a man who engaged in such sins invited calamity. He and Dorinda didn't judge incidents they hadn't witnessed. Their boy was home, and in Thornton and Fidelia, they had family close by.

Thornton was the best farmer Jeremiah had ever met. Men came from all over to learn from him after they witnessed his first harvest. And Dorinda had fallen in love with Fidelia and taken her in like a young, married sister.

Hiram Elliot, Fidelia's father, had visited on a few occasions. Jeremiah liked him immediately. He enjoyed hearing Hiram tell how a destitute Hezzy Jones, whose slaves Thornton had helped free, and whose Missouri farm Thornton's mother had burned to the ground, had tried to sic the law on Hiram for his part in the crimes, to no avail. Hiram Elliot remained a free and rich man.

Thornton never learned for sure whether the people he and the others helped escape made it to freedom, but Hiram had waited year after year for some of them, even one of them, to be caught and marched back for Hezzy to claim, and it hadn't happened. Not one soul who lit out from the Jones place ever reappeared in that territory. Everyone had hope that they made it all the way to some free part of the country.

The two clans—the Guthries and the Barkers and, by extension, Hiram Elliot—formed a formidable bunch. With Thornton and Fidelia so near, Jeremiah felt much less that he let down Dorinda with a life lived so far off from people and things.

It wouldn't be long until the next member of the clan arrived. Dorinda rocked from side to side in her bed to "stay ahead of the pain," she said. Jeremiah couldn't wait to find out whether it was a boy or a girl, for he would also know what the baby's name would be.

Dorinda had decided Thornton should name her child since he had brought home to her Ethan. His nephew had chosen Archibald if it was a boy, in honor of the man who taught his father, William, to read, and Penelope if it was girl, after William's mother, whom William hadn't seen since he was twelve. Thornton said whichever of the two names the Barkers didn't use, he'd one day use for one of his own children.

Two hours later, Archibald Jeremiah Barker was born. Right away, Jeremiah took to calling him Arch. It just seemed to fit.

—◆—

Three months later, on May twenty-third, Thornton cradled the son Fidelia had delivered earlier that day—at four-thirty-one a.m., to be exact, he noted for his father, William, who kept perfect time in his own head and who was bound to ask.

There had been some discussion about the name, but Fidelia had carried the day.

"Now, just hear me out," she had said.

"Of course."

"Polecat Elliot Guthrie. No baby ever did more wiggling than this one did. Felt like a polecat. I think he was trying to tell me something. That he'll be fast and wily and unafraid to climb high to get what he wants."

"Polecat Guthrie. Has a ring, at that."

"Besides, it's fair. Penelope Rosaline Guthrie would have been named for sturdy women. She would have known we expected no less. Polecat'll know we think he can go anywhere."

It was always at the strangest times when he got the urge to kiss her, which he did, right after he agreed that Polecat Elliot Guthrie it would be. She was the smartest person he knew. He had a strong feeling she was right about giving their son such a unique name. And she had stood with Thornton when most women would have run from him. Polecat Elliot Guthrie it was.

Thornton sat down to write to his mother and father about the good news. They lived in a small village in Canada. They sent and received mail at a general post office several miles away. It may be months before the letter reached them. It had taken their first letter to Thornton, back in the autumn of 1835, seven months to arrive.

That was when Thornton learned his mother and father and the others he escaped Missouri with—Ronan, his mother Ella, Henry, his wife Colleen, and their son August—had made it over the Canadian border five days after they and Thornton, Fidelia, and Jeremiah's son, Ethan, had split up on the side of the road in January of 1835, on Thornton's sixteenth birthday. It had been Henry who had insisted they push on and head farther inland to truly be safe from being captured and reintroduced into slavery.

The runaways had stuck together, were still together. They lived in a place where no one cared what anybody looked like. Cabins dotted the woods, and neighbors hunted and fished and toiled with each other.

Henry, who read and wrote with ease, had taken a liking to the word "canyon" after he read it somewhere and turned it into his family name. Over the years, Thornton and Fidelia had received letters from Henry and Colleen Canyon, with stories of how the new clan had turned into a big, patchwork family.

Ronan, Ella, and the Frenchman Ella met in the village and eventually married, lived in a small house Ella and Claude mostly had to themselves since Ronan traveled with Ethan and rounded up horses. Ronan and Ella had taken Claude's family name of Charpentier. Ronan had explained in his own letter that his name was pronounced "shar-PON-tee-ay" and meant "carpenter". He had joked that it was more fitting for Henry, but he was proud that he had chosen the name and that the name hadn't chosen him, as with all the others he had used in his life. He hoped one day to find a wife who would share it with him.

In the very next cottage were Henry, Colleen, August, and their younger daughter, Genevieve. Henry's family lived not a hundred yards from Thornton's mother and father and the son they had in 1837, Thaddeus.

Thornton still couldn't believe he had a younger brother, little Polecat's uncle. He hoped to meet Thaddeus one day. It would have to wait until either he or his mother felt safe leaving where they were. None of them wanted to tempt and irritate fate with that risk. They all stayed put.

Thornton already pushed his luck as part of a system that moved escaped slaves along routes filled with hideouts that led to freedom. Thornton and Fidelia's home, which Thornton and his Uncle Jeremiah had expanded from its original size when a family named Dawson had lived there, had hidden numerous men, women, and children who had fled parts farther east. Some knew to turn north at the Missouri border as his mother, father, and the others had done in 1835. Many, however, had no sense of direction. They often overshot their mark and continued west.

Thornton and Fidelia's home was near the road. In the window that faced travelers who walked west, Thornton and Fidelia had hung a tapestry depicting a bright sun that runaways had been told to look for. It signaled that the owners of the abode would protect escaped slaves. Most escapees traveled at night, and on many evenings over the years, Thornton and Fidelia had opened their door to midnight travelers and fed and clothed and housed them—and when possible, armed them—and pointed them north.

So many had marveled at Ethan's kite. It still hung over the mantle. Ethan had never again flown it. He had seen too much to derive any sense of adventure from flying his kite. In his six months away from home, he had outgrown the toy if not the dreams it planted in him. He had been destined to venture out as soon as he was old enough to head north.

On many occasions, Ethan, who had figured out and insisted on being part of the hidden escape system, had ridden north to scout the road. Based on what he reported, Thornton deemed it safe for escapees' travel. It had naturally followed that one day, Ethan headed north and didn't return. At least that time when it happened, his parents knew.

Jeremiah pretended not to know what went on in the old Dawson place, and Thornton was grateful his uncle kept his secret. In the early years, Thornton's youngest cousin Julius played indoor games—jackstraws and marbles—with some of the runaway children Thornton hid, but Jeremiah was careful not to press his son for details, and he instructed his children not to talk about who they saw at their Cousin Thornton's house.

Thornton finished his letter and folded it into a rectangle. He sealed it with wax and wrote on the blank space that folding it gave him, "Mr. and Mrs. William Newberry," and

added the information for their town and general post office.
When his parents married, his mother had used her maiden
name, Newberry, which William also adopted. Thornton couldn't
wait for Mr. and Mrs. William Newberry to find out they
were grandparents.

————•◇•————

Later that evening, Fidelia Guthrie finally rested on her
first day as a mother. Thornton watched his wife sleep. He
held his son and fingered his tattered copy of *The Sketch
Book of Geoffrey Crayon, Gent.* He found what he looked for
right off. The pages that held "Rip Van Winkle" still had
creases from where he had bent their corners long before.

Polecat was so tiny, he fit in the crook of Thornton's
arm and left plenty of room for his tall, tall father to hold
the small book in both hands. Thornton had to be sure his
son heard on the first day of his life the story of the
farmer who slept and dreamt for twenty years and awoke to
find his problems solved.

Thornton wanted to teach his son that while Rip took the
easy road, up a mountain, to avoid what ailed his life, he had
also missed all that was important and all that made a life
worth the trouble. He hadn't seen his children grow up or had
the good fortune to be present to find his own solutions.

Thornton had been wide awake for all twenty-one years of
his own life, had done a lot of his own deciphering, had been
conscious for some of the worst calamities man could
experience and understood that no matter how long a man
slumbered, his problems would wait by his bedside till he
awoke.

It had been true that he had wondered, more than Fidelia
knew, whether there slept somewhere a hangman he poked and
dared to awaken with his deeds. He never fully relaxed on
that account, but he couldn't fathom where he would be if he
had slept through the part of his life where he met William,

his true father, Ronan, and Henry, and their families, and freed his mother, married Fidelia, and became Polecat's father. And slew the dragon, Marcus Guthrie.

So, he would read "Rip Van Winkle" to Polecat, but as his father had cautioned him to do five years earlier by the side of the road, he would teach his son a much different lesson than the one he had gleaned when his mother had read the story to him. He would make sure Polecat knew that there was no greater gift than being aware of one's own life.

Polecat had drifted off by the time Thornton finished the first page, but Thornton read until he had made it all the way through the epilogue Thornton's own father had handwritten five years earlier. The part about the seed bags and the book drop always thrilled Thornton.

—◦◇•—

Missouri — 1855

THORNTON KEPT one eye on the gun the hangman's deputy pointed at him and one eye on the scaffolding beneath his feet. How far below it would he land when they pulled it out from under him, he wondered. And would he know? Would his neck snap and the rope kill him instantly, as he had been told by so many whose necks had never been in the noose, or would he choke slowly and have time to see the look in Fidelia's eyes as he drooled and swung in the air?

He promised himself he would use whatever strength he had to not kick his feet. He didn't want to leave his children, Polecat and Penelope, with the image of him running in mid-air to nowhere.

Penelope was just twelve and very confused about the family traveling to Missouri to see her father hanged. She was different from how he remembered his cousin Ethan at that age. Ethan had grown into a fine man, but he had been a wily and savvy youngster. As vexing as it was, it made him quick on the uptake about adult matters that were none of his concern.

Other than Thornton's friend Ronan, Penelope was the most straightforward human being Thornton knew. As far as she saw, her father harvested crops, read stories at the dinner table, taught her to hunt, ride, and shoot, and laughed at her jokes. He also caught grasshoppers quicker than lightning, the only game he had played as a child. They hanged bad men, so why were they hanging her father, she had asked over and over and over for days and days and days through tears that made her vomit.

Thornton had insisted she remain at home with her great-uncle, Jeremiah, for the trial, but once the bad news had traveled back and it came time for Polecat to ride out to be with his mother in Missouri, Penelope showed a touch of her relation to Ethan and defied her father and brother. She saddled her horse for the journey east.

She had insisted on seeing what happened to her father. It was the strangest moment Thornton had ever had as a father when he realized he had better let her watch or she might never forgive him. He couldn't die with her mad at him. So she was there, standing on the street next to her mother and brother, waiting to watch.

Jeremiah had almost joined them, albeit as part of a posse he had gathered to stop the hanging, but after much commotion, Fidelia had calmed Jeremiah just enough to convince him to stay home and manage both family's farms. Anything else was no use, she told him through her own furious tears.

As it was, Thornton worried that Polecat might try to rescue him from the noose. On the night they came for him, Polecat had shot at the lawmen through the window and kept them from dismounting their horses for almost an hour. He

had been lucky the men were satisfied to take Thornton, a
large enough quarry, by himself.

Polecat had begged to go to Missouri for the trial and
had only stayed back to ease his mother's mind. With the
verdict in, as soon as he returned to Missouri, he went back
on a tear. In the previous four days, he had told off the
judge and spent a night in the cell next to Thornton's for
contempt of court, taken near-miss rifle shots from hidden
places at men who sat on his father's jury, and railed at
anyone who would listen. Thornton had finally convinced
Polecat his mother couldn't take anymore, and he had quieted
down. It had been a dreadful time for all of them.

Polecat was the same age—fifteen—as Thornton was
when he had been called upon by who knew what or whom to
free his mother and his friends and, apparently, in the doing,
peek his head through the gates of hell. Twenty years had
passed since he killed Marcus Guthrie. Each year he escaped
punishment, he was convinced he had pushed the gates farther
open until he had finally crossed over the inferno's threshold
to take up eternal residence in its fiery cavities.

The day after Thornton killed Marcus, as he stood in the
snow and dug Marcus's grave, he had asked himself how that
deed would be recorded in the Grand Ledger. It seemed he
knew. It had caused his activities as a lawbreaker who helped
slaves escape to come to light. He had been charged with
violating dozens of laws over a twenty-year span, arming
runaway slaves being chief among them and punishable by
death. The charges didn't matter. The pages of the Grand
Ledger would read, "MARCUS GUTHRIE'S KILLING."

Thornton hoped those pages showed his account was
balanced so his children would not have life's tireless
sheriff—Fate—dogging their every step. Her shackles were
inescapable for those whose accounts were not paid. Thornton
didn't want his son and daughter trapped by their father's
debts.

Fidelia disagreed with Thornton with a fierceness only a devoted wife could muster. She told him it was a different gate he would soon stroll through, for having done what many would consider divine. He had helped dozens and dozens, who had been sent to him by others like him. He had provided shelter and food and reassurance for a few days to runaways headed west and north. She would remind him that in saving so many slaves, he had defied laws man had defied God to enact.

But he knew better. If a man committed a crime, high or petty, and it freed him to do good deeds, those deeds would not erase the crime that gave birth to them. He had slaughtered a man, the one who called himself Thornton's father, to save the being who really was his father. Had altruism been a stranger on that January night in 1835 on the upstairs landing of the Guthrie farmhouse? Thornton was unsure. He had pulled the trigger on Marcus and benefitted. Was that day in 1855 the day he would pay for it?

He glanced up at the noose and remembered the night Polecat was born. Thornton had explained to his tiny, sleeping son that even though Thornton had wished as a child to slumber for twenty years, like Rip Van Winkle, and awake to find his problems solved, he had been conscious his entire childhood and had been richer for it, even as he feared the sleeping hangman. No man had figured out yet how to induce the proper coma that would let him escape misfortune, and Thornton hoped Polecat would know that a man was better off if he failed in that endeavor.

It occurred to Thornton that a hangman was different. He had no goal but to take the life of others, even those who didn't deserve the noose but who couldn't prove it. If he napped for long stretches, he would be better off, as far as Thornton saw it, for his waking life was sinister. He could sleep for eternity and suffer none of the penalties Rip Van Winkle had borne for being absent from his own life.

And yet it wasn't that simple, Thornton knew, for the hangman's dream state was often determined by the actions of man. William's friend Archibald had been right. The hangman slept until a man's ill deeds stirred him. He could rest for all time, if man saw fit. Alas, human nature would not allow it. No matter how deep the sleep, no matter how near death the hangman himself was, a man's wicked pursuits would eventually shake him awake.

It was possible that in 1835, the executioner had dozed off, not for a kip that lasted until 1836 or 1837, but for a twenty-year stupor, like Ivan the Terrible, Marcus's watchdog, experienced after he drank a jigger of fruit liquor. And Thornton had slain Marcus just after the winks began and had escaped notice. The drink had finally worn off. The hangman awoke, and he had come for Thornton.

But could a man live his life afraid to do the right thing for fear it may be the wrong thing and he might wake the executioner? One thing was sure: If Thornton had known in 1835 that his deed on the Guthrie upstairs landing would send him to a scaffold in 1855, he would have carried out that deed all the same. He would not have balked and begged, "Wake not the hangman, for I have done nothing and Marcus Guthrie lived to kill an innocent man." He would have saved William and taken his chances with the hangman every time. Thornton wondered how different all the ages would have been if weak men hadn't railed, "Rouse not the hangman, for I have taken no action against evil and therefore must be innocent." It seemed to Thornton that that kind of righteous silence bred shilly-shallying that led men like Marcus Guthrie, Hezzy Jones *et al.* to perpetrate wickedness unchecked.

Maybe Fidelia was right. Perhaps Thornton had simply tried to save the better man's life, had slain the murderer. He found it cruel the circumstances hadn't made it clearer. One guilty man obviously had to be stopped from killing an innocent one. It seemed, though, that Fate believed that if the self-appointed executioner of the executioner benefitted from the bad man's death, a third executioner must be summoned to deal with the second.

Thornton felt there was something wrong with that judgment, for the sum of tragedy and benefit was not always culpability. Sometimes it was coincidence. Some matters were so gray, they were indiscernible to a jury of one's peers. It seemed to Thornton in those instances, when a man's guilt was unclear, the hangman should remain asleep. And if the hangman risked being guilty of executing an innocent man, he should be left to slumber until the end of days, no matter how many guilty men waited for their turn at the scaffold, so that he might never awake and come for the wrong man. And was there no redemptive value in a guilty man? It seemed short-sighted to kill him before time revealed the answer. And what of the guilty man's loved ones? If Thornton was guilty, what of Fidelia and Polecat and Penelope and his parents? What crime did they commit that warranted the murder of a treasured relation? Mere kinship to the one found guilty could not have been sufficient reason to dole out such punishment.

It all made Thornton want to cry, "Let the hangman repose, for he begets murder! He causes the suffering of bystanders! He is myopic and sometimes gets hold of the wrong neck! He freezes in his tracks a man about to do a good a deed who retreats for fear of retribution!"

It was too late for Thornton either way, but he was at peace. Often, when he faced a long day of farming after being up all night with a fugitive, he would recite a well-weathered battle prayer that went, "Lord, Thou knowest how busy I must be this day. If I forget Thee, do not forget me."

The Lord had not forgotten him. He had remembered to send William and Ronan and Henry and Fidelia and two handsome children Thornton's way. Thornton had had twenty happy returns of his birthday since his sixteenth. He had tried to lead a redemptive life in that time, but he would not know until his life ended whether he had been redeemed. He would walk either into the light or into the dark.

There were few gatherers on the quiet side street of the small town where the scaffold had been erected. It seemed to Thornton the law embraced public trials but often hid its executions. They were the excrement all should know about and none should see.

He looked at Polecat, who wore the resolute look Thornton always displayed at that age. He despaired that he had passed on the legacy of Guthrie misery to another Guthrie son after he strove for all of his son's life to keep that ugly bit of history from repeating itself.

He was a better father than Marcus was, had emulated his true father, William, and enjoyed the fruits of that effort through a good-natured, deep friendship with Polecat. Polecat had never hesitated to tell his father that other than Jeremiah's son, Arch, who was there in the street with Polecat also waiting to watch, Thornton was his favorite person. But that day made his son as forlorn as he himself had been at fifteen, and Thornton felt like a failure for it.

He looked at Fidelia a final time. He loved her so. She had made him many promises that morning. She would see about his cremation and till his ashes into the land.

She would also write to his mother and father, who knew not of his fate, for his father, he was sure, would place a stevedore's knot around the hangman's neck to save his son, and he would pay the same price Thornton paid. Another executioner's executioner who would be executed.

His father had already given Fate the first thirty-six years of his life. She was not entitled to more. Her books remained unbalanced when it came to William's account and the account of every soul who had ever been trapped in bondage. When, Thornton wondered, would Fate ever square her books? With so many debits to credit—one for every slave there had ever been and for every woman or child who had ever been stuck by blind and deaf law—Thornton imagined Fate cried bankruptcy each time over the years she had been called on to pay up. She had allowed a run on her bank, had racked up debits every time one more soul was born into or confined by oppression. Her account was horrendously overdrawn. Either way, Thornton would not resign his brother Thaddeus or his mother to a life without William.

William had sneaked back into Missouri several times over the years and checked in on Thornton and Fidelia and his grandchildren. He had waited more than five years to make his first trip, but once Polecat was born, William had needed to be sure the young family fared well. He stayed away from slave territory and used the clan's preferred method of travel: He moved only at night. He had twice brought Rose and Thaddeus with him, the only occasions on which Thornton had seen his mother since his sixteenth birthday. It had done Thornton all the good there was to see how different, how happy his mother was and to meet and know his brother.

Thornton thought, too, about Polecat and Penelope, who loved their grandfather. He had kept close to the house on his visits to see them, but Jeremiah and Thornton's Aunt Dorinda had traveled north several summers after harvest time to visit Ethan, who lived in the same territory as Thornton's parents, and they had taken Polecat and Penelope with them. The children hunted and camped and fished and read stories with the whole family circle and knew their grandparents well. They bragged that their grandfather was the strongest man they knew, and Penelope took special pride in knowing she was named after her grandfather's mother. They had Fidelia and her father, Hiram, but Thornton wanted to be sure they had his father since he would be gone. His parents would learn of his demise after it was too late for William to act. There would be no need to wake any hangman for his father.

It was time.

He looked to the horizon that had given him so much comfort as a child.

His neck snapped. He thought of Polecat and Penelope and held his feet still. Twenty minutes later, he walked into the light.

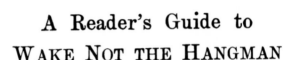

A Reader's Guide to
WAKE NOT THE HANGMAN

1. Discuss in detail the similarities, if any, in the legal issues surrounding the lives, predicaments, and actions of Thornton, Marcus, Rose, William, Ronan, Henry, and Colleen and ones that may exist for some people today. Address why, in a so-called more enlightened era, these similarities exist. Consider: motive for lack of progress, human nature, multi-generational behaviors.

2. Thornton committed a death penalty crime by 1855 standards. Do you believe he should have been hanged? Why or why not? Consider: violation of a death penalty crime versus whether a crime—or any crime—should be punishable by death.

3. In guilt societies, the response to sympathy for convicted criminals who face loss of freedom may be, "He should have thought of that." Is "He should have thought of that" a sufficient response to the *family members* of those on death row, whose loved one will be killed? Discuss how far the death penalty reaches and whether the suffering of the loved ones of those executed is merely tangential to the sentence of death or unfair collateral punishment.

4. When people are part of a mob (a large group of persons behaving in concert to achieve one aim), they sometimes do things they would not do as individuals. Do you believe that if each person who owned a slave when slavery was legal in the United States had to be the *only* person who owned a slave, he or she would have been willing to own slaves? Why or why not? Include mob dynamics in your discussion.

———◦———

5. If, like Thornton, you knew it was against the law to aid slaves in their escape, would you have acted as he did? Consider: what is moral versus what is legal. Can morality be achieved simply by virtue of obeying the law? Can breaking the law be moral? Provide examples.

———◦———

6. Do you believe the action Rose took on the Jones farm was justified, or was it vigilantism that should have been punished by law? Discuss.

———◦———

7. Should Hiram Elliot have been arrested for any of his actions? If so, for which ones and why? If not, why not?

———◦———

8. If you had to be the attorney for one of the characters in *Wake Not the Hangman*, who would it be and why? Consider: the many ways you could represent the character, for example, in family court; as a plaintiff in a lawsuit; as a defendant on trial; as a child in need of protective services. Consider also: representing the government prosecuting a character.

———◦———

9. Do you believe American jurisprudence has changed significantly, not much at all, or to a degree in between since America's inception? Discuss to what extent, if any. Consider: whether the courts today effectively protect the rights of women, children, social subgroups, and workers.

———◦———

10. Are vestiges of American slavery present in American society today? If so, discuss in detail any evidence that you believe demonstrates this.

———◦———

11. "Paternalism" may be defined as a system under which an authority regulates the conduct of others as they relate to the authority and each other or that supplies the needs of a regulated group. Is slavery naturally paternalistic? If so, what are the ramifications, if any, on a society that engages in centuries-long slavery, both during that period and after it ends? Further, if slavery is reflective of paternalism, note the disjunctive in the definition and discuss whether both segments apply to slavery, *i.e.*, whether slavery "supplies the needs of those regulated." In addition, if slavery is *not* reflective of paternalism, what kind of system, if any, does it reflect? Finally, discuss instances of paternalism, if any, present in *Wake Not the Hangman*.

12. If every American slave had been taught to read and write at an early age and had been educated as free children were, do you believe slavery would have survived as long as it did? Why or why not? Further, discuss what you believe to be the effects on a society when an entire segment of the population is kept illiterate for three centuries. Discuss also to what extent, if any, literacy and illiteracy played a role in both the plight *and* the escape of Thornton and the other protagonists in *Wake Not the Hangman*.

13. Ethan's perspective on slavery changed by the end of the book. What or who do you think most impacted his viewpoint?

14. With which character in *Wake Not the Hangman* do you most identify? Why?

15. Parts One, Two, and Three of *Wake Not the Hangman* are titled "Fallow Ground", "Crop Rotation", and "Harvest", respectively. Discuss in detail how these titles relate to the story in *Wake Not the Hangman*.

16. If you were forced to sleep for 20 years, what would you most hope to see resolved in your slumbering absence?

About the Author

Deborah Leigh is a former magazine editor who took a sharp turn into the world of law, which she has inhabited for over a decade. She borrows from both of her pasts and her love of Westerns and classic films to tell tales of justice from bygone times. Born on Los Angeles's storied Sunset Boulevard, she enjoys including worries thought to be intrinsic to urban life in her rustic stories. She has called many cities all over the United States and Europe home and was married in France, where she gave birth in a suburb of a suburb *of a suburb* of Paris. She's had the good fortune to "walk to work" in Wiesbaden, Germany, "run errands in Belgium" when she lived near its border, "catch movies" in Luxembourg while living in Metz, France, and study on a tip of Germany so far south, she once cut her morning classes to go to Switzerland and was back before lunch. She's lived within bicycle distance of the Atlantic Ocean and crisscrossed the United States several times by train and car. Ultimately a hometown girl, she and her only son live in downtown Los Angeles, where she can see Sunset Boulevard from her living room window.

@d_leigh_writes

CPSIA information can be obtained
at www.ICGtesting.com
Printed in the USA
LVOW08s1248111216
516785LV00003B/548/P